# INSTITUTIONALIZED

Stories of

the Deranged

and Demented

# PRESENTED BY
# SINISTER SMILE PRESS

# INSTITUTIONALIZED

## Stories of the Deranged and Demented

PRESENTED BY SINISTER SMILE PRESS

# INSTITUTIONALIZED
Stories of the Deranged and Demented

Edited by R.E. Sargent & Steven Pajak
Foreword by Brian Asman

Published by Sinister Smile Press, LLC
P.O. Box 637
Newberg, OR 97132

Trade Paperback ISBN – 978-1-953112-34-7

www.sinistersmilepress.com

# CONTENTS

FOREWORD     1
Brian Asman

END OF SHIFT     5
Ronald Kelly

MEMORY EATER     19
Jeremy Megargee

MINX     32
Brandon Scott

OUT OF THE BOX     53
Renee M.P.T. Kray

HESITATION CUTS     88
LP Hernandez

SPECTER OF INSANITY     106
Steven Pajak

NEVER BREAK THE CHAIN     124
Janine Pipe

LIONEL AND THE RED RAGE     136
Scott Harper

I AM BUT A SHELL     149
David Rider

LAB RATS     191
Jill Girardi

CASEY'S LAST RIDE     215
Scotty Milder

THE BUZZING     242
Mike Duke

WHEN LIGHTNING STRIKES     261
Richard Clive

NO SANCTUARY     276
R.E. Sargent

SOBRIQUET                                    299
Rebecca Rowland

A CRIME OF PASSION                           322
Richard Chizmar

About the Authors                            339
More from Sinister Smile Press               345

"These walls are funny. First you hate them. Then you get used to them. Enough time passes, it gets so you depend on them. That's institutionalized."

THE SHAWSHANK REDEMPTION

# FOREWORD

## BRIAN ASMAN

**M**adness.

A fertile subject for horror, because it's both intensely personal and as close to a universal fear as there ever could be. Maybe you don't believe in ghosts and therefore don't find them particularly scary. Or demons, if you're an atheist or agnostic. Hell, maybe you think in the unlikely event of a zombie apocalypse you'd be roaming the wastelands in a tricked-out pickup, shotgunning both the living dead and the world's remaining stock of PBR and having a goddamn grand old time, and therefore the thought of walkers running wild over the earth doesn't hold an ounce of terror for you.

Any horror trope, whether it's slashers or found footage or cybernetic undead armadillos of unusual size, you can find a cross-armed, scowling, jaded fan who's totally over it, because it doesn't get under their skin.

But madness?

Oh, that gets under your skin all right. Because for all our differences, we all have a mind, and those minds are completely capable of going haywire, no? Maybe we forget things, people, places. Perhaps we imagine things that aren't there or, worst of all, begin to believe we lack worth, that things can't get better, that happiness is a lie? Madness doesn't always look like a six-foot-tall anthropomorphic rabbit only we can see—sometimes, it's just our brains telling us the world might be better off without us in it.

And that's terrifying.

Insanity's one of the oldest horror tropes there is, the engine of fear behind everything from Poe's "The Telltale Heart" to Lovecraft's oeuvre to Gilman's "The Yellow Wallpaper," and far beyond, all the way to this little volume you're currently holding in your hands. Within its pages, you'll find sixteen tales of creepy asylums, unsettling strangers, bizarre creatures, surgeries and science experiments gone awry, sick and depraved fantasies, and much more. These stories explore the terror inherent when our own brains become—maybe not our enemy, but not our friend either. What if everything we've ever known is an illusion, a fever dream, a—

You get the picture.

Southern-fried horror stalwart Ronald Kelly kicks things off with "End of Shift," the tale of a rookie asylum guard who finds himself inexorably drawn to the notorious mass murderer in Cell 17, a man whom seems to know things he shouldn't.

In Jeremy Megargee's "Memory Eater," an elderly woman struggles with an entity dwelling in her own mind, gorging itself on decades' worth of memories. But even if she defeats it, how much of her will be left?

A lonely and disturbed man on the edge of emotional collapse roams the gritty underbelly of his city searching for answers in "Minx" by Brandon Scott.

Achieving your ideal life is quite a feat, but Kennedy's pulled it off in Renee Kray's "Out of the Box." Too bad her imaginary childhood friend's back, threatening everything she's worked so hard for…

L.P. Hernandez mixes psychosis and domestic turmoil in "Hesitation Cuts," the story of a man who believes his real wife is trapped somewhere beneath her own flesh, and he'll do *anything* to get her out.

Arnold is living his dream life, but at the expense of his dead friend and lover…however, the house of cards is about to all come crashing down. In Steven Pajak's "Specter of Insanity", one seemingly harmless event changes everything.

In "Never Break the Chain" from Janine Pipe, Felicity's languishing in pointless group therapy sessions, grappling with a mysterious affliction, losing hope her doctors will ever figure out her condition. At least until she's wheeled into the operating room...

Sometimes you can't stop madness, you can only hope to contain it...but for the titular Lionel in Scott Harper's "Lionel and the Red Rage," prison's just another killing floor.

In "I Am But a Shell" by David Rider, investigative journalist Sonja must face her own damage when a probe into White Willow Asylum stirs up her tragic past.

Hyper-intelligence is just another form of madness in "Lab Rats" by Jill Girardi. After a lab experiment goes awry, reality itself seems to break down for one rat-bitten scientist.

In "Casey's Last Ride" by Scotty Milder, exhausted office drone Erin meets an odd guy on the subway who's convinced he's already dead. But for walking corpse Casey, Erin might just be his path toward a macabre and final deliverance.

Is something crawling beneath your skin, or is it just your imagination? Mike Duke's "The Buzzing" explores one man's post-surgical experience with formication to gruesome effect.

When a supernatural storm hits the city in Richard Clive's "When Lightning Strikes," the ensuing mass psychosis is the least of Penny's problems, as a long-concealed secret she's kept from her controlling boyfriend becomes harder and harder to hide.

Kristen would do anything for her man, even though it's against her better judgement, but at what price? In R.E. Sargent's "No Sanctuary," she puts her life and freedom on the line for Hudson, but soon realizes she's made a grave error.

Parker's the charismatic managing editor of a high-profile non-profit by day, but he's harbored a dark secret since adolescence. When he meets a confidant who shares his peculiar fetish, fucked-up fantasies become gory reality in Rebecca Rowland's "Sobriquet."

Famed boogeyman chaser Richard Chizmar brings us home with "A Crime of Passion." When a famous author breaks character in his latest series and writes a gritty installment, and the movie adaption paints the book in an even more controversial manner, he realizes he has much to fear when he becomes the target of a radical group with no limits.

So dive on in. Mainline these stories of the deranged and the demented, soak them in, and never, ever lose sight of one simple, inescapable fact.

Yes, this *could* be you.

BRIAN ASMAN

# END OF SHIFT

## RONALD KELLY

Jay Wilmore stood at the guard's station on the east wing of Floor Three—the most dangerous ward in the building, or so he had been told—as the veteran guard on duty checked him in. It was his first night on the job and Jay had to admit his nerves were wired to the max.

"I would be neighborly and say something like 'welcome'," Sam Prater offered, "but everyone we welcome here are the sort of guests who never end up leaving." He nodded toward the long corridor that stretched beyond the safety barrier. Jay stared through the sturdy iron bars at the brightly lit hallway. The walls were painted a sickly sea-foam green and along the walls on either side were heavy steel doors with a single window set at face level. From right to left, there were sixteen in all. And, at the very end of the dead-end corridor, was Number 17.

That was the one that bothered Jay Wilmore the most.

Sam sensed the young man's unease. "Don't sweat it. You'll do just fine. Just keep on your toes and try not to fraternize with the inmates, and this job will be a piece of cake. Oh, you'll see and hear a lot of crazy shit..." Officer Prater caught himself. "Sorry...we're not supposed to use that word. You'll hear a lot of *mentally unbalanced* shit...but don't pay it any attention. Leave it here on Floor Three when you clock out and go home to your family with a clear mind." He regarded Jay, tall and lean, scarcely twenty-five years old —and was curious. "You're married, aren't you?"

The new guard smiled. "Yep. For five years now. Got a beautiful wife and a little girl, six years old. All blue eyes and curly, blond hair. Whatever she wants, she gets from dear old Dad."

Sam chuckled. "I got a couple like that myself, but they're halfway through college now. I'm not going to lie, though. They still have me twisted around their little fingers the same as they did the day they were born."

Laughter echoed from down the green corridor. From the door at the very end.

"You keep looking at Number 17."

"Well, it's kind of hard not to," admitted Jay. "That's the one, isn't it? The one *he's* in?"

Sam took the new man by the elbow and turned him away from the steel-barred gate and the ward that lay just beyond. "Listen to me, son. It kinda bothers me…you starting your first day acting like some kind of true crime fan-boy." The elder guard glanced over Jay's shoulder. In the little window of Door Number 17, a face grinned through the reinforced glass. It looked like a framed portrait of pure, unbridled lunacy. "None of these guys here deserve special attention…not for what they've done…especially not *that* one."

Jay's ears reddened in embarrassment. "I'm just curious, that's all."

The middle-aged man nodded, not looking at all convinced. "So, you haven't read the three books written about him…or seen the Netflix special?"

"Well, yeah…all of that."

Sam looked him square in the eyes. The stare was so intense, he had the young guard's undivided attention. "Take my advice, kid. Don't go down there if you don't have to. Don't look at him…and sure as hell don't *talk* to him. It's better for you and all of us if you just keep your distance and treat him like any other nutcase on the ward. Don't give him what he wants. Don't treat him like a celebrity."

Jay knew he should just keep his mouth shut, but his wife

always told him that he had about as much tact as a skeleton had spit. "Well, in a way, he *is*, isn't he?"

Sam shook his head in wonder. "You're not making any brownie points this morning, you know that? Now, I hate to pull rank on you —I'm really not that kind of guy—but I *am* your superior. And I'm telling you to keep your ass away from him. You don't want him in your head, or everything he can weasel out of you inside his. He's insane, but he isn't dumb. In fact, he's probably smarter than me and you put together."

Jay sensed that he had been walking on thin ice. "I'm sorry, sir. I didn't mean to start out on the wrong foot."

The elder guard smiled and clapped Jay on the shoulder. "Let's just forget it and start fresh. I'll show you the ropes this week and then you go on nights the next. Most of the inmates will sleep through your eight-hour shift and you won't even know they're there." Again, he looked down the corridor to the end. "Except him. It's like he's up twenty-four/seven. He never sleeps."

Jay Wilmore wanted to turn around and see if that grinning face was still in the window of Door Number 17. Wanted to know if he was watching and listening. But he didn't. He knew he had pushed his luck too far already.

A COUPLE OF DAYS LATER, JAY WAS SITTING AT A TABLE IN THE cafeteria downstairs when someone slid into a chair opposite him. It was a fellow guard, more heavy in gut than muscle and sporting a thick brown beard. Jay had seen him around the facility for the criminally insane but didn't know his name.

"You don't mind if I sit here, do you?" he asked, unwrapping a tuna salad sandwich he had bought out of a vending machine.

"No, go ahead." He took a bite of his own ham and cheese. "Jay Wilmore."

"Ted McNair," answered the other. "So, how do you like it here?"

Jay shrugged. "It's a job."

Ted nodded. "Same here. I guess there's worse ways to draw a paycheck, huh?" He opened a bag of chips and ate a couple. "You're on Floor Three, aren't you?"

"Yeah."

"Where all the high-octane squirrels are. So, have you seen *him* yet?"

Jay tried to act like he didn't know what he was talking about. "Seen *who*?"

Ted rolled his eyes. "You know who! Big daddy of the block. Hoyt Hacker."

Jay's heart felt like it skipped a beat. He believed that was the first time he had actually heard the man's name spoken out loud since he got there.

The other guard snickered. "Hacker! The name fits, don't you think?"

Jay looked at the big man across from him, sensing that he was someone he could talk to without it getting back to Sam Prater. "I know. You don't think his name being that, you know, triggered something?"

Ted smiled. "You never know with guys like that. One moment they're as sane as you or me. The next, they're hacking away at their family with a freaking axe."

Jay suddenly didn't feel as hungry as he had a moment before. "Yeah...them and everyone else in the neighborhood."

"Seventeen in all, wasn't it? Jesus, even kids. And one a baby just home from the hospital."

Now Jay definitely didn't have an appetite. "Did they ever figure out why he did it?"

"No," said Ted, "and he's never said either. He's a damn enigma. I guess most looney tunes like that are. Only, he's got a Wikipedia page and fifty pages of links on Google."

Jay stood up and gathered his trash from the tabletop. "Well, I guess I'd better get back to my station. It was nice talking to you, Ted."

"Yeah, bro. Same here." Before Jay could step away, Ted reached out and grabbed his arm. "Uh, hey, be careful, okay? Three other guys have had your job and they didn't last a week. And it all had to do with *him*."

"I'll be all right," Jay assured him. "I know how to handle myself."

Ted's smile told him that he wasn't a hundred percent convinced. "Yeah, right. Well…see you around."

Jay nodded and, dumping his garbage in a trash can, headed upstairs to continue his shift.

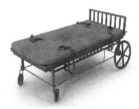

EVERYTHING WAS FINE FOR HIS FIRST THREE NIGHTS ON THIRD SHIFT. Until Thursday. Then it happened.

He was walking down the long hallway beyond the barred security area, checking doors, making sure they were secure. When he reached Door 17, the window was dark. No light inside.

Jay felt relieved. Maybe he did sleep after all. He checked the door and, satisfied that it was locked, turned to go.

"Hey, new guy. Let's talk."

The guard stopped in his tracks. It was the voice. The one on the interviews, the interrogation videos, the loop track in the middle of that song by that death metal band. What was the name of it? "Hacker Hoyt on Bloodstained Avenue," a play on Bloomstead Avenue, the street where all those friends and neighbors had innocently opened their doors and received an axe blade through the forehead or across their throat.

He took a couple steps, trying to ignore him.

"Come on…you've been wanting to talk to me. It's been eating at you since you got the call that you got the job."

Jay stopped and sighed. *Don't do this. Just leave well enough alone.* But he couldn't.

He turned and looked at the little window. Hoyt Hacker had his face pressed all the way up to the glass, so much so that the flesh of his forehead, nose, and cheeks were flattened and distorted. Along with that wicked, mile-wide grin of his, Hacker looked more like some obscene cartoon character than an actual human being.

"Yeah, Hacker? What do you want?" He tried to sound unconcerned, nonchalant. But under his uniform shirt his heart was beating like a jackhammer.

The inmate laughed. "Whoa, buddy. Slow that ticker down. I ain't gonna hurt you. I'm in here and you're out there. No need to piss your pants."

"Don't flatter yourself," Jay said, attempting to keep his voice steady and authoritative. "Now just shut up and get back to…well, whatever you were doing."

"What I was doing was waiting for you, Jay," said Hacker. "I just wanted to talk. Don't you want to talk? Maybe ask me some questions? You do have them, don't you? Questions?"

Something bothered the young guard. How had he known his first name? His name tag only said Wilmore. "No, I don't have any questions. I really don't give a shit about you or why you're in here."

Hacker laughed. It sent a shiver down Jay's spine. He sort of felt like Batman with the Joker standing a few feet away.

"Liar, liar, pants on fire!" taunted the mass murderer. "Come on. I'm bored. I'll tell you anything you want to know. You tell me something, I tell you something in return. Sound like a fair deal?"

He heard Sam Prater's words in his mind. *You don't want him in your head, or everything he can weasel out of you inside his.*

"Sorry. No time for talking. I've got to get back to my desk. Got things to take care of." He turned and started back down the hall.

"Like playing Wordle on your phone? Or is it Candy Crush?" Hacker giggled. "Sandra would kid the living shit out of you if she knew you played that, wouldn't she?"

*Sandra? How did he know about Sandra?*

"There goes your heart again. Boom-ba-boom-ba-boom. You're gonna have coronary before you reach your twenty-sixth birthday, buddy. It's on the 29th, isn't it?"

Against his better judgement, Jay whirled on his heels and glared at the face in the window. "How the hell do you know…?"

Hacker grinned that stupid grin of his but didn't laugh. This time, his eyes didn't match the smile below it. They were bright and shiny, almost feverish. Like a Peeping Tom. Except he was spying on the guard's thoughts and not some naked woman through a bathroom window.

"I don't know nothing, fella. You're a big mystery to me. But not for long. You'll talk to me…and it won't be long, either."

*Get the hell out of here,* Jay told himself. He turned back around, walked to the end of the corridor, unlocked the barred gate, and then closed it behind him.

"Go on!" yelled Hacker behind him. "It's almost lunch time. Eat that chicken salad sandwich on honey wheat bread with the sour cream and onion chips. And the Little Debbie's oatmeal pie for dessert."

Jay walked to his desk a couple of yards from the gate. On his desk was his Igloo cooler. Inside was chicken salad on honey wheat, a bag of sour cream and onion chips, and an oatmeal pie. He hadn't seen what Sandra had packed him for lunch…she had told him it was a surprise.

But it wasn't. He knew they were there.

Just as Hoyt Hacker had told him.

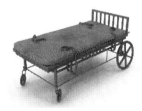

THE FOLLOWING MONDAY NIGHT, JAY WAS SITTING AT HIS DESK, FILLING out inmate evaluations, when Hacker's voice drifted down the hallway. He was singing that song…the one about Bloodshed Avenue.

"Shut up down there, Number 17!" Jay told him, loud enough for the inmate to hear.

The singing stopped. "Oh, we're going by numbers now, are we? So I can call you 8043, then? Or 1277? Which one do you prefer?"

Jay felt sick to his stomach. The first one was the last four digits of his social security number…the second the last four of his cell phone number.

*I've had enough of this shit,* he thought to himself. *I've got to know how he's finding these things out.*

He stood up and, before approaching the gate, checked his belt. Everything was in place. The pepper spray, nightstick, and taser. He wasn't intending on opening the door of #17, but he wanted to know they were there, in case…*what?* What was he afraid of? Hacker was just a man behind six inches of steel security door. There was no threat to him at all.

A minute later, Jay was standing at the end of the hall, facing Hoyt Hacker's cell. "I want to know how you…?"

"What? Know that your mom's favorite flowers are purple iris? Sandra's dream vacation is Venice, Italy?" Hacker grinned broadly and held something up to the little window. He held it against the glass, so Jay had no trouble seeing it. "Or that Jennifer almost screwed up this picture because she got a hold of the scissors in the kitchen drawer by the refrigerator and decided to cut her own hair?"

The little photo the murderer held against the glass was of Jay's daughter. Jenny's first-grade school picture. The one that only looked decent because Sandra had worked half an hour combing their daughter's hair so that unsightly gap in her bangs wouldn't show. The photo Jenny had brought home in the picture package, in her backpack, yesterday afternoon.

"Where the hell did you get that?" Jay pulled his wallet frantically from his back pocket and unfolded it. The plastic window that had held his daughter's photo a few hours before was empty.

"Such a pretty little girl. Too bad about that stutter. I hear Danny

12

Torello has been giving her a hard time about it. 'J-J-J-Jennifer!' he calls her. Bullying is such an ugly thing, don't you think?"

Suddenly, the key was in the lock and Jay was wrenching the metal door open. All precaution and common sense had flown completely out the window. He had to have that photo and he sure as hell was going to find out how the bastard got it out of his wallet.

Jay slipped the nightstick from his belt and took a firm grip on it. Hacker was no longer standing where he had been before. He was in the dark cell somewhere. Jay reached over with his free hand and found the light switch. He turned it on. Nothing happened. The cell remained as black as pitch.

"Hacker," he said, trying to keep his voice calm and even. "Where are you, Hacker?"

Nothing. Complete silence. Not even the sound of breathing.

*Step out and shut the door...now!* he told himself. But the photograph. He had to have...

There was a tug and his belt grew eight ounces lighter.

"Dance for me, new guy."

Then a *pop* and the jab of barbs in his chest. And the sizzle of voltage traveling through the lead wires from Taser to flesh.

A moment later, Jay was on the floor, jerking and bucking and pissing his pants.

And the occupant of Cell #17 was at the opposite end of the hall, slamming the security gate behind him, laughing all the way.

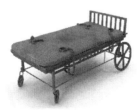

"Let's go over this again, Officer Wilmore."

"But I told you..."

"Again, Wilmore. Give us the reason. Why the hell did you open that door?"

13

He was in the warden's office, sitting in a chair in the center of the room. Still jittery from the tasing, sweating profusely, nervous as hell. There were nine other people in the room with him. Warden Thompson, Sam Prater, two guards, Ted, who he had met in the cafeteria, and another named Henry, the chief of police and a patrol officer, a legal assistant from the District Attorney's office, and two FBI agents. None of them were happy. They had a lot on their plates early that morning.

After all, their most infamous inmate had flown the coop and had been on the loose for the past four hours.

"He...he had my daughter's photograph. I told you that already."

"And how did he gain possession of it, Officer Wilmore?" asked one of the FBI agents, a thin woman with her dark hair pinned back and a severe look on her narrow face. "Are you sure it's not still in your wallet?"

"Hell, no, it's not in my wallet!"

"Could you check for us?"

"Okay!" Angrily, he took the wallet from his hip pocket. "But it's not..."

"Just humor us. Please."

Jay opened the wallet. Daddy's little girl smiled at him from behind the plastic window.

"How the hell did this get—"

Now it was the warden's turn. "Officer Wilmore, you are hereby suspended from duty until an inquiry takes place concerning this grave breech of security." He shook his balding head angrily. "Dammit, man...how could you let this happen?"

"I...I'm sorry."

"Prater, take his belt and equipment, and then escort him from the building. We will be in touch with you, Officer Wilmore." There was no leniency in the warden's voice. Just stern coldness lacking any degree of mercy whatsoever.

Ten minutes later, he was at the time clock. His superior watched in sullen silence as he clocked out and returned his card to its place in the slot rack on the wall.

"This isn't looking good for you, Wilmore," Prater finally said with a sigh. "I warned you, didn't I?"

Jay said nothing, just left the building and walked across the parking lot to his car, feeling stunned and confused, wondering exactly how—and why—he had let his guard down and allowed one of the country's most notorious mass murderers to walk away from a maximum security facility, scot free.

JAY PULLED HIS CAR INTO THE DRIVEWAY AND SAT THERE FOR A LONG moment, still trying to digest what had taken place. He was afraid to go in the house. What would Sandra say about all this? He could already see the worry and disappointment in her pretty face.

Finally, he sighed, climbed out, and walked up the sidewalk to the front door. It was a little after eight-thirty. He usually got home from his shift a quarter after six. Jenny would already be at school and his wife would be in her office, working from home.

He reached for the doorknob.

The door swung slowly open.

Somewhere inside, someone laughed. *He* laughed.

*Oh no…oh God.*

Jay reached for his belt and found…nothing. No nightstick, no pepper spray, no Taser. They were on Sam Prater's desk back at the facility.

Scarcely able to breathe, he pushed the door all the way open. Stepped in. Felt the carpet go squishy under the soles of his shoes. Soaked full of…

"Come in and join the party, Jay."

The first thing he saw was Sandra. She was over there…and here…and *everywhere.*

Hoyt Hacker stood in the center of the living room. His orange coveralls were dark red now. Glistening. His face happy. His hair full of blood and gore and tiny bits of Sandra.

"Daddy's home," the man said softly. "Run and give him a big kiss." And, with that, he slung something in Jay's direction. Something he had been holding in his bloody hand. Something pale and round, with long honey-blond hair.

As it rolled toward him, Jay saw everything. The freckles. The hole in her smile where she had lost a baby tooth a week ago. The glassy blue eyes. The gap in her bangs caused by the scissors.

Jay screamed and ran forward. Hoyt stood there, grinning, holding the axe from the shed in his left hand. He didn't raise it to defend himself. He simply waited and let the ward guard overtake him. A second later, Jay was on top of him, punching, tearing, strangling the life from him.

"I'll kill you!" Jay screamed shrilly. "I'll kill you, you son of a bitch!"

"You can't," said Hoyt with that smile. "Can't kill me."

"Damn...sick...bastard..." Fingers tightening, burrowing into flesh, seeking death and justice.

"You can't." Hoyt's face was as purple as a bruise, his eyes bulging, his mouth grinning. "Can't kill me...can never kill me."

Jay screamed hysterically. Continued to strangle until his hands ached, then grew numb.

"Never," the inmate told him, calmly, serenely. "Never can kill me."

IT WAS JOHN MASTERSON'S FIRST MORNING ON THE JOB. HIS SUPERIOR, Fred Garcia, was giving him a tour of Floor Three when the screaming started.

"I'll kill you! I'll kill you, you son of a bitch!"

"Who the hell is that?" he asked, startled. He breathed deeply, trying to calm himself.

He didn't want his new boss to get the idea that he was a man who was easy to rattle.

"Oh, that's inmate #17," Fred told him. He seemed unconcerned, as though he had heard this type of thing a hundred times before.

"Damn…sick…bastard…"

Garcia sensed the new employee's unease. "Come on. We'll check on him."

Halfway down the corridor, John thought he heard another voice. Strangely calm and serene. "Never. Never can kill me."

"What's going on?" he had to ask.

They reached the door of Cell #17 and peered through the little reinforced glass window. A tall, lanky man was getting up off the floor and walking to the wall next to his bunk. There was a uniform hanging on a peg on the wall. He whistled cheerfully as he began to remove his orange coveralls.

"His name is Jay Wilmore," Garcia explained. "He was a former prison guard here. A good, dependable man for five years on the job. Then one morning, he clocked out, drove home, and killed his wife and daughter with an axe. A horrible thing…him ending up back here after committing such an unthinkable crime as that."

Confused, John watched through the window as Wilmore finished undressing and then began to dress in the guard uniform hanging from the peg. "I…I don't understand. Why do you let…?"

"Let him pretend?" The chief guard smiled sadly. "It pacifies him…keeps him manageable. He's got a whole routine mapped out in his head. Dressing for work, clocking in, walking around his cell all day, like he's making his rounds. He even has a cast of characters to keep him company. A chief guard—like me—named Prater, fellow guards named Ted and Henry, and even a warden named Thompson. He has them all worked out in that warped brain of his, their life stories, wives and children, what they eat for lunch, when they go to the restroom."

"Weird," said John. He watched as Jay Wilmore finished dressing and, taking a timecard from under his pillow, walked over the wall and said, "Cla-click." Then he returned the card to his bunk and began to walk back and forth across the eight-by-ten area of his cell.

"It was terrible what he did...how he snapped like that for no reason at all," Fred told him. "But he's pretty much harmless now. He'll walk around like that for eight hours, clock out at the end of his shift, put on his coveralls, and be an inmate again. It's been going like that for eight years now, just like clockwork."

*I guess you're just going to have to get accustomed to it,* John told himself. *All the wackos and the little games they play.*

"Come on," Garcia told him. "Let's go to the conference room and we'll do your orientation. I'll get us some coffee. How do you like yours?"

"Black," John said absently. "No cream, no sugar."

They were halfway down the corridor when laughter echoed behind them.

John Masterson looked around to see the face of Jay Wilmore plastered against the glass, staring at him through the little window. His smile was broad and seemed to reach from ear to ear...his eyes bright and shiny, looking like someone in the throes of a high fever.

The murderer gave him a knowing wink. For some reason, it sent a shiver down the guard's spine.

"Hey, new guy...let's talk."

# MEMORY EATER

## JEREMY MEGARGEE

There is something malevolent that is living inside my head, and it is eating my memories. What day is it? I thought it was Monday, but now I think it's Friday. I know my sister's name, I'm certain that I do, it's just locked on the tip of my tongue and it refuses to dislodge. Certain things that I always took for granted seem to be gradually fading, and it leaves me feeling confused and outside of myself. How could these things fragment in my mind and fall into obscurity? It isn't possible. I've figured it out.

It's that rancid thing that I see out of the corner of my eye when the curtains aren't properly closed. It gapes with a swollen face, and slobber oozes down its chin from a maw that is permanently unhinged, the jaw bones deformed to the point that it cannot support the weight of its own crooked rictus grin. It looks at me in the wee hours of the morning when I want to sleep and is never fully visible because it wears the curtains like a funeral shroud. But I always feel it. I feel it slouching through the rooms inside of my head, licking at the things it likes, chewing at the tastiest pieces of my past and swallowing with great enthusiasm.

My children do not see it. They claim there is nothing that watches from beyond the curtains, but they are wrong. I want to call to them and ask for their comfort, but it has eaten their names from within me, and it has made strangers of those that were birthed from my own womb. I am alone, and it likes that. It's easier to feed on those that are lost in isolation.

I feel its talons picking at me when I'm simply craving peace, and sour gusts of carrion-scented breath tickle my ears from behind when I'm resting in my chair. I don't know what it is. It is more than an animal but less than a man. It prefers the sick and the wounded, because it knows we make for easier meals. I hate knowing that it is inside me. I hate waking up in the morning and wanting to take my medication but forgetting which pills treat which ailments, and soon they all just bleed together into a handful of purples and blues that make my stomach cramp.

What's the year? I can't recall if I am a teenager or an old woman. Maybe I am just a little girl twisted up in the blankets, doing my best to strangle screams as the Memory Eater lurks in the peripherals of a bedroom with butterflies painted on the walls. It is eating the best parts of me, and time is no longer linear. Time is this vast black dimension where stars don't bother to shine. There's nothing in the long, empty hours but its huge, fish-like irises and the mucus that coats the rims of its eyelids. Each time it laps at my brain like a dog tasting the blood of roadkill on a backroad, I lose more of who I used to be. Where did I meet my first husband? Is he alive, or did he die of cholera?

If he is dead, I think I'll see him soon. It's possible that I'm dead already. I have a little hand mirror and when I raise it up to my face I barely recognize myself. My skin is gray, sagging and loose, and it's like someone has pulled a mask overtop of my skull. Where did those crow's feet come from? Why is there lipstick on my teeth? When is the last time I washed my hair, and when I touch it, why does it feel so brittle between my fingertips?

The television shows that I used to love aren't kind anymore. The people on the shows talk about me and mock me and invite the Memory Eater to take its time devouring what is left. I awaken running through the corridors of my own mind, trying to outpace the fiend, but it limps and it crawls on the walls and it buzzes after me with the sticky wings of a fly, and if I stop for even a moment and turn to face it, that proboscis will slurp up a soul that I promised to God in the muddy river baptism of my youth.

I realize that trying to outrun something like this isn't possible. It doesn't need sleep and it was not born, so it suffers no fatigue like mortals do. It won't stop until all that remains of the person I was is entirely consumed, and I will not let that happen. I will lift withered arms, and I will fight. Tendons creak and muscles feel wasted, but the will still burns, and the will is what I have.

It smiles inside of me, because it senses resistance, but it feels I won't be much of a threat to it. It opens wide the maw, showing jagged teeth coated in strings of moss from the forest path where I had my first kiss at seventeen years old, and it bites into the boy that gave me that kiss, crunching through his face and his limbs, stealing his name, licking up the scraps of that experience and what I'm able to remember about it. It belches out the bones of that special moment in my life, and to seek it now is to find a pit in my thoughts, the ground washed out and no details left of the recollection. Was there ever a boy? Was there ever a kiss? I want to believe there was a forest path, but where, and when, and how did I come to be there...

Its laughter echoes through me, and it pulls the curtains tight around its giant malformed face, making a napkin of them, rubbing the material across the smeared foulness of plump lips encrusted with sores.

There is one thing I'm able to remember, and I keep it locked deep inside of me. It's imprisoned in a room with a thousand rusty padlocks and bells to sound the alarm if the Memory Eater ever gets near.

It's something I'll protect until the last of me is bled dry, and based on the current state of things, that won't be long. I must find a way to kill the Memory Eater.

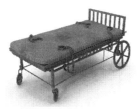

"Look at the cows way down there. They look like little beetles on the hills."

I sit on the edge of the overlook with May beside me, and we're kicking our feet, our scuffed knees drinking in the sunlight. I like the warmth on my skin, and it makes me forget my thoughts. I don't think about Daddy losing his job at the coal mine. I don't think about how Momma frowns so much now that her mouth seems to permanently sag. The hard times don't matter up here, because there's just sunlight, dragonflies, and May prattling on while tugging at the little pieces of rawhide that keep her pigtails in place.

My eyes are closed, and the eyelids are coated in dark orange, the color bleeding through the thin membrane to make little dark motes dance across my shielded vision. I'm focusing on my senses, breathing in the honeysuckle, and I like how the grass tickles the underside of my thighs. May's going on and on about the boy she likes, some scruffy little fella she met at the county fair, and I just smile and nod, swaying in the breeze, feeling the fulfillment of being young and alive in this moment beside my friend.

I let my eyes flutter lazily open, and stretched down below are verdant valleys for as far as I'm able to see, pastures and farmland, hills dotted in evergreen, and it's like some giant painter came down out of the sky to make this scene as close to perfection as it can possibly get.

May is right; the cows do look incredibly small from up here, little more than insects crawling across squares of horizon.

"Wouldn't you like to be a bird, Poppy? It must be something special to fly. Just fluff out your feathers and go. If we were birds, we wouldn't be stuck in this town. My folks say it's going dry. The mines are getting boarded up, and the town is going dry."

I follow my friend's gaze, and I watch the hawk that's soaring overhead, circling and circling, riding the current of the wind. I squint, seeing it so clearly in the realm of memory.

"Sign me up, May. Let's go be birds."

May laughs, and she already sounds like a bird. An excitable sparrow chirping out her approval. I'm resting my arms and chin on the bottom of the rotten fence post, and I'm thinking about how hard it is not to think. I'd like to turn off my brain sometimes, make it be quiet, but that isn't easy. I wish I could think only the thoughts that I want to think.

"What's that down there? The cows are going all red. Is there a glare, or do you see it too?"

My brow furrows, and I return my attention to the valleys beneath us. It's hard to comprehend what I'm seeing. The cows are popping like pimples, fine bursts of crimson spray left in the wake of each explosion, and from this vantage point, the sound is like a little percussive blast each time it happens. There's something down there with them. A rolling brown blur of teeth and eyes and spindly hands where hands have no right to be.

I'm standing up, using the old remnants of fence to push myself up to my bare feet, and I'm watching pieces of hilltop fall away, scooped into a funnel-like gullet, trees and earth falling down into trenches that lead to the infinite.

"No. I was safe here."

"What are you saying, Poppy? What is *that*??"

It is eating all there is to eat, moving lightning quick through the cows and turning them to mincemeat, a razorblade in motion, and it eats the ground, it eats the farmhouses, it reaches up into the clouds and it slurps them down like messy milkshakes, and white foam bubbles from its chin, and it's growing, becoming larger in size and fearsome influence.

"Run, May. Run until your legs feel like they're gonna fall off, and then keep running."

I start running to show my friend what she must do to escape it, and the last thing I see behind me is the Memory Eater lifting its crooked girth up overtop all that there is, and it takes hold of that blazing sun that warmed me so, and it crushes it in its oozing palms. The sun shatters like a lightbulb, and all is dark. The behemoth pulls shards into its gaping mouth, and it chews up what is left of the sun, destroying something that gave me pleasure, chewing on something that once made me happy. It smiles at me in a world of ultimate obsidian, the crunching noises of the hot sun between its scummy teeth giving off dying flickers, and it swallows down the burning.

I'm yanking at May, trying to pull her forward, but she's winded and losing steam, and the fingers come for her, fingers of raw pink tissue shaped like organic forks, and they pierce my friend, they dismember her, they pull her little body apart and her guts splatter on the path and the fingers scoop up the guts and smear them across loveless lips, painting rouge on the scabrous face that wants to eradicate all that I am.

I am running, still holding my friend's severed hand, and it takes me a while to drop it. It falls into a chasm, because that's all there is now, just a chasm, because this memory is being devoured, and the little girl that I was tries desperately to balance on a strip of jagged land that teeters and longs to fall into the abyss.

I'm falling now, and I don't recall anything about that day at the overlook. I can't remember what May's face looked like, where she lived, or how we became friends.

My arms pinwheel, and somewhere in the lost fathoms, I hear a satiated beast digesting precious pieces of my mind.

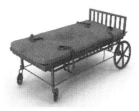

Dark silhouettes loom on all sides, and I can't make them out; they're hunched and faceless and I can only drag my fingernails against the arms of the recliner and keep my eyes shut in hopes that they'll fade into vapor. They whisper, and they sound like my children. But surely they aren't my children, right? They must be strangers from the outer dark. I'm not sure if I have children. I think I did once, in a life that was not this life.

"She's getting worse. We can't keep doing this."

"What do you suggest? She's our mother. She's our responsibility."

"You don't get it, Janet. You only just got into town, and you haven't been around like we have. She's up at all hours of the night. She takes off all her clothes and walks into the road in the wee hours of the morning. She claims there are rats living in her chair. She speaks to people that are long dead, and she constantly raves about something behind the curtains that she claims is eating her from the inside out. It's that bad…"

"I hate to see her like this."

"So do I, but it can't be helped. We're not trained for this, and we all have jobs. We have lives and children of our own. She needs 24/7 care, and she'll only get that from a professional."

"I'll not consent to put her in that hellhole in the center of town. I've heard about the things that go on in Trans-Allegheny Lunatic Asylum. The doctors are barbarians in there. They'll poke and prod her, and they'll leave her to rot on dirty tiles."

"It's better than Moundsville State Prison. The inmates sit in raw sewage and maggots drop down from the ceiling like plump white raindrops. And if this goes on, she could hurt someone, and that's where she will end up."

I want to lift up my hands and clamp them over my ears so I won't hear their endless chatter, but it feels like my arms are heavy, and I'm afraid if I move too much, they'll turn hostile and attack me. They speak about me as though I am not here at all. They are shades and this must be a nightmare. I wish they'd go away. I wish they'd leave me in peace.

"What's her diagnosis again? I'm trying to understand. Why doesn't she recognize us? Why does she seem so locked inside of herself?"

"They call it early-onset dementia. Her mind is eroding. Everything that she once knew is falling apart. She's confused all the time, and I can't imagine what it's like for her."

I grind my teeth, and I want to scream, but I choke the scream down out of fear. I want to tell them that they're wrong. I'm not brainsick, I'm not ill, and I know exactly what is happening inside of me.

It's the Memory Eater. It has always been the Memory Eater.

And just thinking of it seems to give it power, because the room shakes and rattles, the voices of the black shadow things that speak in familiar tones become distant, and I'm swirling and swirling, and it's not the recliner I'm sitting in now, but an ornate chair seated at the head of a dining table that overspills with decadence.

The table is piled high with grimy plates, and candelabras provide flickering illumination, the wax dripping down silver arms while all is painted in the amber-tinted glare of the infernal.

It sits stinking on the opposite end of the table, its skin nothing but meat spoiled rotten, lumpy and leering as it watches me. I don't like to look directly at it. I hate to see the pus that leaks from its nostrils, the centipedes that encircle its veins, and the sagging mouth that can open like a black hole filled with teeth from broken stars.

It eats from several plates balanced in front of it, and I know that it wants me to look. I shouldn't look, but I'm compelled to do so. I see the teddy bear I had when I was little, a frumpy old fellow named Bast. I see the folded wedding dress that I wore when I was thirty-four years old with the frilly sleeves and the sheer back. I see the first car I ever drove when I passed my test and got my license, a purple Ford Pinto, the car perched there on a plate with its wheels spinning and puffs of exhaust billowing up into the air.

It picks up Bast, pinching the stuffed limbs, and it sucks on its head, decapitating the teddy bear and lapping at the stuffing that comes out of him. It eats his button eyes last, and once they're gone, I know nothing of Bast. There never was a teddy bear, and I don't know why I thought I had one.

It cuts up the wedding dress with a steak knife that is encrusted with rust, and it eats it like pasta. It holds narrow hands with twitching fingers under the candelabra, and it collects steaming wax on its palms, and it smears this across the tattered pieces of dress, using it like sauce to make the material easier to choke down. There's a level of pageantry to the way that it eats. It wants me to see how cavalier it is when it devours my memories.

I hate it so, and I simmer like the flames from the candles that light the table. I remember nothing of that wedding, and any recollection of being a bride has vanished down the drain. It is eating the Pinto now, crunching on the metal and popping the tires with its tusks, and the sound of that shrieking metal in its mouth is the worst thing a human being can ever possibly hear.

I know that it will not stop until it has eaten all there is to eat. I'm not fully hollow yet, and there are bits of me that have not had the chance to pass down its gullet.

I will need what remains.

I will use what is left.

I'm staring at the walls and drooling when I hear the music of the bells. Every cell within me switches to high alert, and I'm transported through the dusty corridors of my own psyche until I reach the enormous vault door at the end of a labyrinthine hall.

The door is a massive structure, all plated steel and thick iron rivets, a complex wheel lock in the center, and hundreds of yards of chain crisscrossing the surface of the door with padlocks of various sizes and strengths attached. It's meant to be impregnable, the last holdout in my mind, and it's decorated in antique brass bells should an intruder ever get near enough to sound them.

That intruder stands directly in front of the door, long wet fingertips trailing across the chains and padlocks, jangling them purposefully and making a show of it. It is shrouded in the tattered satin of my black curtains, the material bunched across its abnormally shaped head and falling across its face like a hood. There's only one bloodshot eye visible, the pupil the size of a dinner plate, and the indifference of a shark glimmers in its gaze. No emotion, no complexity, just dead black hunger that cannot be reasoned with.

It's a standoff, and I can only sway there on my weakened ankles, watching the Memory Eater taunt as it studies the door and widens six sets of slit nostrils to smell what is protected inside. It's the last good thing that I remember.

I watch it lean back, a vile phlegmy noise starting from deep in its malformed chest, and then it snaps forward and vomits stomach acid onto the padlocks. I watch the metal drip, turning molten, and the acid eats through the complicated locking mechanisms. Arms emerge from beneath the cape of curtain, first two, then four, then eight, and it takes chains into its balled fists, pulling at them, digging its heels into the floor and gaining purchase, and each time a chain snaps, I flinch and my eyes squeeze shut.

Its lips peel back, and it exposes infected gums with teeth all crowded together, and then those gums peel back too, multiple flaps of incisor and canine and gleaming razorblades that are placed intricately between the teeth to help it shred with impunity.

It's taking bites out of the door, big messy swallows of corroded steel, and the doorframe is vibrating, and it becomes apparent to me that what was built here for defense will not do. No fortress can defend against the Memory Eater, and no door will ever be strong enough to keep it out.

It was foolish of me to choose defense, because offense is all that a thing like this understands.

I don't know how the machete appears in my right hand, but I think I willed it there. It gleams in the endless hallway, catching the light, and the sight of it causes the Memory Eater to pause in its single-minded assault on the door. It looks dumbfounded at the machete, greenish bile boiling out from its gaping mouth and splattering in stringy expulsions across the frailty of its chest. This is something it did not expect, and as it stares and tries to understand, I see it in an entirely new way. Not a larger-than life force of nature that has power over me, but a moronic animal born to scavenge, something that knows only to consume when the host is vulnerable.

I tighten my grip on the machete, and I do not feel vulnerable at this moment. I feel protective. I know that even if it eats every single thought I've ever had in my silly old head, it will not get what is behind that door. That is where I draw the line. That is where this humiliation ends.

It speaks, barely intelligible. Words are dusty coming from its foul maw, as though it has not had the opportunity to utilize them in a very long time.

*"You be old. You be weak. I eats you, all of you, and what be left of an empty head goes to the dirt."*

It shambles forward, cocking its giant hydrocephalic head to the side, desperately trying to figure out where the fear has gone.

*"I be eating old graymeat for time out of time. I eats through your head and then you die. I leave you to the nursing homes and the beds soaked in piss. I do to you, and all that came before."*

It bares its thousands of hooked teeth and sprays out a hiss, phlegm and snot splattering forward, but I do not bend to its will, and I do nothing but stand my ground. When it sees that I am no longer intimidated, something strange happens. The Memory Eater becomes shy, almost embarrassed of how it looks. It grips the folds of curtain with its spindly fingers and pulls them closer over its own repugnant face, looking almost like a scared little child that wants to hide from something and pretend it isn't there.

But I am here, and I am something that it cannot hide from.

I move forward, and without even thinking what I am doing, I begin to hack at the monstrous thing that stands before me. It lifts up arms to block each blow, but it is weakened, confused, and it gets nothing but lacerations and dismemberment for its trouble. A pathetic mewling sound oozes from deep within its throat, and I let the blade fall almost mechanically, a viscous black blood splashing out each time I sink the machete into a new soft part of the Memory Eater's anatomy.

It is perfectly helpless, just how those with dementia feel when their minds deteriorate, and it chokes me up with righteous pride to make this entity feel exactly what its victims felt in the past.

It tumbles awkwardly to its side, scrunching its body up into a fetal position, legs and limbs and even a lashing stinger-tipped tail all drawing up against its sunken belly to protect itself from the cleaving, but it does no good. It drowns snuffling in a pool of the oil-colored substance that leaks from inside of it, and I am standing over it, impaling the machete into its torso over and over again, and it isn't a machete anymore, it's a broadsword, and it is the perfect weapon to slay a monster.

I've hacked through the Memory Eater's ribs, and I leave the broadsword embedded in the sour meat. I kneel down and crack those ribs open wide, and from inside the creature, iridescent bubbles begin to drift up into the air.

Each bubble floats for a few moments and then pops, and inside the bubbles are flashing images from my past. These are my memories, and each time a bubble pops, the memory contained inside of it is returned to me.

I step over the carcass, I walk through the iridescent bubbles, and I turn the twisted and corroded metal of the wheel lock. The great door swings inward, and it falls from the hinges after all the damage it took, sending a loud crash echoing down the hall.

There's a scene playing out in front of me.

A perfect memory, encapsulated in time, and seeing it now takes me back to the night when it happened.

I'm lying in a hospital bed, my hair plastered to my brow with sweat, and I'm beaming down at a tiny pink infant cradled in my arms. The baby is crying, newly born, and a little hand brushes up against the skin of my chest, feeling perfectly warm and smooth. I remember the touch of that hand. I remember the infant's first cries as it came into the world. I remember wiping down my baby's flushed little face, and I remember giving my firstborn daughter a name.

Laurel.

This is the memory I kept locked away. This is the moment I protected. This is the mother that I was, and this is the mother that I have always been.

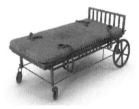

"Laurel..."

The dark silhouettes become visible, no longer specters there to haunt me, and now that the confusion is gone, their true natures are revealed. I see my adult children standing around me in the living room of my cottage. Janet, Bobby, and Laurel.

Laurel spins around, eyes wide in shock, and she leans closer to me, her hand reaching out to brush locks of fine gray hair away from my forehead.

"Mom? Did you guys hear that? She said my name. I think she recognizes me..."

My daughter kneels closer, taking my withered hand into her own, and I look at all of my children. For the first time in what seems like forever, I really look at them, and I'm able to see them as they are. There are tears in my eyes that make it difficult to see, but I see all the same.

"Do you know me, Mom? You remember my name?"

"You're my baby."

I squeeze her hand tighter, and though it is much bigger now, it has the same warmth that it once did when she was just a babe cradled in my arms.

"You're my Laurel."

My children embrace me, and my lips form all their names, and I speak the memories that once were lost. I look to the curtain, and there is nothing behind it but an infinitely blue sky, fluffy white clouds, and trees shedding their leaves as autumn takes them.

I see the world as it was before I left it, and I remember.

# MINX

## BRANDON SCOTT

M inx set his glass down, absent of the bar's chatter-driven atmosphere. He sat alone, running his fingers around the rim of the empty glass. His thoughts twisted and churned like malformed oily smoke, rising high above burning tires.

"Want a reload?" the barkeep asked.

*Where did Cherish go?* his mind whispered.

"Hey, man, I said do you want a reload?"

*She's gone? No—she can't be gone, can she?*

"Yo—" The bartender waved his hand in front of Minx's face in the midst of a whistle.

*I'm going to have to see the old man.*

"Will you get a load of this guy? Hey!" The bartender clapped next to Minx's ear.

"What?" Minx shouted, slamming his balled fist onto the heavy resin bar top. The jovial voices of the patrons were reduced to an immediate silence blended with small whispers.

"I said, do you want a refill on your gin, because if not, then I suggest you leave." The barkeep finished by sucking his tooth. "Ya feel me?" His narrowed eyes tightened with each spoken word.

"No." Minx tossed a twenty beside the glass, and as he got up, drifting toward the door, he found most of the attention in the room was on him. A small blaze of anger erupted in his heart, but he pushed it down.

The air on the street was heavy and thick with the threat of rain. Minx stood on the curb, looking up at the starless night sky. He closed his eyes, tasting the air as he breathed it in. It tasted sweet. It tasted of her. The sound of the distant thunder calmed his soul, and for a brief moment, he felt connected to the atmosphere and even to the sought-after stillness that only the night can offer. The peace within him was short lived, and just like everything he'd ever loved, a darkness came to take it away.

"Hey, sexy, you lookin' for some lovin'?" a woman said, wandering up from an adjacent alley.

Minx frowned as her voice was neither sensual nor seductive.

"Get lost, lady," Minx said.

"Are you sure, baby?" She wrapped an arm around his waist. Her other hand found his crotch and gave it a firm squeeze.

Minx's skin rippled like an ocean wave against her touch, feeling scummy and diseased at the contact. Everything about the woman became shrouded in a pulse of vile greasiness, and he hated her for it.

*Dirty boy! This is your fault—her fault! All her fault—DIRTY! DIRTY!*

Minx took her hand, tearing it away from his bulge. He spun the woman, face to face, before her smile could fade, driving her hand next to her throat. Minx pressed himself against her, looking into the depths of her eyes and finding them dull, bounding soulless, as life on the street had taken its toll.

He sympathized with the street walker and hated her even more. Minx squeezed her hand until the bones in her fingers became jutted folds in his palm. He covered her mouth with his free hand, watching her tears fall into the valley formed between his thumb and forefinger. The warmth against his skin from the liquid disgusted him, driving his anger to intoxicated levels.

Minx pushed through his internal madness, knowing precious time had eroded away. Tick by tick, just time wasted on the ilk of ill repute. He glanced around before electing to walk closer to the mouth of the alley from which she'd arrived. Minx moved her into the darkness as he took great care not to release the pressure over her mouth.

*One scream and we're done, big boy! Just one little scream—*

In the depths of the shadows, Minx freed her. A moment of true silence fell between them, but before she could draw breath to shout, he took her up in his arms and tossed her into the open dumpster behind him. Minx slammed the lid down and stood as sole witness to her muffled cries. He held the plastic firm against the metal as her fists and shoulders beat against it in perfect rhythm.

*One thump—two thump—three thump—and GO!*

Minx lifted the lid. The woman almost catapulted herself free, much to his amusement, and for a brief moment they locked eyes. He brought the lid down hard on top of her head, sending a final thud into the night air.

*If only there'd been more time,* he thought, as visions of cutting her face into little chunks and feeding them to her filled his mind's eye. *Awful small, that one—would probably only be enough for a morsel or two!*

Minx cast that thought aside then returned to the subtle glow of the streetlamps. He looked both ways before he crossed the street and disappeared into the night.

*The old man! Get to the old man! Enough of the games—old man! You must—old man—old—*

"I'm trying—I know, no more games, but—"

*How did it get like this? Your fault—you did this, not her, never her —just you!*

"Life was perfect."

*And now it's shit, just like you—shit.*

"The old man—"

*Yes, the old man—shit!*

"He will help. He will give me answers."

*He won't have a choice.*

In the soft wake of the passing headlights, Minx smiled.

*It wasn't your fault.*

"I know," he said aloud to no one as he walked the avenue. "It was hers."

A stranger sat on a bench that he passed by. He glanced down at her, ending his conversation with himself as she looked up.

"What?" he shouted.

The outburst startled her, and in silence she placed her gaze elsewhere, but not before he saw her eyes in the streetlight.

*Blue.*

Something inside of him burned hot, eating at his ability to rationalize. He wanted to pluck her pretty little eyes out and throw them into the pond, but he kept walking. He needed to keep walking.

His mind was a lit blaze, flaming out of control with heartache, with desire, and fueled by too much gin.

*Oh God, Cherish!* He saw her face in the dry line between light and shadow.

"Why?"

*Why did she leave you when everything was so perfect?*

"He'll know."

*Yes, he will—he always knows—always.*

He paused, leaning against a *no parking* sign as he closed his eyes. Minx clenched his fist in anguish, trying to conjure her face.

"Ah, there you are." He smiled.

Her face was blood-covered and bruised; her eyes were open but sightless.

*What the hell is wrong with you?* His mind cackled. *The old man knows, he always knows.*

The street sign vanished and Minx stumbled. In between blinks, he realized he was on the bright side of town and only three blocks from the old man's place. He sighed before straightening up. The gaps in memory were increasing and ever more terrifying. Minx shrugged it off; he was too close to the answers to be concerned. He spied some thugs out on a stoop about twenty paces up ahead.

"Hey now, lookey what just rolled up. Say, man, don't you know where you are?" one thug shouted as Minx approached.

In the daytime, he would have passed without issue, but now it was open season.

"Yeah, son, you gotta pay the toll!" the other man said, laughing, but Minx paid them no mind.

*They're trying to stop you! Keep you from the truth—slowing you down—don't—old man—old…*

"Hey bro, you deaf or somethin'? You better hand over that paper!" the man said, stepping down to the pavement in an effort to block Minx's advance.

Minx pulled a knife, sinking it deep into the punk's throat. Despite his rage, he laughed in uncontrolled fits. The man choked and wheezed as the blood spattered out of his mouth and onto the back of Minx's downturned hand. The little droplets felt like a touch of warm rain, sending Minx into the throes of unbounded joy.

"Whoa!" the remaining thug shouted, trying to draw his gun.

Minx pulled the knife free, kicking the punk to the cement. He spun, sending the weapon end over end, striking the man on the stoop square in the chest. The guy dropped the gun, clawing at his chest as he collapsed to his knees. Minx stepped up, taking hold of the knife's grip between the thug's hard gasps and pleas. He ignored him as he placed his boot on the man's shoulder and with a tug ripped the blade out. The thug tried to sit up, but Minx stomped him back down. Blood seeped through the man's shirt. Repulsed by the mess, Minx drug the boot's tread down the thug's pant leg, leaving a streak of crimson in its wake. He looked down into the man's fear-stricken face but cared not as he wiped the blade clean on the tail of the punk's shirt. He straightened himself, examining the blade in the streetlight. He folded it, replacing it in his back pocket.

*See what she made you do? All she had to do was stay and she couldn't, could she? It was too much to handle, wasn't it? Why do you need her? Why do you want her? She's trash—straight scum…*

"Because I love her!" Minx shouted down at the dying man, running his fingers through his sweat-laden hair.

*You're not handling this.*

"I don't care." He looked around the street, knowing he needed to get to the old man's place before things went from critical to nuclear. In silence, he resumed his short walk, and within a few seconds he was outside the old man's building.

"Hey! Could you hold that for me?" Minx called out to a young woman as she stepped through the door.

He watched as her eyes studied him. It was as if he could hear her mind pleading with her hands to shut the door and back away.

"Better hurry." She shrugged, offering a small smile.

"Thank you." He returned the smile, dropping eye contact.

*Blue — they're blue.*

Minx took the staircase to the left of the entrance without a second look. The butterflies in his gut swarmed with each new step, but this wasn't the first time he'd gone to see the old man. He didn't understand the nervousness in his stomach that decided to creep into his limbs. Minx had sat many a session on the old man's couch, spilling his thoughts and his traumas, and this would be no different, yet the anxiety remained.

He found himself alone in the long hallway, standing outside room three thirty-one. Minx focused on the chipped white paint around the peephole and the key marks on the dingy brass handle. He blew a small puff of air before he knocked. Silence filled the air as he listened for any signs of life beyond the door.

*And he's playing with ya!*

In a fit of anger, Minx pounded his squeezed fist against the wood slab. Commotion erupted from the other side.

"I'm coming, I'm coming!" a voice announced.

The door opened but was halted by the security chain.

"Hey," Minx said.

The man leaned into the crack, narrowing his eyes as his lower jaw drooped.

*Oh — he's fucking with ya! Fucking with ya hard, amigo!*

"Michael—uhm, Minx, what are you doing here? How did you know where I live?"

"We need to talk." Minx dropped his gaze to his boots.

"No, we don't—our sessions ended two, three years ago? You don't need to be here."

*He's pushing you, man! He's trying to fuck with your head!*

"Nah, he wouldn't do that," Minx said, frowning at the thought as he watched the color leave the old man's face.

*Yeah, he would. What do you even think he's doing right now? Look at that face. Does that brow say, "Come on in"? He's playing you hard, kid!*

Minx kicked the door, breaking the chain. The force from the impact threw the man to the floor. Minx stepped in and loomed over him, realizing the silver of the old man's thick hair and beard made his gray eyes twinkle with a Santa Claus quality.

"Where is she?" Minx asked.

"Who?" the old man choked out between labored gasps.

*More games. He thinks you're stupid, but you ain't—we know better—old man—stupid—shit...*

"Cherish!" Minx shouted.

"No, don't!" The old man threw up his hands to ward off any attack.

Minx stepped back, giving him a bit of space. "Where is she?" he asked again but this time smoothed his tone.

"She's dead."

*DEAD?*

"Dead? What are you playing at?"

"She's dead. I—Minx, I don't know, she's gone."

*Old man's picking his words.*

"How?" Minx demanded.

"You."

*Old man is starting to piss me off! Fix this, NOW!*

"Minx, I don't know anything outside what the cops told me a few months ago. They came to my office and asked questions about you, our sessions, and your mental well-being. Since you were given to me by the state, I waived the medical HIPPA agreement and the confidentiality pact, as it seemed you were a danger to yourself and everyone else around you, but what good did it do? All they told me was Cherish was missing and that you were suspect number one. They never found a body. The only hypothesis I could offer was that you stopped taking your medication. I'm right, aren't I?"

Clear, uncut memories flooded Minx's brain. The blood mixed with violence blended by her screams and the axe. It was all there... even her final plea that echoed in the deep corners of his mind.

The old man made an attempt to sit up. "You know Minx, you could always—"

Minx sank his knife in the old man's throat. He retracted the blade and struck again. Blood erupted from a strong, wet cough, falling onto the old man's beard.

*Look at those colors, just like Christmas!*

He pulled the knife free, only to stab him in the stomach and chest, over and over in a hypnotic rapture, until the old man was no more. Minx wiped the sweat from his brow as he stood, caking more blood across his forehead.

"Damn, I need a drink," he said, cleaning the blade on a paper towel.

*Gin—always does the trick.*

"Yes, gin would do the trick."

*You need her off your mind.*

"I need to get her off my mind."

Within moments, Minx found himself back out on the street blanketed by darkness. He looked up to the apartment building, lost on why he was even there at all.

"I—forgot."

*You've forgotten.*

"Her?"

*Gin.*

"Yes, gin."

Minx began his trek back to the bar.

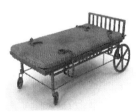

"This seems like a good spot for lunch," Detective David Rivers said, piloting the unmarked car into the back of a vacant lot, away from the stark sodium beams of the streetlights. "Life on the road and not in the fast lane. You know, Kats, I spend more time chewing bread in here with you than I do with my own wife and kids— rotten profession." He chuckled, selecting a foil-wrapped sandwich from the paper bag.

"Yeah, I feel ya on that," Kathy Hallum said, taking the bag from him. "Come to think of it, for the last two years, I've seen more of you than anyone else."

"I'm sorry, can't do nothing about the visual appeal of this mug of mine, but I think we get the job done. Hell, we've outlasted most partnerships at the department—and not to mention two years is a year longer than my first marriage," David said, laughing.

"Oh God, don't start on that." Kathy tossed a napkin at him.

"That woman could cook, lemme tell ya." He took a bite of the overloaded bun. "Did you hear it's supposed to rain? The weather report said it was a slow-moving system and that everyone in the city needed to brace for impact."

Kathy rolled down the misty window a bit, peering up at the blackened sky. The night air reeked of the impending storm; its aroma mixed with the end-of-day heat as it radiated from the blacktop with a heaviness.

"I can smell it." She rolled the window up.

She hated the rain. She hated the memories the angry clouds cast down on her. The memories of her childhood, a place she didn't much like to go. The last remnant of the smells invoked images of a suppressed moment. The street wasn't what she saw out the windshield anymore, but lightning flashes through reinforced plywood slats, and the footsteps—heavy and forceful.

The crack of static across the radio pulled her from the visions of the past, violently into the present. Every time an episode of mental time travel happened, it always concluded with confusion and anxiety. Kathy didn't know how much time passed since she slipped away, if any at all. She glanced at David, who seemed hopelessly lost in his pastrami big boy sandwich, and sighed in relief.

*"We have a possible 187, junction of Blick and Nomad. We have reports of a 10-54 and a 10-45B—units in the area, please respond."*

"A homicide in South End, that's not out of place at all." David took the receiver. "Ten-four, unit sixteen is 10-17, over."

"Well, so much for lunch," Kathy said.

"And I was really getting into this meal...I haven't even opened the chips yet," David said.

"We better get going before the rain starts."

"Roger that." David put the Crown V in drive.

South End was the bottomless pit of evilness for Clydesboro. Most of the time law enforcement looked the other way, so long as the filth didn't spill out into the rest of the city. It was a place where, if you wanted it, you could find, no matter the vice, even a violent death if you desired. Kathy hated going into South End just as much as she hated the rain.

Kathy occasionally glanced at David, who took no notice of her. Over the last two years, they had gotten close, not intimate, but close. She often worried about him, his cholesterol, his wife and kids, and his ego. He'd been the best beat cop in Drexton, and when he came over, he wore his promotion to Lieutenant proudly. So proudly, he gave it up to climb back into the car, because he was a legend, and not just in his own mind. David had a whole trove at the office; they were nothing but fanning enablers.

"Gang territory," she said.

"Yep, we're in the thick of it now, but hey, we got this!" He winked at her.

"Yeah, we got something." Kathy looked out the window.

"GET THE HELL OUTTA HERE! I TOLD YOU WE'RE CLOSED AND NOW YOU go and be a dick about it!" the owner of Legends Pub shouted.

"I don't understand, I just want a drink...do you not like money?" Minx shrugged.

"Kid, I said we're closed—do you have any idea what time it is? Everyone's gone home. Now get the fuck off this sidewalk or I'm getting my Louisville Slugger and we'll have an entirely different discussion—nah, ya know what? Derek, fetch my bat."

"This is bullshit! I just want a drink! Just one drink!"

"You come here, kick in the glass of my front door, threaten me and my son, and think I'm going to owe you some courtesy? I think you've had enough—no, here's the brakes, don't ever come here again! Do you feel me? Don't ever come here again! Now, kindly get the hell away from my establishment."

Derek returned with the well-used Slugger.

"Give me that!" The owner snatched it from his son. "GO THE FUCK HOME!" the man bellowed, pointing the business end of the bat at Minx.

*No more gin!*

"No! They can't do it—they won't do it! I must have it—she had to go away, no—I have to find her!" Minx screamed, clawing at his thick black hair.

The owner lowered the bat, careening an eyebrow.

*Go get the gin!*

Minx made his advance for the front door. The owner lifted the bat, both fists white knuckled onto the handle.

"Man, I said get away! Don't make me do this!"

Minx didn't slow his step against the man's pleas. The owner loaded the bat back as if he were Ted Williams, but before he could let it fly, Minx caught it in his hands.

*Do it!*

Minx's fierce grip was too much for the man as his assailant leaned into him. The owner's arms shook under the weight of the losing battle.

*Do it! Do it! DO IT!*

Minx put his boot into the side of the man's left knee, sending the cap out of position. The owner screamed as the damaged ligaments gave way, folding his knee in on itself. As he collapsed, he let go of the weapon, leaving the bat in Minx's hands.

"Derek, the cops! Get the cops!" the owner demanded, his arms wrapped over his face.

Minx towered over the man as his brain buzzed like a chainsaw, teetering on the verge of a full blackout.

*Do it!*

He raised the bat high as if he were about split logs. Minx watched with reckless joy as the man tried to crawl away but couldn't summon the strength to do it.

"Please—" the man tried.

"Her—she—wanted this," Minx whispered.

"Called the cops! They're on the way!" Derek screamed through the doorway, falling beside his father.

Minx froze with the bat still above him, his eyes full of fire, glaring down at the broken man and his son.

*COPS!*

Minx tossed the bat down beside the owner's head. He stood in the wake of confusion that washed over him. He looked up at the front of Legends Pub, not understanding why he was there. His confusion was so pronounced he began to ask the man why he was on the sidewalk.

*RUN!*

"I—"

*NOW!*

"Good Lord," David said, placing a handkerchief over his mouth.

"Yeah, Sarge—sorry, vic number two expired before we could give aid. We can't pronounce him, but ya know—he's gone. Multiple stab wounds, both vics," the paramedic said.

"This is just brutal—I have no words for this," David said, looking away from the gurney.

"I—" Kathy began.

*"We have a reported 187. Mesa Apartments, number 331, any units, copy?"*

Kathy leaned into the car. "Unit 16, that is less than a block from our position, 10-17, over."

"You think?" David asked, pointing to the stretchers.

"Let's go and see."

They pulled up on Mesa Apartments to a small crowd down front of the aged complex. Kathy stepped out, feeling the intensity in the atmosphere. A woman ran to the cruiser, carrying a bat and crying.

"Officer, I'm the one who made the call—he's dead, he's dead—they killed Doctor Spicer! Butchered him!"

Kathy looked to David.

"I'll call the paramedics down here," David said, pulling out his cell.

"Take me to the body, please," Kathy asked the woman.

"Yes, ma'am, it's up on the third floor."

"Paramedics weren't pleased at the news to say the least, but another unit is on the way," David said, pulling up the rear.

Kathy paused outside apartment three thirty-one, examining the doorframe. "Looks like whoever it was knocked first…the chain was torn loose, but no damage to the brick molding or jamb—and we have a good shoe print here, near dead center."

David stepped in and exhaled.

"Throat destroyed, multiple stab wounds. This matches our perps M.O. for sure, but why this guy?" Kathy said.

"Yeah, Captain Slice 'n Dice strikes again," David said.

Kathy knelt down next to the body. "Wait, I know who this is—the department investigated him a couple years back, yeah—Doctor Hank Spicer, a psychiatrist. DEA busted him for writing under the table Oxy prescriptions. He lost his business."

"Dr. Oxy, yeah, I remember the name… Well, that explains why he's living in South End—you think maybe his demise was drug related? Same with those men back there, just a person needin' a fix?" David asked.

"I dunno," Kathy said, standing back up.

"What became of the good doctor here, after the investigation?"

"He was questioned over a patient of his that was a suspect for a disappearance, but I don't remember how that shook out. That wasn't my case, but I remember Spicer was down at the precinct more than once over it. I'll be honest, I don't remember him being uncooperative with the blue… We'd heard about it, ya know, but something triggered an investigation into his office. A subpoena was served and that's how the DEA found out about his little side hustle. I don't know how the dominoes fell to get to that, but here we are."

"And now here he is," David said.

"Can you believe at one point they were going to use him as our department's therapist, like if you had to shoot someone in the field or something? Crazy world, but yes—here he is."

"We don't even know where to begin and I hate it. We had this in Drexton all the time. Murders in the bad side of town—no one saw anything, knows anything—no leads, it goes unsolved, and a couple years later it's in the cold case drawer. This could be anything… gangs or a simple junkie strung out and needing a fix from Dr. Oxy. In South End, it's a crap shoot, but I'll call this in. Dispatch is going to love us tonight," David said, stepping into the hall.

Kathy stood over Dr. Spicer's body, studying the man's face. It was twisted in anguish, fear stricken, if there were such a thing.

"Kats, we gotta go!"

"What is it?"

"A guy marched up to Legends Pub, covered in blood, and attacked the owner."

Kathy followed David out of the apartment. "Covered in blood?"

"Sounds like our guy."

"Back up?"

"Tried that, no one is remotely close…you know the skeleton we're running on the late shift," David said, bustling down the staircase.

They fell into the car seats. David cranked the Crown's powerful V8, barking tires as they tore off into the night.

"Legends Pub, you say?"

"Yeah, the owner's son phoned in, said the perp beat the piss out of his dad but stopped before killing him—Derek, his son's name is Derek. Apparently, he phoned back within minutes, saying the man took off, but not before having a meltdown," David said.

"You know, we're not that far away. We might—"

A man emerged from an alley on the right, darting into the road.

"Shit!" David shouted, locking the brakes down. The Crown skidded to a stop as Kathy double-fisted the grab handle.

In perfect stillness, the man leaned forward, placing his hands on the Crown's hood. His glare was taut, laser sharp, and Kathy could feel it cut into her skin. There were no sounds outside of David's heavy breath as they sat motionless.

"You see that, Dave?"

"Uh-huh." David gripped the wheel.

The man straightened himself up in the full gulf of the headlights.

"Blood," Kathy said. "That's our guy."

They watched as the man took off into the darkness across the street, vanishing into an alley.

"That alley comes out on Davidson!" Kathy shouted.

"On it." David buried the accelerator.

When the car cut around the bend, they didn't see him. Kathy felt her heart sink, knowing they should've made an attempt when they had him locked in the headlights. She wondered if that should go into the report, fearing the repercussions.

"Oh, you son of a bitch, where are you?" David fumed, pounding the steering wheel.

"There!" Kathy smacked his shoulder, pointing out a glimmer of movement. "You see that?"

"Yes, ma'am."

"He went into that building," Kathy said.

"What is it?"

"Looks like an old apartment complex, but I don't see any lights on," Kathy said as the car screeched to a halt in front of the dilapidated building. Kathy sprang from the seat, her eyes glued to the entry.

"We're going to have to push for backup," she said.

"Warren and Wise are on tonight—I'll make it clear we need them."

"Warren and Wise? Then we might as well be on our own—hell, they're more likely to shoot us at the first signs of life." Kathy frowned, drawing her weapon.

"Yeah, twiddle-dee and twiddle-dip, but I'm calling them

anyhow—hopefully we'll have this resolved by the time they get here."

She controlled her breathing, but the small hairs on the back of her neck stood on end. The building was a multi-floor death trap on the verge of collapse. They made their way up the mold-covered concrete step-by-step, slow and organized. Kathy had appreciated David in these moments; he wore a suit and tie, but he never shook the beat cop from his shoulders.

Against the exterior doorframe, they nodded to each other. Kathy pulled her flashlight, took a breath, and breached the threshold. The entrance led down a narrow, graffiti-covered hallway. The wallpaper hung in torn, disheveled chunks, draping down in long curls, and the place smelled of charred wood. Every shadow her flashlight created among the debris was imposing and unsettling. Kathy caught herself on the verge of calling out HALT, only to discover the assailant was an overturned chair or plastic plant.

With David pulling the rear, she elected for an open door on the right side of the hall, signaling him to take the one on the left. She cut the power to her flashlight, resting at the edge of the threshold. David did the same, and in unison they dipped into their chosen rooms in the amber glare of the streetlights, peering through the windows. Kathy turned her flashlight on again, holding it high above her head and off center. As a weapons trainer, one of the lessons she'd learned the hard way was more often than not, an armed suspect would fire at light itself. Luckily, no bullets came, and after a quick sweep, the room was cleared. When she stepped back into the hall, she'd found David had come up empty as well.

"This building is too massive for just us, and I don't like the idea of splitting up in a place with no power," she whispered.

"I agree, not to mention it's creepy as hell. Let's team this beast, wanna?"

After they worked the lower level room-by-room, they moved the investigation to the second floor. The place was quiet and the weight of the silence keyed into her mounted anxiety. The first door on the left was the first to have been closed. They took to both sides of the entry, guns at the ready.

Kathy drew in a small pull of the musty air as she pushed the door open and nearly choked. The smell was rancid, settling a coating of hateful disgust on her tongue. The room was in total disarray as the flashlight's beam found an overturned table, papers scattered all over, and a bookshelf, face down in the kitchen area. Her light found a pair of shoes shoved between an ottoman and a couch.

David rounded the couch and stopped. Kathy watched as he covered his mouth, doubling over. Kathy moved to his position, halting as her flashlight traveled from the shoes to the pair of thoroughly decayed legs that wore them. She fought hard against the bile her stomach had slammed into her gullet. The stench intensified as she looked on, working the light up the corpse's waist to a shrunken torso. The belly had a severe wound, which opened up to the base of the rib cage. A pulse of terrestrial worms writhed in the bottom of the cavern. Fluids that'd long since dried stained the light-colored carpet in a hideous deep brown. The poor girl's face appeared to have been removed, leaving only a skeletal structure, and Kathy beheld no eyes in the sockets.

Kathy gagged against the aroma of the decay, swallowing hard past the massive lump at the base of her throat.

"She's been here awhile," Kathy whispered.

David sighed, holstering his weapon. Kathy saw his hand shake as he dug the cell phone from his pocket. He still carried an old flip phone, even declining the smartphone upgrade the office had issued, but as he flipped the cell open, a face lit up behind him in the glow of the small blue screen.

Kathy opened her mouth, but before she could even pass the breath over her vocal cords, David's head fell from his shoulders, landing on the girl's corpse. She fired a round but struck her partner's headless body on the right shoulder. Kathy's flashlight caught a man in its path. He was wild eyed, shirtless, and his face and chest were streaked in blood. In his grip was an axe, equally caked in fresh blood that gleaned in the light's aura.

He rolled to her left when she squeezed off another round, hitting only the fridge. She swung the flashlight to the area where he'd dipped out, but he wasn't there. Fear rattled up her spine as it dawned on her that she was alone in the dark with a madman. A noise erupted to her right. Kathy swung the light to that direction, catching the axe blade as it struck the top of her gun, tearing it out of her grasp.

The man took Kathy by the throat, slamming her against the wall. Small pings of stars flooded her vision from the impact. She felt his weight push onto her, forcing the flashlight's beam upward between them. His face was close to hers and his grip on her throat was vise-like.

"She—her," he hissed into her face. "Where?"

Kathy opened her mouth, but no words would come out. He squeezed tighter, placing his forehead against hers.

"Where—her—s-she—where?"

The darkness at the edge of her eyes began to shrink the light between them. The center of his pupils filled every bit of her sight, and all she found in them was death.

"Answer me!" he cried out, tossing her to the middle of the room. The flashlight rolled away, but Kathy didn't care...all she wanted was oxygen. Each new breath was painful and raw, but it was welcomed.

"She's gone—left!" he lashed out.

Kathy watched as the man's silhouette writhed, bashing his knuckles into the side of his head.

"She's gone? She's gone!"

Kathy ignored the babble. *Flashlight and gun!* her mind demanded.

She found the light. It was a small distance away, but she didn't care. If this man was going to kill her, he'd have to do it with a few bullet holes in him. Kathy began to crawl. His words had fallen into an incoherent mess of garble that was close by, then far away. He paced around the big room as if he'd forgotten she was there at all, but as she made it a body's length from the flashlight, a hand landed firmly on the back of her scalp, her hair grasped, pulling her onto her back. In the small beam of light, she saw him above her, axe in hand.

"She—Cherish, I love you—" he sputtered, as if he were crying. "I—"

"Love you too!" Kathy shouted up.

The man fell silent, backing away.

"I love you too," she said again, sitting up from the floor.

"I—" He dropped the axe; the handle landed on her left shin. "—love you," the man finished.

Kathy reached down, gripping the weapon, then with both hands she pulled it to her.

"I'm here. I've never left, not ever," Kathy cooed to the man as he backed farther away. She stood up, her resolve animated in her clench on the axe. "And I'll never leave you."

"Please—Cherish." He sobbed.

"That's right—I'm here, always."

"No!" the man shouted. "This isn't! You're not!" He stepped toward her.

Kathy swung the axe, connecting with the man's upper chest. She felt the blade sink into his meat. She pulled the blade free and swung again, landing in the same wound. Lightning flashed, filling the room with pearly white brilliance, whisking her away in memory. She no longer saw the lumped mass that had fallen to the base of the wainscoting, but only the fixed plywood of the cellar that separated her and her sister from their escape.

This time she was armed with the axe, slamming it into the freshly nailed partition. Each new strike was one inch closer to freedom, bringing her a refreshed source of manic energy. Lightning thrashed around the edges of the splintered gaps in the hateful slats her stepfather had contained them with. The swings kept coming, the need for escape was all consuming, and with a final connection, the boards fell away and the shadowy figure of the past was no more.

Kathy flinched with the crack of thunder, finding herself once more in the decrepit apartment. The air was filled with decay and the copper-flavored undertone of blood. Her palms ached from the clutch she held on the axe handle, but as her confusion cleared, she stepped over to the flashlight.

She brought the beam down onto the figure, then dropped the axe. The familiar taste of bile returned, but she couldn't hold it back as she vomited onto the torn vinyl of the kitchen floor.

"Police! We're coming up!"

"I'm here," she called down. "Get an ambulance!"

Both officers breached the door, their collective flashlights falling onto Kathy.

"What the hell happened?" Warren asked.

"He happened." She pointed to the broken man against the wall.

Wise brought his light up on the body. "Shit!"

"Kathy, where's David?" Warren asked. She heard the note of panic in his voice.

"Over there." She pointed. "I—his head—I'm going to puke, Warren—there's a rotted corpse here too."

Kathy's strength gave out, resulting in her falling to the floor against a kitchen cabinet. She pulled her knees to her chest and cried.

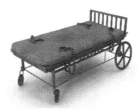

"KATHY, HAVE A SEAT," CAPTAIN RIGGINS OFFERED. SHE SAW THE LOOK in his eyes and it seemed genuine. "So, I don't know where to begin, but I'll start by once more saying I'm sorry. I'm sorry about David and what you've dealt with over this last month. Your report has been analyzed and has been found to be truthful, which is great! More importantly, you had questions, correct?"

"Who was that man?"

"Well, as you know, we couldn't tell you anything until the investigation was concluded. Anyway, his name was Michael North...his friends called him Minx. He was a patient of Dr. Hank Spicer, and no, not one of his Oxy patients, but a legit psychiatry patient. The state had placed him there after several public disturbances. He claimed he heard voices and such, and he ended up a suspect in a disappearance case, but he was never located and the city's memory is short, sadly."

"Cherish—" Kathy said.

"Yes, Cherish Martin. She was a young lady he'd dated for a short time, then stalked after it was over. According to your report, he confused you with her, though her body laid nearby. But we're not going to discuss that. It's over now, and thanks to you, her family has closure." He leaned forward. "So, here comes the wonky news. You're going on administrative leave and your return is on condition of a psychiatric sign-off, if you even wanna come back."

"I'll have to make some decisions, but thank you, Captain." Kathy stood up, handing over her badge.

"Hey now, we're all rooting for ya, Detective. That was all I had on my end. No more questions? Are you sure?"

"Yeah, I'm sure."

He stepped around the desk, giving her a hug. "You're going to be okay."

"I think so," she said with a weak smile.

After the well wishes from her colleagues, she stepped out onto the department's granite staircase. Kathy closed her eyes, finding herself hand in hand with her sister as they stood in the sunshine upon the broken remnants of the reinforced cellar door. She'd feared the ghosts of the past would one day come to claim her, but those ghosts were gone and they weren't coming back.

*Are you still afraid?*

Kathy put on her sunglasses.

"Not anymore."

# OUT OF THE BOX

## RENEE M.P.T. KRAY

Kennedy's car had been parked in her driveway long enough that her back was starting to get cold against the seat, but not quite long enough for Mikey to come outside and check on her.

*Gotta de-stress.* Kennedy had watched enough online yoga guru videos to know that the number-one way to ruin her evening was to bring frustrations home from the office, and frankly she wasn't paid enough to carry her nine-to-five issues over the threshold. She inhaled deeply through her nose, arching her chest out against the seatbelt and letting the cold fill every crevice of her lungs, holding it until the air warmed and her chest started to burn. Then she exorcised the breath from her body in a forceful exhale, imagining that she was pushing out every negative aspect of her workday. The incompetence of coworkers who left splashes of food in the microwave? Gone. The overly bright fluorescent lights that provided nothing but headaches? Out of her mind.

And then of course there was the creme de la creme of crappy situations: Scott, the boss who skimmed off the best of Kennedy's ideas like a stray cat peeling the skin from a mouse. Scott had been in college when his father had started HeartBeat Tech, but by the time it had become one of the more well-known digital payment systems in the United States, he'd graduated with a degree from who-cares-where and Daddy had promoted him to head of public relations. It wasn't a stretch to say that everyone in the company besides Scott himself knew that the snarky twenty-four-year-old with no real life experience was grossly underqualified, but none of them would have dared to voice the truth. As if it wanted to add fuel to the fire, Kennedy's brain dredged up the memory of Scott's voice with its practiced smoothness, reading aloud the email they'd been sent from corporate two weeks ago after they'd been tasked with creating an exciting project to guide new blood into the company's ever-widening maw.

"Scott: we love your concept for the new HeartBeat Tech social media platform! Like Venmo but better. Please have a presentation ready for our meeting at the end of the month to list essential features the app would perform and a few graphics to give us a visual."

*Never mind the fact that we've been trying to get older users on board and they're the slowest demographic to experiment with new social media platforms. Also, never mind that I'm the one who's been researching this shit for the past six days even though my job is customer relations.*

But she wasn't sure that her former frat-boy boss even understood what customer relations was, which explained why he was always treating her less like a fellow professional and more like a secretary that he hoped would rip open her blouse and act out his idiotic fantasies. How many times had he stood just a little too close, let his eyes dip a little too low, and smiled at her in a way that was just a little too creepy to be kosher?

*And I get to do it all again tomorrow.* Kennedy groaned and leaned her head against the steering wheel, fighting back the question that popped to the surface of her mind almost every single night:

*Why don't I just quit?* But she knew she couldn't. There were the usual reasons, like her mortgage, car payment, and grocery bill, but underneath it all was the real fire that kept her burning at this thankless job: Kennedy could not, would not allow herself to be that person who did the walk of shame with all the contents of their desk in a cardboard box. She'd worked too hard for too long to…

*be perfect*

…achieve everything she'd wanted when she was a child: the house, the husband, the job, and the very thought of being forced to slink out of her position by a boss who was embarrassingly under-qualified was enough to make the sides of her face burn with anger.

Kennedy sighed and unbuckled her seatbelt, carefully maneu-vering her black pumps onto the concrete of her driveway. She'd often joked that she could play basketball in heels throughout her twenties, but now that she'd joined the big 3-0 club, she could swear that her balance was wavering day by day. Still, the heels made a satisfying clack against the pavement as she walked to the door.

"Babe!" Kennedy called as she let herself in the house. "Home!"

"Hey, hon!" She heard Mikey's voice a moment before he emerged from the living room and grabbed her in a hug, leaning back to lift her off the ground while Kennedy allowed herself the pleasure of a girlish laugh. Despite being as tall and wide as a foot-ball player and with dark eyes and wavy hair that could make cheerleaders squeal, Mikey had never been on any team beyond the Dungeons and Dragons group that he somehow still maintained. He'd been Kennedy's first kiss, her first boyfriend, her first every-thing, and even all these years later, with her blond hair fading from gold to straw and the extra mid-thirties weight dabbed around her hips and stomach, Mikey still made Kennedy feel like she was, well…perfect. Kennedy sighed and tucked her face into the shoulder of his soft green hoodie, allowing warmth to trickle through her face as she breathed in the scent of being wanted, of being needed, of being enough.

*I could take this drug all day.*

"So! I've got dinner started," Mikey said, peeling her away and jerking his thumb back toward the kitchen. "Chicken piccata with a side of mashed potatoes. It's classy A.F., if I do say so myself. I think we've even got a little leftover wine somewhere in the back of the fridge to really take this over the top." He accented his menu rundown with an exaggerated chef's kiss, and Kennedy smiled.

"Sounds like you've been busy," she said.

"Well, that's just the cooking portion of it," Mikey replied. "I also stopped by your mom's house after work."

Kennedy suddenly tasted vomit up the back of her throat.

When her mother passed away last month, Kennedy had been given an inheritance that might as well have been gift-wrapped with flames from the sixth circle of Hell for all the good it brought: her childhood home, the place she'd bolted from as soon as she was seventeen and could hold a job. She'd been going there on the weekends since the funeral and had managed to pack up the kitchen, bathroom, and the living room, but the next major spot was her mother's bedroom and Kennedy hadn't even been able to bring herself to open that door. Whenever Kennedy had been called to that room, it was only to discuss how bad she was, or how disappointing, or how much Uncle Albert despised her.

It was the headquarters of the Kennedy's-not-good-enough campaign.

"Hey. I know you said you didn't want to think about it during the week. I'm sorry for bringing it up," Mikey said. "But I had an idea."

Mikey took one of Kennedy's hands in his and led her to the garage, throwing open the door and flicking on the overhead light. Neither of their cars fit into the storage bin–filled garage on a normal day, but now there was the additional clutter of three large black garbage bags sitting in the center of the floor, tiny pieces of rags sticking out the tops like flaccid teeth.

"You mentioned that you don't want to go into your mom's room," Mikey explained. "So I cleaned out the master closet and brought everything here instead. I figured it might be easier for you to sort through stuff on familiar ground."

Kennedy stared at the bags and shock swept through her as she processed that these weren't just things from inside the house... these were things from inside her mother's room.

*Kennee crept to Momma's door as silently as possible, which wasn't hard with all the yelling. Uncle Albert's voice was raised so high it was cracking, and that usually meant that his round face and balding head had become shiny red.*

*"Be quiet, Albert," Momma demanded from behind the door, but without any real life to her voice. "Kennee will hear." The slap that whistled through the air in response broke (against Momma's face, probably) with the snap of a whip. Kennee felt a lump roll in her throat. Momma didn't deserve to be yelled at by Uncle Albert; she was always trying to make him happy. It was Kennee who had made the mistake of going into*

*Uncle Albert's things. But Uncle Albert wanted everything just so, and no matter how hard Kennee tried, she was never good enough.*

*"You want to talk about your kid? Then how about this: I finance my sister and niece and what thanks do I get? She can't follow rules, she can't keep still, she's always in the fucking way. If that weasel goes into my things again, I will kill her, Emma. I swear to high heaven, I will swat that little fly."*

*Sweat trickled down Kennee's back as she waited for Momma to defend them both, to push him and tell him to get out, to say that Kennee was her perfectly plucky good girl the way she used to back before Daddy had died. But the quiet sobbing that started trickling from under the door told her that Momma probably agreed with Uncle Albert, that Kennee was a lost cause, a bad girl.*

Kennedy resurfaced in the present with sweat beading the back of her neck and the sound of Mikey's voice in her ear. He was still rambling, a habit he had when he was afraid someone was upset with him. Kennedy blinked hard, willing the memory to disappear into the sands of time like it was supposed to, breathed in through her nose, held the oxygen in her lungs, then exhaled through her mouth.

*You let Mikey see how much that room upset you. Don't let that happen again.*

"Thanks, babe," she interrupted. At the sound of her voice, Mikey's mouth clamped shut. "That was really thoughtful, and honestly it's a huge help."

"I'm glad," he replied, clearly relieved. And although Kennedy wished she hadn't let such an obvious crack in her calm come to light, she had to admit this solved the issue of not wanting to go in that room.

*I'll make myself go in for the rest,* she promised herself. *No more being a baby. But for now, I can get rid of this stuff.*

"I'm going to sort some of it before dinner's ready," Kennedy said as she removed her blazer and handed it to Mikey. Just the motion of it made her feel back in control, ready to show these bags of crap that even though she'd been too chicken to go in and fetch them herself, she was the one calling the shots now.

"Dinner's already just about done," Mikey said.

"Then fish out that wine and have it poured for me by the time I get in, will ya?" she asked, leaning in to plant a kiss on his lips. And with that, Mikey smiled the smile that meant he would have hitch-hiked to Italy in a Walmart delivery truck to get Kennedy's wine if she had asked.

Alone, Kennedy grabbed the sides of the first sack and upended it. The bag vomited a mess of old blouses and a few cardboard boxes onto the floor, and the next two were more of the same, with the addition of some plastic McDonald's Happy Meal toys still in the bags and some old magazines carefully tied in piles. Kennedy shook her head as she knelt in front of the massive pile of garbage and started sorting through it. The work went quickly: old pieces of paper and cardboard went to the green recycle bin, bits of costume jewelry were piled together to donate, and a heart-shaped music box that Kennedy didn't recognize and didn't care to open went straight into the trash. She was almost a third of the way through the pile when she pulled yet another empty shoebox from under a dress. Cocking her arm back, Kennedy was about to throw it into the recycling bin when the image on the front caught her eye, and her breath simultaneously caught in her throat.

It was Num-Num's box.

The logo was the image of a dancing cartoon giraffe in a purple tu-tu that was emblazoned with the words KIDDY KICKS along the hemline, exactly the sort of ploy that would catch kids' eyes and urge them to convince their parents to choose that brand of shoes over others. The cardboard's original technicolor green had faded out to a dull teal, but the rest of it was exactly as Kennedy remembered: wound over and under with gray lines of duct tape that sloppily crossed each other where her mother had taped the box in a fit of passion. Kennedy could still hear the scream of the tape leaving the roll as she'd watched, filled with a six-year-old's concern that surely that box was too cramped for...

*Num-Num. Kennee never knew where she came from or what she was, she just knew that whenever she was upset, Num-Num would be there to help. Whether it was the offense of having to eat soggy fishsticks for dinner or having to listen to Uncle Albert lecture Momma about the financial burden he'd taken on by caring for them, Num-Num was always there.*

*Num-Num was the most beautiful woman ever, coming in top place even before Momma. Her eyes were the bright red of a warm fire and she had dark hair in two bouncing pigtails that fell down her back. No matter what time of year it was, Num-Num always wore an orange summer dress that fell to her knees and was printed all over with dark purple flowers with petals splayed wide open—anemone flowers, as Kennee had discovered when she scoured through a book from the library. Momma hunched over a lot and Kennee was still short, but Num-Num stood up straight and tall, taller even than Uncle Albert, and her tummy had a little flop to it at the bottom because she was always eating everything around her. The grocery bags that Uncle Albert made Momma unpack slowly so he could approve of everything she'd purchased? Gone in one quick snap of Num-Num's jaws. The ash from his smelly cigarette? Licked away by Num-Num. It never stopped making Kennee laugh. Num-Num made Uncle Albert look like he was the stupid one, and Kennee wanted to be exactly like Num-Num when she grew up.*

*After Kennee heard the slap, she went to her room and found Num-Num sitting in a corner with her head resting on the dresser and her bare feet sticking out straight. She wiggled her toes, which had a little bit of lint between them but weren't really dirty even though Num-Num never wore shoes.*

*"Why didn't you do something?" Num-Num asked. Her voice was as squeaky as always, but the red in her eyes burned very hot.*

*"Like what?" Kennee asked as she seated herself on the bed.*

*"Anything," Num-Num insisted, fishing her hand in the wastebasket and bringing up a porcelain doll that Uncle Albert had cracked against the wall earlier that day when he'd found Kennee looking at one of his car books. She'd known that it was against the rules to touch things on Uncle Albert's special shelf, but the book was leather and shiny and had looked so inviting. She'd been so engrossed in the pictures that she hadn't heard the footsteps approaching in the hallway, so she didn't have time to hide the book when Uncle Albert had burst in. He'd ripped it out of Kennee's hands, yelling, "How do you like it when I touch YOUR stuff?" before grabbing the doll and smashing it against the wall.*

*Num-Num sniffed the doll's remains, then put the splintered face between her lips and bit down. The painted smile shattered against her teeth.*

*"Don't you want everything to be perfect again?" Num-Num asked. "Life was great before he came around. Remember?"*

*"Uncle Albert says it's not good for me to question him," Kennee protested, watching Num-Num spool the doll's hair into her mouth like pasta.*

*"When you've done everything you can do and you've been as good as you can be and it's still not good enough, it's time to make your own level of good," Num-Num lectured, waving one finger in the air as she chewed and then swallowed. What had been the doll's face traveled slowly down her throat in a bulge. "Num-num-nummy."*

*"That doesn't make sense," Kennee sighed.*

*Num-Num smiled widely. Bits of porcelain stuck up behind her gums like a second set of teeth, and the silky blond doll hair was wound in between her actual teeth like used floss from the bathroom floor.*

*"Let me show you," Num-Num said.*

The box was light in Kennedy's palms as she flipped it over to look at the duct tape that crossed its diameter, an anaconda's death embrace ensuring that nothing could ever get out.

*"I'm putting Num-Num in this box. You can't see her anymore."*

Because that's what had happened, wasn't it? Momma had claimed that Num-Num was a bad influence on Kennedy, and she'd said that she was trapping her in the shoebox so that Kennedy couldn't play with her anymore. That had been Momma's worst breakdown ever, on the day that…

*Kennee followed strange sounds into the living room. Uncle Albert was propped in his usual spot on the couch, but something was different. His legs and arms were flopped out like he'd forgotten they existed, and there was something in his throat, a bumpy bulge that pushed against him like it wanted to break out through his skin. That was when Kennee noticed how gray his face was except for the purple around his neck, how his eyes weren't blinking, how his chest wasn't moving. The only thing that came out of him was a wheezing gurgle like water draining around old garbage in a clogged sink, and as Kennee stood there, even that stopped. Num-Num was standing over him, and she looked up and winked. Despite her trust of Num-Num and her hatred of Uncle Albert, Kennee heard her own voice screaming in terror.*

*"What did you do?"*

*"I made everything perfect."*

The duct tape along the edges of the box was fading and brittle now, and Kennedy could see that just a fingernail under the ragged edge would be enough to rip it open.

*Why not?* she asked herself as she turned the box again in her hands, as if it had something new to show her from a different angle. *It's just an empty box.*

But it wasn't. It was a relic of her old life, a piece of the Kennedy she'd been when she was…

*imperfect*

…a naive little child who'd believed that her imaginary friend could be trapped in a box. Kennedy added the box to the top of the garbage pile and got up to stretch. The rest could wait until tomorrow; she was suddenly sick of looking through old things from the past and remembering all the burdens that came with them.

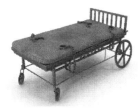

KENNEDY OPENED HER EYES AND GROANED AS SHE TURNED TO SEE WHAT time it was, then groaned again as she saw 4:40 splashed across the face of the clock on her nightstand.

*Crap.* Waking up in the middle of the night seemed to be getting more common the older she got, and Kennedy didn't appreciate it. Her tongue was dry from the wine she'd drunk at dinner, and her bladder was protesting by making itself weigh what felt like a million pounds. Kennedy rolled her eyes and swung her legs out of bed, walking her toes into her slippers before stepping off to the bathroom with a grumble under her breath. Getting up tomorrow for work was going to be hellish if she didn't manage to fall back asleep directly; it was bad enough dealing with Scott when she was fully alert.

*That's a problem you'll deal with tomorrow. Well, later today,* Kennedy told herself as she took care of business.

The bedroom was silent and cold, the way that only a house in the dead of night could be as Kennedy crossed back toward the bed where Mikey lay curled on his side, his giant shape sloped like a sand dune underneath the covers. Kennedy settled back into the cooling indentation that her own body had left and pulled the sheets up to her chin, willing them to warm back up quickly.

That was when she noticed the figure across the room.

For a second Kennedy froze, her mind whirring as it struggled to reconcile the figure it was seeing. She lifted her hand and tried to touch Mikey on the shoulder, to wake him, to have him look around the room and laughingly declare that she was just having a nightmare, but the orders rushed through her body and fizzled out before actually reaching her limbs. Kennedy could only stare stupidly at the shadowy shape whose eyes were the only things she could make out in the darkness, burning with the dull red of embers trying to stay alive.

*I...know those eyes.*

But as Kennedy's vision adjusted to the darkness, the details that emerged around the eyes didn't match what she remembered. The figure was still that of a woman, but she was ancient, her skin hanging off bowed bones as if it had been stretched beyond capacity and then simply given up like a broken rubber band. Her pigtails were barely more than ropey strands now, so coated with grease that they gleamed in the scant moonlight. For a moment the only thing that moved was Kennedy's racing heart, but then the figure leaned forward. A hand emerged from the shadows with a pale saltine cracker pressed between its fingertips, which had nails so tiny and worn on the edges that they looked as if they'd been chewed on for years. Mesmerized, Kennedy's eyes followed the cracker as the hand lifted it in front of a stomach that was pressed round and hard against its faded floral dress like a pregnancy waiting to burst, and then up to an almost comically square jaw protruding outward. The jaw quivered for a moment before popping out with the suddenness of a rusted cash register, and the hand dropped the cracker inside. The jaw receded and started to work up and down, sending bits of cracker sprinkling off into the moonlight.

"Num-num-nummy," the figure whispered. The voice was no longer squeaky.

Kennedy forced her eyes closed and inhaled deeply through her nose.

*You're dreaming,* she reminded herself, though the goosebumps prickling her entire body certainly didn't feel like land of nod material. *You were more upset than you thought from seeing the box. That's all.* She wrenched her eyes open again, ready to see the empty spot by the bookshelf so that she could laugh at her own idiocy.

Num-Num was lifting another cracker to her old mouth, which snapped open a bit faster this time.

*No.* This wasn't okay. This wasn't *allowed.* Kennedy's heart pounded as she stared at the nightmare version of what had once been her best friend, back in the days when she couldn't control the world around herself and needed to dream up a bizarre buddy to do it for her. But she was the one in control of her life now, and she certainly didn't need an imaginary friend as a crutch.

*This isn't real. You're asleep right now, and this is just a dream.* Kennedy was done entertaining this night terror. So despite the uncomfortable racing of her heart and the crawling sensation that had broken out over her skin, Kennedy forced herself to lie back down and pressed up against Mikey.

*Ignore it and you'll wake up.*

Another cracker snapped in the silence and Kennedy squeezed her eyes shut. But even without looking, Kennedy still felt a sense of cold horror that sat in the pit of her stomach as she listened to the crunching of masticated crackers and the stretching of old bones, and she was still able to see in her mind the dying look that had been stamped across the red eyes. It was something Kennedy remembered all too well in the face of Uncle Albert.

Disgust.

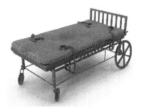

Kennedy's workday started at eight, which left her an hour to get ready when her alarm went off at six thirty every morning. Normally that was more than enough time, but when the beeping roused her out of a shallow sleep that morning, Kennedy felt as if she hadn't slept for a week. Rolling over from Mikey, she looked to the corner where she'd seen Num-Num in her dream and smiled when she noted that it was, of course, empty. The terror of the dream dulled into an ache that would be easily forgotten as Kennedy went through her workday, which promised to bring its own set of horrors. Kennedy got out of bed and set to work readying herself to face Scott, yawning as she went.

*Stupid dream.*

But she was only halfway across the room when she stopped again. The breath froze in her throat as she stared at the space between the bookshelf and her bedroom door, registering the smattering of pale crumbs that was scattered across the carpet like birdseed on a sidewalk.

Kennedy's mouth transformed into hard plaster and she struggled to swallow. She looked around the room, half expecting to see a person—or a thing—watching her.

But there was nothing.

*How did those crumbs get there? And why did that happen on the same night that I dreamed about...*

Like a woman possessed, Kennedy bolted down the hall and through the kitchen, heading straight for the garage. Her silk nightgown gave barely any protection against the early morning cold, but that wasn't the reason why her arms and neck were suddenly prickling with goosebumps. In one quick motion, Kennedy rammed open the garage door and flicked on the overhead light.

In the middle of the floor was the same sight she'd left the night before: bags of garbage, reeking of old perfume and dusty antiques, bits and pieces of a past that was worth nothing to her. And at the top of the pile, mounted above the rest like a corrupt magi's gift for the antichrist, was the empty shoebox, its tape pulled aside and the lid resting gently beside it.

Kennedy took a step in the garage, then pulled back. Her heart was pounding too loudly to be normal while her lips formed a scream for Mikey…but then she swallowed it. She was being ridiculous, she was being…

*scared*

…silly.

*I must have opened it and just forgotten it. And maybe Mikey ate some crackers before bed or something. Now, you're going to go to work, deal with whatever drama Scott has in store, and get through the day normally.*

She pulled the garage door closed, but her hands were shaking too hard to lock it.

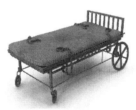

THERE WAS ALREADY A STACK OF NOTES AT KENNEDY'S DESK BY THE time she reached it, and as always, they were all from Scott. Kennedy sighed as she flipped through them, reading ridiculous requests like *send an email to Tina in billing* and *update me on shipping progress* blah-blah-blah.

*I'm not some intern secretary,* Kennedy thought as she crumpled the notes one by one and sat down to power up her computer. *I'm the best one in this department, and he's trying to keep me from outshining him.*

*Are you sure?* another voice asked from deep in her mind, the ghost of Uncle Albert rising to taunt her. *Are you sure it's not because you can't follow rules, can't keep still, and are always in the fucking way?*

"No," Kennedy said aloud. She refused to listen to such anxiety-driven nonsense. She was at the top of her game, she knew it, and everyone else in the office did too. If Uncle Albert were still alive, even he would know it. Same with her mother. Same with Num-Num.

Kennedy stopped, her fingers hovering over the keyboard in the middle of the email to Tina.

*Why did I think of Num-Num? That was just a dream. But the crackers...*

"What crackers?" a voice asked overhead. Kennedy startled and swiveled around. As always, the bane of her existence presented himself smartly in an expensive gray suit with a gold tie clasp and a nametag that read "Scott: PR Lead" despite the fact that no one else wore nametags. He beamed down at her as if his presence was the greatest gift she could have ever asked for, tossing a wave of blond hair back from his suntanned face. He was the owner's perfect son, which meant that this office was his playground and he knew it.

"Nothing," Kennedy said quickly, bending back to her email while cursing herself for not hearing him coming.

*Was I talking out loud?* But that was the least of her worries. If she didn't cut this off immediately, she knew Scott would give her something even more ridiculous to do.

"Hey, if you're planning something, I get it," he rambled. "Charcuterie boards take effort. I'll get out of your hair. I just came by to see if you got my notes."

"Emailing Tina as we speak," Kennedy said. "And then after that I'll be running the STEAM report to check our numbers for—"

"Nah nah nah," Scott interrupted, waving his hand to shush her as he leaned over and propped one of his long legs against her desk. Kennedy stared at her computer screen, acutely aware of his crotch so close to her face.

*One good punch and I could send him crying home to Mama,* one side of her mind whispered.

*Don't you dare,* the other side answered. *You'd be fired for sure. You're better than that.*

"I need you in my corner today, Super K. I'm going to need you to put the pedal to the metal and whip together one of those awesome slideshows you do so well."

The anger that boiled up the back of Kennedy's throat was as palpable and acidic as vomit. He knew she was busy, yet he'd come up with one more stupid task to slip onto her plate, using his empty flattery like a parent trying to get a child to eat vegetables by pretending they were airplanes.

"What?" Kennedy asked.

"Just a few slides to accompany my speech for next week's presentation of the app." He smiled. Kennedy stared at his stupid face in disbelief as she registered just exactly what he was asking for.

"You mean...you mean your whole presentation? Haven't you been working on that this past week?"

"I've been working on my *speech*," he said, and for a moment the charming smile faltered. For just that second the look that flashed in his eyes was the hard light of a schoolyard bully unaccustomed to not getting his own way, warning his victim what would come if they didn't pay the toll. And not for the first time, Kennedy longed to challenge that look with one of her own, tell Scott to shove it and that his degree didn't mean shit, that his whole behavior was disgusting and everyone hated his coddled attitude. But as the thoughts of everything she'd like to say fanned out through Kennedy's mind, she could only latch on to the one hobbling along at the rear of the pack, the slow and ill one that always allowed the predator to get its feast:

*It's not professional.* Hell, who was she kidding? The issue wasn't even about being professional; it was the fact that she'd walked away from a childhood of never being good enough and had made it her life's mission to always be the cool and collected chick who handled her shit so well that no one could see the least bit of disturbance in her world.

She'd never been good enough for Uncle Albert. Well, Scott was just another Albert trying to get her to break.

*And I'll be damned if that happens.*

"I'll start on it right away," Kennedy said.

"I knew I could count on you," Scott replied. "Keep up the good work. I'll let my dad know how great you are." Kennedy couldn't have cared less if he'd told his dad to name her the queen of England; she just needed him to go. Mercifully, his footsteps started fading away until, finally, they were gone.

Kennedy got up and made a beeline for the breakroom, which was thankfully empty. Her mind painted everything in a coat of red as she replayed the idiotic request, the smug smile on Scott's face, his elevated leg so close to her head.

*Calm down,* she reminded herself. *Breathe.*

But her hands were trembling so hard that she could hear the grounds shaking in the coffee container as she picked it up and began to prepare a pot. Pressure was in her head, pounding through her brain and needing release, but she was better than leaking frustrated tears. What Kennedy really wanted was to let out a good long scream of anger, the feral kind that she hadn't made since she was a kid.

*The scream that Kennee's Momma unleashed when she walked into the room and saw Num-Num standing over Uncle Albert was what really made Kennee realize that Uncle Albert wasn't going to wake up from this. Nails dug into her arm and she was whipped around to look into Momma's wild, pale face.*

*"What happened?" Momma gasped.*

*"I don't know!" Kennee said, her voice suddenly choking, matching Momma's hysteria. "I just found them like this!"*

*"Them?"*

*"Uncle Albert and Num-Num," she clarified, spinning around to point, but of course Num-Num had disappeared. Kennee watched as the wild fear on Momma's face drained away and was slowly replaced by a smile, but it was wrong: a crooked, twitching grin that looked as if it were only there to cover up something worse.*

*"Num-Num did it," Momma repeated. She dropped Kennee's arm and walked out of the room, her house slippers thwacking on the floor with every step. Partly out of fear and partly because she didn't want to be alone with the shell of Uncle Albert, Kennee followed. Her Momma's bedroom door was open wide and Abbee tried to follow her in, but her feet stopped at the threshold as if crossing might bring Uncle Albert running in to scream about boundaries and adult spaces. Momma was in the corner picking up a*

*box that contained new shoes for Kennee, a rarity, but she dumped the shoes on the bed as if they were pieces of garbage.*

*"Momma?" Kennee asked, confused. Her momma turned and the wild, desperate look was back, burning across her face.*

*"I don't want to hear about Num-Num ever again!" she screamed. "Little girls don't have imaginary friends! Little girls don't get in trouble! My God, what have you done?"*

*"I didn't do anything!" Kennee protested, and tears clouded her eyes. Was she not good enough for Momma now, just like Uncle Albert said? "It was Num-Num!"*

*"Well," Momma said as she slammed the lid down on the box and grabbed a roll of duct tape from the bathroom, where it had been used to repair a crack in the faucet handle, "I'm putting Num-Num in this box. You can't see her anymore."*

*"You can't do that!" Kennee yelled.*

*"I'm your mother! I'll do whatever the hell I need to do to protect you...!" Her words trailed off into sobs, and she violently ripped the tape from the roll, twisting it around the outside of the box.*

*"Go to your room, Kennee! Stay there and when the ambulance comes don't you say a word! Not about Uncle Albert, not about you being there when it happened, and not a word ever again about Num-Num!"*

Kennedy turned to grab a mug, but one was already being held out to her, the handle clasped delicately between fingers caked with the warm grease of unwashed skin.

She should have been horrified and shocked to see Num-Num standing beside her in broad daylight, but somehow she wasn't. With an almost otherworldly calm, Kennedy found herself thinking, *It's finally come to it. I've finally snapped from the pressure.*

Num-Num's head swayed slightly on her gangly neck like a serpent preparing to strike, but the creature said nothing. Kennedy snatched the cup from between the nail-bitten fingertips and turned away, pulling the coffee pot out roughly even though it was still brewing. She sloshed some of it into her mug as more dripped from the spout to the hot pad, hissing as it evaporated. She always used cream and sugar to cut the acidity, but today the bitterness seemed to sit perfectly on Kennedy's tongue exactly as it was.

"Well, since everything else is going to hell, I might as well just chat with an old imaginary friend, huh?"

She turned back around, and Num-Num was still there in the blinding clarity of the daylight world, on display for Kennedy to see in hideous detail. She was still tall, and if her neck and massive head were not drooping so low, Kennedy would not have been able to look her in the eyes. Her dress was faded and filthy with old stains dark as tea that were positioned in unpleasant places, and all the flowers that used to be open were now closed tightly. Num-Num's knees were rounded and knobby and stuck out of her thin legs, while beneath them the toes on massive feet splayed out for balance, each nail long and curling.

She certainly hadn't aged well. But how had she aged at all?

"Whhhhh," the thing groaned, dragging its teeth across each other as it struggled to open its mouth before finally spitting out the word. "Why?"

"Oh, piss off," Kennedy growled. "You're going to ask me why I put up with him treating me like shit just like Uncle Albert back in the day? Is that why I've started seeing you again? Because stress is high and I just remembered you, so now my brain has gone full-on Freudian explosion as my childhood self judges my current self or yadda yadda?" Kennedy rolled her eyes and took another sip of coffee. The heat agreed with the warm feeling inside, which had grown as she heaped sarcasm onto Num-Num since she couldn't do it to Scott.

"*We* would never let that man control us," Num-Num finally replied, her voice squealing with the protest of a rusted spring bearing too much weight. Num-Num picked up the container of coffee grounds, sniffed it, and poured an ample helping straight into her mouth. She leaned over the sink, her square jaw jutting out from her face, and let hot tap water flow over the grounds. Her mouth snapped shut again, and she swished the contents of her mouth before swallowing it in one cartoonish gulp.

"I can't do anything about Scott," Kennedy argued. Num-Num slowly straightened back up from the sink, looking over her shoulder at Kennedy with a dull smile that exposed teeth flecked with coffee grounds and cavities.

"You don't have to," Num-Num replied. "I'm here now. Haven't

I always been here when you needed me, Kennee?"

Kennedy squeezed the sides of the mug, focusing on the burn that spread through her fingertips.

"I don't need you," she said. "I can handle it myself." But for the first time in years, the mantra that she had formed her life by felt dry and wrong in her throat. Num-Num smiled again, as if she understood exactly what Kennedy was thinking.

"Wah wah, Kennee. You always want to be so good. Please everyone so you'll be the favorite. Let's see how good you'll feel if you stop trying to live by their stupid rules and make them live by ours." With that, Num-Num opened the fridge and pulled out the tray of sushi that Scott brought in every day for lunch.

"Mmmm, dead fish," Num-Num said, popping off the lid. "Could use sauce, though." Leaning her head to the side, the old woman dribbled a thick strand of coffee-coated saliva out of the corner of her mouth and onto the rolls.

Horror coursed through Kennedy along with a few choice warnings—*I'm fired, Scott will kill me, I need to fix this*—but then Num-Num laughed, and as Kennedy stood in frozen indecision, she found herself suddenly grinning, too.

*What am I worried about? This is just my imagination; it's not like this thing is real. Better to picture Scott's food with spit on it than to rub it into his face.*

Kennedy's grin turned into a smile. She walked to the fridge and stood there with Num-Num, looking down at the spoiled sushi and snorting conspiratorially. With a sudden motion, Num-Num grabbed Kennedy's coffee cup and directed it over the tray, drowning the tiny perfect rolls of seaweed and fish in dark liquid.

"Screw you, Scott," Kennedy whispered as beside her, Num-Num giggled. Kennedy looked up at the old woman, and a smile spread across her face.

"Feel better?" Num-Num asked. "I told you you would."

"Why didn't I ever see you again after Mother said she put you in the box?" Kennedy asked. It wasn't the question she'd meant to vocalize, but it was waiting at the tip of her tongue. Num-Num's own large tongue darted out over her thick lips, wetting them before she spoke.

"Because you never let me out," Num-Num said. "You started wanting to please your momma, to be the girl she wanted you to be instead of the girl you were. You forgot about me."

Kennedy nodded. There was something about Num-Num's explanation that made sense, because hadn't Kennee become Kennedy after Num-Num had gone into the box? The little girl who was...

*perfect*

...always good?

She put the lid on the sushi and shoved it back into the fridge. Maybe she would need to go to a shrink later and figure out a reason as to why she was suddenly imagining Num-Num again, but as she looked at the tray of seafood, she realized that this wasn't hurting anyone, and it wouldn't even hurt herself as long as no one found out. This could just be a little coping mechanism, one that worked faster and with better results than the breathing exercises. Besides, it had been awhile since Kennedy had felt so light. The laughing had done her some good, and didn't she deserve to feel good once in a while?

The contented feeling stayed curled up in her stomach like a tiny fetus throughout the rest of her shift, which flew by as she plowed through her work and Scott's ridiculous tasks. By the time Mikey was swooping her up into a hug, Kennedy was downright pleased with the way the day had turned out. Mikey had made dinner again, and this time it was the white bean and chicken chili recipe he'd made the first time he had ever cooked for her.

"By the way, we seem to be out of crackers," Mikey said as he laid two bowls on the table.

"Are you serious?" Kennedy grumbled, irritation rising up in her gut to replace the good feeling she'd been nurturing. Her mind flicked back to the crumbs on the bedroom floor, but she shooed the recollection away. "Well, that blows."

"Babe?" Mikey asked as he registered her sharp tone. "What's up?"

"Why does anything have to be up?" Kennedy snapped.

Mikey's eyebrows raised in hurt surprise at her aggressive tone, and the hot edge of Kennedy's anger wavered.

"I'm sorry. It's just Scott," she sighed as she sat down at the table and dipped her spoon into the chili. "He came up with another thing for me to do...his whole presentation, actually. He'll take credit for all the work I've done, and of course Bill will say it's brilliant because Bill won't believe anything less about his own kid."

"That stinks," Mikey agreed as he shoveled a spoon of chili into his mouth and swallowed it without taking the time to chew. Kennedy blinked in irritation; had he always eaten so loudly and disgustingly? "Maybe it's time to move along. There's gotta be better jobs out there."

"I'm not leaving my job, Mikey," she said, blowing on her spoonful delicately. She had a sudden urge to scream at Mikey for being so childish, sitting there gobbling his vittles like a little boy and lecturing her about her job when he was still working at the same GameStop he'd been in since college.

*He's not qualified to give his opinion,* her mind whispered. *Just like Scott.*

"Well, maybe not, like, tomorrow," Mikey persisted. Kennedy felt the stab of a headache slice up between her eyes and roll through the back of her skull, and as Mikey continued...

"I mean, Kennedy, it's not like—"

*She wished he would just*

"—there's any shame in admitting—"

*shut*

"—that this place isn't a good fit."

*his stupid*

"Nobody's perfect."

*mouth.*

"I am," she whispered.

"What's that?" he asked. Kennedy looked up and met his eyes, wet and helpless like a pet waiting to be coddled by its master, and she was suddenly infuriated.

"I don't need to discuss this," she said, keeping her voice coldly level. Mikey tilted his head like a ridiculous dog, as if she weren't speaking perfectly clear English.

"Maybe you should," he said slowly. "Look, I know you always want to be on top, but everyone has to throw in the towel every now and then and accept that they're not up to the challenge. I know you hate admitting that, but you've got to accept that not everything about your life is going to be something you can make perfect."

"When you've done everything you can do and you've been as good as you can be and it's still not good enough, it's time to make your own level of good," Kennedy said, the phrase popping up in her mind fully formed.

"That doesn't make sense," Mikey pressed. But Kennedy was done listening to anyone for the night. The feeling of lightness, of control, that she had felt when she'd imagined Num-Num pouring coffee over Scott's sushi in petty revenge was back, and she reveled in it. Mikey talked for a few minutes more, but Kennedy was busy replaying the daydream of the afternoon over and over again, and she smiled to herself. After a few minutes of staring at Kennedy with a confused look on his face, Mikey silently got up and left the table. Kennedy finished her dinner alone, which she hadn't done since she'd gotten married, and in the silence her anger faded into discomfort.

*Was I over the line?* she wondered.

"Nah," Num-Num said from across the table. She picked up Mikey's bowl and poured the remnants straight down her throat, then began to dab the inside of the porcelain with her bloated white tongue. "You were right. He doesn't deserve to judge you. You're better than that."

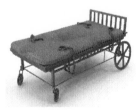

THE NEXT MORNING HAD ALL THE PROMISES OF A BEAUTIFUL SATURDAY, and although it was her one opportunity to sleep in, Kennedy started getting ready to head out the moment she was out of bed. Her phone buzzed with a notification that a yoga guru she followed had just uploaded a new video: *10 Minute Meditation to Clear Headspace- Easy!* but Kennedy swiped it away. For the first time in a long time she didn't feel the need to breathe away her stress. She grabbed the shopping list off the side of their fridge, which had the word "crackers" at the bottom in Mikey's handwriting, and left the house.

The Target was brightly lit and barely busy by the time she got there, so Kennedy was able to move through the aisles quickly and pull what she needed off the shelves. She tried not to wonder, as she placed two large boxes of crackers into the basket of her cart, how a thing that existed only in her mind could have made those crumbs on the floor.

*Mikey must have eaten them. Sleepwalking or something.* The answer was hardly sufficient, but Kennedy realized that she didn't care. She'd forgotten how much fun it was to make her own rules, to not have to measure up to anyone else's expectations but her own for a day or two.

*But it can't stay past the weekend.* Kennedy knew this was a fact just as surely as she knew she was going to work on Scott's presentation on Monday instead of letting him crash and burn. It was just who she was.

*You can't teach an old dog new—*

"—tricks on me, but they're not! Here you are!"

Kennedy jumped at the sound of Scott's voice so close—too close—to her ear. Hearing the sound of the enemy outside of work was so disorienting that for a moment, Kennedy was shocked to see the twin walls of shelves on either side; surely she was at work or in hell. But no, she was still standing in the middle of the soup aisle and there was Scott, dressed in LuLu Lemon pants and a ridiculously tight workout shirt, clutching a coffee from the Starbucks that was located inside the store.

"Aren't you going to say hello to your favorite boss?" Scott asked, still smiling his ridiculous coyote grin as he approached the end of Kennedy's cart and leaned on it.

"Why are you here?" Kennedy asked. Technically it was completely possible that he was there for the same reason she was, groceries, but Kennedy knew enough about Scott to remember that he liked to utilize the "order online and have another shopper pick it up" option. It was out of character for him to be in the actual store itself, unless…she glanced from his venti coffee cup to his other hand, which was empty of a cart or basket or anything else.

*He came in for coffee, saw me, and followed me.* The voice in her head became whiney and rusty, squeaking like bad bed springs as it repeated the mantra.

*Followed me.*

*Followed me.*

*Followed me.*

"Gotta say," Scott was rambling, "I'm surprised to see you here just killing time." Kennedy snapped back to attention.

"I'm not killing time," she said, while the voice in her head asked her why she was even bothering to explain herself at all.

"Potato potahto," Scott said, smiling. "What I mean is, don't we have a big presentation coming up next week?"

*YOU do,* the voice of Num-Num squawked in Kennedy's head.

"We do," Kennedy affirmed slowly.

"Well then, you'd better get cracking. Now before you say anything, I know…I know it's Saturday," Scott said, holding up his hands even though Kennedy hadn't said a word. "Office is closed. But you can do some work from home and really bang this out by Monday."

"It's my day off," Kennedy said. Her voice sounded flat and helpless to her own ears, the whine of a child disappointed that they weren't getting their way, and she hated it. Scott smiled down at her benevolently, but his eyes were as hard and treacherous as black ice.

"I think you'll find that doing as I ask will come with some great bonuses," he all but purred. "Like a secure future at H.B.T. But if you're not willing to be a team player, maybe it's time for me to reevaluate your position on my team."

The sides of Kennedy's temples burned even while her insides turned cold and she felt herself shrinking inside, shrinking until she was Kennee again, a wide-eyed, knock-kneed little squirt of a child who always managed to fuck everything up no matter how hard she tried.

*No!* her mind screamed. *I'm not that anymore! I'm…*

But a perfect person wouldn't have their job threatened. Somewhere in the logic of her mind, Kennedy knew that this wasn't on her, that Scott was being a dick, but it didn't matter.

"Kennedy?" Scott asked, his voice a thousand lightyears away. "Do you understand me?" Behind him a can of soup popped off the shelf and rolled across the aisle, but Scott didn't seem to notice it. Two sets of fingers curled out through the open space and gripped the edge of the shelf, gnawed fingernails pressing roughly into the sleek black metal.

"Get it done, Kennedy," Scott was saying. Kennedy didn't know if she had responded to him or not, but now he was walking away, swaggering in his ridiculous overpriced sweatpants like he was the king of the world, like he was the one who was...

*perfect*

...in charge of Kennedy, Uncle Albert back from the grave.

Num-Num's head twisted out from between the cans of soup, her thick skull bobbing at the end of her stringy neck. She snapped to the side as one shoulder pressed out to freedom, then the other. She reached for the ground with her hands and walked herself forward, bones popping as her legs twisted over each other to fit through the tiny space on the shelf. For a moment she hovered there, the massive rock of her stomach the only thing keeping her dress from falling, then she flipped herself right side up. Her bare feet slapped the tile floor with a dull *fwack*, the sound of Uncle Albert hitting Momma in the face.

"It's time to do something," Num-Num said. Her rusted voice was flat with anger and her eyes were wheels of fire. Kennedy opened her mouth to laugh, but a gargled choke came out instead.

*I've done everything I can and I'm still not good enough, and that incompetent idiot is the one who gets to make that decision.*

But Num-Num didn't seem to be scared; she smiled and slipped her hand into Kennedy's. The hand was not cold or clammy but feverishly warm, and her fingers met perfectly with Kennedy's, more perfectly than Mikey's ever had. Heat rippled up Kennedy's arm, spasming her muscle in an exquisite pain that wasn't entirely horrible, popping through her shoulder and chest and finally rushing down into her stomach until her whole body roared. Num-

Num pulled her forward and they abandoned their grocery cart, following Scott's receding figure across the store.

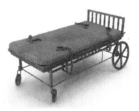

By THE TIME SHE GOT HOME, KENNEDY WAS EXHAUSTED EVEN THOUGH it was barely noon. She filled the bathtub, twisting the knob all the way to red until the liquid belched steam, but when she put her hand in, the water seemed just right. She pulled off her clothes and balled them up, shooting them into the corner of the room as if they were basketballs before slipping into the scalding water with the same pleasure of wiggling into warm sheets on a cold winter night. Kennedy closed her eyes and tilted her head back, allowing the warmth of the water and the heat of her skin to meld together and become one entity. She let her mind wander again, this time in a soothing dream that she was no longer a woman but something else entirely: a being made of heat and confidence, one that everyone knew was good enough.

"Kennedy?" Mikey's voice cut through her daydreams, and she opened her eyes. Although she was still comfortably flushed, the water had grown cold around her.

"In the bathroom!" she called, listening for Mikey's heavy foot-steps to plod dutifully down the hall as she pulled the plug and watched the water swirl away down the drain.

They did not come.

"Can you come out here, please?" Something was wrong. He sounded hesitant, a beat too long between the "here" and the "please" as if he didn't know where he wanted to end the sentence. Kennedy rolled her eyes and stood up from the empty tub, grabbing her robe and wrapping it around herself before heading out of the bathroom. She found Mikey standing in the living room, still wearing his green-and-black work uniform, his ungainly figure blocking whatever was on the television as he stood there watching it. He turned as she walked in and Kennedy prepared herself for the rush of comfort that she would feel when he ran up and took her in his arms.

But Mikey kept his distance.

"What's wrong?" Kennedy asked.

"You tell me," he said as he turned back to the television and pointed at the screen.

A middle-aged woman with short black hair was sitting somberly at a newsdesk, her voice grave as she asked for anyone with information to come forward. Hovering over her shoulder in the top corner of the screen was an extremely grainy image, the type that came from low-budget security cameras. Kennedy watched as a man in sweatpants and a tight shirt walked into view and stooped down beside a terribly parked sports car in a handicap spot. Kennedy recognized Scott with no problem; she didn't need to see his face to know that cocky bastard.

*Screw him,* she thought, crossing her arms.

As if the universe had heard her, a blur in a green shirt and baggy jeans bobbed into the frame. It veered to the parking lot's landscape and picked up a huge rock, which must have made a noise because the man turned around. If he said something the camera was too low quality to catch it, but he took a noticeable step back when the figure got close enough for him to see the rock. He raised his hands, but the newcomer was suddenly rushing him, and though he cowered and tried to put his arms over his head, she raised the rock and smashed it down over his arms and, finally, his skull. Then again. And again. Again.

She hammered until he was crumpled against the hubcap of his car like a broken puppet that needed to be restrung. She then got into her car, its license plate just out of shot of the camera, and drove away.

But that was impossible. Impossible, because that car was the exact same one that Kennedy drove. Impossible, because those jeans and that green shirt were crumpled on her bathroom floor right now. Impossible, because she had no memory of leaving the store or, she suddenly realized, of how she'd gotten home. In fact, she didn't remember anything after Num-Num had taken her hand, but that didn't matter because Num-Num was only a fluke of her mind, a stress reliever, an imaginary friend.

*Right?*

Mikey was watching her now, breathing sharply.

"Kennedy," he finally asked, "what did you do?"

Kennedy's mind clicked around for an answer, a revolver trying to fire on an empty chamber. The phrase she wanted so badly to speak into existence—Num-Num did it—was on the tip of her tongue, but that couldn't be. Kennedy looked down at her hands and noticed something that didn't belong: a smear of red between the skin and nail on the first finger of her left hand.

*No,* she thought wildly. *I'm the good girl.*

But a door in her mind that looked like the one to her mother's room that had been locked just as tightly all these years was slowly forcing itself open. Memories whispered out from behind it, asking Kennedy if there wasn't a spot on her hand where her skin had turned warm under a speckle of blood? And another brought her the image of Scott's eyes, dilated with justified fear as he stared up at her.

*Uncle Albert was snoring with his mouth flopped open like a door on a broken hinge, and he didn't wake up as Kennee entered the room. She stood over him for a moment, glaring at the massive mountain of flesh that had threatened to kill her and had hit Momma. Her hand closed around one of the hotdogs from his plate, the yellow mustard and soft bread squishing between her fingers as she squeezed it tight. He thought he could eat everything in sight: their food, their home, their happiness. But Num-Num was hungrier.*

*Kennee jammed the whole hot dog into his mouth, pushing it down as far as she could reach. He gagged and the muscles of his throat pressed against her tiny fist like the inner workings of a car wash tunnel, but she still held on for a moment, waiting until his eyes opened and met hers. She saw the fear in them, a natural fear that took over when something was wrong, she guessed, but there was something else, too, something buried deeper.*

*Fear of her.*

*Satisfied, she pulled her hand free and left the obstruction to do its job. The noises and clawing motions that Uncle Albert made as he tried to coordinate his failing body to save itself didn't bother her, but Kennee was bothered by the thick ropes of saliva that hung through her fingers and she stepped aside to wipe her hand on the side of the couch. By the time she had finished, so had Uncle Albert. Then she heard her mother scream.*

*"What did you do?"*

*Kennee looked up, surprised at the distress in Momma's voice.*

*"I made everything perfect," she announced.*

Kennedy gripped the back of the couch, suddenly dizzy. It was impossible. She'd never hurt anyone; she'd never been capable of it. That was the reason she'd dreamed up Num-Num in the first place, to have someone she could pretend would be strong enough to do what was necessary since she couldn't and her mother never would. It was only after Num-Num went away that she'd begun trying to be a person without cracks, who didn't care no matter what came their way since Num-Num was no longer around to make light of those situations. But the memories were still slipping into the light, reminding Kennedy of the pulsing of Uncle Albert's throat against her fist and the satisfaction that had risen through her when Scott groaned as he dropped into unconsciousness.

"He attacked you, right?" Mikey's voice floated to her ears without truly registering, as if he were a piece of a lovely dream she'd once had a long time ago. "This was self-defense?"

"Uhh?" Kennedy asked, turning to look at him. He was pale and covered with a sheen of sour, tangy sweat that she could smell even from where she was standing.

The reek of fear.

"Kennedy, that's you! You attacked that guy! What the hell?"

Kennedy snapped back to attention; Mikey had never dared to swear at her before.

"Scott followed me," she said. "He threatened to fire me if I didn't… What, you think I'm just some psycho killer who murders people? Is that what you think?"

Mikey laughed, the same sort of unpleasant bark that her mother had made when she'd heard that Num-Num had killed Uncle Albert.

"There are always bosses that are assholes. That's like saying the sky is blue, Kennedy! But you could have gotten a new job or something; instead, look! Look at the screen! You're the exact same thing you hated in him, because you just went after someone else like a... like an insane bully! And that's how the courts are going to paint you!"

"Courts?" she repeated slowly. The word sounded foreign and aggressive in her mind.

"Well, yeah," Mikey continued, still jabbering. Kennedy noticed a fleck of spit that had accumulated in the corner of his mouth, and she wanted more than anything to tell him to just wipe that disgusting thing away. "You have to turn yourself in."

Kennedy's irritation suddenly morphed into panic that rose through her body like water hitting the boiling point. *You're going to jail!* the voice of her mother shrieked. *You're bad; you let Num-Num out of the box and now* you're *going to a box!* Kennedy saw herself standing behind bars dressed in an orange jumpsuit that would let everyone see how flawed she truly was, her hair getting ragged and her nails growing until she had no choice to gnaw them, gnaw gnaw gnaw them down to the quick just like Num-Num had when she was in her box.

"I can't go to jail!" Kennedy wheezed. "Mikey, please. I don't know what happened, but I can't...maybe we can just leave, or...or something..."

Kennedy buried her face in her hands, and Mikey finally came to her. His arms snaked around her waist and she leaned her head on his shoulder, but he didn't squeeze her close. He held her carefully, as if she were a wild animal that needed to be pacified.

"I don't think you understand," he said. "I'll be with you every step of the way, but we can't run from this. You have to turn yourself in. By tomorrow."

Mikey's words hit like stones against Kennedy's ears and sunk in slowly, dragging her down with them. She swallowed hard.

"What if I don't?"

Mikey said nothing for a moment, and the question hung between them like a palpable beast, a two-faced creature that could ruin or save them.

*Choose carefully, Mikey.*

"Then I'll have to do it." Kennedy pulled away from him and looked at his face, but he refused to meet her eyes.

*So that's it, then.*

He would put her in a box.

Kennedy tore back to the bathroom, tears burning across the skin of her cheeks as she locked the door behind herself. The room was now a place foreign from the relaxing haven she had been in before —could it have been only minutes ago?—with signs of guilt strewn everywhere. The clothes she'd discarded looked sticky and damp with red smears of gore, and she must have stepped on them because there were perfect bloody imprints of her feet against the blue tile leading to the bathtub. And in the corner, beside the scale that she mounted religiously every morning, was the crimson-spattered rock, the proof that she was the monster they were looking for.

"Num-num-nummy," a voice croaked.

Kennedy looked up and saw Num-Num in the mirror, staring out in place of her own reflection. Num-Num's skin was yellowed and dirty under the bright lights of the bathroom, but her red eyes were twinkling and more alive than ever and the tiny petals of the flowers on her dress were open in full bloom. Kennedy put her palms on the counter and leaned toward the glass, and Num-Num reflected the movement until their foreheads were almost touching.

"Tell me the truth. Who did those things?" Kennedy asked, forcing her voice into steadiness.

Num-Num's giant lips cracked upwards in a smile.

"I did," she croaked.

There she had it. The confession Kennedy always preached, confirmed: Num-Num did it, which meant that this was somehow not real.

*Right?*

Kennedy wiped the tears off her face with the back of her hand. In her childhood she had blamed bad deeds on Num-Num and had truly believed that Num-Num had done them, but that couldn't be all there was to it. Uncle Albert hadn't just choked in his sleep while she imagined Num-Num doing it, because why would her mother have been so terrified? Num-Num couldn't have put Scott in a coma, and she couldn't have faked that video footage. Something real had made Mikey see her as an animal to be caged, not an imaginary little game to help her cope with stress. Num-Num was always where stress was, but there was something more to it.

Num-Num was always where Kennedy was.

"*We* did it," Kennedy whispered, understanding at last.

Num-Num nodded, the loose skin on the sides of her chin and neck flopping with the motion.

"Momma tried to keep us apart," Num-Num said, her voice the creak of an abandoned swing. "Momma liked you better when you were the good little pet. And you believed her."

It was true. Kennee had allowed Momma to tell her that she was only a good girl if she was perfect at following other people's rules, creating a Kennedy who needed the appreciation of idiots like Mikey and the approval of assholes like Scott.

"Scott deserved what we gave him," Kennedy said slowly, the word "we" still blocky against her tongue. "I'm not sorry to him. But I am sorry to me. To us."

Num-Num smiled, her wide grin splitting her face like an overripe melon between her two thin pigtails. Kennedy wondered how she could have ever thought Num-Num horrifying; she was neglected, sad, and abandoned. She'd given Kennedy the courage to do what she needed to do, and that's what she'd really been afraid of all along.

"I can be perfect," Kennedy whispered, and for the first time she understood the words. "It's time to make my own level of good." She reached for the mirror. Num-Num, her perfect double, reached back and their fingers met against the glass. "I want us to be put back together again. One Kennedy, with no more forgotten memories and no more flaws."

Num-Num's fingers solidified around hers, and Kennedy helped the crone step out of the glass as if she were helping her over a patch of ice. Num-Num's red eyes twinkled with the joy of a child looking up at a Christmas tree as she caressed Kennedy's chin, her fingers a damp map of crevices and wrinkles filled with the smell of waterlogged memories just waiting to rise to the surface. Then Num-Num pressed her fingers onto each corner of Kennedy's lips and pulled them open. She reached her hand into Kennedy's mouth, then the other, and pushed her forearms through. Kennedy didn't gag, but a sweet heat ripped through her and cascaded down into the rest of her body. The left side of Num-Num's face collapsed inwards with a crack of bone, then her right side, and finally her entire body rolled until she was nothing more than a thick brown worm, stinking of stagnant water and a back-of-the-refrigerator smell. She went down Kennedy's throat with a single sludgy pump, and Kennedy had one odd thought—*I'm giving birth to myself*—before the heat took her.

It filled every pore, burning so harshly that she wanted to die and at the same time was so beautiful that she wanted nothing more than to live and wreak her glory onto anyone who had tried to contain it before.

*I'm finally perfect. I'm a fucking goddess.*

The part of her that had been the good girl was melting down now, crying out somewhere inside that it was too much, she hadn't wanted to go so far, but that voice was weak. It always had been. Num-Num would devour everyone who was in the way, and there would be no boxes anymore.

It was the unmoving darkness of the middle of the night when Num-Num left the bathroom and went to look for Mikey. They found him in the living room, fast asleep in front of the television. Num-Num debated with herself.

*When it came down to it, he didn't protect us. He was going to put us in a box to make everyone else happy. Just like Momma.*

*We love him,* Kennedy cried.

*But he wanted to put us in jail.*

*He was just trying to do what he thought was right.*

*And did you think it was right?*

Kennedy had no response to this.

*He doesn't love us. Not really. He only loves the good girl piece. One of us is going to have to go into the box: us or him. Do you want it to be us?*

Num-Num knew that, regardless of their feelings for Mikey, it would not be them returning to a box.

*Make it quick then,* Kennedy conceded. *He was good to the part of us he saw, before he threatened the box.*

They knew where the duct tape was, and they were out to the

garage to get it and back before the television had even switched commercials. Num-Num made sure to rip off the strips—two long and two short—before they came back in, so that Mikey would not be alerted by the sound. He didn't wake up when they began to tape his wrists together, but he did come around when they started on his ankles.

"Babe?" he asked, his voice foggy with sleep. He tried to move, realized he couldn't, and Num-Num saw the fear of prey light in his eyes.

"Sorry, babe," they replied, and his eyes widened at the new squeak in the familiar voice. "No more boxes." Num-Num placed the last two strips of duct tape across his mouth and nose.

They left the house while he was still thrashing, rolling onto the floor with a colossal thud that would probably wake the neighbors. Maybe they would get there in time, maybe not; or maybe he'd manage to free himself before he drowned on his own spittle. It was no longer any of their concern. Scott was still alive, that much had been made clear by the television report, and they had to take care of that. Num-Num walked down the sidewalk in their bare feet and bathrobe, not feeling the cold of the night.

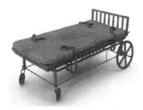

A TRAITOR WOMAN WAS WORKING THE FRONT DESK AT THE HOSPITAL, one who would not allow Num-Num into Scott's room and who, in fact, thought they needed a room of their own. They glared at her and tried to get to the elevator anyway when the yelling started: first from the traitor, and then from the security guard who was barreling toward them. Kennedy wanted to pretend like nothing was wrong and talk her way out, her usual response, but Num-Num refused such abuse. She leapt back at him, ready to swing and remind him just who he was dealing with. But the man grabbed their arms and spun them around, pinning their wrists behind their back. Num-Num butted their head backwards, snapping the cartilage of his nose wetly against their skull and smiling as he bellowed, but the sound brought other men and traitors running. Num-Num's hands were cuffed with cold metal and they licked their lips, desperate to bring these fools to order, but they couldn't even wiggle as they were escorted from the building.

It was when they saw the police car with its back doors thrown open that they understood. There was wire mesh between the front and back seats, ready to lock them in.

"Won't!" Num-Num screamed. "Not back in a box!" But it didn't matter. The man pushed their head down and suddenly Num-Num was in the car with the walls around her again, walls that would stay close until she could be a good girl, yes. She ricocheted their head forward into the metal grate, tearing Kennedy's stupid face on the cold silver, then did it again. She would keep going until she dug out of the box. Then someone yelled, and there was a rush of running legs and the car door opened, and then everything went dark.

By the time they woke up in jail—*back in the box!*—their face had been bandaged and they were all alone. Kennedy and Num-Num consulted on how to handle this new development, teetering between hysteria and waiting, but eventually the waiting decision won out.

Num-Num laid their throbbing head against the cold wall of the jail and licked first their wounded wrists, then a reddish smear on the wall that looked like it could be tasty. The part of them that had been good girl Kennedy was crying softly, wondering if her idiot husband was dead. Num-Num hoped he was. The traitors would find him, and then Scott would wake up, and everyone would say it was all Num-Num's fault, and just like Momma, they would keep her in the box. But she had been in the box before.

"Num-num-nummy," she whispered, their voice squeaking lightly at the end. "You can't keep us here forever, dummy."

They would find a way out of the box.

# HESITATION CUTS

## LP HERNANDEZ

There's something different about my wife. It's the pause before the smile, the confusion in her eyes, as if she is seeing me for the first time. Where do you go when you are not here with me, Anna?

This house is so empty with just us in it. No pitter-patter of little feet, no bird-screech of wonder at a firefly trapped in a glass jar. And now you have become a specter, haunting your old paths with that smile that stops just before it touches your eyes. It is not a happy smile. It is a mockery.

It came to me in a dream, Anna. I dream a lot now, mostly of our life before. This dream was different. It felt real.

You were trapped inside of yourself, dear. Those tentative smiles that never quite coincided with the outside world were flickers of your former self, the YOU hidden within grayed flesh and cloud-white hair. You lay beside me in bed, facing the window as you always do. I watch the swell of your body as you inhale, snores like a mouse chewing a cracker.

I always loved to watch you sleep, Anna. In a marriage of fifty years there are few secrets, just these little slices of reality we tuck safely into our pockets, carrying them around with us throughout the day. That was my secret. I watched you sleep, sometimes for an hour or more. In the dream, I watch you sleep as well, a twitch of the shoulder hinting at your own conjured fantasy.

I reach across the bed to touch your back, something I do not do in life for fear of waking you. You shudder, not from the warmth of my palm but from something else. Your spine stiffens and your hand spider-crawls around your ribs, settling beneath your shoulder blade. Was it the whisper-thin fabric of your favorite nightgown, the tickle of a stray thread? It was a Christmas present from our granddaughter, Layla I think—bought with her own money, she told us with a chest nearly bursting from pride.

You writhe, back arching as your fingers probe the spaces between your ribs. No, not the nightgown. Then I see it, a little bulge in the fabric. I know every inch of you, have loved every inch of you even as our inches, yours and mine, succumbed to the persistence of gravity. There is no bulge here. Or there never was before.

I slide my palm over that familiar terrain hidden by a gauze of plum-colored cotton. I feel it, the bulge, hard as bone but flexible, relenting to the gentle pressure I place upon it. Time takes strange liberties with our bodies. It turned my knuckles into knots, softened your gums until your teeth fell out in your sleep. At night it sifts through your memories, turning familiar faces into smudges, stealing names. But it does not create a growth in a span of hours...

I imagine it is your heartbeat against my palm at first, a little flutter barely noticed. But, no, it is something different. Something that should not be. I gasp, recalling my hand and holding it to my chest as if it was fire I touched and not your body. It disturbs the fabric of your nightgown from underneath, like a beetle crawling over your ribs. Your hand falls limply upon it as if trying to push it back in.

After seconds of holding my breath, I brush your hand aside. There it is, a periscope stretching the cotton. Your nightgown has a scooped back, and I snake my fingers within. There is little light in the room, a warped rectangle of milky orange on the floor. I squint and search for movement. My eyes are not so good, Anna, and my glasses are never near when I need them. But I see something. Maybe. A strip of night hidden within the shadow of your shoulder blade.

The darkness matches the approximate area of the bulge in your nightgown. I inch my fingers closer, avoiding your skin so as not to wake you. Over the course of that brief journey, my curiosity shifts into fear. It is difficult to control my hand, to prevent my twitching fingers from grazing you. And my knuckles block my view of the darkened strip.

I imagine it is a leech, suckling your flesh as its body turns to leather. Did I dream within my dream? Then I feel it, not a leech and not your skin, but warmth and moisture, like steam leaking from the seam between a boiling pot and its lid.

I woke and felt as if my belly was full of boiling leeches, such was the vividness of the dream. You snored like a single autumn leaf skittering over concrete. I rolled onto my side to face you, but there was little to see beyond a spider web of hair on your pillow. The comforter was pulled to your shoulder, nothing bulging beneath it, no moisture spreading. But it wasn't a dream, Anna. It was a message.

The next morning, we resume our wordless waltz, passing each other in silence like enemy ships without munitions. I do not know who is on the other end of the line listening to your gibberish, a very patient person or no one at all, I imagine.

"…just need a couple more days," you said before your words turned to mush. You noticed me watching from the dining room and hid the phone as if it was a bottle of brandy and you were a teenager again.

You sit in your favorite recliner, hands busy with a needlepoint you will never finish. Though so much of you is gone now, this fragment remains, a glimpse of the way things were. I can almost hear our children squealing around your ankles like piglets. They are two things at once, now. Strange to think about it that way. They are both living, some far away, and ghosts—imprisoned in my mind as children.

I sit in my recliner across the room, tugging tufts of cotton free from the broken fabric. Did you do this, Anna? Did you slice up my chair as petty revenge for some offense I do not even remember?

"Anna?"

Your barn-owl eyes lock onto mine for a second. I believe, for a moment, that I have you back, that your name spoken in the midnight stillness of our empty home cracked the facade of your sickness. The moment stretches just as your smile does and the recognition bleeds from your eyes. Of course it would not be that easy.

You're still smiling as you place your project on your lap, left elbow aiming at the ceiling as you scratch your back, your shoulder blade. I inhale sharply, perhaps not loud enough for you to hear, as your hands resume their task and your smile melts into indifference.

Anna, my dear, Anna. You *are* trapped, just like those fireflies the kids used to torment. You're trapped inside of a body that has betrayed you. How long have you been stuck there? Did it happen all at once or by degrees? We are ships, Anna, but not enemies. You listed and sank so quietly, a blade in water, and now this husk sits in your chair.

I have to free you Anna. We only have a few years left if we're lucky. And I won't spend them with an impostor.

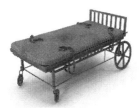

NIGHT TAKES ITS TIME, OR MAYBE IT'S JUST THE SEASON. IN MY OLD AGE I find it endlessly surprising how easily seasons merge and overlap, the familiar touchstones of Christmas or the Fourth of July stripped of meaning without our little piglets to delight in them. I stand in the cold bathroom struggling to read the label of the pill bottle. There is a small army of them between our sinks. I confess I mostly forget what they are intended to cure or keep at bay. Arthritis, a bad heart, a half dozen more things some physician told me about a decade ago. The words are too small for my old eyes, side effects and instructions like fuzzy little caterpillars wiggling on the label. I think I remember which ones made me sleepy.

I dump a few into my hand and tip-toe on cat's paws to the

bedroom door. The TV is on and there are no sounds of movement. Back in the bathroom, I grind the pills into dust, sweep the dust into an empty bottle, then palm it.

And now I wait for the right moment.

YOU ARE NODDING IN YOUR CHAIR, NOT IN AGREEMENT WITH WHATEVER TV judge show you are half-watching, but in defiance of the sleep attempting to claim you. We both nap a lot now, preparing for the big sleep to come, I suppose. Hopefully I can steal a few more good years with you before then.

My feet morph into cat's paws again as I pad to your chair and pluck your iced tea from the tray, a few melted cubes rattling the glass. Your eyes pop open and lock onto mine. I feel like a burglar, Anna, a kid with his hand in the cookie jar. Your lips part but the words come out watery, and you angle your shoulder away from me as if I might strike you. As if I have ever done so in our fifty-plus years.

In that moment you are a stranger to me. Your face melts into a mask, skin pooling where it shouldn't, eyes like ice marbles suspended in a red-threaded spiderweb. Anna, I don't even recognize you when you're like this. I don't even recognize you. And so I turn and shuffle away, no longer padding on cat's paws. It's too tough on my knees, anyway.

Your watery words lap at my back as I reach the kitchen, but you do not follow me. With an ear aimed at the living room, I shake a bit of the powder onto the ice cubes, then fill the cup with more ice and tea. An extra packet of sugar just to be sure and I stir the ice with my finger. I mean to wipe the tea onto my robe and instead streak it across my naked belly. For a moment the world's edges seem to sharpen. The TV judge's voice crackles in the living room.

"What?"

Where is my robe? I think I took a shower, yes. I took a shower and then...but my hair is not wet. I did not take a shower. I take showers at night. Always have. For a moment in that crisp world with the obnoxious, tired judge, I see my pale legs, thighs a road map of blue veins, pubic hair like a forgotten bird's nest above them.

"Where is..."

The judge's voice dives underwater and the world softens, the edges nice and safe now. I blink and find I *am* wearing my robe. How strange that was.

I shuffle back into the living room, spill a little tea on the way. It splashes cold on my toes. You grip the armrests of your chair as if you are afraid there are rockets strapped to the back of it and you might blast off at any moment. I smile so widely it hurts my cheeks as I place your iced tea back on the tray. You smile back, something familiar blossoming in your eyes. I nod as gibberish spills out of your mouth, and claim my seat.

I do not watch you from the corner of my eye, Anna. I listen to the clink of the ice cubes striking glass. You drink small sips. It takes a while. But within fifteen minutes you are slumped and snoring, and I am on my way back upstairs.

The little box of shaving razors is hidden behind a small stack of cloth diapers we stored for a grandbaby who must be approaching middle school by now. Funny what I remember and what slips away. I knew the razors would be there despite not touching them for a decade, but if you asked me the grandchild's name it would have been a struggle. There were three or four babies around the same time and, to be honest, they all kind of looked the same.

I slide the cardboard top off the carton and the razors rattle like sleet tinkling on a window.

"Rats," I mutter, plucking a rust-spotted razor from the box. Moisture got in somehow and each of the razors is similarly corrupted. No matter. I only need the blade to be sharp.

I can hear your snores in the spaces between my steps as I

descend the stairs, razor held away from me in case I take a tumble. It has happened before. My hip reminds me when it rains.

Look at you, Anna. Who carved those lines in your face, turned your plump cheeks into wrinkled jowls? Something crueler than nature, has to be. The same something that burrowed into your mind at night and made a mess of your memories. But I will liberate you. I am only sorry it took me so long to understand.

I place the razor next to the sweating glass of tea and gently turn your body. You snore louder, sleep deeper. Good. The last thing I want is to hurt you, Anna, even though it is no longer *you*. And this will be an exploratory mission, not the real thing I imagine. I tug the sleeve of your house dress below your shoulder, bone white and freckled with a spray of peach pepper flakes.

Where to begin? The dream had a suggestion, but now that I see it, your shoulder blade, I wonder. Are you swimming inside of yourself? You need to be able to see the light when I cut. I don't want to cut more than once. There are marks here, faded pink lines like cat scratches, a dozen or more of them. I think this is right. I think you have tried to escape here before.

Just a test, not the real thing. I swallow hard, the lump in my throat like a cold river rock. I nearly reach for the tea, but my hand slides past it and I retrieve the razor.

My fingers are trembling now, the blade like a chink of ice. How can I do this, Anna? We have been through so much together, so many years, and now I stand beside you with a razor hovering above your skin. As if in response you moan in your sleep, the *real* you, Anna. The you imprisoned within this graying old dough.

Just a test, Anna, a quick cut to see if what has taken over you can sleep through it. My fingers do not stop shaking until the corner of the blade touches your skin, not piercing it, just resting as I gather my nerves.

"It's okay," I whisper as your snores persist.

The blade glistens. My fingers are wet.

I shake my head and sweat sprinkles the chair and your body. A determined drop of it twitches on the tip of my nose.

"Oh…"

There is a line of red above the razor, just a thin thread. I must have pulled it inadvertently. Blood breeches the surface of your skin, overflows it just a little. It was not even where I intended to cut, not that I had made my mind up about that. You shudder, and the razor cuts in a jagged line, deeper this time. I did not mean to do that either. More blood, darker.

"Oh no," I say.

I am not prepared for this. A rivulet courses in the shallow gulley between your ribs. You moan again, louder. The slash is about the length of my thumb, the blood gurgling slowly from it.

DING

The razor blade slips from my grasp and lands on the narrow red stream. It floats an inch or two and then adheres to your skin.

The doorbell...were you expecting someone? I confess I have always left our daily schedule to you and never considered changing that arrangement even as...

Even as you...

Even...

Even as you...

There is a barrier between me and the completion of the thought. For a moment I forget my purpose, forget why I loom over your bleeding back, my thumb a wet cherry above the red smudge beside your shoulder blade.

DING

The door. I shuffle toward it, my thoughts a kaleidoscope, fragments of a dream, slivers of intention out of focus.

"Coming!" I mumble, spittle falling out of my mouth and landing on my belly.

My belly. I stop in the dining room and catch a glimpse of a ghost in the glass of the grandfather clock, a ghost or something like it. It is a haggard thing, beard like dirty snow, wild wisps of hair clinging to a gray, liver-spotted dome. He stares back at me, hunched, caught in the act. Of what, I do not know. Below his wrinkled paunch of a belly is his member, which looks like a sprig of ginger forgotten in the back of the pantry.

"Hey!" I say, and his mouth opens in concert.

I paw at my belly and he does the same.

But I was wearing a robe. I-I've been through this before. I took a shower…no, I did not take a shower. I put the robe on when…

I hear voices, faint, at the front door. That is where I am headed. The reflection of me is wearing his robe again, and I feel its warmth, the stiff but comfortable cotton.

"Coming!" I say, more spit falling out of my mouth.

I peer through the peephole but my eyes are not so good and my glasses never near when I need them. Two people on the porch, that's about the best I can do.

I open the door part way and one, a boy of maybe fifteen, begins to speak. I can't hear him so well. He speaks so softly but I nod my head anyway as he points to the lawnmower on the sidewalk and then makes a few more motions with his hands. I open the door fully and he stops speaking.

He takes a step backward as I take one forward. A boy on the sidewalk, his little brother maybe, covers his mouth with his hand. The boy in front of me is descending the stairs, palms displayed as if I am a rabid dog. He speaks so softly; why can't he speak louder? I take another step forward and he turns to run, slipping over his untied shoelaces.

They've left the lawnmower. I shout at their backs that they've left the lawnmower. But they are jackrabbit fast, and neither breaks stride as they disappear around the corner of the street.

"Ohh…"

Anna, I forgot you. I amble inside, shutting the door and sliding across the tiles as if my feet are skis.

"Ohhh…" you call again from the living room.

I am coming, Anna, bad hip be damned.

You are where I left you, tilted to the side in your chair, your bare shoulder exposed. Blood glistens on your back as you moan again.

"Anna!"

I rush to your side as best I am able.

Who hurt you?

Your hand numbly crawls over your shoulder, fingers dangling like bait worms above the streak of blood.

The razor is glued to your back and I remember now. I

remember who did this to you. Who did this *for* you. I peel the razor free and place it in my...

"Ouch!"

A sharp pain below my hip, a dark snail-trail of blood oozing. My robe is gone again. Must have come loose as I shuffled back from the front door. No time to think about it now. I drop the blade and nudge it under your chair with my toe, then pivot and stagger back toward the kitchen to the sound of your hand slapping at your back.

Where did you put the paper towels, Anna? You are always moving things in this house. Everything is a blur and my glasses are never near when I need them. The blood on my thigh trickles past the knee where the leg hair slows its descent.

"Ooohhh..."

Goddammit, where are the paper towels?

I snatch a dish rag from the oven handle and wipe the blood off of my thigh. It smears around my knee, the leg hairs pasting to my skin.

"Ooohhh..."

I hear you, Anna. I am coming. Just can't have you question why my leg is all bloody. Can't have whatever has imprisoned you question it. That's what this is all about, isn't it? Something about a dream...about how you were trapped inside of yourself, right? I catch a glimpse of the ghost in the grandfather clock, naked again, as I return to the living room. Don't have time to think about him now.

Your head sways as if your neck is made of putty. You are trying to sit up but one hand is still straining to reach the cut on your back. It no longer bleeds, but you must feel it through the drugs. I place a hand on your shoulder and your whole body jolts. I press the dish rag to your wound and you seethe, eyes wide but unfocused.

"S'okay, Anna," I say, or something like it.

Your right hand crawls toward the dish rag like a housecat stalking prey.

"S'okay," I say.

My mind is racing, trying to think of a way to explain the cut on your back. But then you do the most wonderful thing, Anna. I think it is the *real* you clawing to the surface for just a moment. You sit up, blinking, and hold out your hand. Something glints in the afternoon light seeping through the gaps in the blinds. I squint to see. I don't see so good and my glasses are never near when I need them.

It's a needle. And your eyes swell with gratitude as I wipe the drying blood off your back. You, the real you, convinces whatever controls your mind that it was your own fault. You fell asleep with the needle in your hand and accidentally cut yourself. You do this for me. You have given me another chance to free you. I just need to summon the courage to cut deeper.

IT IS NIGHT NOW AND YOU ARE ASLEEP BESIDE ME. THE WORLD BEYOND our window is quiet, no crickets or cars, nothing rising above the sound of your breaths, which pass between whispers and snores. The bandage on your back glows in the darkness of our room, a rectangle of moonlight. Feathers leak from gashes in my pillow and they feel like moth's wings against my cheek. I flip it over but the other side is similarly damaged.

A breath, a snore. Your body swells and deflates and my eyes rest upon the bandage. It's a bit of a blur, and my glasses are never near when I need them. The razor blade is warm in my hand, slick with sweat. I just need a small sign, Anna, a nudge in the right direction. I don't think I can cut you there again, and the bandage would be too cumbersome to remove.

I search the terrain of your back, the lighter flesh blending into the plum that presents as black in the darkness. I need you to move, Anna; find a new place to surface, and I will free you.

I lick my lips and my tongue sticks there a moment...they are so dry.

A breath and a snore and nothing more. I would wait a lifetime to free you, but I am afraid there is not much left for me in this one. I swap the razor for the pill bottle hidden in my nightstand and creep on cat's paws again. Down the stairs, hip hurts—must be rain coming.

You drink half of whatever that God-awful protein stuff is at night and half in the morning. I know this like I knew the razors were behind the cloth diapers. One of your talk-show ladies promoted it a while back, and I've been living with the smell of it on your breath ever since. Even your *change* hasn't altered this habit. It is a part of you, like the needlepoint, like your thoughtless smiles.

Blue-and-white bottle, top shelf as always. I empty the rest of the powder and give the bottle a good shake, take the tiniest sip to test it. It *is* God-awful, but still tastes like a protein drink.

In bed beside you, snoring like you always have. I wonder about this mixture, these flashes of *you* amid the changes. If I hadn't been paying attention, Anna, to you all these years I might have thought I was mistaken. I might dismiss your feeble attempts to communicate as aging, your inability to smile convincingly as the pooled weariness of a long life. It is hard to smile, isn't it? With the light at your back and so much darkness ahead. Is my smile convincing?

I *have* been paying attention. I did not need a dream to tell me you were trapped. I just needed to know how to fix you.

I DREAM OF YOU, NOT IN AN ENDEARING WAY. NO HONEY-COLORED recollection of a Saturday morning on the porch, bumblebees with their black and yellow sweaters hovering around your hips as you water your tomatoes. No soundtrack of piglets in the yard, shoes slick with dew as they chase each other with sticks. Rusty, our favorite mutt, slicing through the grass, mashing dandelions into paste. Instead, I dream we are together, in darkness. It is warm, womb-like. When you speak to me here, I understand your words and not just because we are close but because we are connected. You speak of silent suffering, how fearful you are of the dark, how I can bring light into your world again.

We kiss, as we have not done for many years. I pull away, my tongue throbbing as if a tiny heart is lodged in its tip. Blood fills my cheeks, seeps past my lips.

"Anna..." I say.

But you have swum away to some other darkened corner.

I pull the razor from between my lips, press it against the warm thickness of my enclosure, and cut. The key, Anna, you gave it to me.

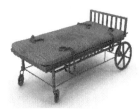

I STARE AT THE WINDOW, MORNING LIGHT BREAKING AGAINST THE curtains with little penetrating. Where am I? It is just me and the window for a minute, a minute that stretches. I have many thoughts in my mind, but they are hazy, wrapped in fog. They flit past, showing shapes and colors but refusing to collect into something recognizable.

The light. The window. A taste in my mouth, like saltwater but not quite. My tongue traces the ridges of my gums. Shapes and colors. The light.

A light, a light after the darkness. A shape coalesces, its colors muted by shadows. Anna pulling her lips away from mine, metal on my tongue.

Anna.

I call your name, try to anyway. Your side of the bed is tidy, comforter pulled tight and tucked beneath the mattress. My heart thunders with the knowledge of what I must do.

"What?"

The nightstand drawer is open. I fumble with the lamp's switch. It's like trying to pinch a tick that keeps moving.

I did not hide the razor blade. It should be right on top, glinting lamplight back at me. I also did not leave the drawer open, which means...

I am not so quick now, not so nimble, and so I scramble to the bathroom as if my right and left leg were swapped in the night. The pill bottles are there, your brush with the snarls of hair like bleached moss. But where are the razors?

Where are the razors? Where did I put that little box? My blood is cold like mud after a November storm. Which did you find first, Anna? The box of razors or the one in my nightstand? The box I imagine. Yesterday I...we...after the incident I...

Here comes the fog again, blunting the edges of my thoughts, softening my memories of yesterday. I sit on the edge of the tub. It is cold, sends a ripple of goosebumps across my thighs. I sit and think —try to think. I think about thinking. I imagine this is what life is like for you, Anna. How terrifying to lose yourself.

*THWACK*

The sound is like an old pumpkin dropped on concrete. I follow it, through the bedroom and down the stairs. Hip hurts, must be rain coming. In the wake of that sound there is no other, no talk-show ladies or angry judges, just the ticking of the grandfather clock with the ghost in the glass.

"Anna?"

The word is clear in my head but comes out as something different, as if my tongue was replaced by a dollop of pudding. I hear something, not above the ticking clock but between the ticks, a voice, a small one.

"Anna?"

It is not your voice. It sounds like something that would come out of a toy.

"Anna..."

You are dressed as if the very next thing you were going to do was leave. You have a kerchief around your hair, knotted beneath your chin. There is a small travel bag on the kitchen island, an empty bottle of protein drink beside it. Why are you sleeping on the floor, Anna?

*Mom! Mom!*

The voice reminds me of our granddaughter's doll, Josie I think. No, that was the doll, not the child.

"Anna?"

It feels like a cord is snipped within me, one that gave strength to my legs and arms. It is a gift, Anna. You have given me a gift, an opportunity to finish what I started. I take the phone from your hand and press it to my ear.

*Mom! What happened! Mom, I'm coming over right now.*

The words lose shape and mean nothing to me. I hang up the phone and leave it on the tiles. It rings immediately. The sight of the protein drink shines a light on my memories, cutting through the haze. You must have known, my dear, even as the *other* you dug through my nightstand and hid the razors, the *real* you knew. There is a little stream of blood leaking from your nose and your eyes are half-open. Your breaths are automatic, short and shallow.

The razors, where did you hide them? I peek into your travel bag, but you would not be that obvious, would you? A knife would suffice, but there are none on the countertops. I open the knife drawer but find only spatulas. You are always moving things, Anna. I understand it is not you but some indefinable *other*, but I don't have time to consider these things.

I need to cut. I need to cut but have no knife. The *other* hid the razors and I have no knife.

Your eyelid flutters and the blood seeping from your nostrils is like sap crawling down the trunk of a tree. No knife and I need to cut.

Then I recall where this all began, not my suspicions about your condition but the knowledge to liberate you. The dream, the glimpse of some shadowed seam on your back. I drag you to the center of the kitchen and roll you onto your belly. There is a little puff in the fabric above your shoulder blade, the bandage from yesterday. Maybe…maybe I can't make a new cut. Maybe I can use the old one.

I am sorry for this part, love. Can't be concerned about modesty now. I strip your blouse, buttons pinging across the tiles like BBs. Your arms are rag-doll loose but still difficult to free from the sleeves. And there it is, the bandage, a little slice of brown where the blood dried. I straddle you, then rip it off and the scab breaks, blood cresting and overflowing the wound.

The phone rings again and I feel your body tense for half a second, in response or in the grip of a dream I don't know. Can't be polite now, Anna. I'm so sorry it came to this. You didn't choose your affliction like I didn't choose for my teeth to fall out in my sleep.

No, that was you, I think.

I carve through the leftover scab grit. It is not a deep cut, but the skin is thin here. I press the pad of my finger into the wound, wiggle it to create more space. In my mind it's easy, just get a hook inside and pull. The reality of it is not easy, especially the getting inside part. I hover my face over the wound. It's longer now but no deeper. Are you in there? I wish you would show yourself to me. The skin tore north and south but not much. I don't have the time to do it this way, Anna, *we* don't.

Where are the razors? They must be around somewhere, the trash can maybe. Where is the trash can? You are always moving things, Anna. Maybe in your needlepoint kit? I shuffle through the dining room past the carved up recliner in the living room. Your needlepoint kit is tidy, Anna, but I can't make sense of it without my glasses and they're never near when I need them. The razors, where did you hide…

My toe touches something cold and smooth. I might not have noticed, but it is also sharp. I kneel, joints popping like miles-off fireworks, and pull the razor from under the recliner. Anna, you left this for me. How did you know I would find it? Tears brim. I am so close to having you back.

NO NEED TO BE DELICATE NOW. NO NEED FOR A STRAIGHT LINE, JUST has to be deep. I press the edge of the razor to the right of the cut already there, not on purpose, just where my shakes lead me. It sinks into your skin and red blossoms to either side. I pull it out. I swallow. You moan and I don't know if I can do this. I press the razor to your skin again, pierce and drag, but my fingers are disconnected from my will. Now there are three wounds on your back, one scabbing over again and two new additions, as if you were scratched by a cat with three different-sized claws, faded scars mingled with fresh cuts.

The phone rings. You moan. I am running out of time.

*You are not doing this **to** her. You are doing it **for** her.*

It makes sense, but it doesn't stop my hand from shaking. I press the razor again, and a new red bulb emerges from your skin.

I am doing this *for* you.

I close my eyes and pull, push deeper and pull harder. You stiffen beneath me and I push harder, pull harder. It feels like miles but is probably only inches. I pull until the razor touches the fabric of your pants. I can't look, Anna. I can't look at what I've done. I made it bright for you. Can't you see the light?

My hand falls into a puddle, fingers probe the seam of your skin. Do you see my fingers, Anna? It's warm, wet, and tougher than I would have guessed. What am I touching? I peek but see only red up to my wrist. Grab my hand, Anna.

The phone rings again. Your body is rigid beneath me. Please take my hand, Anna. Yes, we only have a few good years left, but I would rather a single good afternoon with the *real* you than a lifetime sitting across the room from an impostor.

Please take my hand, Anna. I push deeper, two hands inside now. Bone and organs, muscle and tendons repelling then relenting.

They feel like fingers, like your hand reaching for mine, but it passes.

I sob. I am up to my elbows now. My knees are wet and the room smells like a pail of old, rusty nails. A steady moan from your lips, but your body relaxes beneath me, and the moan passes into a whisper.

I SIT IN YOUR RECLINER. IT SMELLS LIKE YOU HERE, AND THAT'S A GOOD smell. Your unfinished needlepoint is on the tray to the right. I squint to read it. I don't see so good and my glasses are never near when I need them. The letters come in and out of focus.

"H-h-appy...Ann...Anna...v-very s-sorry?"

I think that's what it says. Another message from you I do not understand. The phone keeps ringing, but I won't go back in that room, not while that impostor is still in there, floating on the red tiles.

Hip hurts, might be rain, but through the window I see only blue.

I sit up. My hip hurts, but there is no rain. And you were not where you showed me you would be.

I intend to remove my robe but find that has already happened. I press my hip with a knuckle. The muscles twitch in response.

The muscles or something else. Some*one* else.

You. You were not where the dream showed me.

My hip aches and there is no rain coming.

From here I can see the ghost in the grandfather clock. He holds up a razor blade and I show him mine. We nod to each other.

A little cut to begin. Just need to let the light in, Anna.

# SPECTER OF INSANITY

## STEVEN PAJAK

Arnold Nussbaum sat behind the gleaming Georgian mahogany partners desk—it was an exact replica of the Resolute desk behind which many presidents had sat in the Oval Office—staring blankly at his monitor. He read the email again and felt the warm flush of dread wash over him, starting in his ears and working its way down. His hand trembled slightly as he slowly removed his reading glasses and set them down on the leather blotter, easing back into the chair.

He'd always known this time would come, but he'd always convinced himself this would be the problem of another day. Sadly, today was that day. The email was from his long-time agent and friend, Ronald Carrington. Ronny wanted to know when he'd get the next manuscript in the *Of Kings and Lovers* series.

Arnold's best friend (and lover), Peter, wrote seventeen novels of the saga by the time he was twenty-four and finishing his master's degree in literature, all which were unpublished (at the time), and collecting dust in an old chest in the back of his closet. The novels were a sprawling fantasy-romance saga, spanning generations of characters over decades, a tale to rival that of any created by the greats like Tolkien or Martin.

Pete was completely unaware of his raw writing talent and the potential goldmine locked away in his closet. Arnold recognized it, however. Throughout their six-year relationship, Arnold constantly encouraged Pete to seek publication. Peter never felt his work was good enough, that it would not be well received. Pete suffered from severe depression, and eventually, he took his own life.

Arnold collected the manuscripts before Pete's remaining belongings were shipped to his family in Rhode Island. He shopped the first of the manuscripts around for several months before Ronny Carrington saw the potential and signed Arnold. For the past fifteen years, Arnold had been publishing *Of Kings and Lovers* under the *nom de plume* J.B. Covington. The saga was hugely popular in the U.S. and abroad, was printed in more than twenty languages, and rights had been sold for film and television adaptations. The saga had also made Arnold quite wealthy.

The remaining two manuscripts were submitted to his publisher last year and were scheduled for release in September and the following April. So why had Ronny's email put Arnold in such foul spirits?

The problem was Arnold was a fraud. He'd never written anything of his own other than a few shitty short stories, which were never published. He'd been riding the coat tails of his long-dead friend/lover for more than a decade. *Of Kings and Lovers* was unfinished and he had no idea how to bring the sprawling saga to an end. Ronny was asking for the next manuscript, and Arnold had nothing. Absolutely nothing. Big fat goose egg. He was *fucked*.

Years before the email from Ronny requesting the next manuscript, Arnold worried over the problem (the problem for another day, ha!). He'd spent months trolling through fanfiction forums, hoping he'd find something he could use to start a new manuscript. As he read countless threads created by thousands of diehard fans, Arnold kept asking himself if he was really considering stealing another person's work to pawn as his own. That's exactly what got him here in the first place, wasn't it? It was, but he was desperate, and desperate men took desperate risks when their entire world was one manuscript away from collapsing in upon itself like a black hole.

Plagiarizing a mega-fan's work was dangerous, for sure. If accused, he could just say his work had somehow been hacked, stolen from the cloud by devious, delusional degenerates who lived in the fantasy world. Who would believe some internet troll freak like that over a well-established and respected author? Besides, he was wealthy and could afford the best attorneys—teams of attorneys—and he was willing to bet they could bully the shit out of some cosplaying fantasy-freak who would dare accuse him of plagiarism, or at the very least he would buy their silence—via legally binding and punitive non-disclosure agreements—with large sums of money.

During his desperate search, Arnold had found scores of fora dedicated to his work (ha, his work, right) and the *Of Kings and Lovers* saga, most of which involved shipping characters in strange love triangles, but some were creatively written continuations of, or branches of, the novels published to date. However, the remaining two novels were yet unpublished and unread by the public, so he was unable to find anything he could pilfer that would continue the story. He'd have to wait until the final manuscripts released to see what the fans would come up with, and then he'd need time to put it all together and create a coherent book... That could take years.

Arnold briefly considered hiring a ghost writer. He'd even gone as far as looking up several bios before abandoning that idea. He was concerned his agent or publisher would find out he'd hired someone to write the story and they might start asking questions. It was a bit *too* risky, and he'd not yet reached that level of paranoid desperation. He bookmarked that idea, though, should he reach the level of pulling the pin on this literary grenade.

He continued to brood over the problem heavily. He dreamt frequently that his fraudulent indiscretions were exposed to the public, and his agent and publisher filed lawsuits against him, demanding every penny of every advance ever paid him, every cent of royalties deposited to his bank over the last fifteen years. Peter's relatives also wanted a piece of the pie and hired a team of New York's most ruthless attorneys who immediately filed a multi-billion-dollar civil suit against him. He woke in a cold sweat, heart pounding, breathing labored, a scream always caught in his throat.

Now, he closed the email from Ronny and opened the wall safe, a large unit hidden behind a five-foot painting. Inside, he'd kept the typed manuscripts sealed in plastic to keep them from rotting. Each year, he'd take one out and set about the task of typing the chosen manuscript in Word and saving the document to his cloud storage before finally sending the manuscript to his agent. The safe was once filled with stacks of manuscripts, more than two million words all told. Now, the safe was empty save one last manuscript. Well, one third of a manuscript, if he were being accurate.

He removed it from the safe, swung the door shut, and carried the partial manuscript to his desk. He sat down, switched on the desk lamp, and gingerly pulled the pages out of the protective plastic in which he'd kept it. There were nearly seventy-five typed pages of what would have been book eighteen. Pete had just started on the novel when he'd met his tragic end. It wasn't much at all, certainly not enough to reveal the storyline or give any direction on where he planned to go with the story. Pete had even introduced new characters and hadn't left any notes in the margins, nor had he interspersed between the story any clues that would reveal his plans, as he'd done with the previous manuscripts. Perhaps it was because he'd just started the new novel or maybe he hadn't even had a chance to edit what he'd written before his death.

*What the fuck am I supposed to do with no notes?*

Whatever the case, Arnold was on his own. With the pages in front of him, he switched on the computer with the intention of keying the words into the software. His hope was that he could miraculously just finish the novel on his own. He'd retyped every word of the previous seventeen novels. He knew the characters (well, the old ones anyway) and he knew the story (to date). Why couldn't he finish the story? Surely he could.

The problem was, even if he could, what would he do for the next one? Or the one after that? The saga was not nearly close to an end, at least not that he could tell. There were so many loose threads, so many open questions, so many gaping plot holes that would need filling before he could successfully bring the saga to conclusion. And it was certainly not something he could do with one final novel. No way, not without pissing off his entire fan base across seven continents. He was royally screwed. If only he could ask Pete how it was all supposed to end, perhaps he might be able to see this through.

After typing for nearly three hours, Arnold saved the work, put the pages back into the safe, poured a nightcap, and went to bed, dreams be damned.

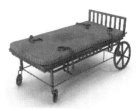

Arnold sat in front of his laptop, staring at the handsome man's publicity photo, framed by an art deco Manhattan skyline. With short-cropped hair spiked up with copious amounts of product, and designer stubble perfectly manscaped, he looked like every other metrosexual trolling the boutique shops on the Upper East Side. His deep blue eyes seemed to be staring right into you, as if he knew your deepest, darkest secrets. He was, after all, Alexander Davenport, the famed Medium of Manhattan.

According to his website, in addition to personal or life readings, the renowned Medium of Manhattan offered spiritual readings, whereby psychic wonder—with the help of his assistant, Maude, a Scottish Fold feline who was sensitive to human emotions and possessed the keen ability to sense the spirts of the dearly departed—would act as a conduit between his client and the hereafter, receiving information from those who had crossed over (as long as it was within a sixty-minute session). His client list included celebrities, doctors, lawyers, politicians, and business owners. He had four-and-a-half stars after more than 1,500 reviews.

Arnold read nearly thirty testimonials and watched several YouTube videos about the Medium of Manhattan. Based on the testimonials and what he witnessed in the videos, the guy seemed legit. If he wasn't, Arnold would be out about a thousand bucks and could laugh about the experience later. But if the Medium of Manhattan was legit, and he could somehow contact Pete from beyond the grave and he could learn how *Of Kings and Lovers* should end, that would be priceless.

He made up his mind, clicked on the flashing *Schedule Now* button, and looked at the online calendar that showed available open sessions. There were sessions available after three p.m. today, and he registered for the first available time slot and pre-paid with his credit card. Within minutes, he received an email confirmation with instructions on how to prepare for his spiritual reading. He was asked to arrive with an open mind and an item that belonged to the individual he wanted to contact in the hereafter. The item needed to be something of importance to the deceased, something that would attract their spirit.

Arnold had only one item in his possession that belonged to Pete. When it was time to leave for his appointment, he retrieved the remaining manuscript from the safe and removed one page from the middle of the stack, placed it into a plastic Ziploc, and then into a folder. He gently set the folder into his briefcase, grabbed his coat and hat, rode the train to East 79th and Madison, and then walked to Park Avenue and his destination.

He arrived ten minutes early, but the Medium of Manhattan was waiting for him with a bottle of sparkling water and a smile. Alexander Davenport appeared less striking in person than his profile photo on the website, but his vibe was energetic and engaging, and he was charming and charismatic. All part of his act, of course.

He invited Arnold into his study—"Where the magic happens," Davenport said and winked—and guided him to one of three chairs at the center of the room, which surrounded a low coffee table. Maude, the adorable feline assistant, sat in one of the chairs. She glanced up at Arnold when he sat, and then she went back to grooming her inner thigh, dismissing him outright. Arnold wasn't sure if that was an omen or just typical moody feline behavior.

Alexander sat in the remaining chair. In front of him on the table was a fresh notebook, which he picked up and opened on his lap. He produced a simple ballpoint pen from his jacket pocket and relaxed back into his chair.

"I'm both a psychic and medium," Alexander said, after making introductions. "This means I can sense and speak about the future and the past, as well as communicate with the dead. I do this through a rare process called automatic writing, which is a form of telepathy.

"Through this process I can accurately access the most relevant information for a person, including illnesses that you and your doctor may not yet be aware of, and predict opportunities and obstacles years into the future."

"That is all amazing, but I'm here specifically to reach someone who has…crossed over."

"Of course, of course. How long has it been since your loved one passed?"

"Fifteen years."

Alexander's right hand began to swirl, the ballpoint pen whispering across the surface of the notepad. He seemed to be making large swooping motions, then smaller, then started moving out again. He focused on Arnold, always making eye contact, as though he were aware of what his hand was doing.

"Do you have an item that belonged to the deceased?"

"I do." Arnold opened the briefcase and lifted out the sheet. He stared at it for several seconds before holding it out in front.

"Please remove it from the plastic."

Arnold hesitated but did as instructed.

Alexander accepted the manuscript sheet in his left hand while his right continued to swirl the pen against paper. He set the manuscript page on his lap and his left hand hovered several inches above it. He closed his eyes, focusing his psychic abilities, reaching out across the boundaries of the living and the dead.

"I'm sensing several presences with us." Alexander's right hand started to scroll more quickly across the paper. He'd shifted from a continuous circular motion from right to left to what appeared to be an infinity sweep. "Perhaps as many as three."

"I'm only looking to connect with the one."

"I understand. But there are others who seem to want to connect with you. One of them is more persistent than the others, pushing through strongly." Alexander's brow creased slightly, and he looked uncomfortable. "I feel…is there is some unfinished business between you and your loved one?"

"Yes." Arnold leaned forward.

The scrolling infinity hand shifted patterns again. The speed at which his hand moved across the paper increased again. Alexander's face indicated further discomfort. "This is strange…I'm getting a sense of…deep anxiety…paranoia…an overwhelming fear that I can't make sense of. I'm experiencing nausea and stomach pain."

Arnold didn't know how to respond, but he knew the medium had made a connection with Peter. He was diagnosed with schizophrenia with paranoia when he was seventeen, after he became convinced his mother and father were plotting to kill him and were secretly poisoning his food. He'd had other delusions, as well, which concerned school officials to the point they required Peter seek medical attention before he could return to school for his senior year.

Upon his diagnosis, Pete was prescribed antipsychotic drugs and weekly counseling sessions, and cognitive behavioral therapy to help him manage his symptoms or test whether he was experiencing delusions. Pete continued his regimen of antipsychotics and therapy for years, until his junior year of college when he suddenly and unexpectedly overdosed on his medication. Arnold found him dead in their room. He'd tried to revive him with CPR, but it was too late.

Arnold saw movement from his peripheral. Maude stopped her grooming and shifted her attention to the medium, as though she sensed the mood change and physical discomfort. Arnold's attention was drawn back to the medium when he seemed to jolt. The notebook and manuscript page spilled to the floor. Alexander stiffened and then threw his head back. His hands gripped the arms of the chair fiercely, and the cords and veins of his neck stood out. He moaned as though struggling against an unseen force…or presence from the hereafter.

The lights in the room dimmed and then began to flicker. Arnold sensed a sudden decrease in temperature, as though the A/C had suddenly kicked on full blast. The overhead light fixture began to sway in a circular motion, gaining speed until it spun like a top. To his left, a solitary book fell from the shelf. Then another, and another…at first each volume slid slowly to the edge of the shelf before gravity pulled it to the floor. The fourth book flew across the room, as if ejected by a sudden blast. Several more books took violent flight before the entire contents of the bookcase exploded all at once from their shelves.

Maude hissed and launched herself from the chair, sprinting for shelter from the paranormal violence. The Medium of Manhattan remained in his chair, his head thrown back, eyes rolled up until only the whites remained. A terrible groan that could only come from agony issued from his lips. Suddenly, his body rose from the chair, just inches at first, and then his ass floated nearly a foot above the leather seat. *He's fucking levitating!*

When the entranced medium at last spoke, Arnold recognized Pete's voice, though he'd never heard his best friend and lover speak so harshly.

"Murderer!"

"Pete, it's Arnie! I'm here."

"Murderer!" Pete repeated through the medium's lips. "Arnold Nussbaum is a murderer."

"What? Pete, what are you talking about?"

"You killed me."

"No, that's not true. You killed yourself."

"Murderer!"

"You overdosed on your pills."

"Murderer!"

A sudden barrage of trinkets and tchotchke around the room launched at Arnold, pelting him with enough force to draw blood on his cheeks, hands, and arms. A framed Ouija board flew past on his right, the corner gouging his cheek, just barely missing his eyes.

"What the fuck, Pete? Stop!"

"You stole my work! You murdered me and stole from me. You took my life!"

The coffee table slid violently against his shins, pinning him with such force he couldn't push it away.

"That's a lie! I did not kill you! Pete, please, I just need to know how the story ends."

"I will have vengeance!"

"Pete, please! How does it end? I have to know."

Pete's presence's-spirit's-force's, whatever the fuck it was, power surged. The lights around the room grew brighter and brighter until their bulbs burst. The books and frames that had fallen from the shelves and walls levitated and started to spiral, a whirling and deadly vortex of wood and glass and sharp edges. The vortex swept violently across the room, growing larger as it collected inanimate objects, sucking Alexander's body into its eye, then suddenly enveloping Arnold. He was lifted from the chair, his body suddenly weightless, spinning, pummeled by vortex detritus, until he was ejected from the twister and flung across the room where he slammed against the wall, the back of his head connecting with drywall and plaster, and then he lost consciousness.

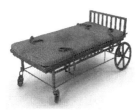

ARNOLD SWAM UP FROM UNCONSCIOUSNESS. WHEN HE OPENED HIS EYES, the waking world was a blur of colors. His eyes focused after a few seconds. Alexander hovered over him. Concern lined his brow, but concern quickly became relief when Arnold shakily pushed into a sitting position.

"Oh, thank God, I thought you were dead."

Arnold looked away from the medium. The study was a disaster. Furniture knocked over, broken trinkets and frames, paintings askew or knocked to the floor, books littering the floor everywhere his eyes moved. He'd never seen anything like it, but he suspected it was the type of damage you'd see after a substantial earthquake.

"What happened?"

Alexander stared at him, incredulously. "You don't remember?"

"No."

The confused look on his face seemed genuine. "You went apeshit and trashed everything."

"That is absurd. I did no such thing."

"You said you don't remember. How the hell do you think this happened then?"

"I have no idea..." Arnold got to his knees, then stood. He was unsteady, but he did not fall. "I remember sitting there, next to your assistant. You were doodling on your notebook. You said...you felt a presence and then everything..." He motioned with his hand, like a fish swimming.

"Yes, accurate. And then you burst from your chair like a madman and did this."

"The hell I did! You...you summoned someone. The presence must have done this. Peter did this."

The medium regarded him suspiciously. "What are you trying to pull here?"

"What am *I* trying to pull? What the fuck are *you* trying to pull? If this is some scam, I don't understand it. You already took my money. You must have drugged me."

"You are obviously not well, sir. I called 911 and they're sending an ambulance. You should just sit down until they get here."

"This is fucking crazy. You're crazy and a scam artist."

Arnold turned away from the delusional man and searched frantically among the mess for his briefcase and manuscript page, both of which were on the floor beneath the overturned table. Thank goodness, the page was unharmed.

He dropped the sheet into his briefcase—he didn't have time to bother with the plastic sleeve—and turned on the medium. "I'm getting away from this place. Away from you, you damn *nutjob*."

Arnold made it to the door before the Medium of Manhattan gripped his arm. "I insist you stay until the ambulance and the police arrive."

"Get your hands off me, charlatan!"

He pulled away from Alexander, raised his briefcase in front of him, and used it to shove the man hard enough to make him stumble and fall to the floor. He pulled open the door, made for the staircase, and pounded down the stairs so fast his heart raced and throbbed in his ears with every thunderous beat. Out on the street, he trotted down 79th back to the subway, completely out of breath by the time he planted his ass on the hard plastic seat. He gripped the stanchion so tightly his knuckles were white.

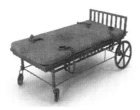

AFTER DEBARKING THE TRAIN, ARNOLD WALKED THROUGH THE PARK, taking the scenic route, hoping his memory of events at the medium's office would solidify and somehow make sense. When he arrived at his brownstone, the police were waiting on the porch.

"How the hell…"

One of the officers spotted him, and they both came down the stairs and braced him, one on each side, as if they expected he might bolt, make a run for it, go on the lam.

"Are you Mr. Nussbaum?"

"I am."

"Sir, I am Officer Williams and this is Officer Papowicz. We received a vandalism complaint from Mr. Alexander Davenport. He alleges you damaged his place of business about an hour ago."

"That's… How did you find me?"

"Mr. Davenport provided us with your address. It was on the form when you booked your appointment."

"Well, that is just preposterous. I did not vandalize his place. He is a fraud and charlatan. He must have somehow rigged his office. He assaulted me, drugged me. Look at my face, for Christ's sake! I should be the one filing charges."

Officer Williams retrieved his phone from his back pocket. He pecked at the screen for half a minute before pulling up a video. He turned the screen so that Arnold could view it and pressed play.

The footage was from the medium's office—*The bastard was*

*filming his sessions! That had to be a breach of privacy. I should sue the sonofabitch*—taken from a corner angle, which covered the entire space. Arnold was taken aback by the surveillance video; he couldn't believe his eyes as he watched himself raging in the office, throwing books and trinkets and flipping furniture while Alexander and his stupid cat stood distraught in the corner, cowering from the barrage he unleashed. Arnold was completely flabbergasted when, in the video, he scooped a vase from a sideboard and smashed it against his own face.

The officer stopped the video at that point and returned the phone to his pocket.

Stunned, still disbelieving what he witnessed on the security footage, Arnold said, "That video is obviously doctored. Someone must have tampered with it. This is a scam to get money out of me."

"Sir, the footage was pulled directly from the security feed just minutes after you fled the scene. It was not tampered with, Mr. Nussbaum."

Arnold shook his head and was speechless. *This is madness. Complete. Fucking. Madness.*

"Sir, Mr. Davenport would prefer not to press charges, as he feels you are unwell. You have two options here: reimburse Mr. Davenport for the damages to his office and property, or we arrest you for vandalism and you stand in front of a judge. The choice is yours."

Officer Williams brandished his cuffs.

"Fine," Arnold relented. "Tell him to send me the damn bill. Are we done here?"

THE WORDS FLOWED THROUGH HIM LIKE AN ELECTRICAL CURRENT, FROM his brain and through the tips of his fingers, which flew across the keyboard at more than one hundred words per minute. He was in the throes of creation, imagining worlds and beings into which he breathed life, developing plots and subplots, forming mysteries and romance and treachery, bringing the unfinished manuscript of *Of Kings and Lovers* to a thrilling conclusion.

He typed the final words, saved the document, and sat back in his chair. He was breathless, as if the act of imagining and writing were physical labors which had exerted him. Arnold had no idea what magic or miracle possessed him. He did not care. All that mattered was the manuscript was complete and he made it happen, proof that he could continue the saga on his own.

*Fuck you, Peter. I don't need you after all.*

Arnold stretched his arms above his head and worked the kinks out of his back. He had no idea how long he'd been at the laptop. He was famished and he had to piss. He stood up, intent on going to the half bath outside his study to relieve himself, but suddenly, a sharp pain seared through his left ear. His hand immediately went to his ear, but the appendage was gone. His fingers prodded a wet mess where his ear had been.

Warm blood started to flow down his neck. When he pulled his hand away and looked at it, it was covered in the red, viscous liquid.

"Where the fuck is my ear?" Panic spread through him, and he staggered several steps away from the desk.

"I won't let you steal my work like you stole my life."

Arnold yelped at the sound of Peter's voice. He spun around and found himself face to face with the dead man. Pete looked exactly how Arnold remembered him the day he committed suicide, young and fresh, dressed in torn jeans, an off-white T-shirt, and navy cardigan. In one hand he held a knife and in the other Arnold's severed ear.

Obviously in shock, Arnold reached for his appendage. Peter slashed the knife across Arnold's arm, opening a four-inch gash across the top of his forearm. Arnold screamed and instinctively pulled his arm against his chest, then clamped his other hand over the wound, applying pressure in an attempt to stop the bleeding.

"What is wrong with you? Why are you doing this to me?"

"You're a murderer and I will have my vengeance."

"Stop saying that! You swallowed your pills and you killed your-self. You were depressed. You were sick in your head, Pete. All I ever did was love you despite your degenerate mind."

Peter stepped forward, slashing the knife left and right. Arnold, operating on panic and instinct, dodged the knife-wielding spirit and ran around the other side of the desk, putting it between him and the maniacal presence.

"You're the sick one. You plotted my demise. You slowly poisoned me, day after day, with small amounts of arsenic in my food. When that didn't work, you used my drugs to kill me."

"Why would I do that? Huh? Don't you see, you are delusional. Your mind is sick, Pete. You made all that up."

"You were jealous of my talent. You always were. And when I made the mistake of sharing my manuscripts with you, you realized I had a goldmine that I was keeping locked away. Your greed took hold of you at your very core and corrupted you."

"You're insane, Peter! And you're a liar and you're dead. I don't need you, so just get out of my life. Go back to wherever you came from and leave me alone!"

Peter hissed and lunged over the desk so quickly, Arnold had no time to react. He did not expect that a manifested presence could make physical contact until Pete's body slammed into him, knocking him to the floor. Pete's ghost hands clamped around his neck. Arnold's mind could not accept that he was being choked by a damn specter. This was insane yet he couldn't breathe and he was getting dangerously close to losing consciousness.

"Murderer, murderer, murderer!"

Survival instinct kicked in, and Arnold flailed at Pete, his wild fists connecting with the manifestation's face. He threw several more punches and then raked his nails across his attacker's face, drawing blood before the steel hands relented. Sweet oxygen filled his lungs, and blood rushed into his cheeks.

Arnold took advantage of the moment to get away. He used his hands to push Pete's face up and away, until he was off-balance, and then Arnold rolled his body to the right, breaking away and out from under. He rolled twice more, putting distance between him and the impossible physical manifestation of his long-dead lover.

On his knees, Arnold pivoted to face the man whom the Medium of Manhattan had summoned on his behalf. He had hoped to make contact with Pete via the medium, but he did not expect a physical manifestation of a belligerent and mentally unstable spirit seeking vengeance for an imaginary murder.

"Pete, can we please just talk? Let me explain."

"No talking. Just dying."

Pete came at him again. Arnold saw the six-inch ornate dagger in Pete's hand just seconds before he felt it plunge into his abdomen. The dagger looked exactly like the one described in the previous novel, which Prince Alexander had used to assassinate King Oren. As Arnold attempted to grip Pete's hand, he wondered where the dagger had come from. He certainly had no such items in his study, nor anywhere in the house. Pete jerked his arm back forcefully, defeating Arnold's weak grip, and then he stabbed again, quick and strong, again and again, shanking Arnold with quick rapid jabs, perforating his stomach and bowels.

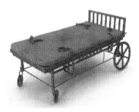

HILDY GOTTLIEB ARRIVED AROUND FIVE, TOTING SEVERAL SACKS OF groceries she'd picked up at the Fairway Market off 86th Street. In the kitchen, she sorted the contents onto the massive island, leaving out the groceries needed to prepare dinner and putting away the rest.

After preheating the grill and prepping her ingredients, Hildy washed her hands at the kitchen sink, dried them on the dishtowel, and then made her way down the hall to Mr. Nussbaum's study. He hadn't come out to greet her upon arrival as he normally did, to chat her up about her day and to share his own. Mr. Nussbaum treated her as a friend rather than employee, and they'd built a rapport and respect for one another over the decade she'd served as his house manager.

She knocked at the door and said, "Dinner will be ready in one hour. You might want to get washed up in a bit. We're having filet mignon and fresh sea scallops."

Hildy paused a moment, expecting a reply. When none came, she knocked upon the door and waited half a minute before slowly pushing the door open. Mr. Nussbaum lay on the floor at the center of the room. His face was horribly slashed. His shirt was completely soaked with blood, the garment slashed open, revealing several stomach wounds.

"My God, Mr. Nussbaum!"

Hildy collapsed beside him, her hands hovering over his face, unsure if she should touch him. Finally, she pressed two fingers against his carotid and felt a weak pulse. He was still alive.

Her cellphone was in the kitchen, and she was out of breath when she reached it and dialed 911. After she hung up with emergency dispatch, she returned to the study and examined him more closely. The scratches across his face looked less like slashes from a knife and more like wounds from fingernails ranked across flesh.

She visually examined his hands. Blood crusted under his fingernails. In his right hand, he gripped a pair of sewing shears, which were covered in blood, as were his hands. She refused to believe he'd done this to himself, but the evidence was compelling.

The ambulance arrived just minutes later, and the police several minutes after that. The paramedics quickly dressed his wounds and placed him on a stretcher, rolling him out to the ambulance with great urgency. Moments later, the siren wailed as they transported Mr. Nussbaum to the nearest hospital, though he was not expected to survive his wounds.

Two officers—Williams and Papowicz—questioned her briefly, while crime scene personnel collected evidence and photos. She saw one of them placing the bloody shears into a clear bag and then a white box.

Hours later, Hildy was alone in the brownstone. She was

exhausted, yet she couldn't go home until she cleaned the blood from the floor before it permanently stained. After scrubbing the floors, she moved to the desk, which the detectives had ransacked. The top drawer stood open, and within, prescription bottles of Haldol were jumbled. Half were empty, but several were full. She tidied the drawer, puzzling over the pills she hadn't known he was prescribed.

Curious, she opened the laptop, intent on looking up the drug on Google to learn what he'd been taking—or not taking, given the full bottles in his drawer—and noticed that the Microsoft Word application was open, but the window was minimized. She clicked the icon and expanded the window to full mode. Hildy gasped and clamped one hand over her mouth. There were nearly 100 pages of the same two sentences over and over again.

Iamafraud. Iamamurderer. Iamafraud. Iamamurderer. Iamafraud.
Iamafraud. Iamamurderer. Iamafraud. Iamamurderer. Iamafraud.
Iamafraud. Iamamurderer. Iamafraud. Iamamurderer. Iamafraud.
Iamafraud. Iamamurderer. Iamafraud. Iamamurderer. Iamafraud.
Iamafraud. Iamamurderer. Iamafraud. Iamamurderer. Iamafraud.
Iamafraud. Iamamurderer. Iamafraud. Iamamurderer. Iamafraud.
Iamafraud. Iamamurderer. Iamafraud. Iamamurderer. Iamafraud.
Iamafraud. Iamamurderer. Iamafraud. Iamamurderer. Iamafraud.
Iamafraud. Iamamurderer. Iamafraud. Iamamurderer. Iamafraud.
Iamafraud. Iamamurderer. Iamafraud. Iamamurderer. Iamafraud.
Iamafraud. Iamamurderer. Iamafraud. Iamamurderer. Iamafraud.
Iamafraud. Iamamurderer. Iamafraud. Iamamurderer. Iamafraud.
Iamafraud. Iamamurderer. Iamafraud. Iamamurderer. Iamafraud.
Iamafraud. Iamamurderer. Iamafraud. Iamamurderer. Iamafraud.
Iamafraud. Iamamurderer. Iamafraud. Iamamurderer. Iamafraud.
Iamafraud. Iamamurderer. Iamafraud. Iamamurderer. Iamafraud.
Iamafraud. Iamamurderer. Iamafraud. Iamamurderer. Iamafraud.
Iamafraud. Iamamurderer. Iamafraud. Iamamurderer. Iamafraud.
Iamafraud. Iamamurderer. Iamafraud. Iamamurderer. Iamafraud.
Iamafraud. Iamamurderer. Iamafraud. Iamamurderer. Iamafraud.
MURDERER!MURDERER!MURDERER!

# NEVER BREAK THE CHAIN

JANINE PIPE

F elicity struggled against the restraints. She knew it was pointless, but it made her feel a little better at least, showed she still had some fight in her. She always thought that if she found herself in such a situation, she would bow down and be a good girl, play the game and do what she was told. Not because she was weak or subservient by nature, not at all. But because if she did exactly what was expected, then she'd gain their trust and be able to pull off the Keyser Soze of her generation.

But things often have a way of not exactly panning out the way one would have liked.

Take even being here for example.

She had supposed that if someone had discovered her affliction, she'd be in some sort of government lab right now, her abilities being honed, being almost honored as a pseudo hero. Should have bloody known that was the fairy tale part of it all.

The only people of authority she ever saw were doctors. Even the police didn't come anymore now that the trial had been set.

Where were Mulder and Scully? Or at the very least some British MI5 version of the dynamic duo. But no. There'd be no Special Weapons Division or visits from Men in Black.

She must have been struggling more than she'd realized as she noticed a figure leaning against the doorframe. He didn't come and see her that often these days, and against all her control, she still felt the shadow of a tingle at the sight of him. Which was so ludicrous that she turned her head away from him, the only part of her body she could freely move in a sign of defiance. Of course, she knew all about Stockholm Syndrome, but that was for kidnap victims, not "patients" (prisoners was deemed too harsh) in high-security mental institutions.

"You've been irritating those wounds again, Miss Jones," he admonished, stepping into the room. Felicity screwed her eyes shut so she wouldn't have to see him.

She felt the mattress sink a little as he sat on the edge, felt his delicate, always cool, but never cold hands explore the bandages under her restraints.

"I'll get Siobhan to change these for you. They'll never heal if you keep rubbing them."

Still, she refused to answer or even open her eyes.

She heard the doctor sigh, felt the mattress springs relax as he rose and walked to the door. Before he left, he said, "Doctor Morfitt will check on you again later." He hesitated, and she sensed him hovering, debating whether to add anything. Then, "I hope you'll open up a little at group tomorrow."

She waited until his footsteps had faded before opening her eyes.

And then she screamed.

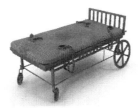

GROUP THERAPY WAS AKIN TO PURGATORY IN MANY WAYS. A SORT OF IN-between world she could never quite seem to escape from. On the one hand, it got her out of her room and away from those same four puke green walls she'd been staring at day in day out but also, she had to deal with other people, her fellow inmates. Oh wait, "patients"...

Although she was extremely certain she wasn't the first and wouldn't be the last captive in one of these places to believe that they were the only sane person in a sea of nut cases, she was sure in this particular instance, it was the correct assumption.

Weekly group therapy was a requirement, and the solicitor had told her if she failed to cooperate, then whatever sentence was finally dealt would be far worse. So she tried to think of it as entertainment since she wasn't allowed to use a phone. She also felt some sort of sense of smugness that she was the only one wheeled in with restraints and that only the staff could look her in the eye. She wasn't there to make friends or allies, and the fact the other loonies seemed to fear her was satisfying. Gotta get your kicks where you can.

The actual "therapy" was the part that made this feel like the eighth circle of Hell. She might not be a doctor, but even she could see that rehashing the same fucking stories over and over was the most mundane and moronic way to spend a morning.

Vera still didn't know why she loved smearing and eating other people's shit.

Les was always happy to share tales of wanking off wherever he could and seemed disappointed every time when Doctor Hunt told him he couldn't share his talent with the group.

Stacy shared the time she'd been abducted by aliens, and Sean recounted in glee how he chose the child he killed—even though he hadn't even hurt a fly in reality and cried like a baby when the goldfish in the communal lounge died.

Finally, it was Felicity's turn, and the entire group twisted around to look in her direction if not directly at her. Her lip curled a little as she relished their discomfort coupled with fascination.

She cocked her head a little to one side and decided today she would be brave. She locked eyes with Doctor Hunt, ignoring the warmth in her groin.

"Felicity," he began, "would you like to share with the group today? We always enjoy what you have to say."

*Oh, do you now?*

And so she began.

Eight years ago at the tender age of just fifteen, she'd snuck out of her bedroom window one night to meet up with her boyfriend, Liam. He was waiting for her at the corner of the street, leaning against a lamppost looking all sexy and much older despite only a year's age difference. He was smoking and had a can of Foster's lager in his hand. She had never wanted him so much. They'd run off into the nearby woods, and after a quick but pleasant fumble, there'd been a cracking noise from behind them.

As she tried to pull her underwear up, she tripped and landed hard on her ass. Before she could call to Liam to give her a hand, she heard him scream, and the fucker took off, leaving her on the ground, pants around her ankles.

And then *he* appeared.

She always believed it to be a *he* although she had no way of knowing for sure. They all look the same, you see, and despite what subsequently happened, she'd never seen him again. She always supposed she would just know if she did.

It fucking hurt when he slashed her anyway, and it was the first of many times that Felicity truly thought she was going to die. For whatever reason, although she was certain she was done for, he had left as quickly as he'd appeared, seemingly content with the deep gash in her thigh and not ripping her to shreds like she'd seen in some of her dad's VHS tapes.

She'd managed to limp home and finally fell asleep, wondering how the hell she'd explain all this to her mom in the morning. She'd slept for twelve straight hours, helped by the fact her mom had gone off to work, leaving her a note pinned to the fridge saying she had a double shift and to get the shepherd's pie out of the freezer for dinner. She braced herself, thinking for just a second that her injury must be very bad since she couldn't feel any pain at all. Yet when she pulled the blood encrusted sheet away, there was nothing on her leg except dirt.

*What the fuck?*

Liam tried to show his cowardly face later, but she slammed the door on him. He was the least of her worries now, the little prick.

She began to wonder if she'd imagined the whole thing, that maybe she'd banged her head and it was all a dream, like JR stepping out of the shower...

Nothing happened for a long time, but she wasn't reassured by this. Instead, she was more in a constant state of confusion. She didn't share what had happened with anyone. Her dad was away on a tour of Kuwait, her mom a busy nurse in a local emergency room. They both had high expectations of her, and learning she'd snuck out for a quickie and had been mauled by a mythical monster would not be what they wanted to hear.

At eighteen, she packed her bags and headed off to college, studying literature but under the provision she'd apply to the police academy or army when she left.

It was pure luck that the first time it happened, she was alone. Both her roommates were staying the night with their respective current beaus, and she'd been feeling under the weather. Due to some complication with her ovaries, she'd only had a handful of periods her entire life and nothing since before the attack. She wasn't old enough yet to worry about fertility, more pleased she didn't have to suffer each month like her friends and spend a small fortune on tampons. But that morning, the sight of blood in her panties had caught her off guard, along with a bellyache which left her gasping for air. Since she was alone, she went to bed with a bar of chocolate and a hot water bottle and settled in for an afternoon of reading.

The sweats started to kick in shortly, along with far more pain, and not just in her tummy.

Thankfully, in a fucked-up way, that first time was so painful and awful that she didn't make it out of her room. She was so exhausted from the transformation and terrified by what had just occurred, she didn't leave the house for the next few days.

The next time it happened wasn't until a good six months later, and this time she was back home for winter break. Again, luck was on her side as her mom was on a night shift, her dad still on maneuvers somewhere in the Gulf. She began to panic as soon as she saw the blood on the toilet roll after peeing. The second change was far more painful, but at least she knew what to expect. Somehow, she managed again to keep herself in the house, barely this time.

After that she began researching. As expected, her studies fell to the wayside as she threw herself into the lore of the lycanthrope. She learned that although unusual, some females are not only controlled by the lunar cycle but also their own menstrual cycle. These women wouldn't automatically turn each time there was a full moon, or when they had their monthly period…both had to coincide.

There was a snigger from one of the other patients as she mentioned periods, and she managed to shut him up with a single glare in his direction. She didn't even realize that she also subconsciously hissed at the guy, sending him cowering into silence.

It put her off her stride, and she debated internally for a moment whether to continue. She'd told bits and pieces of this story over and over again—to the police, to the lawyers, the medical professionals and everyone here, especially Doctor Hunt. She looked at him now and he gave her a quick nod, encouraging her to carry on.

Digging her nails into the palms of her hands so hard they almost drew blood, she continued.

*Although she had more periods now in her late teens than she'd ever had before, it still wasn't monthly, so she didn't have to deal with this "condition"—as she decided to label it—every month. However, one of the many horrific downsides was of course not being regular and therefore never quite knowing when Aunt Flow would appear.*

*She knew she had to be alone and managed to find a small studio apartment her parents agreed to help pay for, so long as she applied herself and got her grades back on target. This wasn't an issue, and she almost became a hermit, only leaving the premises for lectures and seminars, bringing armful of books back to her sanctuary rather than study in the library. And somehow, she coped. She began to excel at her studies again and was able to control the few transitions that occurred by handcuffing herself to the bed when she saw the first signs of her "not quite monthly visitor" during a full moon.*

*It was during the final year of her master's degree that Liam turned back up. A complete and utter coincidence, serendipity or just fucking bad timing, she'd never know, but one minute she was walking back from a meeting with the dean and the next she saw him stepping out of a coffee shop. He hadn't changed a bit. Turned out he was there on some sort of conference and wow, didn't she look amazing, would she like to grab a bite to eat?*

*It had been a while since she'd felt like that, far too long since she'd felt anything inside her, and before she knew it, he was back in her bed and inside her. Soon enough, they were meeting whenever they could, her finding the sex to be amazing. She even managed to laugh when he said she was like an animal.*

*And then…it happened.*

*She'd had a period—a particularly heavy one too—just a week or so ago, so the fact she'd come home to see her parents on the night of a full moon didn't concern her too much. She would never have usually risked it, just in case, but her grandfather had passed away and her father, back in the UK for a few months, wanted her to come and spend the weekend, to grieve as a family. She had a bit of a cold too which was annoying as she tended not to get sick, so the lure of her mom's home cooking and warm hugs seemed like the medicine she needed.*

*As she snuggled into her old bed, coughing and sneezing, she felt dreadful. The next morning, she was full of fever and delirium, and her mom, being a nurse, was sure she had a terrible case of the flu, so it was a good thing she was home. She allowed her parents to fuss over her as she slept most of the day, fighting off the illness. It was only when she woke in the middle of the night in agony that she slipped her hand into her panties and felt the sticky wetness. And then it happened, sudden and fast, and she had no time to warn them…*

*She found out later that some flu viruses hit your body so hard they can affect you in all sorts of weird and wonderful ways, and bringing a period forth is just one of them. Lucky Felicity—she got a two-fer.*

The room was silent as she reached this part. Although she had told it before to the police, it was often the time in groups where she choked, refused to go on. Or got upset and scared the other patients. Or got mad and had to be sedated. She looked up from under her lashes to see the entire room staring at her, collectively holding their breaths. Her glance shifted to Hunt. He smiled. She growled just slightly. The others all uncomfortably shifted in their plastic chairs. They needn't have been scared though. It was a sign of lust, not dominance.

Her heartbeat quickened as she held Hunt's eye. Then she carried on.

*She'd always known what she'd be capable of if she ever turned without being restrained. After all, she was a monster. Her claws and teeth alone were implements of torture, able to inflict agonizing pain and swift, violent death. But nothing could have prepared her for the carnage she woke to that following morning.*

*The walls were painted red, the air thick with the stench of iron and offal. Felicity instinctively knew what she'd done, and before the well of grief and self-loathing set in, she did the first thing that came to mind—she fled. She knew it wouldn't be long before a neighbor reported the smell or someone from work noted her mother's absence. She made a quick decision that would ultimately lead to her ending up in the nuthouse. Before running as far away as she could, she stopped at Liam's. The sex was fast and raw and unprotected.*

*The police caught up with her around six weeks later. She was arrested and questioned. Sensing she had no other option and that just maybe telling the truth would be some sort of defense, she told them what had happened. Of course, a regular detective isn't trained in the ways of the supernatural. One couldn't stop laughing and had to leave the interview room to collect himself and the other looked both thoroughly unimpressed and disappointed at the same time. It was a look she'd come to recognize. They didn't believe her.*

*Still, they believe that she believed it, which was why she was now in this shithole.*

"That's all you get," she snarled.

The other patients all gawked, mouths open, although that wasn't unusual, the trails of drool on the floor proving the fact.

"Okay, people. That's enough for today," called out Hunt, rising from his seat. "Not you, Felicity," he added, "please stay for a moment."

*Aw fuck, now what?* She'd played by the damn rules for once. What did he want?

She sank into her chair a little, prepared for a scolding, although she didn't know why.

Once the others had left, an orderly popped his head around the door and asked the doctor if he needed assistance or would he be okay on his own? He didn't add "with that crazy bitch," but it was implied.

"I'm fine, Neil, but thanks for checking."

And then there were two.

Well, three really.

Or maybe two and three-quarters.

Ish.

Anyway.

Dr Hunt stared at her, and for once, she held his gaze, chin raised stubbornly.

"Dr Morfitt thinks you're almost ready."

*If she'd been able to, she would have placed a hand protectively onto her belly. No, wait, that's what loving mothers-to-be do. One of the many reasons she was almost always cuffed or restrained was she'd tried to rip the life out of her on several occasions. Instead, she merely glared at her protruding stomach where the life she and Liam had accidentally created seemed to be thriving despite the odds. Wasn't it fucking ironic? Years of doctor appointments in her early teens, terms and diagnoses she didn't really understand, at an age where getting pregnant is the last thing on your mind and fertility is something to giggle about during science lessons. The infrequent periods were something for Future Felicity to address. And yet the one time she fucked Liam without a rubber, he knocked her up.*

*She'd had no inkling at first, obviously because she'd more or less been told it was impossible and she had more important things on her mind. Like the fact she was a monster who had just murdered her parents and she needed to find someplace to lay low and be able to control her transformation. Of course, this wasn't a damn movie, and the police soon caught up with her, and well, you know the story from there on. She'd warned them what would happen. That despite being in this so-called safe place for people who were fucked in the head, next time she had a period and it was a full moon, they would witness her turning, and if she wasn't tied up, the carnage that would ensue after would be devastating. All this did, though, was cause furrowed brows and signing of papers basically stating she needed to be constantly under supervision and restrained, since she actually believed what she was saying and would likely enact this scenario in order to prove her story. She had scoffed at that, unable to fathom that these so-called experts actually thought she was so far gone into her own fantasy world that she would pretend to be a wolf and be able to cause that kind of destruction with her own fingers and teeth. What the fuck?*

*So they watched her like a hawk, and in turn she kept an eye on the lunar cycle and for any signs of her own, especially when she started getting sick in the mornings. After losing an argument with a nurse, she agreed to piss in a cup. The next thing she knew, Dr Morfitt was wheeling her into a room with all sorts of odd equipment, including an ultrasound.*

*"Yup," he confirmed. "She's pregnant."*

*Ain't that the kicker? 'Cause you know what doesn't happen, at least for most women, during that nine months of hell referred to as gestation? You don't get a period. No period meant no wolfing out and no wolfing out meant she had no evidence whatsoever. For the next however long this stowaway in her womb lasted, she couldn't prove shit. Over the course of the pregnancy, she didn't bother to keep count of how long she'd been like that, had lost track of the days and weeks, and no longer paid attention to the alignment in the sky. What was the point?*

Felicity locked eyes with Dr. Hunt but didn't reply.

"You're almost full term now anyway, and he thinks the baby is big enough to thrive. We are going to induce you today."

*The fuck?*

With this bombshell dropped, the gynecologist himself appeared out of nowhere, the usual shit-eating smile on his smug face.

"Operating table is all ready… We'll get you prepped and start the C-section as soon as possible. Let's get that lovely little bundle of joy out to meet the world."

Felicity threw back her head and howled.

IT ALL WENT SMOOTHLY ENOUGH, SHE PRESUMED ANYWAY, HAVING HAD enough drugs to keep her woozy and thankfully pain free. She'd asked not to see the child, since it wasn't hers anymore anyway. She wasn't deemed fit to be a parent, not being of sound mind, and the fact she'd be locked up one way or another for most of its life meant it was easier all around to sign the papers and have the baby go straight to a young gay couple who would dote on it and give it a happy life. She opened her eyes for just a second to ensure it wasn't covered in hair and sharp teeth but just saw four tiny pale limbs flapping about. It had a cry to rival Boudica as it realized it has been freed from its warm and comfortable surroundings. To her disgust, her tits started leaking, joining the tears running down her cheeks. Fucking hormones.

She lay in her bed that night, drugged up to the eyeballs and patched up with bandages, a diaper wedged between her thighs, her body leaking all sorts of revolting after-birth type liquids. She sensed rather than saw Dr. Hunt, and for once, she was glad of his lurking presence.

The following day she was mightily pissed off to find not only did she feel like a Magician's Glamorous Assistant who'd been accidentally sawn in half, but that she was still heavily bleeding down there too. Nurse Siobhan came in regularly to help her change pads and give her a sponge bath. She was usually at least allowed to shower and maintain the semblance of dignity, but right then she couldn't have cared less if the entire staff, including Hunt, were staring at her ass since it all just hurt so much and was like a fountain of constant blood spurting out of her. Allegedly, it was all perfectly normal, the womb's way of retracting and clearing out all the stuff it no longer needed, but Felicity was sure she was dying.

Just as she spurted out enough filth to fill a bucket, she called out and was answered by an unknown voice. A head she didn't recognize popped into the room, brandishing a mop and bucket. One of the cleaning crew, but a new recruit she guessed, or they wouldn't dare peek in at the loony.

"Are you all right, my love?" came a motherly question Felicity had not been expecting. It threw her off guard for a moment. Felicity sniffed and turned away. Undeterred, the older lady came inside the room and after a moment of hesitation headed to the small window and opened the blinds.

"There you are, love. You'll be wanting a good view for later. I seen on the news that it's a special one tonight. What did the weatherman call it again? Oh yes. A Wolf Moon."

The woman shuffled off back to her mopping as Felicity felt

another wave of pain and something else. A prickly sensation on her skin, then her eyelids began to flutter. Her body had ejected all the leftovers from the pregnancy and now she was filled with hormonal lust and a desire to slaughter. As her primal urges began to resurface and small hairs began to break through her skin, she hoped she'd find a way to fuck Dr. Hunt before she killed him. They hadn't listened and she had stupidly forgotten to track the days. So pissed off by her body's betrayal in being with child, she'd lost sight of the most important factor. Now the full moon was rising and it called her. She broke the bonds as easily as if they were paper, and as her bones began to reform and her human teeth fell to the floor, the beast took over once more.

By the time she'd finished here, she'd be able to prove once and for all that *she* wasn't the crazy one.

# LIONEL AND THE RED RAGE

## SCOTT HARPER

L ionel expertly performed decline pushups from his jail bed, the soles of his feet anchoring him to the metal frame, his hands flat on the cold stone floor in front of him. His breath was even as he whipped out a quick fifty reps to get the blood flowing through his muscular frame.

He lamented there wasn't much else to do to keep himself occupied these days.

Lionel stood in his county-issued t-shirt and red cotton pants ("county drawers" in jail parlance) and went to the small, grimy sink suspended on the wall. The cell light flickered (as it habitually did all day), momentarily casting him into comforting darkness before relighting. He pushed a thick metal button and frigid water drizzled out in response; he washed his hands with a small bar of white soap, cleaning off the floor gunk.

He gazed at himself briefly in the scratched mirror, beholding his scruffy, bearded face and the wrinkled skin sagging below his eyes. Those eyes, once marine blue, now reflected gray and austere, the face of a dead man pretending to be alive. It made sense to Lionel; his soul had died long ago, and some abnormal force now animated his physical shell.

Lionel looked at the recyclable paper dinner tray he had discarded into the shadowy recesses of the cell corner. The resident rodent picked it over, gobbling down tiny remnants. Lionel could recall the meal's details: rice, beans, fruit, wilted lettuce, and some type of sausage meat. It was a typical institution repast, full of high glycemic carbs and lacking in protein. The county sheriff's department that ran the institution only had to meet very minimal state nutrition standards, and expensive quality protein wasn't high on the list. The dearth of protein made it harder for him to maintain his athletic build. Lacking the proper nutrition, he spent half his workouts burning off the excess calories he took in to get that little extra protein buried in the sugar.

He got back in position on the bed and began another set of pushups. The exercise helped distract him from the claustrophobic narrowness of the room. His world was now limited to a six-by-eight cell comprised of a stainless steel toilet, an uncomfortable metal bed covered with a lumpy plastic mattress, a small writing desk, and a fixed metal stool that accommodated only half of his ass. The thick walls were painted piss-yellow, matching the room's rank odor and Lionel's mood.

He would have liked to have been able to perform dips or pullups, but such exercise perks were no longer allowed in the cells for liability reasons—the jailers didn't want the inmates hanging themselves from the equipment. Or, at least, they didn't want to pay heavy civil fines to the dead inmate's aggrieved family.

Lionel felt the red rage rising inside him, a seething animus always present in the background of his psyche, like a wolf silently stalking its prey from the shadows of the forest line. The rage merged with his pumping blood and flooded his muscles, driving him to perform more repetitions. In quick succession, he had done a set of one hundred.

He stood, his chest and arms engorged in blood, and looked out through the small square window in the heavy cell door. A round, bovine face with a brown unibrow and pubic-hair mustache gazed back at him. It was Olivarez, the deputy sheriff assigned to do the half-hour security walks in his pod. They made eye contact, and Lionel quickly dismissed the deputy. He had little respect for the man. Olivarez was new to the job, young and inexperienced; he was already sporting a hefty gut from too much time sitting on his ass in between walks and eating free food from the officers' dining room.

Lionel dealt with the guard regularly; Olivarez escorted him in waist chains to and from the shower daily and to the rec yard for outdoor exercise every other day. These interactions led Lionel to conclude the man was a coward emblematic of the new breed of millennial officer that had taken over from the old guard. Olivarez lacked the courage to defend himself or his partner in a critical situation.

Lionel had time on his hands, and he spent much of it watching his captors and becoming intimately familiar with their daily routines and idiosyncrasies. He had dealt with cops and sheriffs before his current incarceration. He'd been rowdy in his youth, the type of kid who spent a lot of time in detention. He could recall his superstitious aunt lecturing his father one day after Lionel had been sent home from school for fighting. She'd chewed Dad out, claiming that Lionel was the seventh son of a seventh son and that Dad had ventured even further into bad mojo territory by giving Lionel a forename with six letters. Added to his last name of Mooreau, the combined letters totaled thirteen—very bad mojo, indeed.

Auntie Angelique's warnings had seemed overblown at the time, but now he wondered whether the old woman's concern had been justified. As an adult, he'd spent a week in county lockup after a wild bar fight in which he broke another man's jaw. Alcohol had been involved, and Lionel couldn't recall the particulars of the incident.

His first stint in jail passed quickly. Things had been different then. The inmates knew that if they got out of line, they would end up against the wall on the end of a stiff beating. The intimidation factor had worked then—the inmates knew their place and rarely attacked either the guards or other inmates.

But the world was different now. The inmates and the deputies had changed. The guards were of a new lazy, risk-averse generation and much less hands-on. Consequently, the inmates were empowered to do whatever they wanted, including throwing their body waste on the deputies during security walks ("gassing") or attacking their fellow inmates. Lockup had morphed into a kill-or-be-killed environment worsened by the plague.

Lionel felt right at home.

Although his life circumstances had recently soured, things had not always been so dismal. Lionel caught a lucky break and was released from jail when the battery charges against him were dropped "in the interests of justice." He'd got his life together, gone into the Marines, and eventually done a tour of duty in Iraq. The military had taught him discipline and self-sacrifice. He'd seen his fair share of bloodshed abroad, images of death and cruelty that were indelibly seared in the back of his mind. Lionel had learned to cope with the anxiety that became his constant companion, a condition the doctors labeled "Post-Traumatic Stress Disorder." Or, at least, he thought he had.

After returning home, he'd quickly acquired his real estate license and gone into business with a local agency. The market was good, and he made many sales. He married his childhood sweetheart, Tania, and moved into a picturesque suburban home nestled amongst his clients. With perfunctory diligence that came naturally to him, Lionel had quickly worked his way up in the company and became a supervisor.

Life was good.

And then, one ill-fated day, he returned home early from work, hoping to surprise Tania and take her out for dinner and a movie. Lionel received the shock of his life when he entered the foyer and heard grunting coming from the bedroom. The sight of his naked wife on their bed with her legs raised high and wide as her boyfriend vigorously fucked her, her red-painted nails digging into his pale ass, was forever emblazoned in his memory. He lost all the trust he had built with his wife, years of compromise and work down the drain in one split second. Yet his loss exceeded just his marriage; Lionel lost faith in the world. He had meticulously played by its rules and been harshly repudiated for his efforts. Something broke in him that moment, something he knew could never be fixed. His tie to sanity was severed; a raging fire was lit, one so intense it could never be extinguished.

Anger seethed in his chest, making it difficult for him to breathe. Lionel recognized the other man, a personal trainer from the local gym named Gabe, hired by Tania for private training sessions at the house. Lionel had been unaware of the infidelity occurring in his own home, in the bed he slept in.

Tania screamed as he ripped her naked lover from her embrace and cast him on the carpeted floor, the man's little prick still erect and throbbing, covered in fluid. Lionel encircled the other man's thin neck with his big hands and squeezed with all his strength. The lover's eyes went wide in shock and terror as his air was shut off, his face assuming a red tomato hue.

Tania tried to pull him off, but Lionel was like an enraged bull that could not be stopped. A red haze descended upon his vision as he shrugged her off and continued strangling the man. Soon, Gabe's pupils dilated, and a wet fart snapped out of his relaxed sphincter.

Lionel stood rigid over the dead man, righteous fury still flooding his veins. Gabe's purple tongue lolled out the corner of his open mouth, his cloudy eyes staring vacantly at the ceiling. Tania sobbed incessantly in the background.

Lionel knew that his world had forever changed. He didn't resist when the police arrived and handcuffed him without incident. As he walked out of the house he had worked so hard to have, he realized he would never set foot in it again. It occurred to him that the line between civility and lunacy was ever so thin, and, once crossed, there was no going back.

The trial had gone quickly. Lionel didn't participate in his defense—he recognized that he was guilty. The only truly important thing in his life, what mattered most in the world to him—his marriage—was over. He knew he was broken internally and could never be fixed.

He'd let himself go while in custody. He didn't shave or brush his teeth or get haircuts; his head was unkempt. He perfunctorily showered only to get out of the cell and better understand what was going on in the larger institution. Once, the jailers would have forced him to shave and clean himself. With the pandemic raging and a new generation of hands-off guards in charge, he was mostly left to himself.

Lionel knew he scared the guards and other inmates. When he'd first arrived, they'd made the mistake of housing him with another inmate, a fat pornographer arrested for harassing young girls. The flabby fuck had looked at Lionel the wrong way one day while taking a smelly dump in the cell toilet.

The sight of the man disgusted Lionel. He let the red rage loose, the anger he'd held in check since he murdered his wife's boyfriend. He seized the man by the throat like he'd snatched up Gabe just a few months before. Lionel hoisted his husky cellmate off the toilet and slammed him into the unforgiving wall. The other inmates had screamed and yelled encouragement as Lionel repeatedly bashed in the man's skull, blood and brain matter sliding down the wall like red pudding. The fat fuck was a gory mess when Lionel was through with him. Lionel enjoyed the carnage, the feral lizard part of his brain working in overdrive to absorb all the sensory input.

A second murder conviction assured Lionel would never get out of prison, even though he lived in a progressive blue state that wasn't considerate of crime victims. It didn't matter to Lionel, for he no longer gave a shit. He'd been moved out of general population and into a one-man cell in segregated housing, otherwise known as "high power." He was escorted by the guards in handcuffs everywhere he went.

The days spent in solitude were long, the nights even longer. Lionel would talk to himself, as no one else was available. The red rage still rattled around inside him, seeking release. It was like great sex—once he'd had it, he wanted to experience it again and again.

The jail psychiatrist tried to speak to him. He had nothing to say to her and just stared off into space. He was content to live in his own little mad world and didn't need others (particularly academics) telling him what to think.

While he generally held the guards in contempt, he complied with their orders and did not attack them. Lionel knew that, though weak and lackluster, they served an essential purpose in society, keeping the dangerous animals locked in. And he was an animal now, a most dangerous animal, and belonged inside the institution.

Unable to sleep, Lionel listened at night through the bars as the other inmates chattered, still full of energy after sitting through the entire day doing absolutely nothing. They spoke about their petty lives, the past grand criminal escapades they had participated in, the other criminals they knew, and the women they wanted to fuck.

Many of the narratives were the same: the inmate was tough and street smart, a connected player heavily involved in the illegal activity of his neighborhood. They were too smart to get caught; they were only in jail because someone else had betrayed them.

One name stuck out amidst all the myriad of conversations Lionel overheard, the name of the big man running all the local crime from within the confines of his jail cell. Whether it was prostitution and human trafficking, car theft, drug dealing, or selling guns, the big man was the kingpin, the crime boss whose decision was final and went unchallenged. Anyone dumb enough to cross him met a quick, ugly death, as did their family.

This guy was big-time evil, like a John Gotti or an Al Capone. And he had a name: Thompson Henry Chisholm, otherwise known as THC.

Of course, THC also stood for tetrahydrocannabinol, the principal psychoactive constituent of marijuana, making Chisholm's moniker quite apropos for a drug dealer.

Lionel decided that he was going to kill THC. The red rage was begging for release again, hovering like scarlet fog at the edges of his vision. He couldn't think of a more deserving target.

Chisholm was also vulnerable, which made the thought of killing him even more appealing to Lionel. Although a segregated inmate like Lionel, the crime kingpin was scheduled for the rec yard every other day at the same time as Lionel. Lionel had watched Chisholm in his wire cage on prior occasions. The big man would start by taking off his shirt to reveal a massive frame covered in prison tattoos. Ink teardrops, each indicative of a murder committed, dripped from both eyes.

Chisholm would typically spend the first thirty minutes of his scheduled time in a vigorous workout, performing exercises such as pullups and dips that were unavailable in his housing cell. Then the sweat-drenched kingpin would put his shirt back on and use the phone inside the cage to make business calls for the remaining time.

Lionel had the schedule down pat and memorized.

He was prepared when Olivarez approached his cell that morning at eleven a.m.

"Cuff up, Mooreau," the flabby guard said, looking through the window and assessing Lionel's demeanor. The guards generally addressed the inmates by their last names.

Wearing his full county-issued red attire, Lionel flipped around and faced away from the door. Olivarez opened a rectangular metal tray at waist level with a large key, and Lionel obediently presented his hands behind his back for cuffing. Olivarez handcuffed him, double-locking the cuffs with the pointed end of his handcuff key to ensure extra security.

The guard walked Lionel down the row of his fellow inmates. Typically, the other inmates would stop whatever they were doing and greet the escorted inmate for a brief moment of social interaction. However, the inmates remained quiet; they were familiar with Lionel's reputation and didn't want to antagonize him. Who knew what the crazy multi-murderer in cell number thirteen was capable of?

Olivarez walked Lionel in silence out of the housing module and up a flight of inoperative escalator stairs. The jail had been built in the 1950s, and replacement parts for its antiquated equipment were hard to come by. The ideal solution would have been to tear it all down and build a new jail, but the local board of supervisors was comprised of notorious cheapskates, at least when it came to divvying out money for law enforcement. They refused to fund such a costly venture.

Consequently, the jail husk slowly rotted away, falling apart piece by piece. The decay made life miserable for the inmates confined there and the guards who supervised them.

Olivarez led Lionel by the arm off the stairs onto the second floor and past the tinted windows of a guard booth. Lionel could see inside the booth: another guard, this one named Banuelos, sat in a reclining chair, his dingy black boots on the work counter. Banuelos' huge gut hung over his overtight black leather belt, giving him an unflattering, muffin-like appearance. His head rested against the other side of the counter, his eyes closed, fast asleep as drool dripped from the corner of his open mouth.

Lionel had anticipated the guard would be in such a state—he had never seen Banuelos awake during his previous rec yard visits. The guard's slumber made things much simpler.

They paused for a moment as Olivarez caught his breath. The brief walk up the stairs had winded the fat guard; sweat bullets beaded his brow. Lionel felt his monumental contempt for the man grow even greater.

Olivarez maneuvered Lionel through the open door and into the rec yard. It had rained the previous night, and the enormous stone walls encircling the yard were still wet. The normally smoggy air was crisp and cold. Lionel inhaled, letting his lungs fill to capacity. It felt good to breathe fresh air again. He felt enlivened as they walked toward the row of wire cages.

It was a slow day in the rec yard, with most cages unoccupied. Lionel worried briefly whether Chisholm was there. Then he saw sunlight reflect off the kingpin's shaved bald head inside one of the middle cages and relaxed.

As they passed Chisholm, Lionel inspected the kingpin. Chisholm had his shirt back on and was facing sideways, the cell's telephone cradled in his big hands. The kingpin spoke slowly and softly into the antiquated plastic handset, displaying the casual look of a businessman discussing recent developments with an associate. If he noticed Lionel and Olivarez, Chisholm didn't show it.

The guard stopped two cells down from where Chisholm conversed. Olivarez removed a large keyring attached to a lanyard from his pocket and prepared to open the cell door.

Lionel looked around the quiet yard. No one else was present other than Chisholm, Olivarez, and himself.

Lionel went into action.

He bent his torso forward at the waist and head-butted Olivarez, sending the guard reeling. Shock registered on Olivarez's doltish face as blood trickled down his forehead and into his eyes.

Lionel saw that the man in front of him was thoroughly ill-prepared for his job, that the idea an inmate might one day turn on him had never crossed Olivarez's simple mind. Then Lionel kicked the guard in the groin, hard. Olivarez sank to his knees. Lionel rammed his knee into the guard's jaw and knocked him unconscious. Olivarez slumped in a heap to the ground.

The flurry of activity caused Chisholm to notice; he stood with the phone hanging limply from his right hand, his eyes glued to

Lionel. Lionel laid back on the ground and brought his legs up in a bent position. He agilely slid his handcuffed hands behind his ass and over his feet. When he stood, his hands were now in front of him.

Lionel retrieved the key block from Olivarez's lanyard. He selected one of the larger brass keys he'd seen Olivarez employ on numerous occasions to open the cage doors and positioned it in front of the keyhole of Chisholm's cage.

Lionel looked the kingpin directly in the eyes. Chisholm was not amused.

"What the fuck are you doing, crazy man? Do you know who I am?" the kingpin asked. "I don't need you to free me, you fucking lunatic."

"You do need me to free you. You're the disease; I'm the cure," Lionel said nonchalantly. He couldn't recall the mediocre movie in which he'd heard that phrase uttered, but it didn't matter. His vision went utterly vermilion as he thrust the key home and twisted.

Chisholm was prepared. The kingpin had grown up on the streets, fighting others for scraps since the day he popped out of his teenage mother's womb. Many street thugs had fallen to him over the years—fighting was second nature for him.

The big man smashed the door open with his enormous shoulders, knocking Lionel back. Chisholm pumped his thick thighs, getting up steam as he plowed into Lionel like a pro linebacker and crushed him to the ground. Unlike Lionel, the kingpin was not handcuffed and had free use of his enormous mitts. Chisholm straddled Lionel and began to pummel him, the big man's fists battering Lionel's head from side to side.

An ordinary man would have quickly been reduced to a bloody pulp under the force of such tremendous blows. Chisholm was an experienced fighter and knew how to punch.

But Lionel was hardly ordinary. The blood flowing from his split lips into his mouth enervated him. He reveled in the dismayed look on Chisholm's face when the kingpin realized his punches didn't have the desired effect.

Lionel shot his left knee into Chisholm's unprotected ribs, hearing one of them crack.

"UGGHH!" gasped the kingpin, his mouth agape in pain. Chisholm reached into his waistline and retrieved a shank, a jail weapon comprised of a steel rod sharpened to a razor point. The big man tried to drive it into Lionel's throat.

Lionel blocked the thrust with his forearm, but the weapon still sank into the meat of his upper left pec. Pain exploded throughout his body, and stars clouded his vision.

Chisholm bore down with all his weight, using both hands to push the shank deeper. Lionel concentrated, ignoring the agony. Lionel shoved Chisholm away by employing the strength he had developed from endless sets of pushups. Despite his enormous size, the kingpin sailed off, landing on his back with a heavy *THUMP!*

Lionel stood, shaking blood from his eyes. He pulled the bloody shank from his chest and discarded it like trash. Chisholm recovered quickly, intertwining his fingers into a massive composite fist and raising his hands over his head. The kingpin lunged forward, anticipating a final blow.

Lionel pivoted to his right and brought up his left knee, punishing Chisholm's broken ribs again.

"GAAHK!" cried Chisholm as he bent over and threw up, a noxious mixture of county cuisine and hot blood. The big man collapsed to his knees, winded and in extreme pain.

Lionel went behind the kingpin and smashed his knee into Chisholm's mid-back, digging his patella painfully into the man's spine. In response, Chisholm reared up, exposing his neck.

Lionel wrapped his cuffed hands around the kingpin's wide throat and pulled back, digging the metal links and swivels deep into the skin. Chisholm flailed his hands, trying to grab Lionel, but he was out of position. The big man's face turned red as his air was cut off. He tried to stand, but Lionel held him in check. Blood pumped from the wound in Lionel's chest, saturating his clothing.

Chisholm's eyes went wide with fear, a sensation the big man was unfamiliar with. Lionel wrenched his hands violently to the side and was rewarded with the sound of breaking bone. He released Chisholm, and the man slid gracelessly to the floor.

Lionel watched the kingpin's body twitch. He'd broken something in the man's neck, but Chisholm wasn't quite dead. Not yet.

The big man's eyes were still open, and ugly gurgling sounds came from his mouth. Lionel stood over Chisholm and stamped his foot down on the neck.

*Splutch!* Chisholm's body shuddered and went still. Blood flowed from the mouth and pooled on the concrete.

Lionel stood over the kingpin's corpse and tried to catch his breath. The red haze evaporated from his vision, gradually replaced by the sharp pain of his chest wound. Lionel also noticed a throbbing ache in his left bicep that indicated he had torn it during the fight. The muscle would need to be surgically repaired.

His body was still pumped full of adrenaline when the first of the guards arrived. Olivarez had recovered and was joined by Banuelos. The sleepy guard was now finally awake and already out of breath from the short sprint from the guard booth. Lionel waited patiently for the two millennials to decide what they would do.

"Jeezus, Mooreau, what the fuck did you do?" Olivarez questioned, his eyes glassy from the blows he received earlier.

Lionel remained silent. He knew he must look like a mess, covered in blood and standing next to the butchered corpse of Chisholm. But a man such as Olivarez could never truly understand Lionel's motivations, so there was no point in attempting to explain. It would be like trying to discuss ancient Greek philosophy with a drunk.

The two guards looked at each other in bewilderment, hoping the other would know what to do and take charge. After an awkward silence, Olivarez removed a heavy metal flashlight from a sleeve in his pants. Banuelos shook his head initially, as if he were reticent to proceed, but also drew his flashlight from inside his jacket.

Lionel knew what was coming; he'd anticipated it. When faced with a novel situation that immobilized them with fear, aggravated by the enormous surge of adrenaline that accompanied a critical incident, the guards instinctively defaulted to violence—they began to beat him.

They struck Lionel about the head and torso, weak blows made painful by the thickness of the metal instruments. Lionel did not resist; he dropped to the ground and assumed a nonthreatening fetal position, his body bladed to make it a smaller target.

Other guards arrived, accompanied by a grizzled veteran sergeant named Toly.

"Knock that shit off!" Toly ordered.

Lionel hazarded a glance up as the blows stopped. The sergeant had a look of mixed disgust and resignation on his craggy features, perhaps estimating the time and paperwork required to make an inmate murder accompanied by a guards' use of force presentable to his superiors.

Lionel was carted off on a gurney to the hospital ward, where the nurses stitched his chest wound and cleaned him. News of his actions spread quickly. A Hispanic inmate worker, or trustee, as the guards referred to them, approached his bed. The oval-faced inmate presented Lionel with an aromatic food tray from the officers' dining room. Lionel picked up a shiny red apple and took a bite.

It was delicious, the first decent food he'd had in many months. Lionel looked at the thickly built guard with a handlebar mustache supervising the area. The guard turned his gaze away, tacitly giving his approval for Lionel to accept the tray.

"It's from Montano," the trustee said. Lionel recognized the name. Montano was the leader of the Hispanic inmates at the institution, a figure almost as feared as Chisholm.

"A gift for the kingpin," the trustee added, noting the look of curiosity on Lionel's bruised face.

Lionel smiled and thanked the trustee, who obediently turned and left. Apparently, Lionel had replaced Chisholm at the top of the inmate hierarchy of power. It was a position that did not intrigue him initially—he had no interest in inmate politics.

Then he thought further on the matter. Inmates were like the movie gangsters they so admired—incessantly plotting and manipulating to concentrate power by whatever means necessary. The other jail power players would soon be gunning for Lionel—and gunning hard.

Lionel smiled a vulpine grin. He settled back into his bedsheets, content knowing the red rage would have many future victims to satisfy its unending hunger.

# I AM BUT A SHELL

## DAVID RIDER

### JUNE 1, 2004

"The world is going to Hell in a handbasket."

Sonja studied the withered corpse behind the desk. She'd already gotten the job and was dressed for orientation, but her new supervisor had brought her into the administrator's office to "meet the big man."

Mr. Schick's rheumy eyes appraised her as he shook his head. At this movement, a fresh sprinkling of dandruff fluttered onto his dark suit jacket like the first, weak snowfall of November. "My father built this institution from nothing! With his own two hands!" He raised his palms from the desk's blotter to show his gnarled knuckles—using visual aids in case she didn't understand what "hands" were. "And he kept it running through *two* wars!"

She had done her research. This facility had broken ground in late 1917 but hadn't been completed until *after* the Great War ended a year later. Was he counting World War I and spouting the bullshit claims of his father? She couldn't hold her tongue. "There have been *several* wars since then. We're in one now."

He glared at her. "Are you cracking wise, young lady?"

"No, sir."

"I asked if you're *cracking wise*?!"

She repeated herself, louder, in case his hearing was going.

He spat, "This is what happens when they bring me a *woman*!"

No longer amused, she crossed her thick forearms over the white tunic of her uniform and regarded him with a cold stare.

The man's anger flared, as if the subject of women in the workplace had restarted his heart and he didn't like the warmth. "How will you react the first time a patient hurls feces in your smug face? Or strikes you with a cafeteria tray? Will you cry? Will you quit and run home to mother?"

*How old does this prick think I am?* she thought. "No, sir. I'll shake it off and restrain the patient like any other orderly on your staff."

"Eh," he replied, doubtful, but eyed her large physique all the same.

"I grew up on a farm, sir. I've roped and tied animals in competition larger than any man you have here. Norwegian blood, through and through."

"Helgeson," he sneered. "I knew a jackass named Helgeson on the Morris Chamber of Commerce. Had a snot-nosed punk your age, but no daughters. Where you from?"

"Norway."

"Not *originally*, for Pete's sake."

"Norway, Illinois. Thirteen miles from here, as the crow flies." She tossed in that phrase to sound relatable to the codger.

"Did you attend college?"

She lied for the first time since her interview, doing it with a perfect poker face. "No, sir."

"Then there's at least *one* way you'll fit in with the others." Eyeing her once more, he leaned back and flicked his gaze to the door. Their meeting was over.

Sonja stood. At six-one and two hundred sixty pounds, she towered over the man and his mahogany desk. She held out a hand large enough that she could have palmed his flaky head like a mini-basketball.

He didn't return the gesture. There would be no handshake. She couldn't tell if it was a woman thing or if he just didn't afford respect to anyone. This, more than anything, bothered her a great deal. In the community where she was raised, people were always respectful. Even after she went away to school in Champaign, took her first job in Chicago, and returned on holidays, the folks from home treated her like one of their own.

Now she had come here, to Hills Hollow—an unincorporated village smaller than her hometown—to find herself in the office of Mr. Lyman Schick, Jr. The cranky septuagenarian was incapable of offering a modicum of respect to a new employee, and possibly the patients inside the walls of his facility. It was going to be fun exposing him for the crook he was and shine a cleansing light on this horrible place.

But in at least one sense, she agreed with him.

The world *was* going to Hell in a handbasket—and disrespectful men like Schick were the cause.

She withdrew her hand and crossed to the office door.

He called, "Helgeson..."

She turned.

"Welcome to White Willow Asylum."

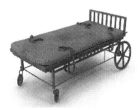

HER SUPERVISOR TREATED HER WITH THE SAME FLATLINE LEVEL OF respect. He mostly communicated in gestures, pointing their way out of the admin wing and down a long corridor. She could only assume he was leading her to the ward where she would be stationed. He had "Clarke" printed on the laminated card dangling from his belt. They came to a pair of industrial doors and he swiped the card on a pad. A beep sounded, a lock clicked, and he walked onto the ward ahead of her without holding the door. No gentleman, Clarke, but she'd expected a minimal amount of courtesy.

He hustled her around a corner—where she caught a glimpse of patients huddled near a television in a wide, dimly lit common area —and into the employee break room. Clarke introduced her by last name to a handful of male orderlies around a table. He didn't give any of their names, calling them only "the second shift."

Her reception was so chilly, she felt like she had wandered into their clubhouse after ignoring a *No Girlz Allowed* sign. They were all thin and wiry and looked incapable of maintaining order at a child's party, much less a mental health facility. She had anticipated her coworkers would be hard-drinkin' country boys and knew the type well. She was looking at a rough start that would get worse once they saw she could do their job.

When they asked to be dismissed early, Clarke said, "Get the hell out and have a PBR waiting for me."

They were gone in less time than it took for introductions.

He patted his pockets and produced a swipe card from one. Printed on it was the surname she had given them—spelled incorrectly with an A in the middle.

"That's not—The name's Helg-*eh*-son. With an E."

"No one'll give a shit. Just put it on."

She clipped it to her belt, grumbling.

He grabbed his car keys from a bank of lockers.

"I…thought you would be showing me the ropes tonight."

"Hell, no. I'm first shift. Only stuck around to make introductions."

"But isn't there…more I should know?"

"Probably, but it's way past quitting time for me. Scotch'll be around presently. He'll give you the rundown."

A sense of unease blossomed in her gut.

He gestured out at the common area, leading the way. "For now, just stand here. Keep your eyes on the goons over there. And don't turn your back."

She had received more thorough instructions babysitting neighbor kids. She eyed him with frustration.

"Don't be fucking needy, Helgason." With that, he walked around the corner and departed.

As she stepped farther into the ward, the hairs on the back of her neck stood at attention. The overpowering feeling wasn't brought on because her research had been lacking. The floor plan was identical to the blueprints filed with the county. The old photos she had studied on microfiche could have been taken today. Everything she had memorized compared to what she was seeing matched. But her prep work painted an incomplete picture because it lacked crucial sensory input on how the place *felt*...

...and this place felt *wrong*.

The soles of her shoes were glued to the floor. Her body overrode her ability to move. Her mind pulled a memory of the only other time she experienced such dread.

*She was twelve, entering the funeral parlor, seeing her father in a casket. Even from twenty feet away, he didn't look right...his waxy, reconstructed face was mannequin-like...and the closer she got, the less he looked like himself...and her grieving, overactive imagination was certain that The Thing That Didn't Look Like Oleg Pedersen was going to jerk to a sitting position and shriek, "But I* am *your father! Come hug Papa, little Sonja!"*

She blinked herself out of her reverie to assess her situation.

She stood in a ward full of mental patients.

*Sonja and the Lunatics. Sounds like an alt-rock band from my U of I years, circa 1989 —*

One of them noticed her.

While the others watched television, a single face swiveled in her direction. He was Caucasian, medium build, average in every respect, down to the brown hair parted on the left. He wore pajamas and sat relaxed in his chair, palms on knees.

*He looks like Rob Petrie from* Dick Van Dyke, *minus the friendly smile.*

At this, the man cocked his head—as if he had heard her thought from across the room. His calm gaze flicked to another patient, making eye contact.

That patient, a white-haired man in a bathrobe, turned fully around to check her out.

Sonja's pulse doubled.

He pushed himself out of his chair and stood facing her like he had been tagged into play. He shuffled in her direction.

*Oh shit.*

She not only felt the overwhelming sense of dread from before, but now anticipation at being approached.

He advanced with careful half-steps, the gait of a man who had broken a hip more than once. His eyes stayed riveted on hers, his breathing ragged with effort.

When he got within ten feet, a gruff voice barked from behind her, "Back to your seat." A middle-aged man zipped from her peripheral vision and intercepted the patient. Catching him by the shoulders, he spun him around with practiced ease. "Go on, Ralph. *Boogeda-boogeda!* Go sit your wrinkled ass down. You're missing the end of *Fraggle Rock*."

"Ralph" gave her another glance before ambling away.

She looked past him at Nondescript Rob Petrie who, her imagination decided, was the one responsible for sending Ralph in the first place—ludicrous though it sounded. He no longer faced her. He stared at a fixed spot on the linoleum in front of his slippers.

She shuddered. The skin on her arms went stiff with gooseflesh. She hugged herself, covering the affected areas with her large mitts.

The orderly caught her reaction. "You got the *Dubba-Yous*."

"Double-Yous?"

He chuckled with a gravelly voice. "You gonna say it, say it right: *Dubba. Yous.* Short for White Willow Willies. You got 'em bad."

She bookmarked the phrase in her mind for notes to jot later.

"We all get the Dubba-Yous here. It's that creeping feeling that God is not on His throne and the lights in the Kingdom are extinguished and He's ditched you to face darkness alone."

Having been left alone moments ago, the explanation was apt—but it didn't comfort her knowing adult men with more experience at this job felt the same.

He extended a hand. "They call me Scotch."

She reached out. "They call me Helgason."

He pulled his hand away before she touched him.

She glared, feeling disrespected and hating it despite having expected such.

"Nope. That was a test. Get in the habit of avoiding skin-on-skin contact. You don't want to know where these jamokes keep their fingers: their mouths, their balls, use your imagination. Asylum life's a big, wet, sticky party. That said, you'll want to pull your hair back. What do you think this is, a Hollywood red carpet premiere?"

She removed a rubber band from her wrist and gathered her long, brown hair into a ponytail.

"You can thank me later. Let me show you around."

IN THE PIECE SHE WAS ALREADY WRITING IN HER HEAD, SONJA ASSIGNED adjectives that fit her new coworker's personality: brief and direct. Her editor would change the names of the other orderlies before her article would be published, but "Scotch" was already a nickname. She had assumed it came from his beverage of choice but learned it was from the butterscotch candy to which he was addicted and consumed every hour, on the hour.

Scotch gave her a short, verbal checklist of their nightly duties. Their main purpose on the overnight shift was keeping patients in their rooms and preventing escapes.

"The worst thing that could happen is being the poor idiot on the clock when one of our lifers manages to hoof his schizo ass to a farmhouse where he carves up the first person to look at him cross-eyed."

"But wouldn't this hypothetical schizo have to get off the ward? Past an orderly?"

"Yes and yes. And his name was Mounds."

"*Whose* name was Mounds?"

"You answered the classified ad in the *Herald* for this job?"

"Yeah. So?"

"Mounds's obituary was two pages before."

"What happened?"

"Hypothetical schizo."

Scotch could be frustrating. After she remarked that the ward had grown noticeably darker than it was when she arrived, he explained it was due to "Cicadan rhythm enforcement." According to him, Schick put the lights on timers that brighten and dim based on the sun's position. Sonja suggested the correct word was "Circadian," but Scotch dismissed it. "No, it's those noisy bugs that hatch every seventeen years. Their life cycle is a Cicadan rhythm." His mind was as made up as his nonsense logic.

At ten o'clock, a soft tone sounded from overhead speakers to signal the hour. He unwrapped his candy, popped it in his mouth, and zapped the DVD player with a remote control. He called, "Lights out, people."

Five patients headed to bed. There were twelve units total on this ward. The others had already retired for the night.

Scotch stood next to the corridor leading to their rooms. When she joined him, he said, "Every night we're judges at the reject parade." As they filed past, he whispered what he knew about each one. "This guy came back from Iraq without a leg or the will to live…Old Ralph here drove drunk and killed some teens…and this jamoke claims he's seen the same girl and her talking dog wandering his hometown for the past sixty years."

Scotch nudged Sonja's elbow, sounding sympathetic for the first time. "Speaking of girls, this little one is Cordelia."

A ten-year-old waif wearing Powerpuff Girls pajamas came up to them. Her short black hair was an unbrushed mess. Her haunted blue eyes touched Sonja's before flicking away. In that brief second, she conveyed such pain that Sonja felt her breath catch.

"Can I switch rooms yet? You promised." She sounded desperate.

Scotch crouched below her eye level. "I promised I'd *ask*. The answer is no."

Her eyes glazed over as she looked to the ceiling. This wasn't the answer she wanted. "But I don't want to be in there!"

"We have no empty rooms. The others have been here longer. They don't like change."

"Why can't I sleep out here?"

"You know the rules."

"Please! I'm small! I can push two chairs together!"

"I'm sorry, sweetheart."

Her arguments depleted, she unholstered the last one in her arsenal. "Then lock me in a padded room."

"Those are only for violent patients."

*"But I just want to sleep!"*

He adopted a measured tone. "Cordelia, you would have to hit one of the others. Or *myself*."

Sonja heard this as a suggestion. He was inviting her to strike him.

Cordelia also took his meaning. Her eyes narrowed. One of her hands balled into a fist. She clenched her jaw. But violence didn't seem to be in her nature. She did nothing.

The moment passed. Scotch sighed as if disappointed in her. He stood, reached into a pocket, and held out a piece of candy. "Let's get you to your room."

In a burst of pure reflex, she smacked it out of his fingers. The candy shattered against the wall into bits of sugary shrapnel.

Scotch paused for two beats, said, "Ow!" and seized the girl by her arm. He mock-dragged her away to the opposite side of the ward. "That is *it*, young lady! You're going straight to the rubber room to think about what you've done! The whole night!"

Sonja noticed Cordelia flash a grim, defiant smirk back at Rob Petrie.

*What the hell's* that *about?*

Again, as if hearing Sonja's thoughts, he lifted his head and looked at her. He made no other movements. He didn't blink. He only stared with a neutral expression.

She waited for some other reaction.

Thirty seconds passed.

She turned to look where Scotch had gone.

The moment she did, a voice growled in her left ear: *"Sonja Pedersen."*

She sprang into the air like a startled cat reacting to a thunder-clap, jerking her head to where she had heard the voice—*had heard it next to her ear*—but no one was present. The Dubba-Yous struck full force, more intense than before—lizard brain giving the flight command. But her rational mind saw there was nothing to run *from*. No immediate danger.

The man observed her in taciturn silence.

He was the source of her fear—she felt it in her core but rejected it all the same.

A hand tapped her shoulder.

She yelped.

Scotch had returned.

"I—"

He raised a finger in warning…a *be quiet* gesture.

*It triggered another memory of Sonja and her father, twenty-one years ago, crouching behind a tree. They both wore fluorescent vests and caps. He had raised his finger. She followed his focused gaze to a buck, grazing a hundred feet away, and—*

"Go to your room," Scotch said in a firm whisper.

*There's no way he heard that. We're too far away.*

The man stood and walked into the corridor, entered the first room on the left, and closed his door.

Sonja eyed Scotch in disbelief.

His tattooed arms were covered with goosebumps. "That's The Shell. If you're going to listen to only one piece of advice, it's this: *never* turn your back on him."

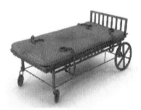

HER EDITOR AT THE *CHICAGO DAILY NEWS* WOULD PUSH FOR VERIFIABLE details. This assignment started as Kritzer's idea, but Sonja fought to come *here*—to this asylum. Mental health facilities didn't even use that word anymore. It had gone the way of "sanatorium." Yet Lyman Schick, Jr. didn't care about negative connotations. He knew people in positions of power in the county and state and networked to ensure the money didn't dry up. From what Sonja had seen so far, however, one wouldn't know *any* funds were coming here. The operational staff consisted of a barely trained skeleton crew. She was being paid minimum wage and assumed the others weren't earning much more. The paint was peeling off the walls, the ceiling tiles were stained coffee-brown, and every wing smelled like her grandmother's house after one of the cats died between the walls.

*So what died between* these *walls? That's what you're here to find out, right?*

At midnight, Sonja said she needed fresh air. Scotch directed her to a fire exit, telling her to use a brick outside to prop the door open. She did this, finding hundreds of cigarette butts in the grass, and walked along the building's exterior under a moonless sky. Her Nokia showed no cell service was available. When she rounded a corner and faced Joliet's distant glow to the eastern horizon, she got a bar. She pressed speed dial one.

A man answered on the first ring. "Hey, honey."

"Is this Bilbo Helgeson, snot-nosed punk formerly of Morris?"

He laughed. "No, it's William Robert Helgeson, baby daddy. But I am, coincidentally, wiping snot from the nose of our kid who can't sleep. What's going on?"

"Schick remembered your 'jackass' dad from the Chamber of Commerce. He considers you a punk."

"Yeah, Dad wasn't fond of that prick, either."

"Language. How's Ollie's fever?"

"Worse. I gave him Benadryl. You okay there?"

She traced her fingers on the brickwork as she walked. "I'm fine."

"Is it as spooky as rumors say?"

"It's just an old building."

"Will we see you this weekend?"

"Not Saturday. I've got to get some pages written for Kritzer. But if you and Ollie want to come out and visit Sunday, maybe?"

"That no-tell motel up Route 47, right?"

"Yeah, room three, under Kritzer's name."

"Got it. Love you, babe."

"Love *you*." She made a kissing sound.

After disconnecting, she reached the chain-link fence surrounding the exercise yard that prevented patients from escaping. Beyond that, too dark to see tonight, stood a grove of weeping willow trees that hid the property from passersby on Route 47.

She wondered how Mounds had been killed.

*Another mystery for an intrepid reporter to uncover.*

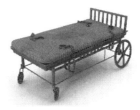

THE FOLLOWING NIGHT IN THE BREAK ROOM, THEY DISCUSSED CORDELIA.

Scotch explained that letting her sleep in the "secure rooms" should be kept on the down-low. After he explained why, Sonja not only agreed with his request, she resolved to leave this arrangement out of her article entirely.

"She killed her folks. Blew them away with the dad's handgun."

Sonja's blood turned to ice water. Speechless, she struggled to accept this revelation.

"Looking at her, yeah, hard to believe. But the county police said there were, like, extenuasive circumstances."

*Extenuating,* she thought, nodding for him to continue.

"Young parents. Whacked out of their skulls on crack. When they weren't neglecting their kids, they were smacking them around."

"Kids, plural?"

"They killed Cordelia's twin brother. That's why she unloaded the gun on them. Three bullets each. Shot them dead. When the cops rolled up, they said she was holding her brother's body and wouldn't let go."

"Christ."

"Imagine killing one parent, let alone two. Now imagine doing it at *ten.*" He shook his head. "Anywho, that kid's all alone. Counselors have been working with her the past few weeks. She'll end up in the system. Foster homes and all that shit. Word is a priest is coming to collect her. I'm trying to make her comfortable until then." He raised an eyebrow. "You all right there, Helgason?"

She had zoned out but blinked herself back into the present. "Y —Yeah."

"Tough kid. Reminds me of my own daughter at that age."

"You've got kids?"

"Just one. Darlene. She's on the other side of the world, starting her second tour. Doing God's work and finding the bastards that did Nine-Eleven."

She stammered, "Th-That's not—They're not—" But she held her tongue. Her opinions on the war would only serve to drive a wedge between them. That wasn't the way forward.

He stood when the midnight tone sounded. True to Pavlovian programming, he unwrapped a candy.

She brought the topic back to Cordelia, attempting to squeeze one more answer out of him. "Why doesn't she want to sleep in her room?"

He didn't seem like he was going to answer.

Sonja waited, willing him to reply.

"She sees demons."

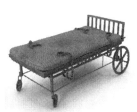

AT ONE A.M., SCOTCH LOOKED UP FROM SOLITAIRE AND ANNOUNCED IT was time for wellness-check rounds. He claimed he had done them yesterday, adding, "Unspoken agreement on graveyard is we take turns every other night."

Sonja set down her newspaper, parsing the unspoken agreement he had spoken aloud.

He nodded to a flashlight on the wall. "You do a sweep of the rooms, peek in to make sure they're breathing, and move on to the next."

She grabbed the flashlight, testing its functionality. "Will any of them be awake?"

"The Shell doesn't sleep. And don't turn—"

"Don't turn my back on him. I know." Before leaving the room, she asked, "What'd he do to get locked up in here, anyway?"

He laid a six of spades on the table. Without making eye contact, he lifted his gaze halfway between his cards and her. "I don't talk about him."

Sonja blurted, "*Hey!*" and regretted her harsh tone—but it pissed her off that she wasn't getting important answers. "I need to know if he's a threat! Did he kill Mounds?"

Scotch put his cards down, now meeting her gaze with steely eyes. He didn't appreciate being challenged. His words dripped with acid. "Mounds killed himself. But he did it because of that monster in room one. If you want to pull his file and learn more, do it tomorrow in the admin building. Because *I don't talk about him.*"

Feeling the color rising in her cheeks, she left to start rounds.

The common room never got darker than it was at the start of her shift. From then until sunrise, the ward lights stayed dimmed to the equivalent of just past dusk on a Midwestern evening. The lights in the corridor outside the patients' bedrooms, however, were on a different timer—one that fully corresponded to the sun's position relative to Central Daylight Time. By five minutes before one, that darkness reached its zenith. It was through this grey-to-black meridian that Sonja crossed.

She swept the flashlight's beam the length of the hallway to confirm the six doors on each side were shut.

One was not.

The second door on her left stood ajar.

*Cordelia's room,* she reminded herself, trying to calm her escalating heartbeat. *She's on the other side of the wing, sleeping on a padded floor. Because she's afraid of...this guy...*

She didn't look through the rectangular window of The Shell's door. She would check his last. Instead, she walked sideways down the hall, intentionally keeping room number one in sight so he couldn't sneak up behind her. She crept to the third door. The woman inside was sound asleep, as were the men in the next two rooms.

As she progressed toward the end of the hallway, approaching the sixth room—from which came abrasive snoring—Sonja realized the temperature had grown markedly cooler. When she swiveled her eyes to check The Shell's door, she saw it had opened. The Dubba-Yous buffeted her, yielding the same physical reaction as an unexpected drop into a frozen lake. She couldn't breathe. When she sensed a presence behind her, only her eyes moved. Her neck muscles wouldn't allow her head to turn because *something was there*, but by not looking she was buying extra seconds where she could believe *nothing was there*.

That belief was dispelled when a voice spoke on her left...

*Your soul.*

...and a different voice came from her right...

*It is cracked.*

Her knees buckled. She stumbled backward—*or had she been pushed?!*—and it took several scrambling steps for her to prevent an awkward fall. She thumped heavily into the back wall, shoulder blades taking the brunt of the force and making it shudder.

She had taken nastier spills as a kid being thrown from her horse. The difference was she had *seen* the snakes or bees that had spooked her horse back then—had been prepared for each tumble. There had been no way to anticipate what just happened.

The flashlight shaking in her hand, she violently dissected the darkness with its beam. It revealed nothing. This only served to scare her more, causing her chest to rise and fall with deep breaths. And when she heard tapping on glass and swung the light to room number six's window and saw the face of the snoring man who had been awakened, she choked out a scream and bolted for the relative brightness of the common area.

Once free of the corridor's darkness, her thoughts cleared. The last thing she should do was run to Scotch in her present state. Slowing her dash to a walk, she angled across toward the patients' restrooms. Her coworker didn't glance up from his cards. She made it unseen to the women's bathroom.

She paced before the mirror. "Okay. It's fine. You're fine. Nothing was there."

Except something *was* there.

She couldn't deny what she'd heard.

*Your soul.*

*It is cracked.*

She stared at her wild-eyed reflection.

*If you're imagining these voices, why are you hearing them from different distances and heights?!*

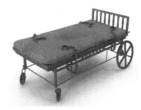

Sonja needed answers. At the end of her shift, she left through the employee exit and headed to administration.

Ever since therapy, it was in her nature to confront issues head on. For several years, her mother drove her forty miles a week to see a psychologist. She instinctively knew *why* they made the long trek to Kingsdale: it was to prevent anyone in their community from knowing how they were coping with tragedy. As far as her mom was concerned, there was no reason to give the Larsens or the Kristiansens enough details to put two and two together. "Say, Marge, ever wonder where the chunky kid with the Smiths shirt and raccoon mascara goes every Wednesday like clockwork? Yeah, me neither." That wasn't how small-town grapevines worked. They flourished from a fertilizer of known fact and idle speculation. The only reason her sessions remained an unverified rumor was because Sonja kept to herself throughout high school and had no loose-lipped friends to spill the beans.

She mounted the steps of the Victorian-style building's porch. She hadn't taken more than three steps into the lobby when a voice said, "I expected you yesterday, dear."

A grey-haired woman sat in an overstuffed easy chair next to the picture window. She was dressed prim and proper in a blouse and long skirt, wearing a shawl to warm her delicate frame from the morning chill. Judging by her tired eyes, life had had its way with her and held no surprises.

"Please." She gestured to the couch and table next to her. A tea service sat on a tray. "I'm about to enjoy my morning tea before my shift."

"Oh, no thanks," Sonja said. "I'm on my way to the records room."

"Yes, that's me, Ms. Helgeson. I've already pulled the file you came to see." She tilted her head to an end table on her other side, indicating a thick manila folder.

Sonja blinked at her.

The woman reached for the tea kettle. "My name is Ms. Duncan." She poured the steaming liquid into the first cup. "Will you join me?"

She walked around the table to sit on the couch.

The woman filled a second cup. "Do you take sugar?"

"Yes, please."

The woman picked up a small set of tongs and retrieved a sugar cube from a bowl. "One lump or two?"

"Three."

She dropped two cubes in the cup, hesitated as her gaze flitted over Sonja's large body, and went back for a third.

*She came damned close to asking if I was sure*, Sonja thought. *But she doesn't want to be rude. She wants to learn more about me.*

"I've been at White Willow thirty years. I started when I was about your age, answering an ad for a secretary. Although I suppose these days the position would be called 'executive assistant.'"

"I'm sure you're right." Sonja blew a curling wisp of steam from her tea. "Although the nomenclature for 'orderly' probably hasn't changed in a century."

Ms. Duncan appraised her before speaking. "Is that what you are, dear? An orderly?"

"Well, I'm wearing all white and didn't fall off an ice cream truck. So I hope that's what I am."

"Mm," she replied.

Sonja cleared her throat. "You, uh, said you expected me?"

"That's right. We're a tight-knit group. We hear things." She passed her the heavy folder. "You'd think this was *The DaVinci Code*, based on how many employees have come here to read it this past month."

"When it comes to recent fiction, I'm more of a *Lovely Bones* gal. But unless there's a new Walter Isaacson biography out," she held up the folder, "*this* will have to satisfy my non-fiction itch." She noticed the label affixed to the folder's tab. It bore a single name. "Shelley?"

"That's right."

"As in Percy Bysshe?"

"In my mind, more Mary Wollstonecraft, due to the horrific nature of the story. But according to the sheriff who delivered that particular patient to us, they named him because of what he had written in blood on—" She pressed her fingers to her lips, keeping her next words sealed behind them. "Forgive me. It's too early to recount such a morbid occurrence in polite company. Rest assured, the gory details of the police report and crime scene photos are the *favorites* of your coworkers."

Sonja started to get to her feet.

Ms. Duncan held her hand in a *stop* gesture. "Oh, you can't *take* the file. You'll have to read it here."

She sat back down.

"I'll give you privacy," Ms. Duncan said, standing. "When you're done, please deliver it to my office down that hall." She took her cup. "By the way, in addition to patient records, I'm also in charge of employee paperwork. There were discrepancies in yours."

"The spelling of my last name, right?"

"Not just that. You didn't complete your W-4 form. For tax purposes, the state of Illinois needs to know if you're claiming a spouse or dependent."

Sonja met her gaze. If she kept her next words simple—and the woman didn't pry—she wouldn't have to lie. "I'm not."

Ms. Duncan's gaze lingered. "For a mere orderly, you're very well read, Ms. Helgeson. Your vocabulary is exemplary."

Sonja shrugged. "I'm just a reader."

Ms. Duncan turned in the direction of her office.

Sonja settled back and opened the "Shelley" file.

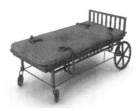

SONJA'S FINGERS TREMBLED AS SHE STARTED HER RENTAL CAR'S ENGINE. The shaking hadn't been there while she perused the patient's intake forms or psych evaluations. Nor were they present when she read the disturbing details of the police report. Had they started upon seeing the crime scene photos?

She eyed her reflection in the rearview mirror. A pale version of Sonja Pedersen stared back. She looked like her thirteen-year-old self again—the one in 1983 wearing a blood-splattered fluorescent cap that stared into the rearview from the police car's back seat.

A strong vibration buzzed against her groin. She twisted her torso enough to lift her ass so she could dig into a front pocket for the phone. She glanced at the caller ID, saw the "Bilbo" nickname, and answered with a calm that surprised her. "Hey, honey."

"Mommy, I miss you," her son said.

She knew Ollie was being fed that line from Bill, but the words sounded heartfelt. The darkness invading her thoughts was almost repelled at the sound of his little voice. Almost.

"Oh, sweetie, I—"

*I AM BUT*

"—I miss you, too!"

She closed her eyes and pinched the bridge of her nose. The grisly details of the police report flooded back to the forefront of her mind.

*He had killed an entire family in a farmhouse.*

*Killed? More like slaughtered like livestock.*

167

*A nighttime breeze pushed their cries across acres of farmland. The nearest neighbors, a quarter of a mile away, heard the screaming. Their 911 call came at three a.m. The responding deputy arrived thirteen minutes later—relatively fast considering the house's remote location. The sheriff pulled up moments later. Neither knew the family living there. As they approached the porch, they passed a minivan in the driveway. The Voyager's window had decals showing a stick family: a father, a mother, and two stick kids holding hands. This detail was noted in the report to explain, perhaps, why the body count inside was different than expected. The officers stated the front door was ajar. They drew their weapons and entered the dark house to see…*

"…to see you, Mommy."

Sonja's mouth was dry. "I want to see you, too. Daddy will bring you Sunday, okay?"

"Okay."

"Why is Daddy up so early?"

She heard Bill whispering his reply to Ollie a moment before the toddler repeated it. "Watching *Turn of the King.*"

"*Return of the…* Again? He's going to wear out that DVD." A thought occurred to her. "He's not letting *you* watch that, is he?"

"Um."

"Tell him I—"

*I AM BUT A*

"—Bill! That movie has too much violence!"

"*…Signs of violence upon entry,*" *read the police report. Furniture was overturned. Windows were shattered. There was no one in the living room. The only light came from around a corner. The sheriff identified himself. No reply. They advanced down the hall, toward flickering blue television light ahead. A skid mark of fresh blood, as wide as if applied to the tiled floor by a large paintbrush, curved around the corner…*

"Daddy covers my eyes at scary parts," Ollie said.

Sonja muttered, "I'm sure he does," and followed that with, "Ollie, I'm driving. Tell Daddy I'll call him later, okay? I love you."

"Okay, love you."

She thumbed the end button and dropped the phone. As she gripped the steering wheel to steady her hands, the gruesome images played out in her mind's eye.

A naked man stood amidst a circle of naked bodies, framed by the TV's rectangular glow. The entire Stick family—the same Caucasian people in the picture frames—had been arranged head to toe around him. Their clothing and IDs had been burned in the fireplace. Two other bodies were present as well: those of a grandmother and her caretaker, a middle-aged Hispanic woman. Six victims total. The coroner would later determine the grandmother had been strangled, but the rest had multiple pre- and postmortem stab wounds. Their murderer stood motionless, arms at his sides, splattered with gore, staring at a wall.

The sheriff ordered the suspect to the ground.

He complied. The brown-haired, brown-eyed man of medium height knelt and lowered himself to lay among the corpses of his victims, in the circle's center.

The sheriff had to step over the children to get to the man. His shoes left red imprints in the spongy, blood-infused carpeting. He holstered his weapon and cuffed the suspect. When he yanked the man upright and jerked him out of the circle, his bare foot kicked the youngest child's head, causing it to snap upward and stare at the ceiling with unseeing eyes.

The deputy vomited at this sight, contaminating that part of the crime scene.

The suspect was booked without uttering a word. He never answered a question in the interrogations. Whether or not he could speak was unknown. A meticulous search of the house turned up nothing to identify him as a family member. Making things more difficult, their last name was "Johnson." His mug shot didn't match the appearance of anyone in the prison system. When entered into the Department of Motor Vehicles database, it yielded hundreds of possible driver's license photo matches but no positive ID. The only thing known about him, after a medical exam, was he had a heart arrhythmia. The sheriff's paperwork referred to him as a John Doe, but the officers called him by another name—based on the only communication left at the crime scene. A forensic investigator had taken hundreds of pictures inside the house. A color photo included in the police file given to White Willow Asylum showed a wall adjacent to the television. On it, written in blood, in large, block letters, were the words, "I AM BUT A SHELL."

Sonja shivered from the same realization she had had after handing the folder back to Ms. Duncan in the records room. She now remembered what caused her hands to shake in the first place.

She had to come back tonight and be near that animal.

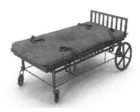

THE TEN O'CLOCK TONE SOUNDED. SCOTCH CAUGHT HIS TOSSED CANDY in his mouth. When Cordelia came over, he offered a piece. She declined. "Can't you get gummy worms?"

"Those'll rot your teeth," he said, holding out his fist. She smacked it with her own. He winced in mock pain. "Ow! That's another night in isolation, you little brat!"

Before he could reach for her arm, Sonja interjected. "I'll take her."

Scotch noticed she had been staring at The Shell since punching in, and she looked frightened. He had seen that specific flavor of dread on other coworkers' faces—usually after reading a certain file. "Go ahead. I only like patients who appreciate quality candy, anyway."

As she was escorted away, Cordelia also noticed Sonja eyeing the man sitting in darkness the same way she did. She put her hand in Sonja's, feeling her respond with a comforting grip.

When they reached the hallway with the three isolation rooms, Sonja paused at the first door. "This one, right?"

Cordelia tugged her farther down the hall and brought her to the last door. "This one tonight."

Sonja crouched on her haunches before her, knees cracking like knots in a flaming log. She brushed the girl's hair away from her face. As always, she averted her piercing blue irises. *Eye contact is tough for her, but she's going to be a stunning woman one day.* She smiled. "Why this one?"

"Because it's farther away."

"Farther away from...?"

"From *him*." She squeezed Sonja's hand with more force. "He's getting stronger. The voices are louder. They found me last night. They know where I am."

Sonja shrugged the Dubba-Yous away. "Tell me about the voices."

She shook her head. "I know better. The doctors got excited when I told them about the voices, even though they don't believe me. They connected wires to my head because they think I'm imagining things. So I don't talk about them anymore. I let the doctors believe the pills are working."

Sonja held her by the shoulders, trying to get the girl to look at her. "Tell me you're taking your meds."

"I am. But they're not helping. I still hear them." She twisted away, turning to the door. Before reaching it, she looked back, making tenuous eye contact for the first time. "Can I ask you something?"

Sonja was startled once again by the turmoil on her face. "Yes, of course."

"A-Are you a mommy?"

Sonja's jaw dropped. "Why do you ask?"

Cordelia's gaze didn't waver. "That's what the voices tell me." Then she turned and went into the dark padded room.

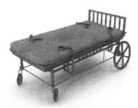

Sonja returned to the common area. The television was off. The patients had cleared out and gone to bed.

Scotch was nowhere to be seen.

The door to room number one was closed.

She moved closer. The bedroom hallway was darker than where she stood, but she could still see the other doors were all shut.

Her next thought posed an alarming possibility. *But what if The Shell's not in his room?*

She hurt her neck whipping around to look behind her and back again to scan her surroundings. Her muscles went rigid. Her heart became a calcified stone from which blood ceased to flow. The resulting fear made her question everything.

*What the fuck are you even doing here? Thinking you could just waltz into this place and expose how the patients are treated. The first thing Schick told you was, "The world is going to Hell in a handbasket." And you had to admit he's right. That's why you're here. Veterans are coming back from the so-called "war on terror," shell-shocked, struggling with PTSD, and ending up in institutions because their government doesn't care once they've served. Then your boyfriend says, "I know a creepy place outside my hometown, and I've heard stories that'll curl your hair..." So you ran the proposal by your editor and here you are. But what you didn't expect is having to deal with disembodied voices or a murderous cypher who writes in blood on fucking walls. And now your candy-addicted coworker isn't where you left him.*

She checked the break room. He wasn't playing cards. Her frantic gaze landed on the flashlight.

*You have to check the rooms—or at least check room number one to make sure the ward's only known actual murderer*

*(other than Cordelia)*

*is in his bed and not wandering around. Once you've done that, you can go find Scotch.*

It was one thing to decide on a course of action and another to execute it. The doorway was a safe haven.

*Christ, Pedersen, act like an adult. How much therapy do you have under your belt to deal with your shit? Look at yourself from the perspective of, oh, say a skinny dude like The Shell who weighs a buck-fifty soaking wet—one with a heart condition, no less. Straighten your back, push out your chest, and march over to his room knowing that if he comes at you, it would be the stupidest thing he would ever do. You could pick him up by his scrawny neck with one hand and body-slam the little prick faster than he could say, "I am but a peanut shell."*

Her interior monologue worked. She strode out of the break room, activated the flashlight, and went directly to The Shell's door. The light revealed an empty room.

*Now* she felt fear.

*Now* she felt thirteen again.

*Now* she felt the horrible memories flow back into her in an undiluted deluge—the ones it took years to acknowledge and accept; that left her psyche irrevocably damaged because of her actions that day.

*Your soul.*

*It is cracked.*

She had said words to that effect in one of her first sessions. "My soul feels fucked up and that means *I'm* fucked up." Her psychologist said he could help her find healthy ways to cope—help her find the strength to overcome dark thoughts.

So what were her strengths now?

*You're a hell of a good journalist. You work for a newspaper doing the job you always wanted. You have the love of a good man and you're raising a wonderful child. And you're a ball-busting, kickass woman who won't let anyone get in her way—especially a pipsqueak sociopath who couldn't carry a hay bale without a forklift.*

She walked out of the corridor with purpose, sweeping the light into every corner of the common room.

"Scotch!" Her voice echoed off the far wall. "Where'd you go?"

She heard a response from that direction—a short, declarative bark of a reply. She crept to the locked door that only opened at the touch of their swipe badges. Behind it were the employee bathrooms. She called him again, holding out her badge, preparing to swipe it on the pad.

"Taking a shit, for Christ's sake!" came his rankled reply through two doors.

She exhaled, shuddering in relief.

*Sonja Pedersen.*

Directly behind her. A different voice than the previous two. Her fingers curled into a fist, ready to defend herself. She spun around, planting her right foot to deliver a haymaker…

No one.

Only a deserted common room. Her eyes darted to the rest of the ward she hadn't yet cleared.

*You will be our vessel.*

This voice came from the direction from which she had just looked. Turning back, she saw nothing.

*Your world will be ours.*

Behind her again.

Her heart throbbed from surging adrenaline. "This is bullshit."

*She does not believe.*

*They never believe.*

*We make her believe.*

Three distinct voices, surrounding her, having a discussion *about* her. She swiveled her head at each sound, pinpointing exactly the locations from where they came. Her eyes strained to see something…*anything.*

*Tell her of escalating conflicts.*

*That will not persuade this one.*

*Tell her of division and discord.*

*That much is already obvious.*

*Tell her of global plague and the deaths of millions.*

*Too far from now.*

*What to do then?*

*Something immediate.*

*What of the little one?*

*She is too strong.*

*She is hiding.*

*Find her.*

The three voices ceased when Sonja spotted The Shell crouched in the isolation wing's darkened hall. He startled her enough to rouse her analytical mind and push back against the absurd notion of invisible entities. The Shell was throwing his voice. That's what was happening. The idea that he was screwing with her was infuriating.

Stepping toward him, she said, "Go to your room," sounding like a parent scolding a bad kid.

He rose slowly, not reacting with the urgency she expected.

She took another step. "Go to your room!"

He stood motionless.

Sonja squared her shoulders and charged. She covered the seventy-five feet at a brisk pace she knew *had* to look threatening. She channeled unfettered rage into her expression. *I'm going to push him through that fucking wall if he doesn't move.*

And then he *did* move, starting to walk in the right direction. One step. Two. Keeping his eyes on her.

By his fifth step, she knew she would overtake him. She barreled toward him like a freight train about to T-bone a slow car puttering across tracks.

Hurting him suddenly seemed like a great idea.

When she shoved him from behind, his head snapped back from the force and his slippered feet left the floor. He sailed forward a full six feet before hitting the linoleum with a sickening splat.

Sonja froze in place, horrified. Her hands went to her open mouth, a shocked, repentant statue.

The Shell pulled his knees under him. He looked back, expressionless, getting to his feet. He continued walking at his own pace out of the common room. His door closed.

Sonja's frenzied thoughts tormented her. *You came here to prove these patients were being mistreated. You're no better than the cruel orderlies you heard stories about. If there were cameras in here, video of you would air during an* NYPD Blue *station break with the Channel 7 announcer saying, "Allegations of abuse in a mental health facility. The shocking video at ten o'clock." And do you think anyone seeing that clip would care that this man killed six people?*

When Sonja found the will to move, she turned away. That's when a voice behind her spoke once more.

*Swerve to the right.*

She spun around, startled and curious at the unexpected sentence, but more frightened by the realization that the best ventriloquist in the world couldn't throw his voice through a solid door.

It all happened so fast.

Sonja was driving to her motel—having left a voicemail requesting Kritzer's help researching the murdered family outside Joliet—when a school bus turned onto Route 47 directly in front of her speeding Camry.

There was no time to brake.

There was nowhere to go except off the highway.

The right wheels dipped off the road at sixty miles per hour. The vehicle's left side yanked upward at a jarring angle. She fought the steering wheel, guiding it off the asphalt completely and missing the bus's rear bumper by inches. The car streaked off the gravel and into the tall grass lining the ditch. With a yellow, blurry wall on her left, Sonja registered another obstacle ahead: a telephone pole. She barely had time for a course correction before miraculously threading the needle between the shoulder and the pole. She couldn't risk hitting the next one. Yanking hard to the left was the only option. She barely had time to check for oncoming traffic and hope her transition back to the road would be a safe one. The Camry lurched as its front end pointed above the horizon and she saw sky through the windshield. The rear end fishtailed and swung wide, and when all four wheels grabbed asphalt and screeched to a stop, she was on the other side of 47 facing the way she had come.

As she stared, saucer-eyed, at the bus—its brake lights only now flaring red—four words played on a loop in her mind.

*Swerve to the right.*

Fɪғᴛᴇᴇɴ ʜᴏᴜʀs ʟᴀᴛᴇʀ, Cᴏʀᴅᴇʟɪᴀ sᴀɪᴅ ɢᴏᴏᴅɴɪɢʜᴛ ᴏᴜᴛsɪᴅᴇ ᴛʜᴇ isolation rooms. Sonja wanted to ask her more about the voices but reconsidered. The shrinks had decided she was mentally fit for release and would likely be leaving next week. The foster care system was going to bring on a slew of other issues that Sonja didn't want to compound, so she held off on her questions.

She returned to the common area to find Scotch staring at The Shell in his usual spot—but he wasn't obeying orders to go to bed.

"Come on, it's lights out," Scotch said in a louder volume than usual. "Go to your room."

The man didn't react.

"Goddammit," he whispered, frustrated. "He never does this."

She wanted to say, "You're an orderly, go maintain order. March him into his quarters." But at the same time, she understood wanting to avoid getting close to him. Had other employees lost their temper and attacked this patient the way she had?

"Go play Solitaire. I've got this."

He eyed her curiously before going to the break room.

She pulled a chair from a checkers table and spun it around to sit on it backwards, facing The Shell.

He lifted his head to acknowledge her.

She stared back, heart pounding.

They regarded each other in silent judgment.

Minutes passed.

She heard Scotch leave the break room but didn't turn. He called to her, "Taking a shit." Seconds later, the employee door behind her beeped and unlocked. Doors opened and closed as he entered the restroom. The ward fell silent again.

She steeled her nerves, exhaling slowly like she was about to *squeeze a trigger* and made the conscious decision to turn her head away from The Shell.

One of the three voices spoke in her right ear—the one facing him.

*Do you believe now?*

Unable to help it, she snapped her gaze back. He hadn't moved. She studied him for another minute before looking away again. "What do you want?"

*We want you.*

Her scalp tightened and her body shuddered. "Wh-Why?"

*We want you to kill this shell.*

"What?!"

*Your soul is not cracked enough.*

"Enough for what?"

*Enough to inhabit.*

"Inhabit?! Wha—? I'm not killing anyone!"

*Anyone* else, *you mean?*

She turned back but kept her eyes on the floor between her feet. "Shut up!"

*She resists.*

*She still needs persuasion.*

"Stop talking about me like I'm not here!"

The voices paused before continuing.

*It will be this one or the girl.*

*Youth is preferable.*

*The girl then.*

A shriek came from the isolation rooms.

Cordelia.

Sonja scrambled to her feet, overturning the chair in her haste.

Between the screaming, the clattering chair, and the pounding of Sonja's running, Scotch could be heard cursing.

She sprinted to the isolation wing. She yanked the last door's handle and, for a second, paused outside the open room. Her urge to protect the girl stalled at an impossible sight.

The ten-year-old was suspended in mid-air at eye level, writhing and kicking, her body closer to ceiling than ground. She grunted in tandem with each straining spasm of effort. Her voice alternated between her own and a different, deeper one. Urine dribbled in a stream from her pajama bottoms. Then she dropped without warning, as if invisible wires had been severed from above. Her body hit the padded floor with a *fwump*. What should have knocked the wind from her lungs did the opposite: she drew breath with a throaty, growling, *"Uuuuuurrrrrr."* It sounded unlike anything that could come from a girl's vocal cords—midway between man and beast. For an intake of breath, it lasted longer than it should. Cordelia's pajama top tightened as her chest swelled. She sprang into an abrupt sitting position. Through the hair hanging over her contorted face, her eyeballs had turned a glossy ebony.

Sonja's abject fear at this spectacle was erased by one simple motion: whatever controlled the girl couldn't stop her from raising a trembling hand and reaching out for help.

She dashed forward, remembering the time she rescued her miniature Schnauzer from a coyote's jaws. Her instinct to protect her pet overrode the warning to never get between two fighting animals, because that situation—like this—wasn't close to a fair fight. Except this time there was nothing for her to kick. No mangy coyote neck to crack in a blind rage like she did back then. All she could do was kneel next to the girl, take her hand, and hold her tight.

*"Our numbers grow on this mortal plane,"* said the voice coming from Cordelia's lips. *"Our influence spreads outward from each shell. Terror has taken root. Fear supplants hope. Constant, unending attrition of the soul will provoke division. Chaos will reign. A dark future is foretold. Before this day ends, a leader will die. The escalation will contin—"*

The inhuman voice was interrupted by a sudden, cleansing scream bursting from Cordelia's lungs. She struggled anew in Sonja's grip. Her feet scrabbled and squeaked against the urine-soaked vinyl floor. When her spasms subsided and she opened her eyes, they were blue again—albeit more haunted than ever. She sobbed into Sonja's chest.

This was how Scotch found them. "What the hell's going on in here?!" He stood tucking his shirt into his pants, looking confused by what he saw. "Oh, goddammit, did she piss—"

Sonja silenced him with an angry glare. "I'll get her cleaned up in the therapy room. Bring me clean pajamas."

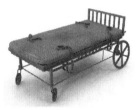

SHE POURED WATER OVER CORDELIA'S BACK.

Other than asking if the bath she had drawn felt warm enough, they hadn't spoken. The girl had merely nodded, peeled off her soiled pajamas, and stepped into the metal tub. She sat hunched forward, holding her knees. Her gaze remained dazed as Sonja cleaned her with a soapy hand towel. She had yellowed bruises on her arms and back, fading evidence of physical abuse her body was erasing. But the girl's mind, Sonja understood, was going to have a harder time correcting its own trauma.

"Is this happening because of what I did to my parents?"

Sonja wasn't sure how to answer. She knew it should be, "No," but wasn't prepared to address follow-up questions. Her experience indicated that the human mind protects itself. *You don't want to deal with this memory? Fine. Lock it behind this door and brick it up behind a wall.* Except Cordelia was dredging up something she hadn't yet shoved into a mental vault. And while Sonja could relate better than most, she wasn't a psychologist.

"I did it because they were hurting Corey. He's my twin, but I came first. That makes me older. He was never as strong as me. So I protected him. Now *they* want me. Except it's Corey's turn to be *my* protector. He won't let them take me to Hell."

Sonja had no response.

"Do you believe me?"

She brushed hair from Cordelia's eyes. "If you say your brother is protecting you, I'll accept that. But I don't believe in Hell. What I *do* believe is if we *think* we did something wrong, we torture ourselves for it. Over and over. That's a kind of hell."

She held out a towel to wrap around the girl as she stepped out of the tub.

When Cordelia saw the CatDog pajamas Scotch had brought from her room, she smiled. "Corey will be happy to be back in his own pee-jays."

Sonja grimaced. *She has such a tough road ahead.*

Once dressed, Cordelia glanced up at her. "*They're* going to come back again. What's going to happen to me?"

It was now Saturday, Sonja's day off. She needed to put a dent in her story and get some pages written. But after everything she had experienced, how could she leave this girl to face it alone?

*You can't.*

She knelt before her. "Listen, I'm off today, but how's this: I'll come back tonight, before lights out, and we'll have a sleepover in the isolation room. How does that sound?"

Cordelia threw her arms around Sonja and squeezed tight.

Sonja held her for as long as she wanted. The hug was so fierce and went on so long, she wondered if the girl had ever been held before.

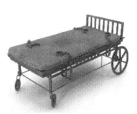

THAT NIGHT, SONJA'S CAR SCREECHED INTO THE WHITE WILLOW parking lot.

She scrambled out of the Camry in the clothes she'd worn all day: a blue U of I shirt, sweatpants, and running shoes. She slammed the door, started to run across the lot, then scrambled back to the vehicle. She had forgotten her badge. She clipped it to the drawstring of her sweats and rushed toward the building.

Her frantic state had been brought on when she came out of her writing trance twenty minutes ago. She had spent half the day furiously tapping away at the keyboard, working on her article, and stopping only for bathroom breaks and a pizza delivery. After saving her progress to disk, she turned on CNN. They were reporting breaking news that former president Ronald Reagan had died that afternoon.

She remembered the voice coming out of Cordelia saying, "*Before this day ends, a leader will die.*" At the time, she hadn't processed the ramblings. Replaying them afterward, she thought, *GWB wouldn't be a huge loss*, and mused, *Even better: how about the Vice President*? But despite her *swerve-into-the-ditch* warning, she still dismissed any acceptance that the

*demons?*

were spouting Nostradamus-like predictions that could happen.

*But now Reagan's dead…and didn't they also say millions would die from a coming plague?!*

This elevated the situation to the next level.

Plans needed to be made, starting with protecting Cordelia.

Sonja swiped her badge and ran into Scotch exiting the men's room.

"The hell you doing here?"

She ignored him and went out to the common area, scanning for the girl among the others. She spotted her curled in a blanket, in a chair far away from The Shell.

He sat in his usual place, seeing Sonja at the same time. He stared as if taking a moment to recognize her out of her orderly uniform. Then he glanced over at the old man with the white hair.

Ralph stood and began to totter toward Sonja.

She headed toward Cordelia.

Ralph intercepted her and reached up to touch her loose hair, which she hadn't tied back. She pushed him away, feeling his other hand grope against her hip, as if reaching for her rear end. Again, she deflected his attempts and got past him.

She stood before Cordelia. "Do you want to go to sleep early?"

The girl gathered her blanket, nodding.

They walked across the ward together. Approaching Scotch, she explained her intention to stay with Cordelia and have a "sleep-over." He said, "Well, I can't make any S'mores for your party. These will have to do," and offered them both a candy. They declined and adjourned to the second isolation room.

Once the door closed, Sonja remarked it was "darker than the inside of a black paint can at midnight." This made Cordelia giggle. They laid on the padded floor. Sonja offered her meaty arm as a pillow. The girl snuggled up close.

The minutes passed. Just when Sonja thought Cordelia's breathing had steadied to the point of sleep, the girl whispered, "Can I ask you a question?"

"Sure, sweetie."

"Promise to not get mad?"

"I promise."

"Why did you kill your dad?"

No one had ever asked this.

There were variations to that question throughout her life. Many of them. But they were of the *What happened?* variety. The police used that one. So did the social workers. Her mother went with *How did it happen?* Even her shrink didn't ask. With him it was *Tell me about that day.* But no one had ever flat-out framed it like she had definitely done it. Only Sonja had ever dared ask that question of herself, again and again from the age of thirteen and every day since.

If there was a Hell, that unanswered question was hers.

Cordelia sensed the mood had changed. She turned her head to check her reaction, but it was too dark. "I'm asking because *they* told me you did it."

Dark memories darkened the room further.

*Her father gave her the rifle because the first time he took her hunting at twelve, she was a natural marksman. When a buck entered the clearing, he put his heavy .270 in her hands. He explained where to aim on its chest —an area he called "the boiler room." He told her how to exhale before the shot and gently squeeze the trigger. Except it didn't budge. The safety was on. "To prevent accidents," he whispered and showed where to switch it off. She braced the rifle's butt against her shoulder, sighted the animal, squeezed the trigger, and her body was rocked at the discharge. The animal went down. An optimal shot on her first try. Her father was so thrilled he gave her a Browning of her own for her thirteenth birthday. The wait for the next hunting season felt like years rather than months.*

*On the first day, she blew her father's brains out.*

*The brief seconds in which it happened were forever lost to the recesses of her mind. Not bricked over…gone. During therapy, following her psychologist's attempts to help recover those memories, she came to the conclusion that that scene was edited out—excised like a botched repair on an 8mm home movie. She only knew she was facing her father one moment —tugging the trigger to confirm the safety was on—and staring down at his ruined, bloody face the next. She hadn't even remembered why the barrel would've been pointed at him. Was it a sudden impulse that most sane people effortlessly shut down? The one that whispers, What if…? And if that was the case, what did it say about her that she didn't ignore the impulse?*

*The police who arrived on the scene, summoned by her mother when they hadn't returned by late afternoon, found Sonja curled into a ball next to her father's corpse. They never once suggested that Oleg Pedersen's death could be anything other than an accident. In the back of the cruiser, when she surfaced from her fugue state, that's the word the deputy used radioing back to the station. This was nothing more than "a hunting acci-dent." She latched onto it like the lifeline it was.*

"Did you kill him because he was hurting you?" Cordelia asked.

At this, she almost said, "No," which was the truth as she remembered it. But to say that would provoke more questions. So she went with, "I don't think so," which was the other truth with which she had learned to live. For all she knew, there were more memories her subconscious had paved over, ones the psychologist hadn't recovered. She repeated, "I don't think so."

This discussion wouldn't lead to a good night's sleep for either of them. She ended it as best she could—by throwing a lifeline like the one she'd caught from the deputy.

"You did what you did for a reason, Cordelia. From what I know, it was a *good* reason. It might not seem like it now, having to explain your actions to cops and doctors. And being in here isn't fun. But at least *you* know why you did it. I envy that. Because I'll never have that knowledge. Do you understand?"

Cordelia nodded and sniffled.

Sonja felt a tear run down her arm where the girl's face rested on it. She stroked her hair. "Get some sleep. Think about happy times with Corey. You were a good sister to him."

She nodded again. "I still am. And now I know something else."

"What's that, sweetie?"

"You're a good mommy."

Sonja's heart swelled. She kissed the top of her head.

They slept.

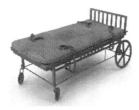

"*Get up!*" Scotch shined the flashlight in their faces.

Sonja squinted into the light. She had slept like a hibernating bear. No disembodied voices, no nightmares, no demonic possessions.

Cordelia pulled the blanket over her face, wanting to sleep longer.

Scotch undimmed the room lights. They revealed his pale, panicked face. "*Come on!*"

*Wait a minute, why is the hallway so bright? What time is it?!*

She clambered to her feet, stepped over Cordelia, and hurried out of the room.

Scotch shut the door behind her. "The Shell. He's gone!"

"Oh my god! Did you check—"

"We checked *everywhere*! Searched the whole ward! We're gonna get shitcanned for sure!"

"How did he escape?!"

"Do I look like I know?! Look, you need to get the hell out of here! Before I notify anyone. They can't know I did anything out of the ordinary—including letting an off-duty orderly sleep with a patient!" He escorted her to the back room, swiping them through. "Christ, I've got to use the can! My irresistable bowel syndrome is fucking with me. I'm giving you five minutes before I call the main building."

Sonja hurried out the exit into sunlight. A thought occurred to her. She felt her pockets, finding only her keys. Then she fingered the ends of her drawstrings and realized what had happened. She sprinted for the parking lot.

She didn't notice her swipe badge in the dewy morning grass.

DRIVING NORTH ON 47, THE REALITY OF THE SITUATION HIT HOME. Full-blown panic surged through her. She could hear her heartbeat in her ears. She had caused this. A sociopath was on the loose because of her.

*Kritzer will know what to do.*

She pressed speed dial two. The call connected. It rang over and over. After thirty seconds it went to voicemail. She stabbed the red button with her thumb and dropped the phone. She pounded the steering wheel.

*This is bad this is bad...*

Ten minutes later, she turned the car into the motel's empty lot and swung into a spot. She yanked the keys out of the ignition and heaved herself out of the car. She bolted for her room across the lot. Locating the room key, she reached for the door, and...

It was halfway open.

Her heart thumped harder. Her skin went bumpy and cold. The Dubba-Yous were here.

She knew who was inside.

She didn't know he wasn't alone.

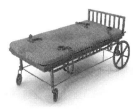

Sᴏɴᴊᴀ sᴛᴏᴏᴅ ɪɴ ᴛʜᴇ ᴅᴏᴏʀᴡᴀʏ. Tʜᴇ ᴄᴏᴘᴘᴇʀʏ sᴛᴇɴᴄʜ ᴏꜰ ʙʟᴏᴏᴅ assaulted her nostrils while she tried to make sense of the horror inside.

The bed had been propped on its side against a wall. The Shell, crouching nude in the middle of the open room, was covered with blood. He was arranging the stabbed, mutilated body of a naked man at his feet. Behind him was a child's corpse. The Shell glanced at Sonja, his face displaying no reaction at what he had done.

White-hot denial subsumed her initial shock. Upon seeing a carryout bag from a nearby cafe on the dresser, the denial vanished like vapor as her mind offered a narrative.

Bill and Ollie had come early to surprise her with breakfast.

The Shell had known they were coming.

He had waited for them all night.

And murdered them both.

She bypassed guilt and welcomed a blinding, familiar rage. It surged through her. The growl building in her chest manifested as an animal roar. She lunged forward, reaching for him. He laid down at her son's stiff feet to complete the circle of bodies. His submissiveness made her angrier. Screaming through gritted teeth, she seized his throat in both hands. It took a fraction of her strength to cut off his air. It took more to feel his trachea crunch. Her fingers kept tightening, forearm muscles becoming steel cords. She gave it her all, keeping her eyes on his, knowing the voices couldn't come if she maintained eye contact.

She was right.

Until his neck snapped.

And her soul further fragmented.

Ancient darkness rushed in to fill the void.

When the voices came, she was no longer there to hear them.

CORDELIA SAT IN THE LOBBY.

A young priest sat beside her. Between sips of tea, he assured her she would make friends at the orphanage. She wanted to believe him. He seemed friendly and had an earnest expression. He'd even taken the time to demonstrate how to fold her clothes and pack her suitcase.

Across the lobby at registration, Ms. Duncan was showing the social worker, who arrived with the priest, where to sign the transfer paperwork. The old woman saw the girl watching and flashed a grin. It didn't touch her eyes. Then those eyes saw something outside and the grin went away.

Cordelia turned at the sound of car doors.

Through the window, she saw two Kendall County police officers by their cruiser at the curb. One of them opened the rear door. He hauled Sonja out of the vehicle.

She was dressed in orange scrubs two sizes too small, her bosom and hips stretching the fabric at the seams. Her wrists were fastened with zip ties. Her ankles were connected by chains only wide enough for her to take half-steps. Her hair was limp and as lifeless as her eyes. She seemed unaware of her surroundings.

Cordelia rose to her feet, excited to see her again.

After the sleepover, all she knew was the scary man called The Shell had escaped. The next day, she had lurked outside the break room as the ward supervisor, Clarke, revealed what he'd learned from friends in local law enforcement: Sonja had strangled The Shell after he murdered two people—presumably a father and son. Their identities were a mystery, as was Sonja Helgason herself. There was no record of any woman with her name, spelled either way, living anywhere in this part of Illinois. As far as anyone knew, she had no dependents. The motel room where the murders occurred was registered to someone named Kritzer—as were her phone and car. The closest Kritzer they could find was someone in Chicago who had died in a freak hit-and-run over the weekend. That particular investigation was ongoing. Detectives found a laptop snapped in half, its hard drive destroyed. They also recovered shriveled lumps of burned plastic in the motel sink, including the remains of credit cards, driver's licenses, and a floppy disk. *How* the items were burned was yet another mystery, since investigators failed to find matches anywhere on the premises. They surmised she must have flushed a lighter down the toilet for some reason—because it didn't seem likely she had summoned fire from her own hands. Fingerprints of everyone involved revealed no criminal records. The murdered man and boy could not be readily identified. Matching the footprint of the child with hospital birth records would take time. DNA testing would follow. Clarke also said Sonja was found standing among the victims' bodies. "And you'll never believe what she'd written on the wall with their blood." That's when he peeked outside the room to check for eavesdroppers. He paled upon seeing Cordelia standing there and chased her away. That was two days ago.

Now she watched as the police escorted their prisoner into the White Willow lobby.

Lyman Schick, Jr. emerged from his office, flanked by two orderlies. He greeted the officers by first names and asked how their sheriff was doing. He told them to send his regards.

One of them handed Ms. Duncan a manila folder. The other officer bent to unlock Sonja's shackles. He instructed the orderlies to grab her arms before snipping the ties from her wrists. "All yours."

Ms. Duncan noticed the folder's blank tab. "What is her name? It seems she gave us an alias."

The officer shrugged. "I'm sure you'll think of something. Any idea who she was?"

Schick answered with a distasteful tone. "Rumors suggest a lying, goddamned journalist."

"Oh yeah?" the officer said. "Rumors from who?"

"A little bird told us," Schick replied.

"Three of them, actually," Ms. Duncan said, grinning that false grin that didn't touch her eyes. "Ones who would know."

The social worker and the priest appeared shaken. The latter picked up Cordelia's suitcase. "Are you ready to go?"

She waited for Sonja to look at her.

The large woman only stared at her feet.

Cordelia began to weep. She followed the social worker to the door, keeping her teary gaze on Sonja.

The priest placed a protective hand on the girl's shoulder and guided her away, giving them a wide berth.

Only when she turned away did she hear familiar voices.

They spoke from behind and on each side, where no one stood.

None of the three sounded remotely human.

*Your world is ours.*

*There is nowhere to hide.*

*We will find you, Cordelia.*

Tears streamed from her haunted eyes as she left White Willow Asylum.

# LAB RATS

## JILL GIRARDI

Regina Silvester tiptoed around the lab, turning out all the lights except for the heavy steel lamp on her desk. She wanted the other graduate students to think she'd gone home, wanted to avoid their subtle insults disguised as concern. Even now, she imagined them lurking in the corridor, their ears pressed to the double doors far to her right, laughing at her, judging her.

*You're obsessed with your research, so much so that you've stopped taking care of yourself. You're secretive, skittish—starting to behave like the rodents you study.*

The same thing had happened a week ago with Brenda, her ex-roommate. Regina remembered the harsh words they'd exchanged the final time they'd spoken. In her disjointed reverie, Brenda's voice melded with her colleagues in a repetitious sermon of mockery.

*Reggi, are you ok? Have you showered today? When's the last time you brushed your teeth? Do you need someone to talk to? Do you need help? What's wrong? What's wrong?!*

She could hear her colleagues through the lab's open window as they left campus, bidding goodnight to each other and the scientists they assisted. Regina had the small Rodent Department almost all to herself. Her meager grant wasn't enough to support another PhD candidate—and while the mice and guinea pigs received moderate

191

attention, no other students elected to work with the rats. Her boss, having doubts about the viability of her research, left her alone for the most part. Of the four animal laboratories in the Beris University Science Department, only the primates received sufficient funding. Wealthy benefactors always loved the spry, mischievous spider monkeys and affectionate chimps, donating generous amounts of money toward their study. Nobody loved the rats.

Except for Regina.

At the far end of the room, cloaked in darkness, three dozen cages housed almost three hundred *Rattus norvegicus,* better known as the common laboratory rat. She'd started feeding them a special diet she'd created for them. Her thesis was a study of the connection between the intelligence of *Rattus norvegicus* and the nutritional content of the food it consumed, but she'd fed the rats the last of her hard-to-find food supply yesterday. The budding scientist lived in a state of agitation, worrying over this snag in what she considered her life's work. No longer satisfied with the standard freeze-dried pellets, the hungry animals rooted through their straw bedding in search of other food. A wave of guilt washed over Regina as she listened to the restless beasts.

She closed the window and pulled down the blinds, then sat on the rolling chair in front of her desk. While waiting for her laptop to start, she scratched a three-inch sore on her right arm, the result of a nasty bite she'd gotten from one of the rats three weeks ago. Within an hour of the bite, she'd come down with a raging fever, chills, and a full-body rash.

Regina self-diagnosed it as the bacterial infection *Streptobacillus moniliformis,* otherwise known as Rat Bite Fever. She treated it with hospital-sized doses of penicillin pilfered from the primate lab, but the sore wasn't healing, and the accompanying fever came and went as it pleased. She could go for days without feeling ill only for her body temperature to soar when she least expected it. Even now, her skin felt hot to the touch, though she wasn't sure if the flush came from the lingering illness or her always-taut nerves.

"Anxiety is nothing more than the amygdala alerting my brain to danger," she said aloud. "Even now, the prefrontal cortex is activating itself to assist me in rationalizing my response."

She laughed to herself. "Better stop talking like that, Reggi, or you'll never get another date. Your last Tinder hookup sure didn't go well!"

As if in answer, a high-pitched squeak sounded behind her. Startled, Regina whipped around and saw an enormous brown rat sitting upright on one of the surgical tables a few feet away. The rodent was round and fat, its beady eyes glittering like tiny rubies in the light cast from the laptop.

"Toolie! How did you get out of your cage again?" Regina stood and approached the rat. She picked it up, stroking its head as she carried it back to its cage. The creature nuzzled her hands, hunting for a treat. It looked up at her and squeaked.

"I know you're hungry. Be patient a while longer. I promise I'll find you something good to eat." She placed the rat inside the open cage. It ran to a corner and burrowed under the straw, with only its snout and winking red eyes visible. Regina locked the door and returned to her laptop.

She reached into the pocket of her ankle-length tweed skirt and pulled out a small pen drive. This she inserted into one of the USB slots on her laptop, then clicked on an encrypted interface icon and entered her password. *RATS101.* The drive contained her precious research from the past two years, the study that was going to make or break her education and future career.

Her research meant everything to her. She'd struggled to find the link that would elevate her study from an often-replicated student project to one that would have serious implications in the scientific world. She'd almost lost hope until the night she'd gotten the rat bite. Up until that moment, she'd tried various diets to prove her theory that what the rats consumed affected their intelligence but had failed every time. Then, on one harrowing night when she was near delirium with fever, she stumbled upon a breakthrough that would change modern life forever.

After entering her daily notes in her digital journal, Regina clicked on an application titled PRE-RECORDED FEED. She waited for the laptop to connect to the external camera she'd rigged in a hidden cave, deep in the forest preserve surrounding the university. The footage was too dark to see anything at first. Regina waited a long moment before a small, black shape sped past the camera, initializing the battery-operated motion sensor and infrared light she'd installed. She took a deep breath, feeling a rush of adrenaline as the picture quality grew clearer.

A large, oblong object lay prone in a hollow on the floor of a cave. Something, or *things* rather, were gathering, wriggling, squirming, searching in the dimness. A mass of small, dark creatures swarmed over the mound. Regina's breath came fast and hard. Her face flushed, her body pulsing with a heat she had rarely experienced in her twenty-eight years. She ran a tentative hand over her breast and sighed.

So engrossed was she in the stream, Regina didn't hear the resounding knock at the door until it was too late. At any other time, her heightened senses would signal the impending danger, but for once, her brain hadn't registered the sound of someone entering the lab and closing the doors behind them. She saw her boss in her peripheral vision only when she was two feet from the computer desk.

Regina jumped to her feet, clicking on the screensaver to conceal what was on the laptop screen. She pulled the sleeve of her sweater over the sore on her arm.

"Doctor Dersauger! I didn't hear you come in."

The scientist stepped a few inches forward, switching on an overhead light as she advanced. Her other hand clutched a clipboard with a thick stack of papers attached.

"Miss Silvester. Everyone has gone home for the night, but I'm glad you're still here. I need to speak with you about some important matters."

Reggi backed against the table, edging herself in front of the laptop to protect it from her boss's prying eyes. She had the strangest feeling the doctor could see through her body, straight through the screensaver, and view the damning recording. Beads of sweat stood on her flushed face as she brushed a lock of hair from her eyes.

"Can't it wait until tomorrow, Doctor? I've been working all day and I'm—I'm so tired. I can't shake this fever." She swayed as she put a hand to her forehead, feeling as though she'd pass out at any moment.

Elizabeth Dersauger ignored her, brushing imaginary dust off her sleek, custom-tailored lab coat.

"Dean Gremmons conducted his annual inspections three weeks ago, as you know. We received his full report this morning."

Reggi nodded. Due to her illness, she'd missed the unpleasant inspections, though she experienced a tremendous amount of distress at the interruption of her work. Unable to see to the feeding of her rats as she treated herself, two reluctant lab assistants from the Primate Division provided them with their standard diet. At least, they'd fed the animals she kept in the lab. The other animals, well, she wouldn't think about that right now, not with Dersauger in shot of her thoughts.

"What did the report say, Doctor?"

"The assessments of the labs have all checked out. All except for one, Miss Silvester. *Yours.*"

She didn't wait for Reggi to respond. "It seems there's a discrepancy between the number of rats we ordered at the start of the year and the number in the cages now. A very large discrepancy."

With almost superhuman effort, Regina stopped herself from shaking, from blurting out the truth and sealing her doom. How should she answer? She had to take care in what she said; a slip of the tongue would give her away.

"I'm sorry, Doctor. I don't understand."

Dersauger consulted the pages on her clipboard. "We ordered six hundred *Rattus norvegicus* before the fall semester started. Now, mid-way, we are missing over three hundred animals."

*Three-hundred-nineteen, to be exact,* thought Regina. Then, "I wasn't aware of any missing rats."

"Let's take a look at the stock." Reggi cringed at the insensitive terminology. These rats weren't *stock*. They were living, breathing creatures—her friends. The doctor strode to the other end of the lab, toward the cages, switching on more lights as she went. Regina followed with reluctance, blinking her eyes in the sudden flood of light. Dersauger peered into the cages one by one, as if she could find over three hundred rats hiding under the straw. Distraught, Regina looked down the line of cages to the last one. Toolie's cage. The door was once again wide open. And Toolie was no longer in the cage.

The boss moved closer to the final enclosure. In a panic, Regina's eyes shot around the room, searching for the rat's hiding place. Although there weren't many areas in the lab where a rodent of that size could conceal itself, Toolie was the most intelligent animal in the Rodent Division. If any of the rats could find a secret space in such a sparse environment, she could. At any moment, the Doctor would look over at the cage and find it devoid of its prize occupant.

Regina was considering a mad dash toward the cage, or even out of the lab, when she felt a rustle at the hem of her skirt. She looked down to see Toolie's small head peering out from the folds, her beady eyes glistening with delight, one forefoot over her mouth as if stifling a giggle. In one motion, Regina swept the rat into her arms and jumped ahead of Dersauger, pretending to pull her out of the cage as the Doctor reached them.

"Look, here's Toolie, the star of the Rodent Division!" Reggi cried, realizing how foolish she sounded. She loosened her grip on the rat's body, allowing her to scramble up her arm and sit on her shoulder. Dersauger wasn't impressed.

"Miss Silvester, how many times have I warned you? You must secure the animals at all times. Training them to sit on your shoulder primes them for escape. We cannot have rodents running loose all over the university!"

"Oh, Toolie would never run away. She's much too clever for that." She didn't dare mention the rat's ability to unlock the cage by herself.

"Put it back, Miss Silvester." Dersauger waited. "Now."

Regina lowered her shoulder toward the open door.

"Kill the bitch!" Toolie squeaked, before scurrying down her arm into a corner of the cage, where she stood on her hind legs, rubbing her paws together and looking for all the world like a common rat instead of the crafty beast she was. The doctor didn't appear to have heard her speak, though she now turned and looked her junior square in the eye.

"I want the missing rats accounted for. I don't care if you killed them, sold them, *or ate them*. I want the full explanation."

"I-I don't know how to do that, Doctor," Reggi stammered, feigning ignorance. "All the rats you see here are the ones I've been working with all semester. If you check my logs since September, you'll see for yourself there were never six hundred rats to begin with. Perhaps…we never got the full order."

She could see her boss hesitating, weighing the possibility of an undetected clerical error. After all, the Rodent Division often went unmonitored. Dersauger nodded, seeming appeased for the moment.

"Have those logs on my desk in the morning."

Regina smiled to herself. She'd already altered the books when she'd begun moving the rats out of the lab. She kept them locked in the drawer of her desk, but she didn't want to get them now, didn't want to risk Dersauger getting too close to her laptop. She hoped no one would find out about the camera equipment she'd taken from the media room.

"I don't know why we need to keep Rodentia at all," Dersauger went on. "We're hardly allowed to do anything with them anymore. Not with those damned Anti-Vivisection people protesting all the time. We can't even do a proper experiment." She sighed, throwing a pointed look at Regina. "We're running up a tremendous food and storage bill, based on the singular research of a lone student. Will your operation ever bear fruit?"

"Yes, Doctor. The rats are showing signs of increased intelligence based on the intuitive diet I created for them. Toolie herself is—"

"Enough!" Dersauger interrupted. "I've heard it all before. This experiment is a waste of the university's resources. If not for the fact that we need to make use of these animals to maintain our grant status, I'd cut your funding in an instant and funnel it toward something useful. The Vacanti Earmouse Experiment—now that was worth every penny spent."

"Yes…I suppose growing a human ear on the back of a mouse did wonders for genetic research, but my theory could—"

Dersauger silenced her subordinate with a wave of her hand. "You've been working on this futile project for two years already.

You have until the end of the week to show me some viable results. If not, I'm afraid we're going to have to replace you."

"You can't do that!" Regina cried. Life wouldn't be worth living without her research.

From behind her, Reggi heard Toolie's shrill voice, and knew she'd escaped her cage yet again.

*"Kill her!"*

The other rats banged against their cages, joining Toolie in a screeching cacophony that filled the room with a demonic pulse, sounding like the siren of a five-alarm fire, their tiny paws rattling the bars of their cages and adding to the unholy din. The sound was deafening to Reggi, but Dersauger seemed unaffected by the noise.

*"Kill her! Kill her!"*

"Yes," the doctor continued, nodding to herself. "That's my decision. I suppose we'll have to euthanize these rats as well…"

"You bitch!" Regina shouted over the clamor, mimicking Toolie's words. *"I could murder you!"*

The rats went silent.

"Miss Silvester!" Dersauger appeared shocked, flustered by Regina's outburst. "I won't stand for this insubordination. If you don't adjust your attitude, I'll find someone else to replace you immediately."

Regina dropped her head, chastened. "I—I'm sorry, Doctor. I don't know what came over me. Forgive me. I haven't been feeling well."

"I can see that. It's clear from the deterioration of your appearance, your odd behavior, and the questionable plausibility of your research. This may be a small university, but we will not have any of our staff besmirch our image. Am I understood?"

"Yes, Doctor."

"Good." The boss looked around, as if she wanted to say something more. Nervous as a rodent, Regina moved and bumped against the desk, which shook the wireless mouse and toggled off the screensaver. The doctor peered into the video stream, shock and disgust oozing all over her face.

Together, the two women watched hundreds of rats feeding on the remains of Regina's bad Tinder date.

"What the—" Dersauger cried out. Then the solid steel desk lamp crashed into her skull.

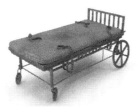

"A H, GOOD, YOU'RE WAKING UP," R EGINA SAID WHEN D ERSAUGER'S eyelids fluttered. The doctor lay supine in the darkness, with her mouth, hands, and feet bound by silver duct tape. Her skull pulsed with searing pain. She moved her fingertips over the cold, damp stone and knew she was in the same cave she'd seen on the video, no doubt deep inside the forest preserve surrounding the campus. A musty odor of musk and animal waste hung in the air, mixed with the putrid stench of decomposition.

With a snap and pop, the area brightened. Regina had moved in front of some kind of motion-activated light, powered by a car battery. Dersauger turned her head and found herself face to face with a grinning skull, so close she could have stretched out her neck and kissed it. She stifled a scream, her eyes traveling down the length of a full skeleton with bits of cartilage and skin still clinging to the bones. Something had chewed through the duct tape imprisoning the body, releasing a skeletal hand that now extended as if pointing toward the entrance of the cave. Toward escape.

With mounting terror, the doctor stared at the skeleton's ribcage. Six pairs of beady red eyes gleamed in the light of the motion sensor. Rats had built a nest of twigs and dried leaves inside the chest cavity. Whiskers twitching, they peered at her from a cage of desiccated rib bones.

Dersauger would have passed out again, but Regina reached down and slapped her on both cheeks.

"Now, Doctor, we can't have you falling asleep. You might say Toolie and I need you to be a...*captive audience*." The grad student let out a mirthless laugh and turned to look behind her. Toolie scampered up onto her shoulder and sat holding her tail in her little paws, peering down at Dersauger.

"Did you know there are no laws against the abuse of rats, though they make up eighty percent of the animals used for laboratory research? We kill over one hundred million mice and rats in the name of research every year. *Every year*, Doctor."

"It's a pity we can't experiment on humans," said Toolie.

"All that's about to change thanks to my—our—research."

One by one, Regina picked up objects, showing them to her prisoner and putting them down again—a hypodermic needle, a small tank of $CO_2$ with a tube and mask, a handsaw, a fire axe, and several other forensic instruments.

The doctor thrashed about, eyes bulging in horror, moaning through the duct tape covering her mouth.

"Hmmmmmmm!"

"What's that, Doctor? We can't hear you. Toolie, hand me the needle."

The rat scrambled to the ground, grabbed the needle in her paws, and brought it over to Regina, who continued in spite of her boss's horrified grunts.

"As you know, there are several common methods to euthanize lab rats. The easiest and fastest by far is an injection of barbiturates, though there is some debate on the amount of pain the animals experience before death."

"Hmmm! Hmmm! Hmmm!"

"Oh, don't worry, Doc. We're not going to use this on you. It's not a high enough dose to kill a human. While it results in a swift death for a rat, it'd only knock you out. We need your flesh for a higher purpose. We don't want to poison your meat, make you unfit for consumption."

"Toolie," Regina said, "we should use something else for anesthesia. What about $CO_2$?"

She put down the needle and sifted through the other objects, her hand now coming to rest on the tank. She picked up the mask with one hand and with the other ripped the duct tape off Dersauger's mouth.

"Help! Help me! Someone is trying to kill me!"

"Scream all you want, Doctor. We're deep in the forest. Did you know my father used to work here at the university? No, you didn't know, because I went by a different name back then. He went missing when I was a kid, and nobody ever found him."

"Help! Help!"

The graduate student continued to ignore her boss, now lost in the reminiscence of days long past. "My father loved exploring these woods. He took me camping here a few times—the grounds weren't off-limits back then, as they are now."

"We stayed here an entire weekend one summer. That's when we found this series of hidden caves—" She stopped, shaking her head as to rid herself of some unpleasant memory. "We almost missed this one. You have to crawl to get into it. I had a devil of a time trying to drag you through the entrance, Doctor, but it opens into a cavern once you're through. Anyway, Daddy put me in here and—and—he went away for the longest time. I don't remember why he left me alone, but he did. And the rats—they terrified me. At first, they inched toward me, timid and skittish. I was only a little girl, too petrified to scream. After a while, they grew bolder. They began coming closer. I could feel their whiskers on the backs of my hands, brushing against my cheek. Then they surged on me, *taking little bites of me!*"

Reggi began to scream, slapping at her face and body like a madwoman. "Aaaaah! Get them off me! Get them OFF ME! Daddy! Daddy, please, help me!"

Dersauger cried out, "Regina! Get control of yourself. You're safe now. The rats can't hurt you anymore!"

The girl quieted, then looked down at her boss, her eyes glazed over. A look of confusion came over her face, as if she were wondering how the doctor came to be in the cave with her.

"You're safe now, Miss Silvester…Reggi."

After a while, Regina's face cleared, her breathing returning to normal. "Yes. Yes, I'm safe now. Daddy came back at the last minute and saved me. The rats were ravenous by then, and they attacked him, too. He didn't make it. He's over there—" She pointed to a dark corner in the recesses of the cavern, then went on. "I escaped while they swarmed on him."

"And now you work with the same animals that attacked you and killed your father?"

"Oh, it wasn't easy. It took years of intensive psychotherapy at Clarks Summit State Hospital and buckets of Risperidone before I became an animal lover. But I didn't put *that* on my admissions form. Now, I'm in danger again. *Because of you!*"

"No, I—I won't tell anyone, Reggi. I won't fire you and I won't hurt the rats. I promise. Please let me go."

"I can't do that, Doctor," Regina said, and affixed the $CO_2$ mask over Dersauger's face, lifting her head to place the elastic strap around it. The woman began to thrash again, but with a twist of a knob on the canister, she was soon unconscious.

Regina picked up the heavy fire axe, testing its weight in her hands. "Cervical dislocation is the fastest and most painless way to euthanize a lab rat, but I'm afraid I don't have much training in surgical procedures. We'll have to go with the second-best method of execution. Decapitation."

She raised the axe high over her head, then swung it down in a wild motion. The blade glanced off the side of the doctor's neck. Regina lifted it again, this time striking the throat, but the blade got stuck halfway through the bone. Dark blood spilled from her mouth, out of the gash around the blade, spilling in thick, red rivulets over Dersauger's neck and chest.

"I had no idea how hard it is to chop off a head!" Reggi struggled to pull out the axe wedged deep in the bone. She braced her feet, then pulled hard. The axe came unstuck with a loud suctioning *pop*, and the woman fell backward into a pile of wet, rotting leaves and animal waste. She uttered a round curse, got to her feet, and swung the axe toward the gushing wound. This time, the weapon hit home, cutting through flesh and tendons and bone. Jet sprays of blood and viscera splashed over Regina's face, her clothes. The doctor's headless body began a violent epileptic twitching and a putrescent stench seemed to burn the air. Reggi wiped gobs of blood from her stinging eyes.

After several minutes, Doctor Dersauger's body stopped

convulsing and lay motionless, a river of blood pouring from her severed neck.

"Sorry you had to see that, Toolie, but don't worry, she didn't suffer. She lost consciousness within a few seconds, due to the intracranial perfusion of blood. We must try to make our kills humane whenever possible."

"It's all right, Reggi," the rat said, grooming blood from her fur. "Now let's cut up that meat."

With the axe and handsaw, Regina took her time defleshing the body. Big pieces of thigh, abdomen, and even a cheek went into a Hefty trash bag she'd brought with her. The fetid stench made her gag and almost vomit several times during the job.

She left half the flesh and all the innards on the doctor as part of her experiment. Now, with only the slightest hesitation, the rats converged on the corpse, devouring all that remained. They chewed through the woman's clothing and the duct tape confining her, fought over scraps of skin and fat and gristle. An extended tug-of-war ensued over the snakelike strings of intestines. Other rodents attacked the eyeballs, pulling them from their sockets and devouring them, even gnawing on the stalks. Reggi left the chest meat for them, mincing it with her ax until it resembled ground beef. The rats went for that first; within minutes, there was nothing left but bone.

EXHAUSTED, HER FEVER RISING ONCE AGAIN, REGGI ARRIVED AT HER apartment building, delighted to find the elevator working for the first time in a month. Broken elevators—what else could she expect from off-campus housing, the only rent she could afford? She wasn't sure she could even pay it now that she'd lost her roommate who'd shared the cost. Still, she couldn't contain her ecstasy over the night's events—another triumph in the course of her research.

Though the cave rats (even the ones bred in the wild) showed remarkable signs of intelligence, the rats in captivity were learning at a faster rate than all the other lab animals. The rats who ate cooked flesh were smarter than the ones on a raw diet. Even the chimpanzees with their natural intelligence couldn't match the rapid rate by which the rodents' brain functions were improving. They wasted far less neurological energy on basic survival and responded to a wide variety of training techniques. Toolie herself was the pinnacle of Regina's research. After all, the animal could speak, could hold a lucid conversation with both reason and accountability. Reggi believed the breakthrough was due to the nutritional value of the meat consumed.

If not for the discovery of fire, humankind would never have progressed beyond *Homo habilis,* the first known cave-dwelling people. The invention of cooked food was essential to human development as the gut more easily absorbed the pre-digested meat. With more sodium and potassium ions pumping across the membrane, the brain could now sustain a prolonged electrical charge. This diverted energy into more important pursuits such as knowledge and progress, as well as increasing bone growth and physical strength.

But mankind had been eating the wrong food for two million years.

Human meat was the key to unlocking the untapped power of the brain, containing a magic cocktail of nutrients needed to boost neurological function by more than four hundred percent. Reggi herself had eaten the cooked meat several times now and found her mind more focused than ever before.

*I need a few more months* and *then I'll reveal my work and change the world forever.*

She'd cleaned up her blood-splattered body as best she could in the industrial sink back at the lab, changing into a pair of medical scrubs from the supply closet. Her shoes now rested at the bottom of a stream near the cave, her clothes deposited in a random dumpster on her route home. Lucky for Regina, the back door of her lab led to a parking lot right on the edge of the preserve. Campus security seldom checked the area. No one had seen her as she left the forest and sneaked back into the building.

Her fever soaring and weak from exhaustion, Regina reached her thirteenth-floor apartment at last. She set down the heavy black trash bag she carried and reached into the laptop bag slung across her chest for her keys. Toolie dozed in the largest compartment but woke at her touch. When Reggi opened the door, she leaped from the pouch and scurried into the darkness of the flat.

She smelled him before she saw him—Michael—her ex-roommate's boyfriend, another grad student who lived on the tenth floor. The odor of Drakkar Noir cologne permeated her nostrils. *Dude is still living in 1989,* she thought, her nose twitching much like Toolie's.

"I've been looking for you," Michael said, his voice cold. Regina pretended not to hear him and picked up the trash bag at her feet. As she moved to enter her flat, he grabbed her arm, squeezing her sore through her sweater. Regina howled in agony as a shockwave of pain rocketed up her arm.

"Let me go!" She looked up at Michael with desperation, her wound screaming. She noticed his disheveled dark hair, the eggplant-colored circles underneath his eyes. He seemed agitated, on edge. He gripped her forearm, squeezing it harder. She howled again, hitting him with her free hand. He didn't let go, but in the struggle, his grasp moved down to her wrist, offering some relief from the pain.

"Where is she, Regina?"

"I told you three times already. She went to the Poconos with some guy she met on Tinder. Stop, Michael. You're hurting me!"

"You're lying! Brenda wouldn't do that to me. She wouldn't cheat and she wouldn't leave me!" Still clenching her wrist, Michael stuck his face close to Reggi's, his face wrinkling in disgust as he caught a whiff of her body odor. "She told me you've been acting strange, talking to someone in your room at night when no one else is there. *Talking about hurting people.*"

"I talk to my friends at night," Reggi said. "Is that a crime?"

"You've never had any friends."

"Look, Michael, are you on Tinder? You can find Brenda's profile yourself."

He dropped her arm, tears of frustration glinting in his eyes. "She said you stopped taking your meds. She was afraid to be alone with you—scared you'd do something to her. She asked to stay at my place for a while, but I—" Michael stopped, something like guilt clouding his eyes. "I know you did something to her, and I'm going to find out what it is!"

He turned as if to leave, but when Regina moved to enter the flat, he pivoted toward her, seizing her arm and twisting it behind her back. He silenced her cry of pain by clapping his free hand over her mouth, then forced her into the apartment and kicked the door shut. Michael tossed Reggi to the carpet. He raised his fist to her as she cowered in the corner by the door, one arm across her face as if to shield off the blow.

"Stay there!" Michael commanded. "If you move, I will beat you within an inch of your life. Got it?"

Regina nodded as if muted by fear. Michael turned his back on her, leaving her by the door as he began searching the apartment.

He'd made a foolish mistake. Even now as he moved away from her, Reggi slid her hand into the messenger bag still slung across her chest, feeling for the hypodermic needle she'd brought back from the cave. Quiet as a mouse, she rose, following him toward the bedroom. He never sensed her behind him, her feet silent as a nocturnal creature, yet another benefit of her new diet. At the door to Brenda's bedroom, Michael hesitated, one hand on the knob as he listened for any sound on the other side of the door. A towel lay wedged at the bottom of the door.

"Bren," he whispered. "Are you in there?"

A loud rustling came from within the room, startling Michael.

"Bren!" he said again. "It's me. I'm here to help you."

The rustling grew louder as if someone was moving about in there. Michael hesitated, paralyzed by uncertainty. Behind him, Regina raised the needle high, ready to strike. Michael turned the knob, kicked away the towel, and pushed the door open. He cried out in horror at the scene in front of him. Reggi peered over his shoulder and regarded her handiwork.

Brenda lay on her back in the bed, most of the meat already stripped from her bones but the flesh of her head and breast still intact. Blue eyes hung from their sockets, coated with an opaque film, the adorable pixie-cut blond hair now matted with blood. A red stain had spread out from beneath the corpse, soiling the flowery bedspread.

On top of two deflated, bluish-black breasts sat the biggest rat Michael had ever seen. The rodent had made the rustling noise, and as he stared in disbelief, it appeared to be laughing. It plucked a decomposing eyeball from the dead woman's skull and popped it in its mouth like an overripe grape. Dark liquid squirted out of its maw as it chewed. The rat swallowed and actually *grinned*.

The stench was abominable, but Regina had insulated the windows and vents with Flexi-seal, trapping the fumes within. The towel kept the smell of decomposition from seeping out under the door. A series of small holes drilled in the wall beside the window allowed the noxious gases to escape into the night air in small increments—nothing more than a passing unpleasant odor offending the tenants, who wrote it off as a downside of living in the slums.

Michael looked around the room and discovered he wasn't alone. From all corners of the room, glowing red orbs watched him. Dozens of eyes gleamed from under the bed, from the flowerpot in the corner, between the slats in the closet door. They peered from behind the curtains, swayed upside down on a hanging plant. The rats gazed at him, anticipation hanging in the air. Almost as if they waited for a signal...

"It's a goddamned colony!" Michael shouted.

He turned to flee, to go get help, to call the police. Something, anything, to stop this nightmare. As he wheeled, Regina jabbed him in the neck with the needle and pushed the plunger down. Then Michael's hands were around her throat, choking her, bashing her head against the wall again and again. She flailed, gasping for breath and clawing at his hands, too weak from her illness to do any damage.

"Die! Die!" Regina heard him screaming, but the sound seemed to come from somewhere outside the flat. She got a knee up and slammed him in his genitals. He howled but didn't lose his hold on her throat. They fell to the floor, still struggling in their fight to the death. He was on top of her now, choking her harder, the needle still jutting from the side of his neck. Regina went limp, her eyes rolling in the back of her head. She was fading, but then, so was Michael. The barbiturates coursed through his veins, invading his bloodstream. She felt his death-grip slackening. He fell forward onto Regina, a dead weight pressing on her. She made a futile effort to push him off but was too weak. Seconds later, she passed out cold herself.

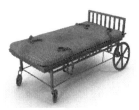

TWENTY MINUTES LATER, REGINA WOKE, HER THROAT BURNING, HER chest constricted from the mass on top of her. With tremendous effort, she managed to push Michael off her. He fell to one side, where he lay on his back, mouth gaping and eyes rolled into the back of his head. The eyes disturbed Regina. She sat up and pushed them down with her fingertips.

Toolie scuttled over and climbed onto the man's chest, looking at his face.

"Is he dead?"

"No, he's passed out. I need to get him to the cave to do a proper kill. It gets too messy here. I had a hell of a time scrubbing up all Brenda's blood. Had to use a black light so I could bleach all the places I missed. I only left her body here so our friends could feed."

"I think he's dead."

"Trust me, he's not. Dead eyelids don't stay closed."

Regina rose, wobbling as she did so. She held onto the doorknob to steady herself. "I need to get him out of here before he wakes up. But I'm so tired…"

All at once, she doubled over, vomiting onto the floor beside

Michael's prone body, remaining in the same position for several minutes before she straightened. She hadn't planned on killing her boss, or her roommate, or anyone for that matter—all were spur-of-the-moment kills. Her boss planned to fire her and euthanize her rats. Brenda threatened to call the police when Regina returned from her date awash with blood. Her Tinder date tried to assault her, and Michael had discovered her terrible secret. In the end, she couldn't allow herself to regret any of it, as all four kills provided her beloved rats with another few weeks of sustenance and furthered her experiment. The need to dispose of her date's body had first given her the idea to feed human flesh to the rats, and the outcome was tremendous.

She'd made a Tinder profile using Brenda's identity and photos and, using the dead man's phone, managed to match him with Brenda. She sent a few messages between the two and arranged a meet-up for later that night, then deleted her own texts with him. *Voila!* A double alibi. No one could prove he and Brenda hadn't run off to the Poconos, never to return. It was all worth it. She'd thrown the phones in the stream near the cave the next day.

But Michael wasn't dead yet—Regina still had work to do. She went out of the room and retrieved the black trash bag, shoving the doctor's flesh into the almost-empty freezer. She'd clean up the vomit later. She got Toolie into the laptop bag, removing the pen drive and leaving it on the kitchen counter for safety's sake. She couldn't risk losing it in the forest during the bloody escapade about to take place. She located her car keys, then returned to the unconscious man on the floor.

With a vast effort, she grabbed him around the waist and heaved his body up, throwing his arm over her shoulders. A thin woman, Reggi nevertheless possessed great physical strength. She drew on this as she maneuvered Michael out of the apartment toward the elevator; his arm still draped across her, his feet dragging on the hall's carpeting.

The early morning hours ensured none of the tenants witnessed her slow, exhausting descent to the ground floor. Luck ran out as Reggi exited the building half-carrying, half-pulling her victim across the parking lot to her Toyota Corolla. One of her neighbors and fellow students, Bill Thompson, pulled up alongside her as she struggled to keep Michael from tumbling to the blacktop.

"Who's your date, Reggi?" Billy called. "Did you have to hit him in the head with a hammer to get him to sleep with you?"

"Very funny, asshole," Regina muttered under her breath, not daring to insult him aloud with so much at stake. Much to her horror, the young man parked his car and came over to help.

"Oh, it's Mike," he said, catching a glimpse of the unconscious man's face. "Drunk and mooning over Brenda again, I bet." He relieved Regina of her burden, holding Michael's sagging body upright as she unlocked the passenger door. Together, they dumped him into a sitting position, his head falling forward onto his chest.

Billy let out a hearty laugh. "My boy got himself *wasted!* You been drinking, too? Sure you're okay to drive?"

"I'm fine. I'm going to drive him around to sober him up."

Regina bent and cranked the passenger-side window open as if to prove they were taking a drive for fresh air. Billy closed the door. "Thanks for your help. I appreciate—" But Billy was crossing the parking lot, heading into the building. He'd already forgotten her. She hurried to the driver's side and got in the Corolla, tossing the messenger bag on the floor at Michael's feet.

Toolie's head popped out of the bag. She crawled out and perched on the center console.

"He saw you, Reggi. You're going to have to kill him now."

The woman groaned. "I know. One at a time, Toolie. One at a time."

The night air blew in through the open windows, chilling Regina and offering her some slight relief from her fever. She sped down the wooded road to the university, blasting the new Fondlecorpse album and singing along to help keep herself awake.

Toolie stretched out a paw and turned up the volume. Still unconscious in the passenger seat, Michael's right arm twitched and he groaned in pain.

"Not a fan of old-school Death Metal, Mike?" Regina asked his unresponsive form. "You always were a square."

She reached the campus and headed downhill, toward the secluded parking lot near her laboratory's back door. A raccoon darted across the road in front of the Corolla, and Regina slammed her foot on the brakes. The car lurched. Michael flew forward, his head smashing against the dashboard.

He came awake with a roar, eyes wide with shock and rage. He lunged at Regina, going for her throat once again. Her foot came off the brake pedal as she tried to fight him off. The car rolled down the slope, picking up momentum as it went. Reggi clawed at Michael's face, his neck, his arms. She used her teeth to bite anywhere she saw exposed flesh. Still groggy from the drugs, he couldn't muster his previous strength and was no match for his attacker's wild toothy onslaught. Toolie jumped onto his head and went for his eyes with her claws as the car continued to speed toward the bottom of the hill. Michael stopped when the rat attacked, fighting to get her off him as she clung to the top of his head. He wrenched her claws from his hair and tossed her backward. The rat hurtled through the air, landing stunned in the backseat.

The car crashed into a tree at the bottom of the hill. Reggi's face met the driver's side airbag as it deployed. She managed to open the door and fell out of it onto the blacktop, her face bearing burns from the airbag. The trees, stripped bare of leaves, were ominous in the pre-dawn light. She went for them now, thinking to get to the cave where she'd left the axe, but Michael was on her in an instant. He tackled her from behind, knocking them both to the pavement and falling on top of her. Again, they struggled, and Regina felt too weak to hold out much longer.

When Michael's face came close to hers, she saw her chance and bit him hard on the cheek, grinding her teeth down until she felt the salty taste of his blood filling her mouth. He screamed and fell backward, holding his bloody face. Reggi got to her feet and tried to make for the treeline again, but he grabbed her by the leg and held on. She shook free and changed direction, heading up the stairs to the laboratory door with Michael close on her heels. He grabbed her from behind as she tried to tap in the entry code on the electronic keypad. From out of nowhere, Toolie leaped at Michael, sinking her teeth into his leg. He shouted and let go of Reggi, who then entered the code and made it into the lab.

When Reggi raced past the line of cages, she began opening all the doors one by one. Ravenous, the rats burst out, their shrill shrieks piercing the air as they went straight for Michael. Regina heard him screaming as she fled across the lab and through the door leading to the other labs. Michael managed to fight free of the rodents and followed after Regina, the small animals chasing him as he went. With Toolie's help, Regina threw open all the cages in the next room. Scores of white mice, guinea pigs, and hamsters leaped from their cages and headed toward the sound of screaming in the other room. Only the rabbits stayed put, lazily watching the mayhem as they lounged on their bedding.

They reached one of the primate labs and freed the primates. Hooting and hollering, the chimps leaped from their cages, seizing loose objects and hurling them at Michael. He dodged a flying microscope, but a Bunsen burner hit him in the face seconds later. Spider monkeys swung from the rafters, raining test tubes and beakers on his head. Still, he managed to get out into the corridor just as Regina burst out of the exit door, heading into the forest. Six chimpanzees followed, screeching as they made for the trees as well, with scores of rodents and smaller monkeys racing along at their feet. The rats forgot their bloodlust for Michael as they dispersed into the trees.

Reggi laughed aloud in the cold, crisp air. Michael was following her, and that was what she wanted. She knew these woods better than anyone else, avoiding the fallen timber buried under ankle-length blankets of wet, decaying autumn leaves. Michael tripped a few times but was always up in an instant. As he gained on her, Regina's exhilaration dissipated, and she began to feel real fear. She knew if he caught up with her, it was all over.

All she had to do was get to the cave where she'd left the axe, and she'd finish this business for good.

Michael put on speed and was inches away from tackling Regina when a shrieking chimp lurched across the path in front of him, throwing him off balance. Another chimp swung down from a tree, landing on his back and pounding him with his hairy fists. As the man fought off the ape, Regina managed to get away.

She reached the cave, dropped to the ground, and slithered through the opening on her belly. Once inside, she stood to her full height. It was pitch-black and Reggi couldn't see a thing, but she knew she'd left the axe on the far side of the cavern wall. With no time to waste, she raced straight ahead toward the weapon. Suddenly, she stumbled over an object in the cave and fell to the ground on her back. Her leg crumpled, twisting beneath her as a sharp pain pierced her ankle. She tried to stand, then to drag herself forward, but her struggle only imprisoned her foot further.

"Regina!" Michael roared from outside the cave, sending a chill down her spine. "I know you're close. You'd better hope I don't find you, 'cause if I do, you're dead."

Frantic, she waved her arms until she activated the motion-sensor and infrared light she'd installed. When the cavern illuminated, she saw her foot trapped between two of Doctor Dersauger's exposed ribs. She could hear Michael outside in the forest, screaming her name as he searched for her. Even if she could get up, she'd broken both her leg and ankle. If she got to the axe, she wouldn't be able to use it.

All at once, Regina knew she would never leave the cave.

Since she hadn't moved, the infrared light went out, leaving her in darkness once again. This time, Reggi didn't bother reactivating the light. She laid still, a sinking feeling in her heart. She'd come so far, done so much with her research. So close—so close!—to proving her theory, only for it to end like this. Bitter tears rolled from her eyes.

She felt pressure on her chest, and then a tiny paw reached out to stroke her cheek.

"Toolie!" she wept. "I've failed. My research will die here."

"No, it won't," the rat assured her. "You left your pen drive at home. Someone will find it and turn in your research. The whole world will soon know what you've done!"

Reggi smiled in the darkness, but only for a split second. She felt it now. Although she couldn't see it, she knew, knew with all her senses, that there were hundreds of rats surrounding her, gathering together in anticipation. They'd developed an insatiable thirst for human meat, and now they were waiting. Waiting to feast...on her.

"Please don't do this," she wept aloud. "Stop them. You're my friend!"

"I'm a rat," Toolie said. "This is what we do."

"No. No, please!"

"Think about it, Reggi. To give your life for your work? What more glorious death could you wish for?"

A calm settled over Regina. Yes! Yes, she would, indeed, become part of her research, her body a sustenance that would forever alter the course of humanity.

Michael shouted from somewhere outside the cave. "I hear you talking in weird voices, you sick freak! Where the hell are you?"

Why did he keep saying she was talking to herself? Hadn't he seen Toolie grinning at him as she devoured his girlfriend's eyeball? Was he suggesting Toolie wasn't real?

*Wasn't Toolie real?*

The rat crawled forward in the darkness. Regina could feel the brush of whiskers on her mouth. The rat gave her a long kiss good-bye, and when she lifted her furry head, a piece of lower lip came away with it. Regina never screamed. She stretched her arms wide and waited—a full, perfect, and sufficient sacrifice.

The rats swarmed.

# CASEY'S LAST RIDE

## SCOTTY MILDER

I know it's hacky to start a horror *story with a dream. But that's how this one starts, so you're gonna have to bear with me.*

*In this dream, I'm at a bonfire out in the middle of nowhere. At first I think I'm up at Bates again, at another one of Doug Rochester's epic Sabattus Road house parties. Doug lived in a white, two-story Dutch Colonial gifted to him by a dead aunt or grandmother. The place was tucked way back in the trees, and all us misfits—the theater dorks, the radio nerds, the gothy music students—gathered there on Saturday nights. The long back yard sloped gently toward a black wall of forest, and right in the middle of that yard was this big pit where people would throw in old textbooks, warped 2x4s, splintered chunks of furniture, whatever...as long as it would burn, it was fair game. Then Doug would upend a gallon of gasoline over the whole mess, and within seconds the fire would be raging.*

*Except it's not kids here, not in the dream. There's just me and this bonfire, and all these faceless people sliding around in front of it like phantoms. I hear conversation, but it's not party talk, you know? There's no joy in this anxious chatter; it's like what you hear if you're at the supermarket or on the subway and the text messages start flooding in about a major disaster, like a tornado or school-bus crash.*

*I can't make out any words. I'm not sure I even want to. Because whatever they're saying, I know it's no good.*

*There aren't any trees. There's no Dutch Colonial behind me. Everything around me is just this pregnant dark that's sticky...and right in the*

215

*middle of it, there's this bonfire and all these moving shadows, and maybe those shadows don't look so much like people at all anymore.*

*The fire roars. Except it doesn't sound like a fire at all. It sounds like the sea.*

*And then an arm grips mine. I turn, and it's you. This girl I used to sort-of know. Marla Ciccone. I'm surprised to see you here, and even more surprised by the way you're smiling. It's like you saw me across a crowded room and your heart skipped a beat and you just* had *to come over and talk to me. A love-at-first-sight kind of thing. Not the kind of look I should be getting from you. Because you were the* cool chick *in college. Half Japanese, half Italian, all beautiful. I remember your face, but mostly I remember your arms; they were roped in these intricate, Delphic tattoos, the meanings of which were entirely mystifying. That was back in the mid-nineties, when being covered in ink was still sort of exotic. You always wore these ruffle shirts and this wide black fedora, cocked all jaunty on your head. You carried a bone-handled switchblade in your back pocket, and you liked to show it off. You'd whip it out, press the button, and then cackle when everyone jumped at the* snick. *You'd make a big show of picking your teeth with it.*

*You were in a punk band, you DJed for the college radio station, you threw all the best parties with your roommates (even better than Doug's), and you were basically better and more interesting than anyone else I knew.*

*You're wearing the fedora now, still cocked back on that avalanche of dark hair, but otherwise you're naked. I see it's not just your arms that are covered in tattoos — it's your whole body. The black lines squiggle all over your bronze skin like worms.*

*I see your gums bleeding through the grin. Blood dribbles over your bottom lip and etches lines down to your chin.*

Casey! *you yell, in a voice that isn't yours. You sound genuinely happy to see me. And this is weird for two reasons.*

*One: I don't think I ever actually exchanged two words with you. You were the sun and I was some faraway dwarf planet circling you in a wide, elliptical orbit. You knew who I was, I think, but I'd have been shocked if you could remember my name.*

*Two: you were murdered nine years ago. What I heard was that you got yourself all strung out after we graduated, fell in with some terrible people, and the kamikaze plunge of your life culminated in your fiancé—yoked to the gills on meth—taking it in his head one night to smash your face in with a hammer. I looked up his mugshot online. He was every glowering, slack-jawed, hollow-eyed redneck that you see in these stories. His face was a blasted topography of pockmarks and divots, like an aerial photograph of some distant, war-torn desert. His nose was bulbous and red, and it canted distinctly off to the left. His teeth were yellow. His eyes were Cro-Magnon. The snake tattoo on his neck looked homemade.*

*I couldn't believe you were with him. I couldn't square the circle.*

*You still have a Facebook page, but now it reads* "In Memory of Marla Ciccone." *The profile picture hasn't changed in almost a decade, and the only posts I ever see are from your friends and your older sister. They pop up every year around your birthday, everyone talking about how much they miss you.*

Casey! *you yell, spraying more blood.* I'm so glad you came!

*And that's when I realize that I'm dead, too.*

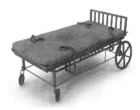

ERIN GETS ON THE OUTBOUND RED LINE TRAIN AT TEN MINUTES AFTER nine, like she always does. She boards at Downtown Crossing, and —for the moment, at least—she has the car to herself.

She hopes there isn't a game at Fenway tonight. She has a headache from hunching over her computer all day, and the only thing she wants is to ride the forty-five minutes back to Davis Square in relative quiet. She wants to get to her apartment, where she can bring up *The Great British Baking Show* or *Jane the Virgin* on Netflix and veg out on the sofa. Her fat Maine Coon, Thomas, will flop into her lap and lay there, the purr rattling out of his chest like a lawnmower engine. Maybe if she's feeling real adventurous, she'll DoorDash some Chinese food from that all-night place over on

Dover. It isn't the most exciting life, but it's the one she's got, and she's happy enough with it for the time being.

If there *is* a game, though, a bunch of juiced-up dudebros in Red Sox jerseys will pile on at Park Street. She'll get to listen to them chant, *"Yankees SUCK! Yankees SUCK!"* for the next half hour. It won't matter who the Sox actually played. It could have been the Indians or the Royals or the Orioles or some fucking visiting team from Japan; Boston sports fans are admirably focused in their animosities.

And since it's Boston, twenty minutes in, someone will probably throw a punch. Someone will call someone else a "FAHkin' queeah!" Someone will start dry humping his buddy. The n-word will be thrown around liberally. The car will stink of beer and sweat and hot dogs and fresh vomit, and she'll sit here appreciating the impulse to become a mass shooter. She'll think about how great it would feel—how absolutely *divine*—to whip a pistol out of her messenger bag and start blasting.

Erin's been in Boston eight years—four years of college, another four working at the ad agency—and it's just now dawning on her that everything everyone told her about the city was correct. Boston changes you. There's a poison under the surface—a thick, tumescent pus—and after a while it seeps in.

But tonight she's in luck. When the train rolls into Park Street Station, the platform is nearly empty. That means the peace and quiet will remain at least until Kendall Square—and even if it starts to fill up then, it'll mostly be students from MIT or Harvard or Tufts. They usually behave themselves.

The doors whisk open. Three people board. Two wear masks, like her and everyone else for the past two years. The first is a middle-aged black woman in a business suit. She crumples into the seat by the door and jams earbuds into her ears. The second is some white college kid. Even under the mask she can tell he has one of those bland, featureless faces you immediately forget.

The third is a tall, thin man of indeterminate age. He wears light blue pants and a poofy red jacket with a faux-fur collar. He's maskless, and seeing his naked mouth after all these months of only looking at eyes is oddly disquieting. She can't help but focus on his lips: too wide and too thin, dry and gray with dead skin flaking away like old paint.

She wrenches her gaze from his mouth and looks at his eyes. They're ice-chip blue, and they skate over Erin with a look of such startling sadness that her breath catches in her throat. She glances quickly away.

He sits, almost dainty, across from her.

She gazes down at her hands, wishing she had a book. At least then she'd have an excuse for not looking up.

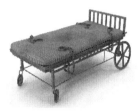

*IT'S THE SAME EVERY NIGHT, THE DREAM.*

Casey, I'm so glad you came!

*And then we're away from the fire but I can still hear it thundering out in the black. We're laying down. The ground is soft and cool, like we're on a bed of moss. I'm naked too. Your limbs entwine in mine. I can feel your breath against my neck. The stench slithers into my nostrils: smoky and foul, rotten with something spoiled. I imagine the maggots that must be making short work of your insides.*

*I remember those bleeding gums and think* don't kiss me don't kiss me. *But of course you do.*

*In college, I wouldn't have allowed myself to even imagine kissing you. You're MARLA FUCKING CICCONE, after all. Such fantasies inevitably collapse in a crash of self-loathing so complete that the only thing left to do is hurl yourself into the sea.*

*But I have no control over this dream, and in it, you kiss me. You crane your neck and the black circle of your face descends upon mine like a rogue planet caught in a gravity well. Dry lips mash together. Teeth clatter. There's no spit in your mouth: just this cavernous, sucking dryness. You're chewing at me, hungry, and you push all that rottenness down my throat* until I choke. I taste the blood and the corruption inside you, and I want to scream.

You're on me. Riding me. But as we make love—or whatever it is we're doing—you arch your back and now you're silhouetted against the flame. I see that there are pieces of you coming off. Skin liquifies and sluices from your bones like foam. Hair slithers off your scalp in tangled clumps.

I know it's happening to me, too, because when you grind your pelvis against mine all I can feel is bone scraping against bone.

The murmuring rises from the shadows: a formless deluge of nervous syllables that refuse to coalesce into words.

I try again to scream, but my lungs have long since shriveled to dust. All that's left of me is a ribcage and many white yards of bone.

You're dead. I'm dead.

And this is all that there is.

Then sunlight wedges into the slit between my blackout curtains and I wake. The alarm on my phone is going off. It's set to "Mr. Roboto," because that's one of the only songs obnoxious enough to ensure I'll get up and shut it off.

I silence it and flop onto my back. I stare at the ceiling.

I'm still dead.

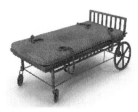

Sometimes, when she rides the train, Erin plays this game. It's a holdover from her years at Northeastern, where she was a creative writing major.

She'll sit there and quietly observe the other passengers, make up stories about them, try to figure out who they are. The object is to lean as hard away from the typical as possible. Avoid cliché. Go specific and idiosyncratic.

Take the black woman over by the door. She's wearing a business suit, and is coming from downtown where all the big law firms are. The *typical* thing would be to turn her into a lawyer. So let's come up with something different, shall we? But this is where things get thorny. You can lean away from one boring cliché and overcompensate your way into an uglier stereotype. For instance, if the black woman isn't a lawyer, maybe she's unemployed and the suit is borrowed. Maybe she wore it to some job interview for an entry-level position. But that's…well, that's just *hella racist*. Why does the black lady need to be unemployed? What, did her baby daddy run out on her? Are the welfare checks not enough? *Come on, Erin. You can do better than that.*

Erin decides the lady is an audience outreach liaison for one of the big theaters on Tremont Street. The Wang, or the Shubert. She studied theater education at Emerson, with a minor in theater management. Part of her job is to coordinate shows for local high schools. It's part of a larger education initiative, and the woman (*her name is Sandra*, Erin decides) is basically building it from the ground up. She's been toiling away at it for four years and hopes to have a shot at being named Managing Director someday.

Sandra lives up in Medford, and she's on her second marriage. Her first husband was one of those stupid college flings that got out of hand; they limped along for three years until he realized he was gay. They parted on good terms because—thank *God*—they didn't have any kids. He's a landscape architect and lives in Sweden with his husband. They still send each other Christmas cards. Sandra married again in her thirties, this time to a nice, boring accountant. No, wait. Why does the accountant have to be boring? *Typical.* Let's try again: he's mild-mannered, sure, and good with numbers, but he's also athletic and charming. He awakened a dormant spirit of adventure in Sandra. Whenever they can, they get out of the city to mountain bike the White Mountains in New Hampshire or raft the West River in Vermont. Still no kids, because they both agree they don't want any. All in all, a good life, even if Sandra's tired from her job a lot of the time.

And what's she listening to? Maybe she's trying to quit smoking, and it's one of those self-help affirmation tapes—*smoking will kill you, you have the power and the motivation to resist cigarette cravings.*

But that doesn't track with all her mountain biking and river rafting. If Sandra had ever been a smoker, she would have quit years ago. So maybe it's old-school hip hop. Or maybe she needs a crystalline flood of New Age—*Pure Moods* volume whatever—to cycle herself down at the end of the day.

Or maybe when Sandra was at Emerson, she got sucked into the Allston music scene—all those hardcore, punk-rock bruisers—and decided against her better judgment that she liked it. Maybe it's something that stuck, even as she inched her way into her comfortable forties. So maybe right now she's rocking out to Blood For Blood's *Wasted Youth Brew*.

Erin snickers. She always drives the imagination cart into the ditch eventually. That's half the fun.

The bland, college-looking guy clutches the center pole. She decides his name is Danny. He presents an even bigger challenge because—like so many of the white college guys she sees riding the train between Boston and Cambridge and Somerville—there's an inherent samey *sameness* to them that borders on an actual nothingness. Danny looks like every other engineering major at MIT, or business major at Suffolk, or pre-law student at Tufts. But maybe he's older than he looks. His face is a facade of casual disinterest, but there's a nervous *something* happening in his eyes. So maybe he's actually in his mid-thirties and he's going back to school after serving two tours in Afghanistan. Maybe the blandness he projects is a carefully constructed mask, because he's afraid that if you see the *real* him, you'll see all the terrible things he did. That he was forced to do.

Typical.

Danny isn't as much fun as Sandra. Maybe someone more interesting will get on once they get to Kendall Square.

And what would someone see if they look at her and play the game? They'd see a slight, half-Asian woman in her late twenties who's being practically swallowed by a heavy gray overcoat. They'll assume she's half Chinese, because in this country it seems like no one understands there are Asian countries *other* than China. So of course they'll think she's coming from Chinatown. Will anyone look beyond the obvious? Will they see that she's actually three-quarters

Thai, but with an Irish maternal grandmother who provided her name, the spray of freckles across the bridge of her nose, and her green-tinted eyes? Will they see the D.C. suburbs in her? The five years of Judo in middle and high school? The My Bloody Valentine tattoo on her left bicep and the black rose on her right forearm? Will they see her goth/emo past, when she dyed her hair green and listened to My Chemical Romance and Marilyn Manson and dreamed of becoming a poet one day? Not Poet Laureate or anything—fuck all that pretentious bullshit—but one of those underground rabble rousers who screams recitals in dive bars and has her words printed in the back pages of rock zines. Will they see how that girl took a temp copywriting job at an ad agency right after college, and how the temp job is going on four-and-a-half years now, and how she hasn't even tried to write a poem in almost three? Will they see all the ways she gave up?

Erin pulls her eyes away from Danny and they land, involuntarily, on the man sitting across from her.

He stares, smiling vacantly through great slabs of teeth. His back is ramrod straight, and his hands are folded primly in his lap, the long fingers interlaced like a basket. Even beneath the poofy jacket, she can see that he's impossibly thin. His graying hair is cut short and swept back behind his ears. Those blue eyes crouch deep in their sockets, and the skin all around them is puffy and purple, like maybe he's been crying.

He smiles. But his eyes...they're so *sad.*

She can't read him. There's no story here for her to write.

"Hi, Marla," he says, in a voice like tape being pulled from cardboard. "It's really good to see you."

THE DOCTORS CALL IT COTARD'S DELUSION. THE INTERNET CALLS IT *Walking Corpse Syndrome.*

A few weeks back, my sister came by my apartment and found me in the kitchen carving my forearm with a paring knife. The blood that came out was lumpy and brown, half coagulated. The muscle and ribbons of fat were dried out. Desiccated.

A stench oozed from the cuts. I could feel them in there: all the microbes, all the maggots, chewing and turning my flesh to gas.

My sister freaked out. She's a gentle sort, a worrier, and I didn't like seeing her like that. I tried to explain, to show her what was coming out of me, but my tongue had gone stiff with decay. My vocal cords were frozen solid. I can't imagine what I looked like to her: skin the color of ash and flaking off in chunks, dust-filmed eyes tumbled back into the sunken holes of my skull. My gums were nothing but blisters, the teeth gone all loose like stones in wet mud. She cried and called 911. A man and a woman in blue scrubs pounded up the stairs and pushed into my apartment. They shot something into my arm and loaded me into an ambulance. Someone turned on the siren. I tried to tell them not to bother, that they should just haul me off to the morgue.

They didn't take me to the morgue, though. They checked me into the Department of Mental Health at Mass General, which is this red-brick block swallowing half of Boston's West End. It's the type of place you see from the outside and you don't want to go into because you don't think they'll let you leave.

They put me on a seventy-two-hour hold. I don't remember any part of those three days, but I found out later that my sister lobbied and somehow succeeded in securing a more permanent commitment. By the time I woke up, I was an inpatient.

The first doctor was Emmanuel Feldstein. He had a Jewish name, but he was black and his voice carried a hint of the Caribbean. He made me think of a Voodoo priest, and I wondered if I was his zombie. He asked a lot of questions. I don't remember what I told him. But whatever it was, he didn't like it. He frowned and jotted notes on a clipboard.

The next day the orderlies brought me to another doctor. Her name's Sarah Bouchard. She's also black, and she seems way too young and too pretty to be a psychiatrist. She has something close to an English accent, but not quite. South African, maybe.

*She sat me down in her office, her on one side of this big oak desk and me on the other.*

*"How long have you felt this way, Casey?"*

*"What way?" I croaked. I had managed, in the last couple of days, to find a way to work my dead vocal cords. It felt like someone was pulling barbed wire through the pinhole of my throat, loop by bloody loop.*

*"Like you're dead."*

*I didn't know how to answer that question. I didn't want to tell her about you.*

*Dr. Bouchard looked at her notes. "I see you were diagnosed with clinical depression six years ago," she said. "Your family doctor gave you an initial prescription for Buprion and referred you to a psychiatrist. But I don't see anything here indicating that you actually made an appointment."*

*I shrugged. I hadn't made the appointment because, frankly, it didn't seem to matter. Nothing mattered. Even back then, before I knew I was dead, everything had gone flat and gray.*

*Dr. Bouchard made a whistling sound. "Okay," she said. "Here's what we're going to do. You're going to stay with us for a little while and we'll see if we can't get you better. How does that sound?"*

*I didn't have the heart to tell her that the only thing that would get me better was a quick trip to the crematory.*

*"We're putting you back on the Buprion, and we're going to add in some olanzapine. We'll see how you do on that. If we don't see any progress, we'll switch over to a combination of lorazepam, olanzapine, and escitalopram."*

*I nodded. Why not? It was all just words. Disconnected syllables signifying nothing.*

*"We'll give that a go," she continued, and clapped her hands together. "And if that doesn't work we'll try ECT."*

*"ECT?" I asked, and immediately regretted it. Speaking was agony.*

*"Electroconvulsive therapy," she said and then interpreted something off my look that must have suggested fear. "Don't worry," she said. "It's not like what you see in the movies, and ECT has proven very effective in managing this condition."*

*I wasn't scared. I just wanted to get back to my room, which had the comforting stillness of a tomb. I could lay there in the dark and imagine that I was in one of those above-ground mausoleums in New Orleans, laid out on a slab and left to molder away.*

*"Casey," she said and smiled. "You're* not *dead. I know you don't believe me, but you're very much alive. I'm here to help you see that. Okay?"*

*I nodded, but her words brought the first flutter of fear.*

*Alive?*

*No.*

*No no no no no.*

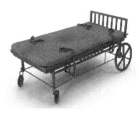

I SEE DR. BOUCHARD TWICE A WEEK. HER DRUGS NUMB SOMETHING IN ME —*a vestigial something still trying to feel—but they don't make me any less certain that I'm dead.*

*I've learned to say what she wants to hear. She says I'm making progress. That I might even get out soon. That's okay. Or not. It doesn't matter.*

*On the way back to my room, I always see you. You sit in what I guess must have been the rec room. You wear a thin hospital gown and you're always hunched over a checker board, moving the pieces randomly back and forth.*

*You look up at me as I pass, and the only thing left of your face is bone and a few gamey strips of dried flesh. Your eye sockets are gaping caverns. Dead black space with no galaxies to light them. Things wriggle in there, just beyond the reach of the fluorescents. Your teeth chatter, and I know you're trying to smile.*

*Now that it's over, now that everything else has rotted away, you're more beautiful than ever.*

*I smile back.*

"HI, MARLA. IT'S REALLY GOOD TO SEE YOU."

Erin's first thought is to say *my name's not Marla,* but that violates the city's rule number one when it comes to interacting with nut-jobs: *don't.* She looks away instead.

What feels like minutes go by. The train is rattling over the Longfellow Bridge now, and the glistening ebon ribbon of the Charles unspools toward the Atlantic. Clouds churn out there, heavy and black, and much closer, there's the bright *whisk-whisk-whisk* of streetlamps floating by. She can't see the moon, but maybe she can feel the lunatic energy of it pushing down.

She's aware of the way the train rocks, of how the bland guy (*Danny*) is sort of watching her, his mouth pulled taut. The black woman (*Sandra*) stares out the window and bobs her head to whatever's going on in the earbuds.

Erin shrinks under the hot, liquid press of the man's gaze.

"I didn't see you in the rec room yesterday," he says. "Where'd you go?"

She steals a quick glance, not because she wants to but because she can't help herself. His lips pull back in a too-wide grin, exposing a row of spit-slick teeth. She looks quickly away. But before she does, she notices that, under the puffy coat, he's not wearing regular blue pants. He's wearing scrubs. That's weird. What's weirder is that they only come halfway down his shins. He wears no socks, and his tennis shoes are untied.

This isn't adding up.

"Where'd you go?" he asks again. His voice still sounds like a wood rasp, but there's a joviality in there that raises the hair on the back of her neck. "I looked all over for you."

"Hey," Danny says. "You okay?"

She catches his eye. He doesn't look so bland now. She swallows and gives a little shake of her head.

"Marla, where'd you go?"

"I'm not Marla," she says and stands.

DR. BOUCHARD IS DRONING ON AND ON ABOUT SOMETHING—SAFE SPACES *and personal agency and whatever else—and I'm fighting this headache and this cramping pain in my jaw because I had my first ECT session yesterday and now it's like someone took one of those electric egg beaters to all the moldering tissue inside my skull and whipped it into mush. I hear this buzzing noise, papery and thin, and I think that it might be what's left of my thoughts. They've separated from me, gone alien and insectile, and if I wasn't an empty shell before, I definitely am now.*

*I think my name used to be Casey and that this person Casey who once existed might have had a sister. Her name is Carrie, maybe. But I can't remember her face. I try to picture it and all the features dance away, leaving this pink void fringed by an explosion of auburn hair.*

*Dr. Bouchard says something about this being a process, about how I need to be patient. I wonder what she's up to. Why didn't she just have me cremated, instead of propping me up and dragging me all through this hospital like the old guy in* Weekend at Bernie's*? I used to think that movie was a comedy. Not so much now.*

*Dr. Bouchard's mouth keeps moving, and sounds keep coming out of her, but I'm not sure anymore that they were ever words. All I hear is this keening moan, like wind at the end of a long tunnel, and the way her tongue flaps around in her mouth makes me think of the way a lamprey will press its many-toothed face to aquarium glass.*

*She's dead, too, I think. And maybe that's a revelation. Maybe that's something I hadn't considered before.*

*Maybe we're all dead. Maybe I'm the only one who knows it.*

*No. That's wrong.*

*YOU know it, too.*

*The orderlies take me back to my room, and when we pass by the rec room, I look over to where you're always sitting by the checker board. But you're not there. There's another Asian lady, hunched over the board and shuffling the pieces, but she's in her fifties and her hair is mostly gray. The skin sags off her face like candle wax.*

You're dead, too, *I think.* But you're not Marla.

*The orderlies open the door to my room. One of them—the tall blond one named Paul, the nice one—smiles and makes mouth sounds at me. A meaningless series of faraway* wah-wah-wahs, *and I look into his eyes and see things moving in there. Little wriggling things. Paul smiles, and there's a crust of dead froth at the corners of his mouth. The boreholes of his nostrils are lined with sludgy ridges of spoiling meat.*

*He's rotting from the inside out. Putrefying and sprouting mold.*

*And then the door closes and I'm all alone in that dark.*

You weren't in the rec room.

Where are you?

*That's when I start to panic.*

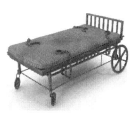

ERIN MOVES HASTILY TOWARD THE DOOR. THIS ISN'T HER STOP, BUT SHE needs to get off before the guy tries to talk to her again.

The train plunges into a tunnel. The lights flicker and for a few seconds she's in the dark and she can feel the guy creeping up behind her, grin contorting itself into a death rictus as he reaches. But then the lights snap back on and she sees his reflection, still sitting behind her on the bench.

The train spills out of the black and into a pool of fluorescent light. She sees the parallel red stripes along the white-tiled wall and the sign for "KENDALL/MIT."

The train wheezes to a stop. The door whisks open. She hurries onto the platform.

It's not until the train rumbles away that she realizes the platform is empty. *What the fuck? Where is everybody?* For a moment it's like the world has completely emptied out. She thinks back to a crazy movie she watched in college, *Night of the Comet*, where these two valley girls in LA wake up to discover that everyone on earth has disappeared. Except for some zombies, she remembers.

But Erin can hear the receding roar of the train, and the steady drone of traffic overhead. A horn blares up there and someone shouts in thick Bostonese: *"The fahk're ya' doin' ya goddamned retaaaaahd, pull ya head outcha fahkin' ass!"*

That steadies her a little. She takes a deep breath.

*Damn, that dude really freaked you out, didn't he?*

She looks toward the stairs: dark concrete ribboned with rubberized yellow bumpers. The escalator is out of order, but up at the top she can see the graphite haze of the city sky, framed in the open square of the station exit. That steadies her too. She'll wait for the next train, where there'll be no crazy guy in scrubs, and she'll be at Davis in no—

"Marla."

She squeals and spins, and *of course* he's there, lurching toward her. The fluorescent light spills into the crags and canyons of his face like shimmering silver. He's grinning, and his eyes don't look sad now. They don't look like anything at all.

"I wanted to tell you that I found it," he says and slides those long fingers into the coat pocket. He pulls out something thin and cylindrical. "It helped."

There's a *snick.* The sound ricochets across the subway platform like a gunshot. The cylindrical thing sprouts eight inches of sparkling steel.

"It helped," he says again, showing her the switchblade. He takes another step.

*Fuck this*, she thinks and turns to run. Just as the guy slides out of her vision, she sees a flutter of movement behind him. Then her feet pound across the tiles. The guy shouts after her, and there's another voice, a lower one. She hears the *thwock* of something hitting flesh.

Her foot plunges for the first riser, misses, and the rubberized bumpers rush up and fill her vision with yellow.

She hits first on her knee, then her shoulder. Her head smacks one of the risers, and for a microsecond everything shatters into black. But her shoulder took most of the impact; after she blinks a couple of times, she's okay.

She rolls onto her back.

The guy in the red jacket is tussling with someone. She recognizes Danny. Thank Christ for bland college kids. Danny's mask hangs askew and she's surprised to see that he has a mustache. He's got the guy's wrist in one fist and pounds the side of his head with the other. The guy squawks like a bird.

The silvery light glints off the switchblade as the guy wrenches his hand free. Erin opens her mouth to shout, but before she can, he buries the switchblade into Danny's throat. Now Danny is the one who's squawking, except it's more a wet *urk-urk* sound. His Adam's apple bobs. He claws at his throat, but it's too late. The guy pulls the blade free and then plunges it into Danny's eye.

Erin's mouth hangs open. There's a scream in there, but it refuses to come out. She can feel it coiled in her throat, swelling like an inner-tube and shoving all the air back into her chest.

Danny staggers backward. One hand goes to his eye. Blood and something gelatinously white spurts between his fingers. More blood pulses out of his neck. His other eye finds her, and she has just enough time to register the shock and hurt before he topples over the lip of the platform and vanishes from sight. There's a metallic *bong* as his body hits the tracks below.

The guy turns back to her. He's still got the switchblade. And he's still grinning.

"See?" he says. "It helped."

*The dream is gone.*

*Five nights in a row now. I lay on my cot in this room* (mausoleum), *and I stare up at the overhead light. It's just a bare bulb wrapped in a white metal cage, so the crazies like me can't break it. Its buzz is like a single wasp trapped in a jar.*

*When it finally snaps off, I roll onto my side and let the dark envelop me. It's a different dark than in the dream: glacial and antiseptic and filled with nothing. There's no bonfire. There are no promises.*

*I wasn't obsessed with you, you know. Was I attracted to you? Of course. You were MARLA FUCKING CICCONE, for Christ's sake; it simply wasn't possible to be in your presence for more than a couple minutes without falling at least a little bit in love with you. But I wasn't alone. Everybody was caught up in your churn: the dudes, the chicks, probably even the professors and the hair-netted ladies working in the cafeteria.*

*I left college a year before you did, got a job working for the city, and I barely thought about you still up there in Lewiston, hurtling toward a hammer-smashed future nobody could see. I went on with my life. The color started draining out of everything, but I didn't know yet that I was dead. I wouldn't understand that for a long time. I just knew that the world felt increasingly separate from me, like I was wrapped in a layer of cling-film and was slowly suffocating.*

*I didn't think about you for years. Not until the flurry of Facebook messages—ohmigoddidyouhearwhathappenedtomarla?!?—followed by the tearful memorial posts and pictures. Here I am with Marla at one of her shows. Here I am with Marla at that frat party on State Street, both of us festooned in Mardi Gras beads and sticking our tongues out because we're having oh-so-much fun. Here I am with Marla on a road trip. With Marla in the DJ booth. In our dorm room. At Kim's Kitchen, sucking down bowls of noodles. Basking in Marla's glow, taking in as much as I can* before the moon of time drifts between us and casts me in the penumbra of an eclipse.

I didn't have any of those pictures to share. I just had a few scattered memories: mostly of me somewhere in the background and you playing with that switchblade, pretending to pick your teeth with it.

At first I thought the dream was terrible. But then—after I realized what it meant, what was happening to me—I came to depend on it. Because I found YOU in it. Not the cool girl with the tattoos and fedora and chaos in her eyes, but the REAL you: the bones and the viscera and all the hollow parts. The most gorgeous version of you that there could be.

I came to depend on the dream because when I'm in it, I feel like I can let go. I can stop clinging to the illusion of life and accept the dusty, worm-filled truth of what's become of me. As long as you're there with me, I can let go. Because you're the only one who understands.

I let the dark swallow me, and eventually something like sleep takes over. But this sleep is dreamless and cold. A tunnel with no end. I drift through it, alone and incorporeal. I'm in it for aeons. And then I wake.

Once my body finishes its slow decay, is that what's waiting? That vast, eternal absence?

Marla.

They took you away from me.

I may be dead, but I can still make them pay.

SIX NIGHTS NOW. I WAKE, AS ALWAYS, TO THE CORPSE-GRAY SUNLIGHT pushing through the dirty, wire-meshed window. The wall eight inches from my nose is a flat expanse of featureless white. I feel like that white is trying to tell me something. Whatever it is, I don't want to know.

It was the tunnel again. But this time it was different. There were *voices in there: a murmuring, feverish drone. I think they're the same voices from the bonfire, but I still couldn't make out what they were saying.*

*And—finally—there was this pinprick of light way at the end of all that black. YOU, Marla.*

*A grinning skull, chattering at me from the dark.*

*And I could hear your voice, floating above all the others.*

Casey, *you said.* Come find me.

NOW I CAN HEAR VOICES IN THE HALLWAY. NOT THE DREAM VOICES, BUT *a light and cheerful (and* lively) *banter. It's shift change; the morning nurses have arrived.*

*I go to sit up, and as I do my hand slips beneath the cardboard-flat pillow and encircles something. Whatever it is, it's small and hard and cylindrical.*

*I pull it out and look.*

*Your switchblade. I know it's yours because of the bone handle.*

Casey, *you said.*

*I press the button.*

Snick.

Casey. Come find me.

# CASEY'S LAST RIDE

*When Paul comes to take me to Dr. Bouchard, I'm waiting.*

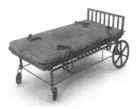

THE GUY'S COMING TOWARD HER, LOCK-KNEED AND LURCHING LIKE there's something wrong with his legs. Erin feels a fog coming over her, swirling into her brain like smoke being pumped through a bellows. She's thinking about Danny—how he'd looked at her right before he went over the edge. One eye was spurting blood, but the other rolled toward her...and was there an accusation in there? *But I tried to help you!* Was that Danny's last thought before he tumbled face-first to his death?

Once, when she was in high school, Erin watched a guy get stabbed outside a rock club in Cardozo. The band were some post-metal bruisers called Ratnation, and the show had been a turgid and depressing affair. Even the two grams of shrooms she took before the concert didn't do much to enliven the experience.

She didn't know what sparked the fight. She and her friends were standing under the awning, smoking, when shouts erupted from up the street. She looked just in time to see a bearded guy in a leather jacket toss some scrawny kid with a mohawk up against the side of a building. A girl with pink hair tried to get between them, and the bearded guy shoved her aside without a second look. She landed—ass-first and screeching—on the sidewalk. Everyone around them scattered like pinballs.

The bearded guy moved in, fists raised, and then the kid sprung forward and the bearded guy screamed, and when he staggered backward into a parked car Erin saw the blood sieving out of his abdomen, soaking his pants and turning his white tank-top a glistening scarlet all the way up to the chest.

Erin thought herself a tough girl, take-no-prisoners and suffer-no-fools. But seeing all that blood, hearing the screams, and watching the way the bearded guy's legs turned to water as he sank to his knees…it undid something in her. Knocked something irretrievably loose. The next thing she knew, she was on her hands and knees, puking into the gutter as the shriek of approaching sirens rolled through her head like a tidal wave.

That was nothing compared to what the crazy guy did to Danny.

He zombie-walks toward her, switchblade held out like a gift, and all she can see now is the way the knife handle flapped beneath Danny's jittering Adam's apple, how the blood and white stuff spurted through his fingers. How that one indicting eye grabbed onto her.

Blood smears across the crazy guy's hands. More spatters his red coat and those too-short scrubs. He's saying something, but the words are lost under a throaty rumble that pours out of the tunnel. Behind him, hurtling through darkness, is a stab of light.

*Are you just going to lay here and let him gut you?*

She thinks she might. But then she looks back into his eyes, sees all the madness in there, and before she knows she's going to, she levers herself into a crouch. Her mind flashes back to the Dojo, where once upon a time she'd worked her way up to a green belt. The tough-girl thing.

The guy takes another step and then her hand is under the knife-wielding arm, shoving it upward, and her other arm is around his waist. She relishes the snap of surprise in his eyes as her leg hooks behind his.

Then she's shoving, and he's falling, and the train explodes out of the tunnel like a lunging eel. The rest of it clicks past in a series of snapshots: the conductor's wide eyes and gaping "O" of his mouth, the switchblade clattering across the tile, the poofy jacket billowing as the guy goes over the edge.

In that last second—right before the train obliterates him in a cacophony of flesh, bone, and steel—their eyes meet. The sadness is gone. So is the insanity.

What she sees instead is relief.

Then the train roars past, metal wheels screaming. Erin spins away, that thing inside her knocked loose all over again. Acid splashes up from her stomach, etches raw grooves in her throat. Tears sting her eyes, doubling and then tripling her vision.

That's why she can't quite make out the person crouching there, pinned beneath the fluorescent lights. She sees tangles of dark hair, diamond-chip eyes, a Cheshire-cat grin. The rest is lost in a prismatic haze.

Erin staggers and collapses to her side. Her stomach lurches, trying to expel its contents. She claws at the tiles as she gasps for air.

The train rumbles to a stop.

Doors slide open.

The person kneels and picks up the switchblade.

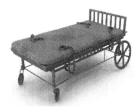

*I MANAGED NOT TO GET TOO MUCH OF PAUL'S BLOOD ON THE SCRUB pants, but the shirt is a total loss. Rorschach patterns of gore turn the blue fabric stiff and black.*

*Luckily they let me wear a plain white T-shirt in here. I strip off my sweatpants and pull the scrubs on in their place. They're six inches too short, but they'll have to do. I also squeeze into his tennis shoes. They're a little narrow, but otherwise okay.*

*The buzzing is still here, ricocheting around the back of my head like an errant bullet and trying to tear apart my thoughts. But there's also YOUR voice, murmuring from some place just behind my eyes. That helps. It helps. Like the switchblade.*

*I shove Paul's body under my cot and unhook his magnetized ID badge. I wipe the blood off on my discarded sweatpants. I don't look anything like Paul, but once I swipe my way off of this floor, I don't think anyone will ask to see the badge. All I can hope for is that no one thinks to check on him for the next ten minutes or so.*

*I look down for a moment, wondering if he's going to ripen like a gourd before my eyes and disgorge all his rotten contents. Revealing him to be what I know he is. But he doesn't. No eruptive gasses. No maggots.*

*One eye gapes at me, still as startled as it was when I jammed the switchblade into his ear. There's nothing wriggling in it now.*

*As I leave, hoping no one notices my change of pants and shoes, I remind myself to stop by the employee lounge. It's Boston in mid-October. Someone is bound to have a coat.*

The wind has picked up by the time I push through the side exit *and stumble out into the loading dock. It needles at me with icy teeth. The red behemoth of Mass General looms behind me. A massive gray-and-white brutalist nightmare rises in front of me.*

*I head for the narrow corridor of Fruit Street and cinch the coat's zipper up around my throat. I'm glad for the faux-fur collar; October in Boston is no joke, even for the dead.*

*I lucked out with the coat. Not only is it fur-lined and down-filled, there's also a CharlieCard in the inside pocket. If I go left, I know, I can work my way around the hospital to the Charles/MGH Station.*

*But you tell me no. That's the first place they'll look.*

*So I turn right, instead. The rolling green expanse of Boston Common is somewhere that way. Beyond that is Park Street Station. The hub of the city. From there I can go anywhere—inbound, outbound, doesn't matter.*

*But where will you be?*

I'll find you.

*Fall in Massachusetts means the sun drops like a stone when it's ready to. The wedges of sky above the buildings have gone a smoky, purplish gray. It looks like flesh caught in the grip of putrefaction. By the time I get to the Common, it'll be full dark.*

*I shamble up the street, willing the rigor in my legs to ease enough to let me keep walking. I need to keep moving, or they'll grab me and take me back inside, pump me full of their drugs and their lies, try again to convince me I'm still alive. They'll keep me there—unburied and half decomposed—forever.*

I'll find you, *you say.*

I'll set you free.

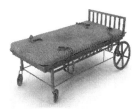

THERE ARE POLICE, AND THEY SAY SOME THINGS TO ERIN, AND SHE'S pretty sure she says some things back. But she has no idea what. The fog has flooded into her brain again. It's pulsing throughout her body now, weighing her down and making her limbs feel sluggish. It stings her lungs, and she thinks she might choke on it.

The EMTs worked on her for a while, disinfecting the abrasion on her forehead and stabbing a light into her eyes, telling her to follow it. Now she's sitting on the bottom riser of the out-of-order escalator. They've cordoned off the area. Yellow tape encircles the platform, flapping in a rank breeze that wafts down occasionally from the street.

They managed to move the train. She watched them inch it forward into the outbound tunnel. Now there are white-overall-clad forensic techs down on the tracks, scraping up what's left of Danny and the crazy guy. The fluorescent light glints off their plastic goggles, making their faces look detached and inhuman.

At least her vision has cleared. Uniformed cops stand on the platform, having an intense, mumbling conversation with two rumpled detectives. They all wear cloth masks except for one of the detectives, who wears one of those N95 deals. His name's Halloran. He's fat and white-haired, with the ruddy cheeks of a hard drinker, so Erin figures he must be in the high-risk demo. His voice is gruff, but his eyes are kind as far as a cop's go. His vowels carry the faintest vestige of South Boston.

Those eyes keep flitting over to her. She told him about the switchblade, and the mystery person who knelt and picked it up. He'd nodded, jotted something down in his little notebook, and told her they'd keep looking. She doesn't think he was lying, exactly, but she knows he didn't believe her.

The person was a woman. Erin is almost sure of it. She grabbed the switchblade and smiled and then started picking her teeth with it.

Then, before Erin could catch her breath, she was gone.

Halloran breaks away and shambles over to her.

"Ms. Preedan," he says, "we've got your statement, so you're free to go. But I may need to get in touch with you later, if that's okay."

"Sure," she hears herself say.

"Are you able to get home? I can have one of our uniforms give you a lift up to Somerville."

Erin peers up the escalator. The night is still the color of charred stone, fringed in the glow of streetlights. More honking. More shouting. Some girl's laugh explodes out of the dark like a frightened bird.

The city and all its poisons.

But *real.*

*Home.*

"I think I might walk for a while," she says, thinking Central Square is only a mile or so up the way. She can grab the next train there or—if she doesn't think she can handle that just yet—dial up an Uber.

"You sure?" Halloran asks. "It's pretty cold out."

She runs a hand down her overcoat. "I'll be okay," she says. "Thanks, though."

He nods. "There may be a news camera or two up there. Just put your head down and keep walking and they'll leave you be."

She stands. A soul-deadening tiredness has leeched into her bones, but as she climbs she can feel it start to loosen. She can feel her muscles coming back to life.

"Ms. Preedan," Halloran calls.

She turns.

"I know this is gonna be hard for a while," he says. "But you fought back. You survived. Hold onto that."

"Thank you," she says and means it.

"You've got my card if you need anything," he says.

"I do. Good night, I guess."

He chuckles humorlessly behind his mask. "Good night."

She turns back toward that oily square of night and continues to climb.

# THE BUZZING

## MIKE DUKE

Through a Percocet-induced fog, Clark Phillips's fingers scuttled along the large incision running from the top of his left shin to just above his knee. They scrabbled and scratched without any real conscious direction but somehow managed to deftly adjust pressure and not irritate the puffy scar tissue.

The home health nurse had removed the staples a week ago. It was three weeks now since the total knee replacement surgery, and the constant pain had finally subsided. Therapy wasn't as bad as it had been those first two weeks either. Except bending his leg for max flexion and holding it there. That was still excruciating. Unbearable, even, and it wore Clark out each time he did it—which was supposed to be a good three times a day.

The scar was a clean line except for the very top portion. That was wider than the rest. A thick scab occupied the center still, while the surrounding tissue was almost paper thin and redder than Clark thought it should be. The doctor had told him to keep an eye out for any signs of infection. He had asked the nurse about it, but after looking, she didn't think there was anything to worry about.

"Not uncommon," she had consoled him.

Clark was scratching at the top of the scar still when he opened his eyes, blinked, and glanced down at the wound, which was now exposed. The Lycra support stocking the doctor told him to wear for the first month post-surgery normally came up over his lower thigh. But it had rolled down to his kneecap while he slept, enabling Clark to pick and scratch at the healing flesh.

What he saw caused his hand to freeze mid-motion and his lungs to suck air in, one quick gulp, and then he held it.

He had scratched the scab completely off and opened a hole above his knee. His fingers were covered in blood, and red smear marks dotted his skin and the stocking. But what really disturbed him was the sight of a tiny fly sitting in the center of the open wound.

*Is that a fruit fly?* he thought.

It took off, buzzing loudly for such a small insect, moving up into the air above Clark. Its black form blended in with the background of the living room, giving Clark's pursuing gaze the slip.

He shook his head and rubbed his eyes, not trusting what he thought he saw. His mind was dubious, to say the least, but the purported perception was vying for dominance.

*Was that damn fly just sitting on the incision, or did it crawl out of it?*

Clark's instinct was to stand and try to catch the fly. But it only took one movement too far, and a jolt of pain to make him cease all efforts. At three weeks out, he still couldn't move around without the walker, and getting up and down was a complicated sequence of actions, not one smooth maneuver.

"Goddammit!" he exclaimed at the sharp bite in his knee.

Clark reached over to the table next to his recliner and grabbed the small flashlight and a piece of gauze pad he had there. Leaning forward as much as he could, he dabbed at the bloody portion of his scar and then shined the light on it, inspecting the flesh and prying the skin apart with thumb and forefinger, trying to look inside if possible.

"Nothing," he mumbled after some time and sat back in the chair. He tossed the gauze pad in a small trash can next to him, grabbed some antibiotic ointment and an extra-large Band-Aid, then dressed the open wound.

Before long, he fell back asleep. Fitful dreams of flies swarming about, landing on him, itching, and him swatting them plagued his unconscious mind.

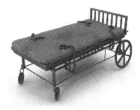

"Hey," the voice called to him, soft and comforting. "Hey," the female voice repeated gently. When Clark eased his eyelids open, his wife, Nancy's, face was just a foot away from his, smiling at him. She extended her hand and rubbed the side of his face.

"How's my Papa Bear doing? Are you hurting after therapy earlier today?"

"Not too bad," Clark muttered, trying to rouse himself. "I think I'm due for another Percocet, though. But, damn, this shit knocks me for a loop. Can hardly stay awake once I get still."

"Well, honey," Nancy said, standing up, "it's better than being in tons of pain, like you were the first two weeks."

"Yeah, I know," Clark conceded. "Just after three weeks of sleeping half the time, I feel like the most unproductive person alive. I can't even stay awake long enough to finish movies or properly binge-watch a TV show, much less do something legitimately useful with myself."

"Well, Clark, don't be so rough on yourself. Nobody in their right mind expects you to be productive right now, other than keeping up with your physical therapy exercises and stretches. Your only job is to regain range of motion and recover. Once you do that, you can start being 'productive' again. Kapeesh?"

Clark bowed his head slightly. "Yes, ma'am," he mumbled, then grinned at her. "Thank you. I needed that."

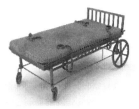

OVER THE NEXT WEEK, CLARK CONTINUED TO CHECK THE SCAR TISSUE beneath the Band-Aid. It didn't appear to be infected, but it refused to heal up all the way. The scab would not reform, and the skin around the edges stayed red and appeared to be puffier than before. However, it wasn't painful, and there wasn't any pus oozing or anything alarming like that. The most annoying development of all was it growing progressively itchier, to the point that hydrocortisone cream wasn't helping one bit anymore. The nurse informed Clark that itching at this stage of healing was normal, but he thought by this point it should be starting to ease up a bit instead of getting worse each day. The nurse wasn't concerned.

*I don't think she's taking any of my concerns seriously*, Clark thought as he rubbed and scratched the scar through the compression stocking. *Not one damn bit.*

The day before his one-month follow-up visit with his surgeon, Clark was struggling not to claw the hell out of the wound. The itching was maddening, and when he wasn't scratching, Clark would swear he felt something moving inside his skin there. Nothing overly dramatic. Just a wiggling perhaps. A ghost sensation that tickled one moment and itched like crazy the next. He had been told by the doc that the nerves on the outside of the knee would likely never provide normal sensation again. He hoped this wasn't the new norm. He was definitely going to ask the doc about it the next day.

Nancy was in the kitchen making dinner and not paying attention to him.

*Yes,* he thought. *If she saw me clawing myself like this, she'd give me hell and make me cover it up and good.*

Clark nonchalantly placed a throw pillow on the couch arm, obscuring his knee from Nancy's view in the kitchen, and proceeded to slide the stocking down and remove the Band-Aid. As he pulled it back to reveal the wound, Nancy called his name.

"Clark? Are you hungry yet?" she asked, without looking at him.

Clark's head jerked up, guilt spreading across his face. He saw she wasn't looking at him and glanced back down before she could get a glimpse at him and know she caught him with his hand in the proverbial cookie jar.

His eyes came to rest on the hole in his skin just in time to see a small black fly crawl out, shake its wings clean of blood, and then take flight.

Clark's mouth fell open as he gawked at the surreal scene unfolding before him.

*How the fuck...* was all he could think until the fly's movement broke his bout of disbelief.

"Holy shit!" he shouted and shoved himself into a standing position in one burst of movement. Clark grabbed the cane he had just started trying out in the last couple of days and started hobbling around, straining to maintain eye contact on this fly and see where it would land. If he could track it that far, he might be able to smash it with a magazine or book. He needed that fly to carry to the doctor appointment tomorrow. Proof he wasn't seeing things.

"What the blazes are you doing, Clark?" Nancy yelled at him and started hurrying his way. "You're gonna hurt yourself trying to move that quick! Slow down and let me help you. What do you need?"

Clark could hear the fly buzzing steadily. It flitted in and out of his sight, but the noise helped him reacquire it each time. Until the noise ceased and it disappeared completely.

"Dammit!" Clark blurted out, frustrated. "Do you see it, Nancy?" he asked her.

"See what?" she questioned him, not understanding what was going on.

"That damn fly! Didn't you hear it buzzing?" Clark continued scanning all around the area he last spotted the insect.

"A fly? No. I didn't hear any buzzing, and I didn't see any fly. What's the matter with you, honey?"

Clark turned and looked Nancy square in the eye.

"I just watched a *motherfucking* fly crawl out of this hole in my knee, shake my blood off its little wings, and then fly the fuck away!"

Clark's eyes were big and round as he pointed at his leg for emphasis and then waved his hand erratically through the air, indicating the flight path of the culprit. His face scrunched up, his nose raising in a half snarl. Disgust and utter consternation on full display at the same time.

Nancy shook her head back and forth, looking at Clark like he was hallucinating or something.

"Clark. Did you take an extra dose of Percocet by accident?" Nancy eyed him with concern.

Clark's hackles rose, insulted at her insinuation.

"No, I did not, dammit. What are you trying to say?"

"Well," Nancy began and hesitated for a moment. She recognized how antagonistic Clark was becoming and tried to choose her words carefully, though she could only tread so lightly given the nature of events. "I hear what you're saying, Clark…what you saw…or at least what you *think* you saw…"

She paused, seeing his neck and shoulders tense, his eyes squint and narrow at the perceived affront to his basic rationality.

"But, seriously, honey, do you really think something like that could have happened? Have you ever heard of such a thing?"

Clark eyed her with a look of betrayal and more than a bit of dismay, but at the same time, her questions rang true.

"Maybe you drifted back off and dropped into a dream. Wouldn't be the first time since the surgery. Right?"

Clark looked down, not wanting to relent but finding it impossible to deny the fantastical aspect of it all.

"Baby," Nancy tried to console and comfort, "let me pour some hydrogen peroxide in the hole and bandage it up better for you. I'll put something bigger than a Band-Aid on it. How does that sound?"

Clark looked back up at her, face still stiff. It wasn't easy letting go of something you knew in your gut was real, even if it sounded insane to anyone else.

"You'll take a good look inside it with the flashlight too, right?" he asked, eyes pleading with concern. "Before you bandage it up?"

Nancy could tell right away this would be a non-negotiable demand if he was going to let it go.

"Of course I will," she said. "Go sit down in the recliner and prop your leg up. I'll get everything together and take care of you right there."

Nancy smiled lovingly at Clark and walked into the bathroom.

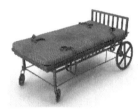

"Look at it, Doc," Clark pleaded, pointing at the hole in his knee, the bandage removed. "That shit don't look normal."

"Of course, it doesn't look normal, Clark!" Doc Morton chided him. "You've been digging at it like a dog does a hole in the dirt. What the hell, man? You're lucky it hasn't gotten infected!"

Clark wanted to object, but the doc didn't give him the opportunity.

"All right, Clark. Here's what we're going to do. I'm going to treat this now and bandage the hell out of it. I don't want you or Nancy or anybody to touch this bandage. You're back to sponge-bath rules for the next couple of weeks. Every three days, I want you to come in here and I'll get one of my nurses to bring you back and change the dressing. You can't allow yourself to scratch this thing anymore or you're going to end up with a severe infection, maybe even an abscess or gangrene. That kind of stuff could lead to major complications. Even amputation. So this isn't something to play around with. You feel me?"

The doctor canted his head and looked down his nose at Clark, eyes like slits, challenging him to argue.

Clark mumbled in the affirmative but wasn't happy about it.

Doc Morton looked at him, confused. "Clark, is there something you're not telling me? Your response is not what I would expect under normal circumstances."

Clark glanced up, hesitated for a moment as he caught the look Nancy was giving him out of the corner of his eye, and then decided to just spill his guts and get the whole thing off his chest, no matter how crazy it might sound.

"All right, doc. I didn't tell you everything. Nancy, here, thinks it was just a dream, but I swear to God, I saw something crazy happen yesterday."

Doc Morton had a mixture of feelings vying for expression on his face. He felt baffled, confused, and amused all at the same time.

"Well," he prodded Clark. "Hit me with it."

Clark took a deep breath and mentally said *Geronimo* before blurting everything out.

"I saw a freakin' fly crawl out of this damn hole in my leg yesterday," he insisted, pointing at it for emphasis. "Clear as I see you right now. Little bugger sat for a few seconds shaking blood off its wings—my blood, mind you—then flew off across the living room. I tried to get up and spot where it landed so I could kill it, but it disappeared."

Clark stopped and finally took a significant breath of air, staring at Doctor Morton, expecting to be treated like a crazy man. Doc Morton scrunched his bottom lip, chin rising in contemplation for a moment.

"A fly, huh? What kind?"

"I'm not sure. 'Bout the size of a fruit fly or a little bigger," Clark informed the doc.

Doc Morton nodded his head up and down.

"Well, I can't say it's the strangest thing I've ever heard of," the doc confided, "but it definitely defies rational explanation. I can't see how any fly larvae could have gotten into your wound."

"Doc!" Clark exclaimed. "I don't have a god damned clue either, but it's been itching like three hells for a week or more now. Something isn't right." Clark's fist slammed down on the counter next to him, unconsciously emphasizing the last word. Doc Morton jumped a little in surprise.

"Okay, Clark. Okay," he tried to reassure his patient. "How 'bout I look inside and see what we can see before bandaging it up? Sound good?"

Clark nodded, relaxing after finally feeling he was being taken seriously.

Doc Morton donned a head lamp and grabbed a small fiber-optic camera and made sure it was transmitting to the computer screen. He gave Clark a local shot to numb the flesh and proceeded to irrigate the hole with distilled water while a nurse spread the wound with her fingers. With his other hand, Doc Morton pressed the fiber-optic camera into the edge of the wound, continuing to flush it with water in hopes of seeing inside better.

"Hmmm, tweezers," the doc mumbled to himself and sat the camera down to pick a pair up, probing inside the hole. Clark felt a tugging sensation but couldn't see what was happening. Anxiety gripped him suddenly.

"You see something, doc?" he asked, a crack in his voice betraying the borderline panic he was experiencing.

"Nope, Clark. Not a thing. I thought I did, but it was just part of your remaining tendons. That's it."

Doc Morton looked Clark in the eye. "All's good. Now, I'm gonna put a couple of stitches in this and bandage it up," he said and patted Clark's good leg to reassure him. "But to cover all bases, we'll draw some blood and do a CT scan as well. My nurse will get you set up with that, and I'll call you with the results as soon as I get them."

A half hour later, Clark headed out the door with explicit instructions to not scratch the wound and to come back in three days and have the dressing cleaned. His head spun with doubts. He questioned his own senses. *Was it the drugs?* he wondered. *Was he crazy?* Even more terrifying—*Was he sane and Doctor Morton was covering something up?*

Nancy observed Clark's posture shift beneath the weight of fear and distrust, though she suspected it was more frustration than anything else. She rubbed his back as he walked slowly toward their vehicle using the cane for support with every step he took.

CLARK AWOKE TO SUNLIGHT STREAMING IN THROUGH THE LIVING ROOM window and a buzzing in his ear. He jerked his head up and looked around, scanning for the fly he was sure he had just heard.

He had fallen asleep in the recliner binge-watching *X-Files*. He listened intently but heard nothing else. *A dream perhaps?* he wondered, but then he noticed the sticky feeling of his left-hand fingers. He looked down and saw layers of blood covering his fingertips–dry, mostly dry and congealed–fifty shades of crimson.

"Fuck," escaped his lips as his eyes glanced down to see his knee smeared in blood and trails of red running down the armrest as well as the inside of his knee. The bandage was in tatters, the stitches busted, and the ragged edges of flesh spread apart.

And that was when he saw something odd.

Movement. Pulsating, wriggling movement of some sort, just beneath the skin of his knee below the hole. Almost as if something soft was crawling about. The itching hit him like a hammer, and his stomach did a belly flop.

*Maggots!!!* his brain shrieked.

"Oh, fuck me! Fuck me!" he blurted out, fingers scrabbling at his knee, pushing, prodding, squeezing, trying to press the offending fleshy form toward the opening and force it out of him. His digits slipped and skidded across his blood-covered skin. Whatever was inside seemed to squirm deeper.

"Oh god, oh god, oh god," he muttered, desperately trying to rid himself of this invader, overwhelmed by the foreign nature of its presence, the absolute violation of his tissue. It mocked every notion of security, blasphemed the sacredness of a man's own body—corrupted his temple.

He manipulated the area surrounding the wound relentlessly,

but nothing emerged except a steady stream of blood as he pinched the skin from all angles.

"Clark!" Nancy almost shouted.

He froze, eyes locking with hers–his were the deer, hers the proverbial headlights. Guilt flooded his mind, and he peered back down at his knee. It looked like he had slaughtered a small animal atop his leg.

"What in God's name have you done, Clark?" she pleaded with him, her face begging for a rational answer, though not really expecting one.

"I...I woke up like this..." he began with a truth, his instincts debating on whether to stick with that strategy and confess or deviate with a seat-of-the-pants deception. He stared at Nancy and knew he couldn't lie worth a damn to her.

"But then...then I swear I saw something moving under my skin. It rippled and moved like something was squirming underneath...like a maggot maybe..."

His voice trailed off and he couldn't stand to hold her gaze any longer. The look of shocked pity that filled her eyes was too much for him to bear. He felt ashamed, forsaken, and frustrated beyond words, all at the same time.

"Oh my goodness, Clark. Bless your heart..." Nancy stepped forward and reached out to cup his cheeks in her hands.

Anger welled in Clark, and he jerked his head back and checked her hands with his own.

"Bless my heart? Really?" His stiff neck, pursed lips, and raised nostrils communicated the degree of insult he felt at that moment. Nancy recoiled as if a snake had reared its head at her.

"I don't want to hear another word or see another sympathetic look from you. Just carry me to the ER."

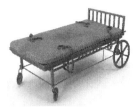

C<small>LARK HAD CLEANED UP, DRESSED HIMSELF, AND WALKED DOWN TO THE</small> vehicle without saying a word. He didn't speak the entire way to the urgent care facility either. He signed in on his own, and when the nurse called his name, he stood and immediately held up a hand to stop Nancy in her tracks. She sat back down and stayed in the waiting room while he went back to see the doctor.

He emerged forty minutes later, face frozen in a scowl, nearly striking the floor with the cane at every step. Nancy stood and simply walked in front of him, opening the door for him and then going ahead to the vehicle to unlock the doors and start it. She knew better than to ask him anything right now. She had never seen him look so angry. Never seen him glower with such intense rage. This was not like her husband. Not at all.

They drove in silence for a few minutes. It was Clark who broke it.

"That motherfucking quack job doc in a box," he sputtered. "Told me I was imagining it all. Told me I needed to take some Valium." Clark waved the prescription about violently in protest. "And I need to wear mittens to sleep or something to stop me from picking at it and messing up the stitches."

He paused long enough to take three deep breaths, then continued to rail against the curveball life wouldn't stop throwing at him right now.

"Can you believe that shit? Valium and mittens? *Valium!*" he spat. "And *motherfucking mittens!*"

Nancy drove, listening but refusing to speak. *Just let him vent*, she thought.

Clark shook his head back and forth. "Valium and motherfucking mittens," he muttered to himself. "I'll be damned."

Nancy pulled into the pharmacy parking lot, took the script from

Clark, and walked in to fill it, all without a word. When she got back in, she set the bag in his lap and drove the rest of the way home. Neither of them said another word.

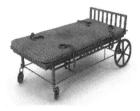

"HELLO," CLARK ANSWERED HIS CELL PHONE.

"Hi, is this Clark Brady?" a female voice asked. "This is Nurse Beckett with Doctor Morton's office. He asked me to call you with the results of your CT scan and bloodwork. Everything looked fine. No abnormalities in your blood tests and nothing but bone, metal, and normal tissue in the scan. Everything is fine. Just leave the stitches alone and let it finish healing up, Mr. Brady."

Clark's stomach knotted. He wanted to scream at this young lady but knew it would do zero good. He swallowed back hard on his emotions and just said, "Thank you, ma'am. You have a good day," then pressed end.

He sat there, stewing in a cauldron full of bubbling angst, rage, and paranoia. He knew something was not right, but everyone else kept telling him there was nothing wrong. Everything is *A-OK*, they assured him.

Well, someone was lying, and it wasn't his eyes. He was sure of it. But how to prove his senses were working in proper order? It took some time, but the idea finally came to him. So simple a middle schooler could have thought of it.

Clark stood and embarked on a small scavenger hunt, rummaging through drawers, cabinets, boxes, and even out in the garage. When he had all the items, he came back to the living room and sat down in the recliner. Nancy left for the store to take care of the big grocery shopping trip.

When she was gone, Clark removed the bandage, snipped the stitches, and set about applying his improvised fly trap. A small mason jar with a rubber gasket he had laying around from a failed car repair would allow him to capture any escaping flies and observe them. There would be *no* other explanation for where they came from. He used some flesh-toned stretch wound wrap to secure it firmly to his knee. Once done, he stuffed some pillows under his knee to prop it up, started up another episode of *X-Files*, and settled in to wait.

After staring at the jar more than the TV for a half hour or more, Clark decided the old adage "a watched pot never boils" was probably accurate in his situation as well. He made an effort to not look at it and tried to pay attention to the show. Of all the episodes he could have started, it was the one with the insects that came out of the old trees the logging company had cut down, cocooned the workers, and dehydrated them. It made Clark shiver, but eventually he nodded off anyway.

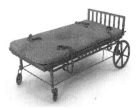

SOMETHING TICKLED HIS SKIN, MADE IT ITCH. HE REACHED TO SCRATCH it, but his fingertips hit glass first. The jar. He heard a mild buzzing. Light and distant but clear, nonetheless. He glanced down at the jar, and every muscle in his body spasmed in a violent startle response. He saw a small black fly beneath the glass. It flew about, buzzing, landed, crawled, then took off to fly and buzz again. It could not stay still.

Clark gaped at it, his jaw hanging slack for some time before he picked up his phone and took video footage of it. The skin around the hole began to quiver, pulsating in a rhythmic fashion, and then everything surrounding it joined in, the jittering flesh extending out beyond the edges of the jar. Clark's eyes stared in horror at the alien movement of his skin.

*This is not right,* he thought. *This is so not fucking right.*

Clark decided to press at the afflicted area. He placed his thumbs just above the jar, where quadriceps and knee met, and pressed in and down toward the wound. His hands jerked away as if bitten by an electrical current. A swarm of black flies poured forth from his knee. His eyes blinked rapid fire with disbelief. The buzzing noise multiplied a hundred-fold, filled his ears, and vibrated in his skull. His entire body trembled and grew weak. The need to evacuate all contents gripped his stomach. He turned his head to the right and leaned over the armrest. Vomit sprayed onto the carpet. The hamburger and French fries he had for lunch mixed with bile produced a revolting odor. His abdomen continued to contract, forcing him to wretch until nothing was left. The contractions continued, and he dry-heaved over and over. Agonizing spasms wracked his entire midsection and stabbed with a vicious intensity beneath his sternum. He thought he might disgorge his entire esophagus and stomach, turning them inside out in the process. When at last the dry heaves relented, Clark collapsed back into the recliner. Eyes squeezed shut, he struggled to calm his labored breathing.

The pain subsided at last. He opened his eyes and instantly they were drawn like a magnet back to the jar, to the black flies plastered across the interior. Some crawled over one another while others buzzed about in flight, all of them searching dutifully for a way of escape. Despite having believed his senses and fears the entire time, now, with what seemed to be undeniable proof, Clark felt the greatest feeling of disbelief.

He realized with absolute certainty in that moment, he did not *want* to be right.

*But I am right,* he thought. *God help me, I was right all along.*

He wiped his mouth and stared at the flies.

"Holy fuck. What do I do now?" he asked himself out loud.

"Clark!" He heard Nancy call from the back of the house. "Are you okay?" Her voice was already closer. "I was bringing the groceries in. It sounded like you were throwing up."

Nancy walked in and immediately saw the vomit on the carpet. Then she looked at Clark's leg, the jar taped to his knee too, at odds with its surroundings to blend in.

She stared for a long moment at the contraption and then looked him in the eye with a painful degree of concern.

"Clark," she began, trepidation filling her voice. "Why do you have a jar strapped to your knee?"

Clark looked at her like she had grown a third eye or something similarly foreign and absurd.

"What the fuck do you mean, 'why do I have a jar strapped to my knee?' Are ye daft as well as blind, woman? Can you not see them?"

Clark's head jutted forward and bobbled to and fro in disbelief.

"See what?" Nancy asked him, enunciating each word with care.

Clark's whole body went rigid. He spoke his next words slow and precise.

"You have got to be fucking kidding me."

Nancy clamped a hand across her mouth, face scrunched up, breathing erratic, eyes unable to accept what had become of her husband.

"Don't tell me you can't see the flies in the jar, Nancy!" Clark screamed at her, his whole body shaking with the violence of his demand. "Don't you fucking dare tell me you can't see them! There are hundreds of them inside that jar. They're crawling all over the inside, flying all around. And buzzing. Holy shit! Don't tell me you can't hear the buzzing!"

Nancy's hand gripped her mouth like a seal. Tears burned in her eyes, flowed down her cheeks to be flung through the air as she shook her head back and forth.

"I'm not fucking crazy, Nancy!" he shouted. Clark reached for his phone again and took more footage now that the rest had emerged. After several seconds he stopped it and played it back.

"There they are!" he declared. "Right on candid fucking camera video. I've got it. I'm not nuts!" He glared at Nancy, and she cringed, shrinking away from the fury in his eyes.

"It's right here, Nancy! On video. Proof! Look at it."

An almost imperceptible shaking of her head occurred, but Clark picked up on it. "Dammit, Nancy! Look at it!" Clark shoved the phone screen toward her. "Look at it!" he snarled and pumped his hand twice reinforcing his command. Nancy retreated, back to the wall, head wobbling back and forth in a terrified refusal to look at the video.

"Goddammit, Nancy! You're in on this too, aren't you? You've been in on it the whole time." Clark palmed his forehead and shook his own head. "Oh my fucking god. How did I not see this? You traitorous bitch! How can you stand there and go along with this whole conspiracy? They've incubated flies inside my skin! Flies, for god's sake!"

Clark clamped his hands over both ears all of a sudden and cried out.

"Gaaaahhhhh! The buzzing! It's getting too loud. I can't stand it."

Without warning, Clark put the recliner down, stood up, and started hobbling into the kitchen where he grabbed a knife and cut the bandaging holding the jar to his leg. As he ripped the jar away with one hand, he covered the opening with his other and moved to the sink. Numerous flies escaped and flew about his head. He pursed his lips and blew at them to shoo them away while he turned the faucet on full force. He quickly removed his hand from the opening and tried to drown as many of the flies as possible. More escaped, but Clark watched as several were drowned by the water flooding over them. He watched them swirl within for a moment before setting the jar down and picking the knife back up.

There were more flies still crawling out of the wound on his knee. He laid the blade along the edge of the wound, pressed down hard, and drew it down the length of his knee cap. Blood poured down his leg. Nancy screamed and ran for the phone, knowing she was not capable of stopping him. She called 911 and pleaded with them to send police and rescue to stop her husband from harming himself.

Clark proceeded to pull the layers of skin apart and dig his fingers inside, feeling all about for any more flies or larvae, dragging his nails over both bone and metal implants, tendons and ligaments, searching for any more foreign bodies to expunge. He was getting ready to cut sideways along the inside of his leg when officers rushed him, tackling him to the ground, his face striking the corner of a countertop on the way down and opening up a gash that bled worse than his leg.

Nancy shrieked and sobbed and wailed, "I'm sorry, Clark," the whole time they strapped him to a gurney and loaded him in the ambulance.

And Clark kept yelling at them all. "Look in the jar! They're there, I tell you. The flies are there! Just look in the jar, for god's sake!" Over and over, Clark and Nancy's duet continued until the doors of the ambulance shut and the trip to the ER and psych ward began.

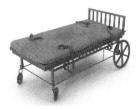

CLARK WOKE UP IN A SOFT WHITE ROOM WEARING A STRAITJACKET, HIS whole body strapped down to a bed. All he could move was his head. He had no idea how much time had transpired. Hours? Days? He had no clue.

He just knew his face hurt...and it itched.

He contracted the muscles in his right cheek, testing the waters. It bit him with a jolt of pain when he moved, but it didn't help the itch. Or the feeling of something small and very light touching his skin. Clark cast his eyes down as sharply as possible, and out of his peripheral vision he made it out. A tiny black fly crawled out from between the stitches in his cheek. It shook its little transparent wings and flew into the air, buzzing. Clark tried to follow it, but the door opened and light flooded in.

A doctor—Doctor Morton—walked in and scrutinized the room, searching here and there, then suddenly plucked the fly out of the air between his forefinger and thumb. The man smiled at Clark, walked out of the room, and shut the door behind him.

Clark screamed, but nobody answered him. Outside all he could hear was Nancy crying and saying she was sorry. But inside the room...and inside his head...he heard the buzzing flies...multiplying and growing...in his knee and in his cheek. Felt the tiny, itching vibrations as they buzzed and crawled beneath his skin. Cutting his eyes, he strained to see the flesh covering his cheekbone twitch and undulate but he could not. The straps held his head and body immobile. But Clark knew the truth. He wasn't crazy. He was a guinea pig. Being crazy would have been a blessing by comparison.

Clark breathed deep and screamed again. He felt tiny legs crawl onto his face and then they were gone. In the dim light, he could see the fat-bodied fly lazily making its way across the room like a drunk man staggering home from the bar. It landed on the rectangular window inset in the door then sat there, rubbing its legs together. The sound was a mix between a buzz and a scratch and dug at his brain. But it was the glossy black ichor exuding from the fly's mouth and dripping from its legs onto the glass that made Clark's skin crawl.

Dr. Morton appeared at the door window, smiling at the fly, and tapping on the glass. He looked at Clark. One eyebrow rose slowly as the doctor tilted his head downward and grinned with a devious charm. He waved his fingers up and down at Clark, then returned his attention to the amorphous fly, whose body was transforming into a white, bulbous, undulating form with double the wings, double the legs, and double the mass, and it was growing.

Clark's stomach did a somersault cannonball right before ejecting its contents in a projectile geyser, arcing upward before falling onto his chest. He panted like a dog in July seeking shade, and spit, but there was no relief in sight for him. He'd never leave this place. Not alive anyway.

# WHEN LIGHTNING STRIKES

## RICHARD CLIVE

"Y ou're keeping something from me," said Tom, putting down his cappuccino. He was staring at her from across the table. "Something's wrong."

"Nothing's wrong," said Penny, her hand sheltering her eyes from the sun's glare. The pavement café was packed with people enjoying the outside service, the city streets bustling on a warm summer's day. Beside them, a floppy-haired vendor sold popcorn from an old-fashioned cart, his machine's glass box popping with kernels of corn.

Penny knew Tom knew...*something*. He always did. But it was *her* body, and she'd be damned if she was going to let him control her. Like he had the past four years.

"When it ended, with Jodie—"

"Your ex has nothing to do with us," she said.

"Trust is important in a relationship."

Was it even a relationship anymore? Sometimes she felt it was more like a dictatorship. When Tom first set up the joint bank account and offered to pay her phone bill, she thought it was a sweet gesture, an old-fashioned guy wanting to take care of her. Little did she know it was a seizure of power. Concealing her movements had become increasingly challenging.

"Trust works two ways," she said finally.

"So…there's nothing you want to tell me?" he said, pushing his horn-rimmed glasses back up to the bridge of his nose.

"Nothing," she said, her heart quickening.

Sometimes she even felt guilty for the most trivial acts of deceit. She resented him for that, for turning her into a liar. But this was far from trivial. She had considered ending the relationship. But he'd created such a web of co-dependency that splitting up would require an almighty level of resolve.

"Right," he said, tapping a teaspoon against the glass tabletop.

"*Right*," she repeated.

She'd read somewhere people looked to the left when they lied. Or was it right? She kept her eyes on him, holding his gaze, remembering a magazine article speculating whether liars blinked infrequently or excessively. Anxiety spread from her gut, her head trembling like one of those wobble-headed car toys, a bead of sweat running down her forehead. She resisted touching her face.

"I want you to sign something," he said, reaching inside his jacket and producing a folded sheet of paper and a stainless-steel ballpoint pen. He placed them on the table in front of her.

"What is it?"

"Open it."

She did. The A4 form was embossed with the bank's letterhead. Her heart skipped a beat.

"Sign it," he said.

Her eyes scanned the text, but her mind was racing, and she couldn't gather enough composure to process the words on the sheet. The letter might as well have been written in ancient Hebrew. Then she read something about their accounts requiring a joint signature.

"*Sign it*," he insisted.

She signed reluctantly, knowing deep down what this was about.

She handed him the form, which he refolded and placed back in his jacket pocket. She tried to give him the pen, too, but he waved his hand dismissively, so she clipped it to her blouse's breast pocket.

At once, the heavens above the city's skyline darkened, brooding thunderheads arriving from nowhere.

"Looks like rain," she said. "We should finish up."

Tom ignored her weather concerns.

"That document prevents you from withdrawing money from our savings account...at least without a double signature." He sighed deeply, closed his eyes, then said, "Why is £600 missing from our savings account, Penny?"

He made her feel like a child when he used her name. That bead of sweat finally dripped onto her skirt, and she felt heat rising to her cheeks, her pores prickling. His coffee breath wafted from across the table, and it sickened her. She was hot, uncomfortable, desperate to get up and walk away.

"According to our banking app, the money was withdrawn at the branch three days ago," he said. "We agreed not to touch that money. Babies are expensive. They need clothes, toys, nappies...and that's not even factoring in your maternity."

Her mind grasped for an excuse she knew she should have already prepared. They never touched the account, had saved nearly £2,000. She'd planned to replace the money in the coming months. He never checked the savings... *Never...*

*Stupid...stupid...stupid...*

"Well—?"

"I'm not pregnant, Tom."

"If we keep trying, it's a matter of time," he said.

Lightning pulsed.

An old memory flickered in her mind's eye, one best forgotten. They'd never meant for the old man to break his arm. She shook off the random thought.

"Where's our money?" he demanded.

The sky cracked with thunder.

Again, the memory flashed in her mind.

"*Well?*" he said.

The body hit the pavement with a sickening thud, warm pink mist spraying Penny's bare ankles. She stood, lurching away from the table. Her cup toppled to the ground, porcelain shattering like the fragments of the human skull at her feet. Gray matter leaked from the body's left ear.

People screamed and ran, knocking over tables and chairs as a hot wind arrived, whipping the café's parasol umbrellas.

"Shit," shouted Tom.

Penny checked her ankles and found them spattered with blood and a fleck of what looked like gray porridge. The dead man's shattered teeth were scattered like dice about the remains of his head, but as luck would have it, his business suit remained intact, a wet sack of mush seeping internal organs. The body was flat, like a deflated balloon. Despite the commotion, she checked her lower legs for any breaks in the skin that might allow infected blood in. She was clear. Disgusted, she used a serviette to wipe her lower legs.

"J—Jumper," Penny stuttered, looking up at the six-story building towering over them. Above, she spotted an open window where curtains bloomed in the wind. But as her eyes surveyed the upper reaches of the apartment complex, she saw a second man standing on the edge of the penthouse suite's open roof.

Bright streaks of lightning blazed in the sky.

She grabbed Tom's sleeve and pulled him away from where she feared the second man might land. They had barely moved five feet when another body hit the pavement with a nauseating thwack.

More screams echoed amongst the city's glass and concrete.

"The fuck?" shouted Tom.

Crowds of distressed and screaming people ran into the road, away from the bespattered sidewalk, stopping cars and delivery trucks. Horns hooted. Somewhere a siren wailed, and when thunder roared, so did the motorcycle that weaved between the stationary traffic. The sports bike let out an almighty growl as the rider opened the throttle and careened into a crowd of a dozen people at hurtling speed. Bodies flew. A man and woman lay motionless, crushed between the bike and a white Honda Civic, the car painted with fresh blood.

Tears filled Penny's eyes as she turned and started to jog down the street, away from the chaos. Ahead, a woman was digging a broken glass bottle into her wrist. "The lightning," the woman screamed. "I didn't mean it…I'm sorry, I'm sorry…I didn't mean it…"

In her peripheral vision, far above her, climbing scaffolding attached to a towering Victorian theatre, Penny saw a construction worker step over the safety guardrails. Lightning blinked, momentarily turning the man into a lonely silhouette, a superhero surveying the city below. Then, at once, many of the buildings' highest windows opened like eyes...of surrounding office blocks... of apartments...of city hotels... The people inside the concrete and glass structures clambered to reach the windows before their colleagues...friends...family...

Penny covered her eyes.

The next peal of thunder was the loudest yet, but Penny could still hear the bodies hitting the pavement, one after the other, the sound like the kernels of corn popping inside that glass box.

ANGRY THUNDERHEADS ROLLED ABOVE THE CITY'S SKYLINE, THE bulbous topography of every cloud backlit by the pulsing lightning.

Penny felt like her head was spinning due to sensory overload and anxiety, beads of sweat slaloming down the slope of her nose. The atmosphere was charged, the small hairs on her arms and neck standing on end. The air tasted like coins, too, tinged with the distinct chlorine-like scent of ozone. On went the distant screams, a chaotic chorus carried by the raging wind.

They were just outside the city center, in an area she knew well, populated by university buildings both old and new. The architecture varied from modern office blocks to neo-gothic revival, glass-fronted student halls neighboring ornately designed art galleries and grand-looking libraries. A maze of footpaths and walkways cut through the campus' parks and leafy gardens. Here, the streets were deserted, the light oddly tinted with a pinkish hue.

"Follow me," said Tom, jogging ahead. "Don't talk to anybody."

She followed.

A lightning bolt struck a nearby elm tree, splitting its trunk—and her mind flashed again with the childhood memory of the ball hitting old Mr. Carter's kitchen window. The kids had feared for their lives when the old man stormed out onto the street, waving a kitchen knife. He popped the ball before their eyes, tossing the deflated case into a nearby hedge. Later, one of the other kids tossed a firecracker through his mail slot, startling the old man. He fell, breaking his arm on his kitchen floor where he lay for four hours until help arrived.

Thunder detonated, every violent fulmination vibrating in Penny's bones.

In her twenty-eight years, she had witnessed surreal events. As a young child, she remembered her family crowding around the TV as the first jet-propelled airliner exploded when it hit the World Trade Center's North Tower; she remembered, too, recent news coverage of huge apocalyptic fires consuming Californian forests, and she had watched Chinese doctors dressed in hazmat suits on YouTube, investigating a worrying plague.

But *nothing* like this.

An entire city's population had been driven to a state of insanity, seemingly by an electrical storm. And she thought she understood, at least to some extent. Because when the lightning flickered, pictures pulsed in Penny's mind's eye in perfect lucidity, memories replaying in high definition. Memories she wanted to forget.

*Flash…*

She sees Annabelle, the snotty little girl with no friends, her ginger hair tied with red bows. She sees her best friend Jess shoving her, the other girls joining in, pulling Annabelle's frizzy hair, ripping her blouse. She watches everything but says nothing…

*Flash…*

She sees Arthur, the school hamster she took home for holidays, running in his little plastic ball like he hadn't a care in the world. He hadn't—until his ball reached the edge of the top of the stairs. *Somebody* should have been watching. She sees her father holding a rusted garden spade, digging a little hole in their back garden…

*Flash…*

She sees her dying grandmother lying on a bed in a piss-stinking old people's home, the room thick with heat, her body a used-up husk of skin and bones. She hears her younger self promising to visit again soon. But seeing her nanny struggle in her final days was an ugly sight. She sees a coffin and a bigger hole…

When she closed her eyes, thunder boomed, and she felt its aftershock, stirring echoes in the vault of her mind, waking the past from its slumber.

The visions were as toxic as venom, irrefutable evidence infecting the minds of the masses with unreasonable guilt. God help those who had committed more serious sins. Humans were self-centered animals, weren't they? But unlike less sentient creatures, people were cursed with the affliction of withstanding their conscience.

For many, it was too much to bear, instigating a wave of insanity. If judgment came from above, punishment, it seemed, would come from within.

The storm had brought the lives of the city's population into sharp focus. And there was something stranger: *sometimes* the lightning showed new memories…things that hadn't happened…*to her.*

"Keep up," said Tom.

Sheets of newspaper drifted in the deserted streets. A page caught on a lamppost, flapping in the breeze: SUMMER STORMS, the headline predicted

"We need to get out of sight," said Tom, taking a path veering between a modern office block and a much older library building. "You see people, stay away. We are too visible on the main street."

They hurried down the narrow walkway, and the man stepped out from the shadows where he had been sheltering beneath an office block portico. "I know what you've done," he said.

Tom stopped, turned toward him.

The man drank from a plastic bottle, a brand of cheap white cider favored by juvenile delinquents and tramps. His wiry form was concealed by a filthy-looking pea-green parka, the architecture of his face altered by a jaw shrunken from tooth loss. He wore a scowl on his haggard face, his being permeating a sickening miasma of ammonia, alcohol, and vinegary sweat.

"I know what you've done," the man repeated.

Tom ignored him, turned, and beckoned Penny to keep up.

Tom's skin was pale and clammy looking. He appeared nearly as sick as the alcoholic rogue attempting conversation.

"Hey," said the man, shouting at Tom. "I'm *talking* to you."

Homeless gangs often congregated around the university campus, smoking, drinking, wasting away the hours of the day, begging students to part with spare change. Penny sympathized with them, imagined spending a single night on the cold city streets. If she were homeless, she thought she might drink too. But this man was aggressive in his approach, threatening, confrontational.

"Just ignore him," said Tom, reaching for her hand.

"Think you're better than me, do you?" said the man, spraying white-flecked saliva bubbles on his unshaven chin. "I know what you did."

Tom momentarily locked eyes with the man, and Penny noticed the vagrant's own contained a purplish glow, a trick of the storm's light perhaps.

"Finally got your attention, did I?" said the man, still looking at Tom, a toothless smirk forming on his skeletal face. "What you did—"

"Shut up," shouted Tom, stepping forward, fists clenched.

"I were you, missy, I'd get as far away as possible from this one."

"What are you talking about?" said Penny.

"He's a lunatic," said Tom. "Pay no attention—"

From the corner of her eye, inside the nearest office block, Penny saw a body violently launch itself headfirst against a ground-floor window. A shower of glass exploded. Penny reeled away. Writhing in the window's jagged glass, the blond-headed woman screamed, a shard piercing her cheek, spiking up and into her right eye. Another glass fragment penetrated her neck, blood pooling on the red-brick walkway where they stood. She flailed, arms outstretched, the glass cutting deeper into her throat as she thrashed.

"Damned," the woman croaked, "all of us…damned."

The homeless-looking man gulped his cider, then began to laugh.

Penny's eyes met Tom's. His eyes were bright beacons, glowing with a purple, ethereal light.

Lightning strobed.

She sees a smashed dinner plate lying on the black-and-white tiles of a kitchen floor, the gravied remains of a home-cooked dinner beneath broken porcelain. She sees a bottle lying on its side on a checkered tablecloth, red wine pooling beneath the flickering candle. She sees a young woman, head in hands and crying, her bruises as dark as storm clouds. She sees a younger Tom, throwing a packet of pills onto the table, blister pack jutting from a box she recognizes as a brand of oral contraceptives. She sees his fists balled, his scowl fixed, staring at this other girl…

*Jodie? His ex…?*

The drunken tramp was now hysterical with laughter.

Tom pulled Penny farther along the path, at which point she snapped fully from her trance—and saw something fall from the sky. The body hit the ground face down with a wet slap, bones audibly breaking on impact. The fallen man then began to twitch gently in a final seizure, lower teeth protruding through his upper lip, face flattened beyond recognition.

Then another body fell—and another, and another.

They dropped from the buildings above. When Penny looked, she saw people on the roofs, their eyes wide and glowing purple.

Still, the woman in the broken window thrashed, and the drunk shouted, "I know what you've done, *Tom*. I know what you've done."

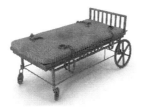

"It's just like that movie," said Tom, pacing, his eyes their usual blue. "On Netflix."

"With the blindfolds?" said Penny.

"No, the old one."

She shook her head. This was nothing like a movie. This was fucking Old Testament.

They were holed up in a grotty crack den on the city's edge, the abandoned high-rise apartment a scene of depravity. Candy wrappers and cola cans littered the tattered carpet, and dirty needles lay scattered, too, the syringes' blood-stained barrels evidence of probable heroin abuse. Tom had kicked the nearest hypodermics away. The place reeked of stale cigarettes and wet socks, the warm, damp apartment incubating mold or mildew.

"You've still not told me where that money went?" said Tom.

Penny remained silent, sitting on a tattered armchair facing her disheveled reflection in a cracked mirror on the wall.

The door to the balcony was open between a pair of curtains that billowed in the wind. Penny stared at the city's skyline, observing the pulsing storm as faint screams traveled on the howling wind, echoing between the distant tower blocks, the sound reminding her of a long-ago trip to a theme park. *Rollercoaster screams.* But *these* screams were real, the modulation rough, their harrowing acoustics unlocking a primal brand of fear buried deep within her DNA.

Back at the university campus, the purple glow in Tom's eyes had terrified her, but he was yet to throw himself from one of the high-rise buildings' concrete balconies or cut his wrists with broken glass. Did he have a conscience? She wondered.

Did she?

For her, the storm had stirred difficult memories, but that was all. Her bladder had nearly let go when the bodies first began to drop. But she was yet to lose control of her emotions. Yet to turn mad with regret. There had been no suicidal impulses or wanton acts of violence. What she feared most was Tom. If the storm could show her things, surely it could show him too.

"I need to be able to trust you," he said, his voice low.

"You can," she mumbled.

"Then what did you do with that money?"

She tried to keep her breathing steady. Now was not the time for this discussion. Their lives were in mortal danger. Their relationship *was* a serious commitment—or *had* been. But this wasn't about commitment, was it? It was about control. Always had been.

270

"Not telling me is as good as lying."

Not telling him was her only option. Back at the university campus, she had seen his potential for violence, had seen what he had done to poor Jodie. The lightning had shown her. Tom's fury had been palpable, such was the intensity of the vision.

*"Tell me."*

Outside the sky flared.

"Penny?"

Thunder snapped.

She thought again of lying but feared he would know.

*He would know...*

The ceiling's cobwebs wafted as the wind intruded from the open balcony door, the light fitting, too, swaying. Then the bare bulb flickered. Thunder crashed, the sound like a mountain avalanche, and in the cracked, dirty glass of the mirror she faced, Penny saw her eyes contained an ethereal radiance. A purple glow.

*Shit...*

"Tell me."

"I—"

"The money, the fucking money?"

Her eyes were bright in the mirror, and so were Tom's, and again the thunder cracked like her sanity, its symphony orchestrating her darkest thoughts and the truth she withheld. If she looked at him, he would know...

He was standing between the balcony door and the chair in which she sat. Again, the lights flickered, and so did the lightning, momentarily silhouetting his profile against the dark sky.

He marched toward her and clamped his thick hand around the back of her neck, trying to maneuver her head so her eyes met his. It was the first time he had laid a hand on her this way.

Tom kneeled on the chair, straddling her, and pushed his face against hers. His breath was sulfurous, tinged with a fecal odor that suggested severe constipation. She had never noticed the smell before. It was as if her spouse was turning bad from the inside.

*No, he had always been bad, hadn't he? Just ask Jodie.*

"Now, tell me what you did with my money," he ordered.

Not hers, not theirs, *my* money. Struggling to breathe, pinned by his weight, her mind seized. The armchair rocked.

He kissed her forehead gently, with purpose, a saliva stream breaking as he slowly withdrew. She kept her eyes from meeting his, fearing they might reveal the truth. Again, the chair rocked under the weight of them both.

"Where's my money?"

She struggled and the chair toppled, its back thumping against the floor, knocking the wind from them both. For a split second, they lay on the filthy floor, his weight still crushing her, the left lens of his glasses spiderwebbed with cracks.

She would never have hurt Tom. Despite everything, part of her still cared for him. But she was in fear for her life, and his anger was evident in the creases around his eyes, in his downturned mouth, the pressure his hand applied to her throat.

"You stupid—"

So when she saw the hypodermic lying on the dust-furred carpet, its barrel glistening and filled with drug addict blood, she reached for it.

"I need to know where my money went," he insisted.

His hand was tighter around her throat now, the veins at his temples bulging, the syringe slipping from the tips of her sweat-slicked fingers.

"Where is it?" he said, choking her.

The cylindrical barrel rolled away as she pawed at it, but then the bare needle caught in the carpet, allowing her fingertips to gain purchase. Still pinned by his larger body, she swung the syringe, sticking him in the side of his thick neck, not caring if she infected him with hepatitis or worse. She raised her knee into his balls for good measure.

His face contorted with pain and shock, and he rolled off her onto his side, screaming inwardly. A lion darted by a tranquilizer gun.

She was on her feet, dodging his swiping hand, and she ran, out of the derelict squat and into the maze of damp-filled corridors where the ceiling's lights fizzed and flickered, the faulty electrics a strobing runway above.

"*Penny,*" he roared, his vocal cords strained, his pitch hemorrhage-inducing.

She'd never liked elevators and knew using one was ill-advised during a fire or, indeed, an electrical storm as violent as this. But Tom was faster and now a wounded animal, and he would catch her. If he knew the truth, he would catch her and…

She reached the elevator doors, slapped the flashing button, and waited. She heard the lift ascending, the creak of the arthritic pulley system and the hum of a strained motor. When the doors finally opened, she squeezed through and hit the "G" for the ground floor, and that's when Tom came crashing around the corridor's corner, still clutching his bleeding neck.

"Wait," he shouted. "We can sort—"

*Fuck…*

He was six feet from the sliding doors when they closed, sealing her in a tomb of duskier light. The elevator jolted and began its slow descent, and she counted the thirteen numbered buttons on the lift's panel, knowing Tom would be racing down flights of stairs, a man possessed.

The lift came to a grinding, juddering stop, and she waited for what felt like eternity for the doors to open. When they did, she slid between the slightest crack and ran toward the abandoned lobby and out into the storm.

She emerged in a concrete wasteland under the shadows of rundown tower blocks, surrounded by neglected playgrounds, a burnt-out car, and obscene graffiti. If anything, the storm had intensified.

"Penny," he screamed. "Come back, Penny."

She turned and saw Tom close behind, the wind beating his hair, still clutching his neck, hobbling from the blow to his crotch.

"Penny—"

Ahead, she spotted the entrance to a network of alleys where she prayed she could lose him. Breath ragged, throat burning, blood thumping in her ears, she ran.

She rounded a corner—and went sprawling over an abandoned supermarket shopping cart, twisting her ankle. She lay hopeless as he approached, not daring to meet his glowing eyes.

Dozens of jumpers perched on the surrounding tower block

roofs, poised like gargoyles. Even from a distance, she could see their eyes burned bright as they prepared to plunge to their deaths.

The menacing clouds darkened still. Then the rain came, ice-cold nails against her skin. Veins of lightning forked, the pulsing storm synchronized to the synaptic electrochemistry of every human brain, connecting neural circuits, resurrecting episodes of memory, shocking the city into a collective state of psychosis.

Tom bent to Penny and placed his index finger under her chin, gently raising the tilt of her head so her eyes met his. Again, the lightning flashed, alighting the belly of the pregnant black clouds, and in the cracked lenses of his spectacles, she saw her reflection, her eyes glowing as purple as his.

*Flash…*

She sees bodies entwined, writhing beneath thin sheets, hurrying toward climax.

*Flash…*

She sees the white porcelain rim of a toilet seat, her hand between her legs, holding a color-banded plastic strip.

*Flash…*

She sees the hospital sign. She sees white scrubs. She sees long tunneling brightly lit corridors.

*Flash…*

She sees doctors, nurses, and lightning blazes, scratching bright white streaks into the graphite sky, scratching like cold metal against her cervix as she lies observing the surgeon's shadow on the theatre's white ceiling, her sedation failing to suppress the emotional pain of the abortion.

She sees it all. The £600 she handed over in crisp twenty-pound notes, the spotting in her underwear, the clotted remains of the pre-fetal form that had come away.

"You *bitch*," said Tom, eyes neon bright and full of realization. "*Our* baby, you murdered our baby."

*Murdered*, his accusation was ironic. Because when the lightning flashed, Penny had seen Jodie too, her body battered and bruised yet *this time* lifeless, all because she refused to bear his children. All because she refused to surrender control. Yet he was immune to guilt, it seemed. He was a father only to fear.

A tear welled in Tom's eye, splashed onto Penny's hand. He clasped his hands around her throat—and throttled her in the torrent of the storm, controlling her life until her last shuddering…

*Breathe…breathe…breathe…*

Gasping, she tried to pry his hands from her throat by pulling at his wrists, but his forearms were so thick, so strong.

The world was graying out, her existence slipping away, was defined by pain, by his thick hands around her slender throat, by his power over her…She felt the ballpoint pen digging into her left breast.

*The pen…*

The needle wound on his neck glistened: a red target.

With her last reserve of fading strength, she let go of his wrists and fumbled for the pen clipped to her breast pocket. Tom was too focused on the job at hand to notice her wielding the makeshift shiv.

She stuck him hard. He released his grip, staggered back, and she gasped, air flooding her oxygen-starved lungs. Tom clutched his neck. The pen was far more substantial than a flimsy needle, and blood sprayed from the wound like water from a punctured hose.

Again, the lightning strobed, and Jodie's image flashed in Penny's mind's eye, cowering beneath Tom, begging him for mercy. He had shown none.

Neither would Penny.

Before Tom could recover, Penny drove the pen into the gristle of his neck, puncturing muscle and tendons and cartilage. She stabbed him again, and again…and again, her adrenaline driving her blood frenzy.

He fell to the ground, holding his ruined throat, blood pooling on the cold concrete. Had she punctured his carotid artery? Severed his spinal cord? Cut his jugular vein? She did not know. But she felt nothing. There was no guilt.

Wet hair clinging to her face, she stood over him exhausted, watching him die where he lay, gasping like an old faucet.

Lightning flared as the sky rained bodies that burst when they hit the ground, the pink mist as bright as her luminous eyes, the drains running red with the blood of the city.

# NO SANCTUARY

## R.E. SARGENT

There was a chill to the air, and Kristen involuntarily shuddered. The dull orange glow from the instrument panel did little to dispel the inky darkness that surrounded the Challenger. The purple exterior—the salesman at the dealership had called it *Helraisin*—disappeared into the shadows as easily as a chameleon blended into the colors of the foliage of its environment. The night was still, quiet, moonless. She could not make out anything beyond the windows of the car.

Kristen turned the temperature a little higher to ward off the cold—she had left the car running, positive that no one would hear the purr of the supercharged 6.2-liter Hemi at normal idle.

Glancing at the clock at the top of the media center screen, she wondered how much longer she would have to wait. It seemed like it had been hours already, but she knew time seemed to drag when she was bored.

She pulled out her phone again, smiled at the picture of her and her pittie on the lock screen, allowed the Face ID to unlock the phone, and started watching TikTok videos, a bad habit she had when she was bored. She didn't detect the danger until it was too late.

The passenger door abruptly opened, and Kristen froze, her breath momentarily stalled as if all the oxygen had been sucked out of the vehicle. The world seemed to stop spinning, the events happening like a video that had been slowed down to a crawl. But then, a large man was sitting in the seat before she even realized what was happening. Then, everything sped up to three times normal speed.

Kristen screamed.

"GO, GO, GO!" the man yelled.

"Who the fuck are you?" Kristen yelled, the passenger not being the person she had been waiting for.

"Just fucking drive!" he yelled.

"Get the fuck out! I'm calling the cops!" She brought up the keypad and dialed a nine before the man swatted the phone from her hand.

"Kristen, what the hell are you doing? Get us out of here before they discover me missing!"

Kristen stopped, her eyes wide, searching the face that was sitting across from her, looking for some familiarity. She turned on the interior light, and the shadows raced from the car, joining the ones outside in the night sky. "Who are you?" she asked cautiously, her eyes blinking at him. "Did Hudson send you?"

"Kris, it's me!"

Kristen looked at him apprehensively. The voice was familiar, but this definitely wasn't Hudson. Although the immediate sense of danger had decreased, she was still on edge.

"Seriously, please drive! We don't have much time."

Kristen stared at him, unable to move. Finally, Hudson reached up and pulled the mask off his face, revealing his true self. He watched as recognition changed her features, some of the fear melting away.

"Drive," he said sternly.

Without another word, Kristen flicked on the headlights, shifted the Challenger into drive, and tore off down the rutty dirt track.

"I DIDN'T THINK YOU WERE GOING TO MAKE IT." SHE TURNED AND looked at him, his expression stoic, hard.

"I told you I'd be there."

"You freaked me the fuck out."

"Why? You were expecting me."

"Yeah, you. Not some stranger's face."

"I had to get past the guards somehow."

Kristen turned on the reading lamp and gave him a once-over. "Where is that uniform from?"

Hudson pointed at the road. Swing on the main road here and work your way over to the interstate. We need to head south."

Kristen followed his direction and then turned back to him. "The uniform?"

"I took it off a guard."

"Is he okay?"

"Depends on your definition of 'okay.'"

Kristen studied Hudson's face, frowning. It was then she noticed the smear of blood on his face. "Babe! You're bleeding!" She reached out to touch his face, and Hudson grabbed her wrist and pulled it away.

"It's not mine."

"N…not…then whose is it?"

"The guard's."

"Hudson! You promised me. No one was supposed to get hurt."

"It was the only way I could get out. I had to take his clothes. His keys. His…"

"His what?"

Hudson mumbled something.

"His what?"

"Face, all right? I took off his fucking face and wore it as a mask."

"WHAT THE ACTUAL FUCK, Hudson!! Are you fucking kidding me right now? Get that fucking thing out of my car!! I can't even believe this shit!"

"What do you want me to do with it? Just throw it out the window?"

Kristen pulled off the road onto the dirt shoulder and rolled down the passenger window. "I don't care what you do. Just get it out, now!"

Hudson got out of the car, walked over to the barb-wired fencing that bordered the vast parcel of barren land, and flung the flesh mask as far as he could into the brush, like one might toss a tortilla. Kristen rubbed her forehead and then her temple. When Hudson got back in the car and shut the door, she rolled up his window, turned off the reading light, and pulled back out onto the two-lane blacktop.

"Happy now?" he asked.

"That's an overstatement. Maybe a tad less freaked out. Maybe half a tad if there is such a thing. Did you really have to take off his face?"

"Seemed like the right thing to do at the time."

"Jesus, Hudson. Sometimes I wonder if I should even be helping you. If we get caught, I'm fucked... I'll spend the rest of my pathetic life behind bars too."

"Come on, babe...stop with the righteous act. You were right there beside me when everything went down. I think you even enjoyed it. The difference between you and me, though, is when I got arrested, I told them you had nothing to do with it. I took full blame, so you weren't locked up too."

"I already thanked you for that. And for the record, I never enjoyed it. I was scared. I tolerated it, because I love you."

"Either way, it's the least you can do, helping me bust out of that place. It's been two years. Two miserable fucking years. I would have been there for the rest of my life and you know it. It'd be bad enough if I was just a prisoner and they left me alone, but no. They have to test me, psychoanalyze me. Fuck with me. I mean I might be a little psycho, but there are guys in there that make me look like a Sunday school teacher."

"Okay, okay. I get it. But I'm never gonna like it. Do you think they know you're gone?"

"I'm hoping not, but you never know. They won't know what vehicle I'm in, though. By the way, damn. This is a sweet ride. When did you get it?"

"Three months ago."

"Things must be good on the outside."

"I've got a huge payment. It's worth it, though."

"You've got to let me drive it."

"Maybe."

"Oh, you WILL be letting me drive it."

"Chill, Hudson. I'm your girlfriend, not your bitch."

Before she could react, Hudson's hand reached out and grabbed the steering wheel and yanked hard, causing the Challenger to fishtail around in the opposite direction, however she threw all of her one hundred and thirty pound body into trying to take control of the wheel to keep them from crashing. Simultaneously, she hit the brakes and the car slid sideways to a stop.

"Are you trying to get us fucking killed, you asshole? Not to mention you could have wrecked my car."

"You've got a little more sass coming out of that mouth than I'm used to. What's that all about? Are you fucking around on me?"

Kristen banged her head on the steering wheel. "Are you serious right now? I stand up for myself for once in my life and suddenly you deduce I am seeing someone else? If that was the case, why would I even be here? Wouldn't I have reported that you were going to escape instead? Jesus! What's your mental?"

"My mental? Is that supposed to be a joke? Just because I was institutionalized doesn't make me crazy."

"That was just an expression, not a jab at you. Stop being so sensitive."

"Then stop disrespecting me."

"I wasn't." Kristen studied his eyes, which burned white hot. She decided to back off before she ignited an explosion she couldn't come back from. Memories of his temper—of his terrifying crazy side—flooded through her mind…memories she tried to suppress, possibly to the point of even fooling herself that he had changed in his two years of lockup.

Kristen looked down. "I'm sorry, babe. I didn't mean anything by it. I love you. Here, you drive."

Kristen shifted the Dodge into park, opened the driver's door, and got out, circling the back of the vehicle on the deserted road. When she got to the passenger side of the car, she opened the door and Hudson got out. She could still see the rage in his eyes. She wrapped her arms around him, but he remained an arm's-length away.

"I'm sorry, baby," she repeated and kissed his lips. She felt some of the tension leave his body and she pulled him in closer. Finally, he relaxed and kissed her back. Then, he pulled away.

"Just be gentle with me, Kris. You have no idea what I've been through."

There was so much she wanted to say to him, but she held back and instead said, "You got it, babe."

Hudson walked around the car and got in the driver's side while Kristen got in the passenger side. He shifted the transmission into drive and whipped the car back around in the right direction, stepping on the gas pedal hard, the tires barking when the transmission shifted to second and then again when it hit third.

"Take it easy," she told him. "This car stands out enough. Don't give them a reason to pull us over."

"I know you're right, but fuck, this car is begging to be *driven*."

"She's a damn beggar, all right," Kristen said, laughing, trying to lighten the mood. "Just don't get us arrested."

"I'm not going back to that shithole."

"Yeah, I can imagine it's not much fun."

"Understatement of the year."

"Where are we going, by the way?"

"I have a friend that lives on eighty-seven acres in the Arizona desert. Things disappear there. I plan to follow suit."

"The desert. Yay." She said this sarcastically, half-heartedly.

"You'll like it okay. He has this bunker. I hear it's amazing.

Everything we need, and all underground. Our own little sanctuary. Stays pretty cool down there from what I hear."

"And the car?"

"He has a huge barn. It'll be hidden from prying eyes as well as from the air."

"Arizona it is, then."

"Yeah, but first I need to eat. Taco Bell?"

"You certainly know how to get a girl's attention. Let's go."

Kristen made Hudson park in an empty area of a grocery store parking lot that was in the same center as the fast-food restaurant. There was no way she was going to let him spill greasy taco meat on her leather seats.

"Oh my god."

"What?"

"Do you know how long it's been since I have had Taco Bell? It's been forever."

"Sorry."

"It's all good. But damn. I'm so happy right now."

"Glad that's all it takes," she said, smiling at him.

When they were done eating, Hudson changed into some clothes that Kristen had brought with her and they threw their trash and his stolen clothes in the dumpster behind the store. Having already used the bathroom when they ordered their food, they got back on the interstate with Hudson still behind the wheel. A few hours later, Hudson exited the interstate and pulled into a gas station. At the pump, he opened the filler lid and inserted the nozzle, pressing the button on the pump. He pressed the handle, but nothing happened.

"Gotta prepay, babe."

"Hand me your bank card."

"Eh. My account is empty. I pulled out everything I had. Don't want to leave an electronic trail. I'll go inside and prepay cash."

"How much is *everything you had*?"

"A couple hundred bucks. Not nearly enough, but things are tight. The car payment and insurance on this thing are killing me."

"Shit."

"We'll figure something out."

Hudson nodded.

"Do you want me to pick you up a snack while I'm in there?" she asked.

"Nah. I need to take a piss anyway. I'll go in after I pump the gas."

"Kay."

Kristen headed inside and handed the clerk forty dollars, hoping it was enough to fill the tank. At this rate, they wouldn't have enough to get to Arizona, which concerned her.

As the clerk preauthorized the pump, Kristen looked out at Hudson as he began to pump the gas. She remembered the first time she had seen him. She had been walking her pit bull and a car had driven by slowly. She remembered looking at the driver, thinking he was cute. The next day, he coincidentally drove by her again as she walked her fur baby. This time he waved. The third time, she waved him over to the curb and introduced herself, later finding out that his drive-bys weren't coincidental at all. After that first day, he had driven around for hours hoping to cross paths with her again.

There was something about him…rugged good looks with an air of confidence. Kristen could see that person she had fallen quickly for, right on the other side of the glass pumping the fuel, his face expressionless, his eyes staring off into the distance, at everything, at nothing. But what she had quickly come to find after dating him for a hot minute was a man who was troubled—even his demons had demons—but he refused to admit he had a problem, refused to get help. *"I'm not damaged, you are"* seemed to be words he lived by. He was never the problem. Everyone else was.

Despite his issues, they had fun. Kristen chalked some of it up to a rebellious phase she had been going through. The product of strict parents, she had escaped as soon as she had turned eighteen, crashing on friends' couches, sometimes sleeping in her car (back then, she owned a beat up Ford Taurus), and she had even forced her way into vacant houses from time to time just to have shelter. Within six months, she found a little more stability, landing a job that paid enough for her to rent a room and keep food in her belly. Within days, she had gone to her parents' home and kidnapped Sarabie, her pittie—her best friend. And a month after that, she and Hudson were a thing. To Kristen, he was the spark in life that was missing...a wild child. She would never have admitted to herself back then that she was into bad boys, because she didn't even realize it herself. She just wanted to breathe! To live!

"Can I get you anything else?"

Kristen snapped out of her daze and turned her attention back to the lady behind the counter. Reaching over, she grabbed a pack of gum off a display and handed it to the cashier.

"Just this."

"That's two dollars and nineteen cents."

Kristen gave her the cash, took the gum and the change, and joined Hudson outside. He was just hanging up the gas nozzle when she approached.

"Okay if I still drive?" he asked.

Kristen knew it really wasn't a question.

"Of course."

"Cool. I'm going inside to pee. Be back in a bit."

Kristen climbed into the passenger seat of the car, stretched her legs out, and put on her seatbelt. She watched Hudson through the glass again, this time with her on the outside and him inside. He made his way to the back of the store where the restrooms were and disappeared inside one.

Things had been good when they were good. When she was with him, she felt alive. Life was fire. But then she noticed the cracks in his personality. An occasional uncomfortable moment, then some outright red flags. Then the full-blown manic episodes. She had thought about leaving him, but it wasn't something that was easy to do. She loved him...was downright addicted to him, self be damned.

The time of his arrest—their arrests, actually—was one of the lowest times of her life. She knew what he was doing. Had discovered it by accident. Why she hadn't called the cops, she still didn't know. Instead, she had kept quiet. And somehow, he had justified it and convinced her that it wasn't as bad as she was making it out to be, that everything was okay, that what he was doing was perfectly normal.

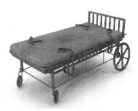

THE HOUSE WAS DARK WHEN SHE ENTERED. SHE CALLED OUT HUDSON'S *name, but there was no answer. He had promised to be home, yet the house was dark, quiet. She went room-by-room, flipping switches, chasing the shadows away, and replacing them with the brilliance of hundreds of lumen. Unable to locate him, she pulled out a dining room chair and swung it around, straddling it, the back of the chair against her chest. She'd wait for awhile, the plans they had made to go on a long drive in his truck the only thing she could think about. That was when she heard the scratching. Faint. Rhythmic. It came from below.*

*Rodents, she thought. But no, that seemed wrong. Hudson was too meticulous. Too clean. He would never have vermin. But what was under the house? Was there a basement? Kristen tried a door in the hallway. A coat closet. Another contained towels and linens. No stairs. She slipped out the front door and around the side of the house. She saw no sign of a lower level, but as she rounded the corner at the back of the house, she spotted them. Three low windows at the bottom of the structure, three single panes of glass in each, all three windows spaced equally apart along the back of the house. They seemed to be frosted, but as she approached them, she saw the brush strokes. They had been painted over…from the inside.*

*Kristen worked her way around the exterior of the house twice, inspecting every inch, looking for some way to get in the basement. Obvi-*

*ously if there were windows, there was a way in. Convinced the entrance was not hidden outside, she went back in the house.*

*Inside, she looked everywhere a staircase could be hiding. Originally curious, she soon became obsessed.* People don't go to great lengths to conceal something unless there's a good reason, *she thought. Finally, unsuccessful, she ended up back in the hallway. This passageway felt like the answer, as all the other walls in the house backed to another room, an outside wall, or they had fixtures attached to them, such as in the kitchen and the bathrooms. The house was old. It appeared to never have been remodeled. Paneling covered every wall. She ran her fingers over the seams, putting pressure on the wood. Nothing. Just a solid wall. That was until she got to the fourth panel over. As she was pressing on the wall a few feet from the top, she heard the distinct click of a latch letting loose. A portion of the wall popped a half an inch out. Taking a deep breath and holding it, Kristen popped open the door.*

THE CAR DOOR OPENING MADE HER JUMP. SHE HADN'T REALIZED SHE had zoned out. Hudson got in and started the car without a word before shifting into drive and pulling out of the parking lot. She glanced over at him, his profile slightly illuminated by the dash lighting. He looked serious, almost stern, and his thoughts seemed impenetrable. She decided not to pry.

"Are we going to stop for the night, or keep driving?" she asked.

"I'm not tired. I've been cooped up for way too long. I can drive all night. It will get us there sooner. Plus, we need to save our money."

"Mind if I kick the seat back then and close my eyes for a few? I'm exhausted."

"Go for it."

"Thanks."

Kristen reclined the seat and adjusted her body to get more comfortable. Finally, she pulled a hoodie out of the back seat and balled it up to use as a pillow, settled back into to the seat, and closed her eyes.

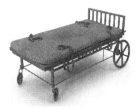

*SHE FELT FOR A LIGHT SWITCH INSIDE THE OPENING AND FOUND A METAL box mounted to the wall, a single switch attached. She flicked it up, not expecting anything to happen, but the stairway in front of her was washed in bright light. She looked at the single bulb light fixtures that were mounted to the ceiling of the stairwell, three of them in total. Something seemed off, and she couldn't reconcile what it was in her mind, but then it clicked. This was an old house. Everything on the main floor was old and outdated, but the light fixtures, the conduit attaching all of the light boxes together, the clear bulbs that were screwed into the fixture…all of them were shiny and bright, as if they were recently installed. And they were all tucked in behind a hidden door leading to a basement with painted windows.*

*Her breathing got heavy and she stared at the bottom of the staircase, but she could only see a wall and nothing else as the stairs took a hard turn to the right once they reached the lower landing.*

*"Hello?" she called, afraid to hear an answer. There was none.*

*She turned back toward the interior of the house.*

*"Hudson?"*

*Still silence.*

*Knowing there was no way she could not check out what the mystery was at the bottom, she grabbed the handrail and descended the stairs sideways, ready at any given second to swing around and race back up to the main level of the house. The stairs didn't creak, which she thought was odd.*

*The entire situation was odd. She tried to claw through the swirling tornado of her mind to come up with any reasoning that made sense, but it was almost like her thoughts wouldn't let her go there. Nothing good could come from the puzzle pieces falling together in her mind. She would either be conjuring up something that poor Hudson would have no part of in a hundred years, or something so grotesquely fucked up—yet real—that it would be unfathomable.*

*At the bottom landing, she made the right turn and descended the three additional stairs, finding herself in a big room with concrete floors and workbenches lining the walls. Dozens of tools hung from pegboard or littered the workbench top.*

*An explosion of air escaped from Kristen's lungs and it was then she realized she had been holding her breath. It was simply a workshop and that was it. Kristen shook her head and chuckled at her stupidity.*

*Her short-lived relief was broken by the scratching sound she had heard earlier. Curious if there was an animal trapped farther back in the room, she walked toward the sound, the light giving way to shadows as she worked her way back.*

*At the back of the room, a metal shelving unit sat against the wall, the shelves littered with old paint cans, a couple rolled-up tarps, and some other miscellaneous items. Pulling out her phone, Kristen turned on the flashlight and peered around in the inky shadows. Just walls…nothing sinister. But then, she heard the scratching again, and it seemed close.*

*Kristen turned toward the metal shelves and removed a paint can and then another. She felt a little like Nancy Drew in the moment, sleuthing a secret passageway.* The Secret Staircase *was a title that would certainly fit this situation. She turned her flashlight toward the unit and peered between the shelves. She saw wood, where the rest of the basement—so far—was concrete.*

*Working at a faster pace, Kristen emptied off the rest of the paint and miscellany and slid the shelving unit out of the way. The wood she spotted was actually a door.* So why hide a staircase? And a door? *She would soon find out. Kristen flicked open the deadbolt lock and yanked the door open, the hinges emitting a loud groan. She placed one foot inside and swung her phone flashlight through the doorway.*

KRISTEN AWOKE TO THE CHALLENGER SLOWING AND THEN STOPPING. She cleared her vision, sat up, and looked around. They were at a gas pump. She looked over at Hudson, who was taking off his seatbelt.

"We need gas already? How long was I asleep?"

"A few hours. We still have half a tank, but I'm hungry. Thought we could top off and drive through that Jack in the Box."

"I could eat."

"Be right back."

Hudson got out of the car and walked toward the convenience store. When he got inside, it dawned on her that he would be right back out since she had the money and he forgot to ask. A minute later, Hudson came back out and walked to the car, opened the gas cap, put the nozzle in the car, lifted the handle, and started pumping. Kristen got out of the car.

"Oh, this one's not prepay?"

"No...it is."

"Um...okay, but I didn't give you any cash." Kristen ran her hand through her hair.

"Don't need it."

"Of course you do."

"Nope...I'm good."

"Okay, what are you not telling me? What the hell am I missing?"

"Just hold on, Kris."

Kristen noticed his forehead was bunched up and he had a scowl across his face, so she decided she would table the conversation...at least until they were back on the road.

When the tank was full and Hudson was back in the car, he pulled over to the drive-thru and pulled up by the menu board.

"What do you want?" he asked.

"A number three, large size, with a Coke. Also could you please ask for ketchup?"

"Yup."

The speaker barked and the employee on the other end asked to take their order. Hudson ordered for both of them and then pulled up to the first window to pay. A sign directed them to proceed to the second window. Kristen reached for her backpack and started to pull her wallet out, but Hudson placed his hand on her arm, then reached into his back pocket and took out a wad of cash, peeling a twenty off and handing it through the window. Kristen's eyes grew wide.

"Not now!" he whispered, giving her a stern look. She gave him a look back, letting him know the conversation was far from over.

When they had their food, they found a place to park.

"Okay, don't think I'm not going to ask again. What the fuck, Hudson? Where did you get the money?"

"You don't need to know."

"The fuck I don't. I'm wrapped up in the middle of this with you. If you did something illegal, I'm going to suffer the consequences as well. We're in *my* fucking car."

"I knew you would get bent about it."

"What did you do?"

"Borrowed a little money."

"Borrowed?" Kristen looked at him incredulously. "Borrowed"— she used air quotes—"from whom?" She had a feeling she already knew the answer, but she needed to hear it from him.

"The last gas station."

Kristen rubbed her hand over her face and took a deep breath.

"Are you just wanting to get caught? The cops have got to be looking for us now. And we stick out like a sore thumb."

"Relax. We aren't going to get caught."

"How can you be so nonchalant about it? I'm sure she already reported it."

"She isn't going to cause us any problems."

Kristen's eyes went wide. "Hudson!! Please tell me you didn't fucking kill her!"

"I didn't."

"Are you lying to me?"

"No."

"Then why do you say she won't cause us problems?"

"Cause she doesn't know who took the money."

"Explain."

"I knocked her the fuck out while she wasn't looking. She literally doesn't know what—or who—hit her."

"HUDSON!! Fucking really?"

"Well, we needed the money."

"Don't you think we could have gotten some another way?"

"Like how, Kris? Are you gonna suck dicks on the corner?"

"You don't have to be an asshole."

"And you don't need to be all over my ass for everything. I'm doing what I need to do."

"And putting me in a bad situation for it. It's not just your ass. I helped you escape. Add all your other crimes to the list and I'm fucked. Sometimes I wonder why I'm even helping you."

"That's a pretty fucked-up thing to say."

"This isn't my life, Hudson. Never was. I mean, I love you and all… Maybe that's the reason I've put up with all your crazy shit… stayed right by your side even when…"

"Even when what?"

THE ROOM WAS ESSENTIALLY ONE BIG SPACE WITH CONCRETE BLOCK WALLS. *The floor was bare cement as well. A single lightbulb sat at the center of the ceiling, one hundred watts of bright intensity that lit up the center of the room but did little to reach the shadows in the corner of the area.*

*Kristen's breath caught in her throat, her eyes wide open, disbelieving.*

*Along the far wall were two cells—cages really. They were about five feet high, not tall enough for a person of average height to stand upright in, and each was approximately five feet wide. The cages sat a few feet apart from each other and appeared to be made of steel rods that had been welded together, although definitely not by a professional, as the spacing of the rods was inconsistent and the welds looked like something an amateur would produce.*

*Each contained a bare mattress…no sheets, no blankets, no pillows. But it was the other contents of each cage that twisted Kristen's stomach in knots.*

*In the cage on the left, a women was curled up in the fetal position, clearly lethargic and probably in shock. Her blond hair was tangled and ratty, her frame extremely thin, gaunt. She lay naked, her skin splotchy and discolored. Where her feet used to be were merely stumps, the angry, scarred tissue discolored and swollen. Kristen wondered if infection was setting in—the amputations clearly not performed by a medical professional. They had the same crudeness to them as the cage construction—both most likely done by the same person.*

*Kristen held back the bile that started working its way up her throat, her stomach churning at the horror in front of her. She turned her attention to the cage on the right. The redhead was in a similar condition, but her feet were intact; instead, one entire hand was missing and just the fingers and thumb were missing from her other hand. Her feet hung off the mattress, her toenails scraping across the concrete.* That scratching sound I heard.

*Kristen covered her mouth and tears leaked from her eyes as she tried to process the scene and figure out what she was going to do next. Neither girl looked at her, like they didn't even notice her there.*

*Finally, a huge sob burst from her chest and she ran toward the stairs, anxious to get out of this place, to get out of this house. Once she was a safe distance away, she would figure out what to do.*

*When she got to the top of the stairs and pushed the door open abruptly, stepping into the hallway, she stopped short.*

*"Kristen."*

*She stared at him, mouth agape.*

*"Well, this is unfortunate."*

*Panic lined her face. "I didn't see anything. Let me be…I'm going home."*

*"I'm pretty sure I can't let you leave. Besides, I have a great afternoon planned for us. I went to a lot of trouble."*

*"I'm not going anywhere with you, you sick fuck!"*

*"It's unfortunate you feel that way, but trust me when I tell you that you'll change your mind."*

*He moved toward her, and she let out a scream.*

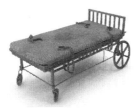

"Well?" Hudson asked. "You stayed by my side even when...? When what?"

"You know."

"Say it."

"The girls."

"As I said before, don't act all innocent. Once you got past the shock, you were into it just as much as I was."

"No, Hudson, I wasn't."

"Cooked just right, the fingers and toes are better than any hot wings you've ever had. Admit it."

"I don't think that's what they had in mind when someone coined the term 'finger foods.' And for the record, I only ate it because I was scared you'd hurt me if I didn't, but I never swallowed it. I spit it out and slipped it in my pocket and then flushed it when I used the bathroom."

"I don't even know what to say, Kris. After all these years, after everything. Why did you even show up last night?"

She sat there, silent, thinking. Then, shrugging, she said, "You asked. You needed me. I didn't feel like I could say no. I still love you. That's something I've never been able to get out of my system, even when I've tried. You wouldn't believe how many therapy sessions I've attended, hoping to heal from everything: the victims, the shit you got me into, you holding me against my will until I saw things your way. But if I'm being honest, also hoping to figure out how *not* to love you anymore. Obviously, it didn't work, because one message from you and I'm putting *my* life, *my* freedom on the line to help you."

Anxious, not knowing how he was going to react to her admission, she turned to look at him. He was staring at the road, his fingers white-knuckling the steering wheel. Their speed had crept up again, and Kristen noticed he was going about eighty-three miles per hour.

"Hudson?"

He didn't respond.

"Talk to me…I'm sorry if I pissed you off. I'm just trying to be honest with you. I'm not the scared little girl anymore that you knew when you went away two years ago."

"I have nothing to say to you. Obviously, what I thought we had didn't mean shit. I feel like you were playing me the entire time."

"Playing YOU? You were the one who was controlling. You were the one that threatened me. I did what you wanted. I did what I did to survive."

"But I thought you *wanted* to be there."

"You paid attention to me. You wanted to be with me. I mistook bad attention for good attention. But I know better now. These two years you were locked up, I was conflicted, confused. That's why I came. But I finally see it clearly now. I can't be with you anymore. We aren't the same…and I'm not idly going to sit by and watch you hurt people any longer. It's bad enough I never reported the girls in your basement. You may have never gotten caught if they hadn't died and if you hadn't made mistakes when you dumped the bodies."

Hudson was silent again, a deep scowl setting in on his face, his fingers still holding the wheel in a death-grip.

"I care about you, Hudson," she continued. "I really do. And I'm glad I could help you. I'll get you to Arizona…to your friend's place. But I'm not staying once we get there. I'm dropping you off and heading home…to my normal, boring life."

Hudson responded by slamming the accelerator down to the

floor, the speed shooting up over a hundred, then one-twenty, then one-forty. Kristen grabbed the "oh shit" handle and held on for dear life, wondering how much of it she actually had left.

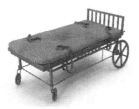

"HUDSON, SLOW THE FUCK DOWN!"

"What's the matter, Kristen? Is Crazy Hudson scaring you? Do you not trust me anymore?"

"It's not that," she said, her voice a higher pitch, her words delivered through gritted teeth.

"Maybe we are better off on the other side…you and me, Kris. Burning for eternity together." The car was ripping down the road at a speed faster than she had ever ridden before.

Kristen held on tighter, her muscles tensed up. "If you want to kill yourself, then by all means, do it, but don't take me with you. I'm not ready to die!"

"What? You're too good for me now? Is that it?"

"No, it's just that I'm finally being honest with you. I'm not that scared little girl that is afraid to tell you how I feel. I don't feel good about hurting people, Hudson. I never have."

Hudson was silent for a fifteen seconds, his eyes on the road ahead. Finally he spoke. "You have the power to make this stop, Kris. Just say the word. Say you'll stay with me in Arizona—at our own little sanctuary. We can make it work. I will be better. Just promise me and I'll stop the car."

Kristen looked hesitant…conflicted. "I dunno, Hudson. I can't be a part of all this."

"Please, Kris. I need you by my side."

She gripped the bar tighter and looked down toward the floor-board. "I'm sorry," she whispered.

Hudson immediately reacted by whipping the steering wheel left and right, the car swerving across both lanes of the deserted highway, the tires chirping as they tried to hold tight to the asphalt, the car dangerously cutting a zig-zag pattern across the black surface of the road.

"Damn it, Hudson!!! Fucking knock it off! You're going to kill us!"

"What does it fucking matter, Kris? Huh? You don't care if I live or die!"

"I do! I want you to live, but if you decide to take yourself out, I don't want to go with you. Please stop the fucking car! This ride is over!"

"It's far from over, sweetheart."

The left front tire slipped off the asphalt onto the shoulder and the car began a slide toward the ditch that ran parallel to the road. Hudson yanked the wheel and the car whipped back onto the hard surface, but the aggressive correction forcefully carried the car all the way across both lanes and toward the ditch on the other side. Hudson fought the steering wheel, trying to get control and get the Challenger back on the road.

"HUDSON!!!!!"

Kristen's scream pierced the interior a split second before it happened, but then everything slowed down as the worst imaginable scene played out in front of her. The car completely left the road. They grabbed air as the front end caught in the ditch and then they were flipping, first end-over-end, but then the car felt like it was spiraling before it started rolling. The contents of the car seemed to be void of gravity as the items floated in the air and then pummeled their faces, their bodies. Kristen couldn't count the number of rolls, but it seemed like twenty or more—it was never ending. And then, when she thought they would never stop, the car rolled one last time and slammed into something so hard, it stopped abruptly. Kristen felt like every bone in her body had been turned to powder, then seconds later as she was trying to pull herself out of a surreal haze, the real pain set in and she screamed again.

Yelling through the agony, she tried to get her bearings. She was slumped against the passenger door, her head resting against the cool ground, the window now devoid of glass. She looked around and found Hudson suspended above her, the seat belt being the only thing keeping him from falling on her and crushing her. He was passed out...or dead. Kristen tried to dredge up any type of emotion toward that last thought. She was sad, but not surprised, when she failed.

As she tried to unbuckle her seatbelt, she saw it. The flickering light behind the car. Flames dancing in the night air. They were on fire. They were fucked.

Frantically working at the buckle, Kristen got the seatbelt undone. She stood up and tried to negotiate her way past Hudson, but his body was slumped toward her and in the way. She shook him.

"Hudson. Hudson! HUDSON, wake the fuck up! We're on fire!"

Hudson didn't move, so she tried pushing him to the side and pulled the door handle and tried to push the door up. It didn't budge, a result of the damage it had incurred during the rolling.

The flames grew bigger and Kristin's heart pounded harder, uncertain if the car could or would explode like in the movies, but not wanting to be around to find out. Out of options for a way out of the car, she laid back on her side in her seat and projected both feet at the windshield. She kicked out—nothing happened. Determined to bust the safety glass out, she kicked again and again, and finally the corner of the windshield tore away from the frame. Six more kicks and the glass on her side of the windshield was flopping in the wind. She started shuffling her body through the opening. The flames grew brighter. The cracking sound became louder. She had to hurry, and just as she was wiggling her shoulders through the opening, she heard him.

"Kri...stennn," he whispered, then a gasp and a wheeze followed. It sounded like something was wrong inside him—in his body this time, not his head.

"Hudson! You're alive."

"Ye...yes. Hurry. Get me...get me out...of here."

Kristen stopped, reached her arm back through the window, and touched his shoulder.

"Oh, Hudson...you don't look so good, sweetie."

"Hu…rry…help me. We have to…to go. Arizona. Safe there."

Kristen grabbed his hand, held it to her face, kissed it.

"Look at you, my love. You don't look so good," she repeated.

He looked at her, the look of an animal that knows it's time, but hoping they are wrong.

"Arizona, Kristen. You…me. Sanctuary. I love…you."

"I love you too, Hudson." She let go of his hand. "Unfortunately, though, there will be no sanctuary. Not now. Not ever. Goodbye, my love."

Kristen pulled herself through the window and rolled away from the car. Every inch of her body screamed at her as she scrambled to her feet, her eyes landing on the Challenger, the body so badly damaged that it was unrecognizable, the flames more consuming than she could have imagined. She turned and ran, her survival mode kicking in, trying to get as far away from the burning car as she could. She made it fifteen steps before the explosion happened, the ass end of the car flinging itself up in the night air before settling back down with an ear-deafening crash.

As she used the pale light from the fire to follow the debris trail back to the highway, hoping someone would eventually come along, she started to concoct a story in her head. He showed up at her house and kidnapped her…made her drive him and then demanded he drive. He must have still been obsessed with her after all these years. She was scared for her life and didn't know what to do. The only way to get away was force him to crash the car. She'd be real convincing. She had to be. She would finally be free. Knowing he would never come back into her life and draw her into his web of sickness, that was *her* sanctuary.

# SOBRIQUET

## REBECCA ROWLAND

*'m sorry for everything.*

Parker typed this quickly under the hardwood shroud of the conference room table. He knew she'd respond eventually —she always did—but he kept his fingers pressed against the back of his phone case to feel the vibration of her acknowledgment. Sure enough, before Mac finished his opening remarks, a buzz tickled his palm.

*You know how you can make it up to me.*

To ward off the flush slithering around his neck, he rested the cell on his lap and folded his hands casually on top of his papers. Mac frowned on bringing laptops to the weekly staff meeting, insisting instead that his editors print out their notes or else just bullshit their way through section updates. Parker generally selected the latter approach, but with news of a visiting investor scheduled to appear, he'd jotted down a few points on the back of a few sheets snatched from the recycling bin. It took him a half second to realize Mac had finished speaking and was staring blankly at him.

Parker cleared his throat and listed the progress on the projects his freelancers were juggling and stated with exaggerated enthusiasm his *sincere faith* that each would be delivering their stories ahead of schedule. Parker worked for the media division of a high-profile nonprofit agency. He freely admitted that he took the position not out of selfless altruism or a deep-seated belief in philanthropy but rather with the goal of adding a prestigious notch to his resume. He never understood why people refused to admit to such motivations. What was wrong with career planning? A yearning for advancement? Or even just wanting to look like a good guy?

He looked like a good guy.

At least, he thought he did.

The phone tickled his crotch, the vibration sound seeming to amplify against the overpriced fabric of his trousers.

Mac was staring at him again.

"I'm sorry," Parker pretended to cough into his elbow. "Say that again."

"Mr. Dickens, Parker here is our editor-in-chief," Mac said, his eyes still fixed on his employee.

Dickens was a slight man: thin, with a few slivers of gray slicing through a thick head of black hair. His face was carved with deep wrinkles and hollow circles incongruous to his younger stature. Parker guessed he was fifty, perhaps fifty-five at the most, but the roadmap of creases hinted that he was likely a half sip away from a twenty-eight day stint at the local substance abuse clinic.

Parker focused on the bright maroon line—only a half inch in length but painfully apparent under the glare of the obnoxious overhead lighting—that marred the visitor's vampirishly pale face. Likely a broken capillary. He wondered if it was possible to taste the ethanol in an alcoholic's blood.

"Parker?" Dickens repeated with obvious mock interest. The muscle below the red spot twitched a bit. "That's an unusual name."

"It's a family name," Parker said, the explanation tumbling out of his mouth icy and automatic, like a spray of newly fallen snow caught in a gale. The truth was, he had no idea why his parents had chosen the moniker, but it was the topic of unending sobriquets when he was young, the most common being Parker Brothers, after the game manufacturer. He had been given it because he had proven himself a skilled strategist.

At least, he once thought that was why.

"Nah, dude," his friend Jason confided a few days before their high school graduation, the two of them tying the laces on their skates before a marathon of street hockey. "It's 'cause talking to you, I don't know, sometimes there seems like there's multiple Parkers. Like one minute you're laid back and chill, and the next, you're all hyper and aggressive and shit. For no reason."

Parker frowned at this explanation. "What do you mean, like Sybil?"

Jason rolled his eyes. "No—I don't know, man. Forget I said anything."

"Who thinks that? That I act like I have multiple personalities?" Parker flipped through an index of familiar faces in his mind.

"Everyone, dude." Jason shrugged. "Sorry." He hopped from the bench and skated quickly away toward the rest of the team.

"It was the last day I talked to Jason, actually," Parker told Bonnie as he rehashed this stubborn memory to her over lunch behind his closed office door. "He and I didn't bother to change back into our sneakers; we just skated home that night. And then, when he—"

"It's dissociative identity disorder," Bonnie said, stabbing a pile of dressing-soaked lettuce with her fork.

"What is?" Parker asked.

Bonnie sighed audibly, the way she often did that made Parker feel like a five-year-old who'd wet his pants. "They don't call it multiple personality disorder anymore. It's D-I-D." She didn't look up from her bowl but kept stabbing. "And you don't have it."

Parker smirked. "How do you know?"

"You're just a hypochondriac. And a moody bitch." She smiled into her lunch bowl. "You feel things intensely, and that makes people uncomfortable. Envious, even."

"You're not a psychologist."

Bonnie looked up. "No, I'm just your work spouse, your partner on the side." Her eyes narrowed slightly. "On the *sly*."

"Neither of us is married," Parker said.

"Then I guess I'm your everything partner. The front and center." Bonnie winked. It was a gesture he'd never seen any woman do but her, unless he counted the women he'd seen in movies or on television. It made her seem like a hologram, a wax figurine suddenly come to life. She put her bowl onto his desk and laid the fork, still spearing mouthfuls of salad, gingerly atop her mostly uneaten lunch. "Why didn't you ever talk to Jason again?" she asked. She folded her hands daintily in her lap but crossed one leg over the other, the position pushing her skirt higher up her thigh and exposing the bare skin above her boots. A pale blue vein snaked from just beneath the surface of her bare knee and disappeared under the tweed hemline.

Parker smiled. He wiped his mouth with a napkin and slid his dish next to hers. "I think you already know."

She tried to suppress a grin: Parker could see her pursing her lips with effort. "I want you to tell it again," Bonnie said. She ran her hand slowly along the side of her thigh, tracing the blue line as if to punctuate the request.

Each time he told her one of his stories, the colors of the memory deepened, the edges darkened, like he was delineating figures in a favorite photograph with a fine point pencil.

That night, he and Jason had played hockey with a group of other boys from the neighborhood until after the sun set and they could no longer see the ball even when they squinted. Jason had been in such a hurry to get home, he insisted they leave right from the park, skate the two miles along the long stretches of busy streets to save time. There were sidewalks, of course: the boys had walked to the park instead of driving, but the cracks and chasms in the concrete formed by frost heaves made the journey back on wheels less than ideal. They decided to take their chances on the road itself. The glimmer of oncoming headlights would provide enough of a warning of oncoming traffic.

"What's so important about getting to Julie's house?" Parker asked him, his eyes fixed on the back of his classmate's muscular thighs matted with sweat and grime as Jason skated quickly along the black pavement two paces ahead of him. The silver curbing that edged the carefully manicured tree belts seemed to flash like a strobe light as the two sped in and out of the shadows between yellow streetlamps.

"Got a date," Jason called back quickly. "You know how it is. Gotta get ready."

In the heavy, humid dusk, Parker could smell him: a wave of salt and hormones sailing behind Jason like a banner. "You can shower at my house," he offered. Then, after a carefully timed pause, "My mom's working second shift tonight."

It had been their private cryptic message, one that materialized years earlier when the two were in middle school, two pimply-faced boys drowning in puberty. What began as a convenient release evolved quickly into a semi-regular routine, even as the boys planted their feet firmly in high school, though the covert visits had petered out in their senior year. Parker blamed himself: in their final naked tussle in the seclusion of his bedroom, Parker had bitten Jason on the shoulder, hard enough to draw blood, and had continued to suck on the wound until Jason wrestled his clenched jaw from his lover's skin. Although his friend had been furious—so furious that the two had not spoken for months after, the episode took on a starring role in Parker's masturbatory fantasies for many weeks following.

Jason stretched his neck slightly, appearing to search farther into the distance of the dark road, mentally negotiating for the upcoming curve. Then he slowed his gait and turned his body to look at Parker. "That's all done with. You know that, right, Park?" When his classmate didn't respond, he continued, "We were just messing around. We've got girlfriends to do that with now. Understand?" He met Parker's eyes and held them, frowning slightly to emphasize that his mind would not be changed.

"Yeah, yeah, I know," Parker responded, glancing down at the double yellow line a foot to the left of Jason's ankles.

"I mean, in three months, we're leaving for college," Jason continued. When Parker only stared straight ahead, his classmate slowed his pace further until the two boys were skating side by side. "No more kids' stuff, right?"

Parker smiled at him. "No more kids' stuff," he repeated. After a carefully planned pause, he added, "But one thing?"

Jason raised his eyebrows as if waiting for his friend's verbal request. He wasn't prepared for Parker's sudden dart sideways, toward his torso. His body did not respond in time to correct the dramatic shift in balance when Parker pushed him, hard, over the yellow dividing lines and into the next lane.

He most certainly was not ready for the Lincoln Continental speeding around the corner and directly into his pelvis, knocking his body like a rag doll over the car's hood and windshield until it rolled over the side and onto the opposite curb, one wheel on Jason's skate smashing the passenger-side mirror, then striking the roadway's cement edging with an audible crack.

The car skidded to a stop just as Parker calmly dragged one toe behind his other foot and glided over to his friend, now a whimpering, mangled pile huddled over in a shadow on the ground. Jason's face had also struck the side of the curb—the corner, it appeared, as there was a visible dent in his forehead just above his left brow. Something dark and wet poured from the laceration and into Jason's eye.

Parker leaned forward until his face was nearly touching his friend's.

"How did he taste?" Bonnie asked.

She was the only one he had told about his secret.

"Terrified." Parker grinned. "And salty."

Bonnie said nothing to this, only stared at him, a slight smile tipping the edges of her lips.

"How many times have you heard this story?" Parker asked.

"About a million," Bonnie said. She stood up slowly and walked closer to him. "I know all of your stories, Parker. It doesn't mean I don't love hearing you tell them over and over again." She lifted her right leg and swung it over his knees, then sat down daintily, straddling his thighs without touching his chest. He was already excited from the memory, the image of Jason, his friend's countenance slowly enveloped by a sticky sheet of blood. The warmth of her body on his legs ratcheted the intensity even further, and he closed his eyes and willed himself to calm down.

It had been this way between them almost from the beginning. He only vaguely remembered meeting Bonnie; if someone had a gun to his head, he'd still have to guess at how long ago it had been, but they'd progressed from awkward acquaintances to intimate friends almost immediately. Her hair smelled like a tropical island, its dark strawberry blond waves parted in the middle and swinging about her chin like Clyde Barrow's notorious partner. She even wore one of those felt berets in the winter. He'd remarked that she should buy one, one chilly November afternoon as the two of them walked side by side toward the subway entrance, her golden curls flying everywhere in the wind, and sure enough, the next day, she arrived at his door still wearing the hat, looking like one of those cult photographs of the infamous moll he'd seen in his perusal of library books on gangsters as a teenager.

He touched her face briefly, then glanced at the clock on his computer screen. "I have to get back to work," he said, dropping his hand. "Save some for tonight."

Bonnie's face fell, but she climbed off his lap without argument. She had removed herself just in the nick of time: without bothering to knock, Mac opened the door to Parker's office and stuck his head inside.

"All set for the benefit?" he asked, not bothering to acknowledge Bonnie's presence.

Parker cleared his throat. "Lynn's going instead," he said, then shrugged as if the matter was out of his hands.

"Parker," Mac began, crossing his arms in front of his chest. "You know this position has never ended at five o'clock. It's important for you to be at this fundraiser. Shake a few hands, stroke a few egos."

"Lynn has it under control," Parker said, tapping his mouse and studying his computer screen. *And her tits are better at stroking than any bullshit I could manufacture*, he thought.

Bonnie rolled her eyes, reading his thoughts.

"Besides," Parker added, "I'm visiting with my father this weekend." He knew this was his Get Out of Jail Free card; Mac liked to brag that he cultivated employees who maintained tight family relationships. It read well in his monthly briefings to the corporation's executive officers, and Parker was a man who valued his family above ambition and fortune.

At least, it appeared that way.

The truth was, Parker's only connection to his father were through blurred snippets from his early childhood, yellowed film reels gathered from the cutting room floor of his memory: an older, dead-eyed version of Parker carrying a weathered brown suitcase, climbing into the passenger side of his mother's light blue Buick; an even deader-eyed version sitting perfectly still beside a window that would not open, the overhead lights of the painfully unadorned room incessantly buzzing, a million insects screaming to be released.

Parker would not be visiting anyone this weekend. He and Bonnie had another project to contemplate.

"Oh." Mac frowned slightly and thought for a moment. "You're sure Lynn has all of the information?"

"I quizzed her on the curriculum vitae of every guest of honor," Parker said, keeping his voice level. He glanced at Bonnie. She was nodding solemnly at Mac, but his boss kept his gaze focused on Parker.

This seemed to be enough to appease him. "All right. Good work, Parker," Mac said. "Enjoy your weekend." He jutted his chin once to reinforce his wish and retreated, shutting the door quietly behind him.

Bonnie stood to leave as well. "Until tonight, then?" She smoothed the fabric of her skirt and walked slowly toward the door. "'You still intend on making it up to me?"

Parker considered what they had discussed, what they'd been discussing for months now, their own private vision board. He felt his heart race with excitement. "We'll be there by eight. Room seventeen."

At this, Bonnie's expression blanked, all emotion wiped clean from her face. Just as quickly, however, her smile returned. "I'll be waiting," she said, her hand on the doorknob.

"Wait—" Parker leaned forward. "Where do you go? Just now, when that happens, where do you disappear to?"

Bonnie shook her head. "Don't be silly," she said. Her eyes softened. "You'll never be rid of me, love. That's what being a partner means." She winked again, and before he could respond, she was gone.

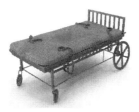

HE DIDN'T KNOW WHY HE TOLD HER. WHY *HER*, EXCEPT IT HAD SEEMED like a natural progression. They worked in different departments; there was no reason for them to interact at all except by choice, but he saw her daily—sometimes hourly—if the circumstances warranted. They relished indulging one another with the most grue-some of revenge fantasies, ones often featuring work colleagues in starring roles. When his frustrations could not wait until after a staff meeting, Parker typed Bonnie a message, spewing his unedited dysentery of anger in blocks of text that filled the screen.

*Mac put the kibosh on the alternate sources of funding piece. Two weeks of research in the garbage. Right now, he's stuffing his face with some sort of artisan cheese and pesto wrap. I can smell his noxious fumes from here.*

Less than a minute passed before she replied.

*People choke on food all the time.*

A slight pause, then,

*Sometimes, they die. Not a glamorous way to go, but dead is dead. You'd have a built-in excuse to stab him in the throat, though. Claim you were creating an airway.*

Parker scanned the area of table in front of his supervisor. On his waxy sandwich wrapper was a white plastic fork and knife still encased in their clear packaging. He imagined himself calmly bran-dishing the utensils, driving the tiny serrated edge alongside Mac's stubbled lump of Adam's apple. The carotid artery was the main pathway for blood to the brain. If he drove the weapon with enough force, he could sever it, cause the blood to gush from the wound, pour onto his hands, perhaps even onto his arms, a warm stickiness smelling of copper.

He swallowed.

*Of course, a takeout knife isn't going to do the job,* Bonnie noted. *You'd have to saw through the trachea. Better off shooting for the jugular vein.*

Parker's fingers flew across his screen. *Are you certain? I feel like an artery is the way to go. And it can't be that hard to cut: you can feel the pulse right below the jawline.*

A second passed.

Then another.

Then:

*Maybe just go for the femoral artery. Those bleed like crazy.*

Parker sniffed. *How the hell would I explain stabbing him in the groi—*

An over-accentuated clearing of the throat.

Mac was staring at him from the head of the conference table. Parker's eyes drifted to the green globule of oil dangling from his boss's lower lip. He pantomimed wiping his mouth, and Mac wildly pawed at the refuse in front of him, searching for a napkin. When the offending remnant had been removed, Mac made another guttural noise then continued speaking, turning his attention to another employee. Parker dropped his eyes back to the phone in his lap. Bonnie had replied before he'd had a chance to hit return.

*I've always wanted to fuck someone while being covered in blood.*

Parker read the message, then quickly tapped the power button to blacken his screen. He silently willed his heartbeat to slow down, resting his arms on the table and pressing his fingertips together to form an awkward tent shape. Mac was a fan of meditation, had sent the whole team on a weekend retreat one year to learn *conscious relaxation* and *self-discovery.* Parker spent most of that Saturday banging one of the yoga instructors in the resort's boathouse. The only *discovery* he'd gleaned from the experience was that gonorrhea was still very much a concern and a bitch to treat.

He closed his eyes and inhaled deeply, then leaned back in his chair. He couldn't resist looking back down at his phone. The screen blinked to life again.

*Was that too much?* Bonnie asked.

Parker rubbed his thumb along the hard shell of the phone's protective frame, then responded.

*Your blood?*

*No.* A pause. *A stranger's. Some sad sack I pick up from a bar or off an anonymous website. I ride him cowgirl-style, then sit him up and slice him with a box-cutter, feel the hot blood pour over my naked body.*

A thick muscle in his groin clenched. He closed his eyes again and measured his exhalation, slowing the release of breath, but jumped with a start when he felt the hand on his arm. He turned to see Lynn, both of her hands now brandished limply in front of her as if she were being held at gunpoint, staring at him wide-eyed. "I'm sorry," she whispered nervously. "I didn't mean to startle you." She moved one arm toward the table, picked up the stack of copies Mac had passed along for distribution, and offered them again to Parker.

He shifted his legs, hoping to disguise the erection pulsing in his lap. "Thanks," he said curtly, accepting the papers.

How long ago had that been? In his office, Parker stared at his computer screen, searching his memory. He sniffed. The garlic tang of Bonnie's abandoned salad still permeated his nose. At times, the days blurred together. Sometimes they somersaulted and played hide and go seek, mischievous children purposefully lagging behind until forced to behave. If he were honest, Parker admitted that when he tried to chronologically affix an event from his past, he second-guessed his recollection.

"That's what happens when you have no spouse or children to go home to at the age of forty-two." Bonnie's voice echoed from his memory and bounced playfully off the white walls of his office. "Thank goodness you have me, or you'd go completely off the rails." He remembered her teasing him about this soon after his most recent birthday, the two of them alone at a table in a seedy, out of the way pub, nursing their drinks and assessing the clientele as potential donors.

Tonight, they'd make their shared fantasy come to fruition. Parker had planned the evening meticulously. As he opened his email, he allowed his mind to briefly consider the brackish tang, a gush of warmth spreading along his bare chest, how Bonnie would look, her ethereally white skin splashed with deep red ichor.

Parker swallowed hard, shook the images from his mind, and returned to his work.

Flashes of sporadic tunnel lighting disco lit the windows of the subway as the train ticked quickly toward Kenmore Square. The car was packed; Parker and Bonnie were fortunate to snag two seats together, but fellow commuters on both sides continued to push on them so incessantly, they surrendered their bodies to fit into one. It was a particularly cold autumn, so the smothering body heat of strangers was not altogether unwelcome.

"Did you ever think of asking Lynn out for a drink?" Parker asked in a low voice, his breath making the soft wave of hair framing Bonnie's earlobe dance.

Bonnie was distracted, scrolling through the technicolor feed of her social media on her phone. "No," she said without looking up. "Have you?"

"I'm her supervisor. It would be considered inappropriate," Parker said. He studied the side of her face. There was a large freckle positioned nearly parallel to her nostril. He hadn't remembered seeing it before and wondered if Bonnie had been out in the sun too often recently. He lowered his voice to a whisper. "Besides. That's not what I mean."

A slight grin leaked from the side of Bonnie's lips. "Oh, I know what you mean," she said, continuing to slide her finger up and down her screen. "And we both agreed. It's too risky to choose someone from work. It needs to be someone who can't be traced back to us. Preferably, someone outside of the city." Her eyes flickered sideways at him.

"I know that," Parker said.

She turned her head toward him and raised an eyebrow. "Do you?"

The car squealed to a stop. The doors opened, and a smell of diesel mixed with food truck hot dogs wafted inside. Half of the car's contents spilled onto the platform, and the remaining passengers seemed to simultaneously exhale with relief. A few new riders stepped into the car and grabbed hold of the balance bars before the doors closed again and the train resumed its journey toward Brookline.

Parker looked down at Bonnie's lap. She was wearing the same black skirt she always wore to work, the one that grazed her knees, and boots that tied at the top of her calf. In the distorted illumination of the train car, her exposed knees glowed yellowish: not jaundiced, but slightly golden. Without thinking, he placed his hand on the space of skin just below her hemline. Her thigh was smooth and cold, like a sheet of fresh cream or a marble column in a museum display.

Bonnie smiled sweetly at him but gently placed her hand on top of his and moved it onto his own leg. Her eyes darted covertly at the passengers around them. Without turning her face back to him, she whispered. "It will be worth the wait. When we find the one. You'll see."

THE SAME PROMISE ECHOED FROM THE SPEAKERPHONE OF HIS CELL where he'd placed it in the dashboard tray. He'd borrowed the Honda from his elderly neighbor, a woman whose cats he fed and plants he watered every time she left on vacation.

On the car's radio, a Heart song from the seventies played, Ann Wilson crooning about dreaming of being a willow that leans over a stream, her sister Nancy riffing the guitar in a sequential downward spiral as the chorus soared. Parker tapped the steering wheel in time to the beat and glanced at his reflection in the rearview mirror. Only his eyes were visible in the dim light cast from the instrument panel. "Where are you?" he asked, glancing back at the double-wide dark road in front of him. "I just got off route 1. There's an L.A. Fitness on my left."

"We're just ahead." Bonnie's response was punctuated with a metallic giggle through the speaker. "See the girl with the jean skirt? You can't miss her."

Sure enough, a block farther on the right, a gaunt woman leaned against a public bus stop sign. She wore an oversized white t-shirt with a neck hole that creeped along one shoulder, the strap of a silvery blue bra digging into freckled skin. Bonnie stood a foot behind her, both arms held behind her back like a captured prisoner.

Parker slowed the car to a stop in front of the women and pressed the button to lower the passenger-side window. "If you're headed south, I can give you a ride..." he offered, his voice sounding strangely mechanical as if he, too, were speaking through the car's speakers.

The girl glanced up the road. "Are you going to the casino?" she asked, her eyes still fixed on the expanse of distance behind him. "I want to go to the casino."

Parker's eyes fluttered up to Bonnie. She was grinning but said nothing. "Sure," he said. "I don't mind stopping there to drop you off. I'm just grabbing a few things from my room, then I'm headed back into the city. I can drop you on the way." He felt along his arm rest until his fingers massaged another button and the door locks released in a synchronized click.

Bonnie leaned her head slightly forward. "Mind if I come along, too?" she asked, but the girl was already climbing into the front seat. She shimmied her ass slightly against the plush upholstery, read-justing her acid-washed skirt with her hands.

"Of course," said Parker. "The more, the merrier, right?" He sounded cheerful. Neighborly.

At least, he thought he did.

"Aces," Bonnie replied and slid softly into the back seat.

Parker pretended to squint at the stranger. "You look really familiar. Is your name Beth? Becky? Did we meet at the gym the other day?" He motioned with his head at the building behind them in the distance.

The girl rummaged through her purse, an oversized, shiny black sack with a small tear growing along the bottom of one strap like a worn Hefty bag. "No," she said quickly. "I'm from New Hampshire. Just down here for the weekend. My name's Tammy."

Parker turned back toward the road, checking for passing traffic before he pulled back into the lane. "Oh? Were your parents big Debbie Reynolds fans?"

"Who?" Tammy said, already sounding slightly bored. Parker snuck another look at her when they passed under a streetlight. She wasn't more than twenty-five years old—closer to twenty, he guessed, but already with a decade of hard living under her belt.

"Never mind," Bonnie whisper-groaned from behind them.

Tammy continued to ransack the handbag. She pulled out a small white plastic container, a miniature ibuprofen bottle, the kind sold in gas stations or hotel concierge stands, and shook it like a tiny maraca. "You got any water," she asked, "or anything else to drink?" Her eyes flitted nervously around the front seat and foot wells.

Parker reached an arm behind her seat back and felt around for the cooler he'd placed on the floor earlier. Bonnie's soft hand touched his wrist and squeezed, and he felt his fingers close around a plastic soda bottle. "Funny you should ask," he said, bringing the cola in front of the gear shift. "It's about half rum, though—my own mobile cocktail. You never know when you might need a pick-me-up, am I right?" His own voice sounded strange to him again, like he was hearing it from somewhere far away.

"Just not while you're driving, right?" Bonnie interjected quickly.

"But not while I'm driving, no," Parker said. He glanced at Tammy, but she didn't seem concerned. He tilted the bottle toward his passenger and she accepted it greedily, unscrewing the cap and guzzling a hearty swallow or two before tossing a few small pills into her mouth and chasing them with another gulp.

"This is it," Bonnie exclaimed and reached over the seat to grab the top of Parker's arm. He felt himself flex his bicep in response. He could hear the excitement in her voice; it seemed to bubble out of her, a dark effervescence leaking from her pores and jumping onto him in a million pieces like fleas. She let go and pointed to a large billboard on the side of the road—*Pheasant Inn*.

Parker tapped his directional signal but only slowed to a stop in the road. "That looks like a car dealership," he said, squinting at the lot in front of the sign. There was a smaller placard fixed beneath the larger one reading *JP's Auto Sales: Cash for Vehicles*.

"Are you selling your car?" Tammy asked, replacing the cap on the now half-empty cola and trying unsuccessfully to smother a burp.

Bonnie waved her hand as if shooing both of them away. "It's behind it. Just turn in. You'll see."

Sure enough, his headlights illuminated a larger lot piggy-backing the front one; this expanse of blacktop was much wider than the first and framed by an unending row of white-shingled, single-story buildings broken only by a picture window and door every fifty feet. Only five or so cars dotted the back area, and Parker pulled the Honda into a space between the entrances to rooms thirteen and twelve. He thrust the shifter into PARK but left the engine running.

After a long moment, he felt Bonnie's warm breath on his ear. "You ready?" she whispered. She was leaning her body against the back of his seat, her chin nearly resting on the back of his shoulder.

Tammy unscrewed the cap and took another swig of the cola. "Is this where you live?" she asked in a tone that indicated she would be unimpressed with the answer either way. When she pulled the mouth of the bottle away from her face, Parker saw with some disgust that she had dribbled a bit of the liquid onto her chin. A small brown splotch was visible on the swath of t-shirt fabric near her collarbone.

Parker turned the key backward and the engine silenced. "I need…" He paused. Tammy wasn't looking at him. She was gazing bleary-eyed out at the row of motel doors with cool disinterest, twirling her wrist to rotate the plastic soda bottle so that the brown liquid, what was left of it, swirled like a small vortex inside. "I need—"

*"I need us to do this." Bonnie's voice was soft but insistent. Parker had been sound asleep, but the sound of his cell ringing somewhere far away jarred him awake.*

*He pawed at the nightstand and brought the phone to his ear without opening his eyes. "Yeah?" His voice came out as a hoarse whisper, and he cleared his throat. "Hello?"*

*"I need it. Do you understand?" Her voice drizzled like honey into his ear.*

*Parker opened his eyes and blinked rapidly. The single white dot on his Apple TV console cast an eerie hue about the dark bedroom, an eye of mechanical moonlight watching over him. "Yes, yes," he replied. "I know."*

*Bonnie's breathing was audible. She inhaled sharply and continued. "Do you?" she whispered. She exhaled, and Parker thought he heard her muffle a small sob. "You're the only one who can do this for me," she said softly. "For us."*

*Parker licked his lips. His mouth felt dry, tacky, like he'd been breathing through his mouth in his sleep. "Tomorrow night," he said. "I'll secure a room in the morning." His eyes were beginning to adjust to the dim light, and he shut them. There was silence on the line. "Bonnie?" he whispered into the receiver.*

*But she was gone.*

And now he was here, sitting in the front seat of his neighbor's sedan, a woman half his age bouncing her knee incessantly only two feet away. Tammy placed the cola bottle in the cup holder between them; it was nearly empty. "I think I've been here," she said, her eyes still scanning the doors. Her demeanor had changed; the generous amount of alcohol and pills he'd mixed with the soda hadn't acted like a depressant but appeared to do the opposite: Tammy was a magician's hat of jumpiness, nerves hopping and sizzling from her body so palpably that Parker suddenly feared they'd jet propel her from the car.

"I thought you said you were from New Hampshire," Bonnie noted flatly from the back seat.

"Have you visited this area before?" Parker added quickly, trying to smooth any discomfort.

Tammy flipped the visor down and studied her face in the lighted mirror. "Yeah, I come down here a lot." She rubbed her bottom lip, then turned to look at Parker. "You know, to party." She smiled coyly.

Parker swallowed. "This is a good place to do it. They take cash if you pay double. The rooms are decent, too. And you're not too far from Boston—or Salem, even, if you're into that." The cell phone's vibrating alert buzzed from its holder on the console. "Excuse me," he said and checked the text message.

*Enough with the small talk, Chatty Cathy.*

Parker glanced in the rearview mirror. Bonnie was staring intently at him, a small smile peeking from the side of her mouth.

*Ask her inside. I'm sure she could be wooed with the prospect of making a bit of quick cash.*

Parker stuffed the phone into his breast pocket. "Do you mind if we go inside for a bit? Maybe have a quick party before we head to the casino?" He held his breath. If she turned this offer down, he'd be stuck driving her to Everett and they would have to find another target.

His fears were eased when Tammy leaned back in her seat and bowed her head so that her eyes gazed upward at him: a deer pleading in the glow of his headlights. It was clear she'd practiced the move ahead of time. "Sure, that sounds like fun," she said. "I'm all out of cash to gamble with, though. Do you think you could float me a few bucks?"

Parker grinned. "I think we can make that happen." He pulled the key from the ignition.

The room itself was sparsely decorated: a king-sized bed, its dark coverlet stretched tight as a drum across the firm mattress; a wide, low dresser of drawers painted grayish-blue; a simple side lamp with a trim, white shade. The floor was not carpeted but instead dark wood tinted to a deep mahogany. In the dim light, there was a shadow in one corner, stained remnants from a previous evening.

"This is me," Parker said, tossing his keys with a satisfying clink onto the nearby table, barren save for a three-ring binder of local restaurant menus and tourist attraction brochures, his leather-bound shaving case, and a half-empty box of cheap facial tissue. "Make yourself at home. I'm just going to use the little boys' room."

*Little boys' room.* Why had he said that? That was a phrase old people used. A snippet of memory film ticker-taped across his mind: his father, the words barely audible under the ceaseless buzzing above, asking him if he needed to use the facilities. Or had he been defending his son's nervous shifting from foot to foot when his mother had scolded Parker for his incessant fidgeting during their visit? *Maybe he has to use the little boys' room.* Each time they visited, the droning monotone in his voice was tamped down further by the brightly colored capsules the nurses delivered. His father's facial skin seemed to blend seamlessly into the pale yellow walls of his small room until Parker wasn't sure if he existed anymore at all.

Parker studied his reflection in the interrogation lighting of the small bathroom mirror. The tiny schisms of broken capillaries dotted the whites of his eyes. Bonnie's voice drifted from nearby, asking the girl if she wanted another drink. Parker removed his cell phone from his pocket and placed it carefully on the sink, then walked back into the room.

"The rest of the bottle is in the trunk if you'd—" he stopped when he saw her. Tammy had undressed and was sitting—sprawling, really—in the simple wooden chair next to the table, her gaunt frame starkly rigid and angular like a wire hanger in the glow of the table lamp. He could see that her toenails were ragged and chipped with ancient navy-colored polish.

She smiled dreamily at Parker, the effects of the alcohol finally taking hold. "Hi again," she said slowly, clearly trying her best to properly enunciate each word. On the other side of the outside wall, a group of garrulous partiers whooped and hollered as they passed the door, their voices fading just as quickly as they hurried away to their room at the other end of the lot. Tammy wrinkled her nose slightly at the cacophony and pushed herself to standing.

Parker unbuttoned his shirt and laid it carefully on the bed pillow. He did the same with his pants, his boxer shorts, and his socks until he, too, was naked and his clothing pig-piled against the headboard. He glanced at Bonnie. She was standing motionless on the other side of the room, her arms crossed in front of her like a linesman at a sports game, her eyes darting to and fro between Parker and Tammy.

Parker nodded once to her, then pulled Tammy toward his chest. Her skin was cold, prickled with gooseflesh. She leaned her head back and looked up. Her glassy eyes seemed to droop as she did so, maintaining an arduous fight against gravity, and her blinking was noticeably slower.

"You're not nodding off on us, are you, Tams?" Bonnie asked, her expression amused. She smirked at Parker. "How many of those sedatives did you put in that bottle?"

"I didn't expect she'd demolish the whole damn thing," Parker hissed back. He guided Tammy back over to the chair, sat down backwards on it, and awkwardly tried to balance the girl on his lap.

Bonnie exhaled one of her trademark sighs and walked over to help him.

Tammy adjusted her legs to straddle her host and stared into Parker's eyes. "I'm not drunk, silly," she said. "Can't a girl have a good time?" She reached out to cradle his face in her hand, then leaned forward to kiss him hungrily on the mouth. Her saliva tasted like chalk and vanilla extract gone rancid.

Parker moved his mouth away from hers and to the bottom of her ear, kissing her softly. Locking eyes with Bonnie, he ran his lips softly along the side of Tammy's neck and into the curve beneath her jaw until he felt the rhythmic beating of her pulse. He pressed the tip of his tongue firmly against the faint throbbing and closed his eyes, pictured the thin layer of skin, the diaphanous partition separating his teeth from her carotid artery. Her blood pushed urgently against his mouth, aching to escape.

When he opened his eyes again, Bonnie was sitting behind Tammy. She grinned, then winked at him, her eyes traveling purposefully toward the table. It all seemed to happen in slow-motion: Bonnie wrapping her arms around Tammy's elbows and pulling her forearms backward, Parker reaching over to the unzipped shaving kit and removing the new straight razor from inside; Tammy, unaware of the significance of either action, smiling wickedly at Parker as she ground her pelvis deeper against his.

Bonnie leaned forward to kiss Tammy softly on the top of her clavicle, the girl thrust her head backward in appreciation, and Parker made his move. He stabbed the tip of the blade forcefully into the side of Tammy's neck, then yanked it sideways as hard as he could. A gaping chasm opened and yawned, first exposing sinewy pink muscle, then vomiting a wave of bright red blood. Tammy's eyes opened wide in surprise, and she jerked spasmodically in an attempt to thrust her hands forward but Bonnie fought to hold them back. Sprays of crimson pulsed within the gory tide like a metronome, bathing Parker's neck and chest in sticky warmth.

When the arterial spray slowed down to a nearly imperceptible beat, Bonnie pushed Tammy's limp corpse sideways and onto the floor. She encircled Parker's torso with her arms and clutched his body against hers, alabaster arms and legs like marble soon swirling with vermilion ripples and blotches. Their bodies entwined so tightly, blood spurted from between their shoulders and splashed Parker's face.

*Thank you. Thank you.*

Bonnie's voice wasn't coming from her mouth but instead sounded somewhere far away, like it had in the car, on the speakerphone. Like it had when she'd phoned him in the middle of the night. *Yes*, it said, *yes, this is it. This is what I needed.*

What *we* needed.

He opened his mouth, tasted the spray of blood on his lips, and pushed his fingers into Bonnie's back. Wisps of her strawberry blond hair dragged through the streaks of blood on his face and stuck to his cheek. The force of his orgasm erupted and ran him over like a freight train, violent, and his body buckled in near seizure. For a moment, his vision clouded, and Parker wondered if he were having a stroke. He squeezed his eyes closed as tightly as he could, warding off a wave of nausea and willing his heart rate to slow. After three deep breaths, it did.

"See? And you thought Mac's weekend retreat was a total waste of time." Bonnie's voice was only a whisper in his ear.

When he opened his eyes again, Parker's arms were folded

across his own chest, the hair on his arms matted and tangling in the downy black fur between his nipples. Tammy's body lay in an awkward heap beside his left foot. Her left shoulder appeared torn, the flesh ripped aside and the musculature below pricked heavily with teeth marks. Outside, the raucous group of partiers passed by again; someone yelled incoherently about locating an ice machine. After the last vestiges of their voices faded away, total silence permeated the room like a thick fog.

Bonnie was nowhere in sight.

Parker stood up. His balance felt wobbly, his muscles weak and malnourished. He tried to remember the last meal he'd eaten. Lunch with Bonnie? Was it today he was recalling or sometime long ago? He walked unsteadily to the bathroom, his bare feet making audible wet smacks as they tracked Tammy's blood across the hardwood.

Bonnie was not in the bathroom.

His mind had softened gradually as the years passed. It had evolved into a warming round of pungent cheese, the stagnant air forming tiny pinpricks and spaces of nothing.

It seemed like an eternity since he'd first told Bonnie about Jason.

But she'd already known, hadn't she?

Parker examined his face in the mirror. The ghost of his father's face stared back at him. The silence that surrounded him was deafening. The incessant buzzing had finally ceased, at least for now. The insects trapped behind the plastic covers encasing the blinding fluorescents had escaped. There was no putting them back.

He checked his phone screen. It was blank. Bonnie would text when she needed him again: he was certain. She would appear in his office doorway, and their fantasy, their plan for room seventeen, would materialize, simmer, and solidify. When his hunger returned, Bonnie would become corporeal once more. Always the strawberry blonde, always pale, always beautiful, always his partner. The dark blue vein of deoxygenated life-force pulsing through him, struggling to breathe.

Front and center and on the sly.

Parker ran his fingers along his chest, drawing a roadway of pale skin within the sticky layer of quickly cooling dark red. He closed his eyes and stuck the fingers in his mouth, allowed a metallic surge of the briny substance to dance along his tongue and drizzle down his throat.

He opened his eyes and smiled. His father smiled back, square white teeth rimmed with red.

Someday, he would no longer crave it.

At least, he thought he wouldn't.

# A CRIME OF PASSION

## RICHARD CHIZMAR

**P**ast midnight. A dark cabin nestled in the wilderness. Night sounds…invaded by the whisper of heavy tires. Doors slamming. The crunch of gravel under footsteps.

Many footsteps.

Instantly awake, Drake lifted the .38 from the nightstand and slipped out from beneath the bedsheet. He crouched to a knee, listening, staring out the open curtains at the front yard below. He glimpsed a flicker of sparks in the darkness, then the orange tint of flames, and thought: *My God, they're going to burn down the cabin.*

### Chapter 1

Thomas Drake sold his first novel, *Nightlife*, on his thirtieth birthday. He celebrated both events with a carry-out pizza and a solo trip to the movies. The book—an urban crime thriller—sold well in hardcover and the paperback edition snuck onto the *N.Y. Times* list for three weeks. The resulting four-book contract allowed him to quit his job as a social worker and write full-time.

Despite the lucrative deal, Drake continued to live a comfortable, rather conservative life in the suburbs outside Baltimore. He was a bachelor by choice, rarely dated, and had never dated the same woman twice. Whose fault that was, he claimed he didn't know.

Drake did admit—and too often, his few friends scolded—that except for his bank account, he didn't offer a very attractive or exciting package. He was barely of average height, and at least ten pounds underweight. Receding hairline. Pale skin. A face of little character.

And he was far from daring or spontaneous, writing in an upstairs office six days a week, eight hours a day, preferring mornings and early afternoons, walking his two-year-old Labrador retriever several times a day, playing poker on odd Monday nights (more out of habit than actual enjoyment) and golf twice a week. And, no matter what the day had been like or what the next had to offer, he always read himself to sleep.

## Chapter 2

DRAKE SCRAMBLED CLOSER TO THE SECOND-FLOOR WINDOW, HIS HEART pounding at his bare chest. Their van was parked at the bottom of the cabin's gravel driveway, parking lights still on. Cocky bastards. Surprised they didn't just toot the damn horn to announce their arrival. A small fire burned to the side of the van, a safe distance from the cabin. The flames threw distorted shadows across the lawn, and Drake watched as the figures took form. He counted all four of them and found a hint of relief in knowing that no one was lurking beyond his view. They didn't appear to carry weapons, but Drake knew the firepower was there.

For just a moment, he contemplated opening fire on them from the window but ruled against it. Despite an extensive book knowledge of weapons, he'd never actually fired a gun until a week ago. And a week's practice hadn't helped much; six bottles out of ten remained his best score. He knew his only chance was at close range.

The woman remained by the fire—it was now waist high and growing—while the others returned to the van. The back doors stood open and Drake could see several stacks of boxes inside. The men waited in turn, then carried armloads of what he immediately recognized as books—his own novel, *The Prey*, he knew—and took turns dropping them onto the fire. With a flush of surprise and anger, he realized that they were replaying the book burnings from New York and Chicago and the other cities they'd followed him to.

None of them made a move toward the cabin, content for the moment with the destruction of his books. He could hear them mumbling through the slightly open window. Nothing loud or clear enough to understand, but he guessed that they were congratulating themselves for finding him again, for destroying more of his evil work. Crazy fuckers. Probably thought he was cowering in fear. *Let them think it*, Drake thought. It'll make my job that much easier.

He remained at the window and watched, recognizing each of their faces in the glow of the fire. The woman named Jessie. Strikingly beautiful and clearly insane. She was their leader. And the three men. All large and equally crazy.

Six days. It had taken almost a week, but they'd somehow tracked him across hundreds of miles. Drake had known they'd eventually find him—in fact, he'd spent most of the six days at the cabin trying to prepare for this moment—but he couldn't help but wonder how they'd done it. He'd told no one where he was going. No one, because, quite simply, there'd been no one left. Drake shifted his weight and flexed the fingers holding the pistol. *Let 'em come*, he thought.

Outside, the fire spat gray smoke, and Drake imagined he could feel its warmth wash his face. He touched a finger to his cheek. It was hot, but only from anticipation...and yes, he admitted, from fear. As the three men returned to the van for another load, Drake pushed the curtains aside and thought, *That damn* Times *critic was right: I never should've sold it to the movies...*

## CHAPTER 3

DESPITE HIS USUAL INSECURITIES, THE FOLLOW-UP NOVELS DID WELL AND continued Drake's success. His main character, Robert Steele, was an aggressive New York City attorney (by day), a street-smart vigilante with a penchant for breaking the law and serving his own brand of justice (by night). A rather trite theme, Drake admitted, but he'd added what proved to be an irresistible quality to his character. He had made the lawyer a hopeless romantic, a puppy-eyed tough guy with a heart of gold and a body to match. Steele chased criminals while gorgeous women chased him. Steele's audience grew into a wide and loyal one, and it showed in Drake's royalty statements.

By his fourth novel, Drake was a major force in the crime and mystery fields. A regular on the bestseller lists. Guest-of-honor at conventions. Major awards winner. Book club selections. Frequent appearances in the media: television, radio, newspapers.

Foreign sales from his first four novels had even allowed him to buy a lakeside cabin in the hills of Western Maryland. A place to escape the creeping closeness of suburbia, a place to really be alone and write. No neighbors. No telephone. No mail. Just a two-story cabin with spacious rooms, a double fireplace, and an office with a view of the lake.

Then…came trouble.

*The Prey*, Drake's fifth and most daring novel, drew more attention than all of his previous books combined. Part of the reason was that, for the first time, a Thomas Drake novel had debuted in the top five on both the *Times* and the *Publisher's Weekly* best-seller lists. The other, more publicized reason, however, was the novel's controversial theme.

*The Prey* was darker—and more ambitious—than the typical Steele novel. Less romance and more gritty drama. The book followed Steele as he infiltrated the seedy New York underworld of child prostitution and pornography to search for the killer of his lover's teenaged sister. The world Drake described was ugly and dark and violent; his characters breathed hate and perversion. The writing itself was grim and graphically violent, and the ending was not a happy one.

Drake, his agent, and his editor all agreed that it was a risk, moving away from the popular Steele formula, but when the book debuted so high on the bestseller lists and stayed there, and when the critics lauded it as "chilling and thought-provoking" and "disturbingly real," their concern changed to delight.

So, when Warner offered close to seven figures for the motion picture rights to *The Prey*, no one was particularly surprised; and, despite his reservations about the book's graphic nature, the offer proved too much for Drake to resist. He signed the contracts, kept his fingers crossed…and waited anxiously for the movie's premiere.

The film was a disaster, bearing little, if any, semblance to its source material. Warner's final creation was a tasteless ninety-eight-minute, new-wave-director-on-speed's version of hell on earth, a thumbnail away from an NC-17 rating. The film was overly violent and obscene and grossly erotic. Pornography for a mass audience, the angry reviews shouted.

Concerned citizens protested the movie's showing in dozens of cities. The critics hated it, the public hated it, and Drake hated it.

And an underground group of fanatics who called themselves Mother Earth branded the movie "filthy" and "evil"—and hated it enough to kill.

## CHAPTER 4

ONE OF THEM WAS GONE.

Drake leaned closer to the window and frantically scanned the yard. Christ, he could only see three of them. They were standing next to the van, watching the cabin, talking low. Drake squinted, trying to focus on their features.

Too dark.

The fire had eventually weakened, thanks to a limited supply of books. *They must've bought out a dozen stores*, he'd thought, watching them dump the last load. Drake had suspected that, with the book burning nearly complete, they'd make a move for the cabin soon. So, he'd left the window momentarily and hurried back to the night-stand, grabbed a full box of ammunition, and then returned. The process couldn't have taken more than five or six seconds, but they must've known all along where he was watching from and taken advantage of his mistake.

He finger-tipped a flannel shirt from the chair near the window and slipped it on. Then he emptied the box of bullets into the pocket over his heart. Again, he considered opening fire from the window, surprising them, and hopefully taking advantage of the confusion.

He tensed. It just might work...no! *Damn it!* Drake thought. It would just force their hand that much quicker, show them that he wasn't going to surrender so easily. *Damn it!* He thought he'd be ready for this. Ready for anything after what had happened back at home.

The roof creaked and Drake flinched, almost dropping the gun. He imagined one of them standing directly above him, motioning to the others and laughing. Then lowering his weapon and drilling machine gun fire through the roof.The second-floor windows were unprotected, but the doors and windows downstairs were heavily boarded from the inside. They wouldn't withstand constant battering, but they'd prevent a quick and easy entrance and allow Drake the time to defend the breach. He'd begun transforming the cabin into a fortress during the second day, feeling, at times, both paranoid and silly. Now, he knew he'd been right.

Suddenly, he heard a crack of breaking glass and wood downstairs. Den window. Side of the house. Another crack followed.

Drake glanced out the window again, a chill tracking his spine. Only one of them remained by the van now; the others had disappeared. Another board cracked. Louder this time. Closer. He sprinted for the stairs.

## CHAPTER 5

MOTHER EARTH'S REIGN OF TERROR HAD STARTED TWO MONTHS EARLIER with a two-page letter to Warner Studios. The group had determined that *The Prey* was an "evil movie, a deranged portrayal of America's youth," and condemned the movie studio for making the film and blamed the book's author for producing such trash.

Over the course of several weeks, Warner and Putnam forwarded a total of twenty-three letters to Drake from the organization. None of the letters listed a return address, and the postmarks on the envelopes were from various states.

Shortly after, similar letters began arriving at Drake's post office box, an address he'd been certain only business associates were aware of. Finally, they began showing up at the house.

All the letters were written in the same handwriting and all carried essentially the same warning: if you don't stop the paperback release of *The Prey*, withdraw from your upcoming signing tour, and seek redemption for your sins, we will have no choice but to punish you. And each letter was always signed the same: the faithful disciples of Mother Earth: Jessie. Carl. Randy. Willie.

No one Drake spoke with had ever heard of the group and considering the apparent size of its membership, he wasn't surprised. His publisher ran a check through the research department and even checked with the FBI, but nothing turned up on either's computer files. The postal service tried but couldn't help, and the police claimed that they needed more to go on than a stack of crazy letters. Their only advice: just ignore the freaks and they'll eventually forget all about you.

But they didn't forget him.

They sent more letters. Then packages. Cardboard boxes full of black ash and charred copies of *The Prey*: burned, they claimed, to symbolize their contempt for the novel's author.

Mutilated publicity photos of Drake.

Mangled baby dolls, signifying the author's ill effect on the country's youth.

Then, during the signing tour that Putnam had arranged, he'd begun noticing the same face in the crowd in different cities. A tall, raven-haired woman. Thin and very attractive. Well-dressed. Intense. Always closely watching him.

He initially spotted her during a book signing, staring at him through the store window. Then...sitting alone at a corner table in a Detroit restaurant, walking in a Houston airport terminal, and in the passing crowd at several other signings. Only her professional appearance had kept Drake's suspicions to a minimum. *Perhaps she's a stewardess*, he thought. Curious and strangely attracted, he twice tried to follow her, but both times, she'd vanished.

The woman finally confronted him during a signing at a Midwest Kroch's & Brentano's. She waited her turn in line, unnoticed by the author, then while Drake scribbled a signature, she leaned over and quietly introduced herself as Jessie from the organization Mother Earth.

The words froze Drake, and instead of grabbing the woman—as he would later wish he'd done—he was too terrified to even look up. After a moment, he dropped the pen and slowly lifted his head. The tall woman's red lips spread into a smile, and he immediately recognized her as the woman he'd been seeing in the crowd.

Before he could react, she doused the book-covered table with a container of clear fluid and set it afire. The crowd panicked and scrambled, and Drake knocked over two rows of paperback racks trying to escape the small fire. The woman disappeared in the ensuing commotion.

The woman did not appear again, but there were six more book burnings. Each time hundreds of copies of *The Prey* were set afire on the sidewalk in front of the bookstore in which Drake was appearing. And each time the culprits escaped without a trace. Witnesses in each city reported that there were four persons involved: three men and a woman.

Finally, after a bomb threat was phoned into a Washington, D.C., mall bookstore, the tour was cut short and Drake was granted an early vacation.

He returned to Baltimore, where the county sheriff's office agreed to give him protection outside his home. But after a week passed uneventfully, the police left.

Then, the phone calls began…

The first call came late on a Sunday night, during the local weather broadcast on the eleven o'clock news. Drake had called it an early night and was reading an old Dean Koontz paperback in bed—half-listening to the news—when the phone rang. He picked it up after the first ring, startled and annoyed by the shrill interruption.

"Hello."

"Is this Thomas Drake?" A woman's voice.

He immediately knew who it was on the other end. He shivered and stared at the closed bedroom door, the drape-shrouded window. His number was unlisted. Always had been. Only his agent, two editors at Putnam, and a few relatives and friends had the number. He couldn't believe that they'd found it. He went to hang up the receiver and then changed his mind. Just play it cool. Play their game.

"Yes, this is Thomas Drake. And who is this?"

"I think you know who this is. And I suggest that you listen very carefully to what I have to say."

"And if I don't?" He got up from the bed and began pacing the carpet.

"We are a very powerful organization, Mr. Drake. With resources beyond your comprehension. Trust me, we will find a way to make you listen. We always have in the past."

"You mean…Christ, you mean you're done this before? I'm not the first person you've—"

She laughed, an angry, ugly sound. "Oh, yes. There have been others. None as popular as you, of course, but there have been others." She waited, then said. "Alex Forrester wouldn't listen either. Do you remember him?"

Jesus, he remembered. It had been in all the newspapers. Alex Forrester. Rock and roll musician. Heavy metal. Accused of head-lining a satanic movement, using his music to recruit devil worshipers. Paralyzed last year in a highly publicized automobile accident. Brakes failed. Oh my God.

"You…you were responsible for that accident—"

"Do you know why we chose Mother Earth as our title?" she asked, ignoring the question. "Because we live by nature's laws. There was a time when this earth was free of darkness and evil; it was pure. It is our mission to make this country pure again, to cleanse it of all filth."

"You're crazy," Drake whispered. "Absolutely crazy." He'd known from the start that this woman and her Mother Earth followers were a bunch of lunatics. But until now, the real danger of the situation had failed to sink in.

"The choice is yours to make," she said, her voice rising. She was enjoying it now, taking pleasure from the control she held over him. "You still have time to seek redemption for your sins."

"What sins? Have you even read my book? I haven't done anything. I'm not responsible for what ended up on the screen."

"Of course you are, you miserable man. The film is simply an extension of your vision. It is your message that must be stopped. Do you think the people see anyone else's name on the movie credits? No, of course not. Only yours. And yours is the only name on the book cover. It is you who is responsible."

"No, that's not true. Why are you doing this to me? You have no good reason to—"

"NO GOOD REASON?" She was shouting into the phone now, her voice trembling with rage. "I have a fourteen-year-old daughter lying comatose in a hospital room because of…of filth like you."

*My God*, he thought. She was crying.

"My baby was once an innocent child, a pure person, Mr. Drake. But she was too trusting, too easily swayed. I didn't see the warnings. I failed her. Her group of peers were evil; they read the filthy books, watched the filthy movies, and they acted as characters from those evil worlds. They lied to their parents. They drank and partied and dressed like sluts. They did things with boys. My baby was high on drugs when the car she was a passenger in went over an embankment. Now, she just lays there in that horrible hospital."

"What is it that you want from—"

"The predators in this world," she continued, "the spreaders of evil like you, think they are powerful and strong, but under nature's laws, we know that evil breeds only weakness and purity offers eternal strength. Remember that, Mr. Drake. Remember that."

Drake sighed. "Just tell me what it is that you want me to do? We cut the signing tour in half. The paperback release is a week away. I couldn't stop that even if I wanted to."

"You must repent for your sins. Speak with your public, to your readers. Warn them. Tell them you have repented. Tell them that the book is wrong, full of filth and lies and evil messages—"

"I'm hanging up, lady. I can't listen to this anymore. And don't try to call back, because I'll have the police put a tap on the phone and—"

"Come now, Mr. Drake. We both know that the police will be of no help to you. They went through the motions for seven days and now you are all alone."

Drake shivered again and walked to the window, parting the white curtains with a finger. The side yard and street were empty.

"Besides, if you keep calling, the police will just think the whole thing is a publicity stunt for the book. They didn't believe Alex Forrester when he called, you know?" She was under control again, teasing him now, taunting. "Trust me, the police will be of no help. We are much stronger than you think."

"Fuck you."

"Such harsh words." She laughed. "The oldest rule of nature is that the strong shall survive and the weak shall perish. Don't be weak anymore, Mr. Drake. For your own sake, don't be weak."

He hung up, silencing the awful voice, and called his agent and told him of the latest incident. He didn't call the police. Afterward, he left the phone off the hook.

The next morning, Drake drove into town and bought an answering machine. He installed it that same morning and screened his calls the rest of the week. He counted over a hundred hang-ups before deciding to disconnect the line completely.

Things went downhill fast after that night.

Six days ago, on the exact day of The Prey's paperback release, Mother Earth went over the edge and took Drake with them. He found the dog on his way to fetch the morning paper. The black Labrador was sprawled on its back, legs stiff, mouth open, and definitely dead. A smear of blood on the walk revealed that it had been killed in the grass—single bullet to the head—then dragged onto the concrete front porch. Stuffed between the dog's teeth was a ball of glossy, colored paper—a wrinkled book cover.

He buried his companion in the back yard, then showered and packed a single bag. He didn't consider, even for a moment, calling the police.

After a trip to the grocery store for supplies and food, he drove downtown to a pawn shop and picked up a brand new—at least that's what the owner claimed—.38-caliber pistol and a dozen boxes of ammunition. Then he loaded the car and headed for the cabin.

An hour later, he stopped at a crossroads convenience store and phoned Colin at the office. But instead of hearing Colin's ever cheerful voice, Drake found himself speaking with one of Colin's literary partners. "I'm afraid I have some tragic news to pass on to you, my dear Thomas."

Drake immediately knew what had happened.

"The police were here this morning. It seems that poor Colin was…was shot to death in his apartment late last night. A foiled robbery attempt, the police suggested. There were signs of a struggle and the lock was damaged.

"There was something strange, though. It seems that the killer tried to burn down Colin's apartment by setting a pile of books afire atop his magnificent Persian rug. Now that makes perfect sense: the police think that the murderer was simply trying to cover his tracks. But what is so puzzling is that every single book on the pile was one of yours. I wonder where they all came from? Don't you find that queer? It's just so terrible—"

Drake hung up, cutting him off in mid-sentence. He felt nauseous and sat inside the parked car for almost an hour before his head felt clear enough to continue.

He arrived at the cabin late in the afternoon, an emotional mess. Anger. Fear. Disbelief.

He was sure they would search for him; they'd gone too far now to turn back. The disciples of Mother Earth. He didn't know who or what in the hell they were, but he was sure of one thing: they'd look for him and eventually find him.

And he prayed he'd be ready.

## CHAPTER 6

DRAKE CLEARED THE STAIRWAY IN TWO STRIDES AND RAN FOR THE DEN window. He could hear the wooden boards groaning, surrendering under pressure. He crossed the kitchen and walked right up on the man who was climbing, legs first, into the cabin. The man's blue jeans were pushed up above his shins, exposing thick, hairy ankles. He wore no socks, but a leather holster holding a small pistol was strapped to his right ankle. The man was obviously stuck—probably caught on a jagged piece of board or a nail—and was grunting with effort.

Drake stopped short of the den carpet, hoping the man hadn't heard his approach. Close range. In the back. He raised the .38, his arms shaking wildly, and took aim. Steele would never do it, he thought in a flash of sanity.

He lowered the gun. Steele would just knock the bastard unconscious and tie him up.

Drake looked up at the man again, at the gun hanging from his leg, and wondered if the same gun had been used to end his agent and longtime friend's life. He imagined the man breaking into Colin's apartment and pressing the gun barrel to Colin's bald head and firing. He imagined the man stuffing the tattered remains of a book cover into his dog's lifeless mouth, and…

…Drake raised the .38 and pulled the trigger twice in a quick, jerky motion. The man spasmed, his legs kicking at empty air, and a pair of red mouths opened near the center of his back. He went limp.

The adrenaline rush was overpowering and, for a moment, Drake felt as though he might faint. He steadied himself against the back of the sofa and brought the gun to eye level, as if he were unsure if he'd actually pulled the trigger. A loud crash and a sudden flash of light in the next room snapped him back. He moved cautiously through the kitchen, searching the shadows for movement, turned the corner, and froze at the base of the stairs. A pile of broken boards lay at his feet, and the bay window stood wide open, the van's headlights shining bright white into the cabin. The lights were blinding, but Drake leveled the gun and forced himself closer to the window. Holding his breath, he leaned over the windowsill and peered around the right side. Nothing. Then, to his left. Again nothing.

He backed away from the window, shading his eyes with his

gun hand. He was about to return upstairs when a long, silver canister flew through the window and exploded with a loud pop as it hit the floor. A second can followed, landing with an identical pop. A cloud of white smoke erupted with a hiss.

*Tear gas*, Drake guessed, his eyes already beginning to sting and water. *Trying to smoke me out*. He shaded his eyes and ran for the stairs…and tripped face-first on the pile of broken boards. The gun flew from his hand and slid across the floor, settling somewhere near the bottom of the staircase.

Drake crawled on all fours, fingers groping for the lost weapon. The gas was overpowering now; he could barely open his eyes. His throat felt on fire; he couldn't stop the coughs that racked his body. *No*, his mind screamed. *It can't end so easily. Don't panic now.* Suddenly, his fingers touched something metal and cold and he knew it was the gun. *Okay, get yourself together now,* he thought. *Find your way back upstairs*. His fingers closed around the rubber hand grip…

…and were crushed beneath an unseen boot.

He screamed with pain.

The boot released.

Drake sensed movement above him, then felt strong hands pick him up and fling him backward out the window, onto the waiting lawn several feet below.

## Chapter 7

"It is nature's way, Mr. Drake." The voice was soft and calm. Unbearably confident. "And it is our way."

Drake was stretched out on his back on the dining room table, his arms and legs bound with thick rope. A piece of tape covered his mouth. Jessie sat on a chair at the end of the table. Two men stood behind her.

They'd surprised him at the bay window, and he'd surprised them right back by fighting like a wildcat. It had taken both men to take him down. One of the men sported a two-inch gash across his forehead and the other man's lips were cracked and swollen. The third man was still inside the cabin, stuck in the window; he was dead.

The men rarely spoke, but the woman had spent the past fifteen minutes repeating the same crazy sermon she'd told him earlier over the telephone. "We live by nature's laws, Mr. Drake. It is our duty to make this earth pure again." She motioned to one of the men and he removed the tape from Drake's mouth.

Drake sucked in air, coating his dry lips with a sweep of his tongue. The back of his head ached from where he'd been struck, and he longed to massage it. His eyes were the worst, though, red and raw.

"Kill me now," he hissed. "Just get it over with."

"Oh, but we have no intentions of killing you. We only kill when necessary to achieve our final objective, and you, Mr. Drake, are exactly that. By allowing you to live, by allowing the world to witness our power, we will set the highest possible example and hopefully deter future sinners from walking your path. Mother Earth's message will be heard across the country very soon, thanks to you."

"You're...you're all crazy. My God, you killed Colin for no reason. You chased me all over the country because of a damn book."

"Ah, but a very popular book. A book that will, unfortunately, be read by millions. We told you, the film is only an extension of your vision. It is your message that must be stopped."

He spoke without thinking: "I'll never stop writing."

"But you will, Mr. Drake. We will make sure of that. I know we have met once before, but allow me to formally introduce myself. I am Jessie Moore. Doctor Jessica Moore. And these two gentlemen with me are..."

## CHAPTER 8

Excerpted from the Monday evening edition of the *Baltimore Sun*:

BALTIMORE—Bestselling crime novelist, Thomas Drake, was

discovered early this morning suffering from shock and severe dehydration at his country home in the Western Maryland wilderness. The local author was flown to the University of Maryland's Shock Trauma Unit, where he is listed in serious but stable condition.

Though officials declined to discuss details of Drake's condition, the father-and-son team of hunters who stumbled upon the gruesome scene, Jim and Jeffrey Cavanaugh of Cumberland, claimed that the local author was suffering from bizarre wounds and was close to death when they first found him.

"The first thing I noticed was that both his hands were missing, gone right at the wrist," said the elder Cavanaugh. "There were bloody bandages wrapped over the stumps, but they were full of dirt and green pus and he didn't even seem to notice. He was crazy as a goat, eyes staring all big and wide, slobbering all over himself, mumbling about his mother and the earth and something about nature's way. It was spooky as hell."

"And then we figured out why he was so hard to understand," continued the son, Jeffrey Cavanaugh. "Someone had cut out his tongue."

Ironically, Drake's latest novel *The Prey*, sparked by controversy over the recent film release, debuted at the number one spot on the *New York Times* paperback best-sellers list yesterday and...

## Chapter 9

"STUPID." ALTHOUGH WHISPERED, THE SINGLE WORD ECHOED ABOUT the small hospital room. It was a small white-walled room, a private room with a washing sink, sitting couch, a single bed, and the usual tangle of hospital machinery. A skeleton of a girl lay stretched atop the white sheets, a clear mask covering her nose and mouth. Her long dark hair, its luster faded, snaked across the pillow. Her eyes were closed.

"How could I be so stupid? I failed you again, my dear Chelsea." Jessie, dressed in a conservative business suit, held a page from the *New York Times* vertically for her daughter to see. Thomas Drake's

*The Prey* was still perched atop the paperback list: eight weeks and counting. After a moment, she lowered the paper to her lap.

"How could I be so stupid?" she repeated, as if insisting on an answer. "We knocked him out of commission, sent an important message, but our actions were merely counterproductive. The damn book is selling: even now his filth is spreading to the people."

She stood and unlocked the safety rail on the left side of the bed. "What shall we do, sweetheart?" she asked. "Help me see the light." The bar lowered and Jessie leaned down and cuddled against the cool side of her daughter's body. She slipped the mask down and softly kissed the girl's lips, then replaced the mask.

She sat down again on the stiff hospital chair and, as was her custom, began reading to Chelsea. Sometimes she read books or magazine articles, but always the newspaper first...to keep her daughter abreast of current events. Now, she read from the *Times* entertainment section. The lead article was about New York's revitalized publishing world. Industry numbers were skyrocketing. Hardcover sales were up forty percent, softcover sales nearing fifty. Companies were expanding.

She finished the article, dropped the newspaper to her lap, and watched her daughter's lifeless face for a reaction, for an answer to her plea for help. Chelsea had targeted both Forrester and Drake, but Jessie knew it was she who had failed in the latter plan's execution. Now, as Chelsea told her what to do next, Jessie's pulse quickened.

"Yes, yes," she said, her enthusiasm mounting, a plan forming in her mind. "We won't fail you, baby girl. We'll go right to the top this time."

She ran a polished fingernail over the black-and-white photograph—of Putnam's CEO and Vice President, standing together, smiling—then slashed the photo to shreds with a sweep of her nail and said: "We'll go right to the top."

# ABOUT THE AUTHORS

RONALD KELLY - Born and bred in Tennessee, Ronald Kelly has been an author of Southern-fried horror fiction for 35 years, with fifteen novels, twelve short story collections, and a Grammy-nominated audio collection to his credit. Influenced by such writers as Stephen King, Robert McCammon, Joe R. Lansdale, and Manly Wade Wellman, Kelly sets his tales of rural darkness in the hills and hollows of his native state and other locales of the American South. His published works include *Fear, Undertaker's Moon, Blood Kin, Hell Hollow, Hindsight, The Buzzard Zone, After the Burn, Midnight Grinding, Mister Glow-Bones, The Halloween Store, Season's Creepings, Irish Gothic,* and *The Web of La Sanguinaire & Other Arachnid Horrors.* His Silver Shamrock collection of extreme horror tales, *The Essential Sick Stuff,* won the 2021 Splatterpunk Award for Best Collection. Kelly lives in a backwoods hollow in Brush Creek, Tennessee, with his wife and young'uns. Find out more about Ronald at www.ronaldkelly.com.

JEREMY MEGARGEE has always loved dark fiction. He cut his teeth on R.L Stine's Goosebumps series as a child and a fascination with Stephen King, Jack London, Algernon Blackwood, and many others followed later in life. Jeremy weaves his tales of personal horror from Martinsburg, West Virginia, with his cat Lazarus acting as his muse/familiar. He is an active member of the West Virginia chapter of the Horror Writer's Association and you can often find him peddling his dark words in various mountain hollers deep within the Appalachians.

BRANDON SCOTT crafts tales of Supernatural Suspense and Dark Fantasy from the mountains of Western North Carolina. He is an

Active Member of the Horror Writers Association and has been featured in various anthologies such as *Killers Inside, 19 Gates of Hell, 25 Gates of Hell, Campfire Macabre,* and *From The Depths.* His debut novel of the Vodou series was launched in 2019 by Devil Dog Press.

RENEE M.P.T. KRAY grew up in Michigan with eight siblings and a small army of cats. Her love of reading and writing went into maximum overdrive when she read *The Lord of the Rings* at age 10, and since then she's spent her time obsessively scribbling story ideas into notebooks. After being homeschooled all through elementary and high school, she earned her BA in Literature from Ave Maria University and her MFA in English and Creative Writing from Southern New Hampshire University. She has self-published two collections of short stories: *Think Again: A Captivating Compendium* and *Restless: A Year of Ghost Stories.* However, none of these pursuits have been as challenging as trying to get her pug, Potato, to stop eating dirt. Find out more about Renee at www.reneemptkray.com.

LP HERNANDEZ is a writer of horror and speculative fiction. His work is regularly adapted as audio dramas by The NoSleep Podcast, including the finale of Season 16. In addition, you can find his short stories in many recent anthologies. When not writing he serves as a Medical Service Corps officer in the United States Air Force. He loves his family, heavy metal, and a crisp high five. Find out more about LP at www.lphernandez.com.

STEVEN PAJAK is the author of novels such as the U.S. Marshal Jack Monroe series and the Mad Swine trilogy, as well as short stories and novellas. When not writing, Steven works as an administrator at a university. He continues to be an avid reader of Stephen King and Dean Koontz, John Saul, Richard Matheson, and many other favorite authors in the horror, suspense, thriller, and general fiction genres. Steven lives in the Chicagoland area with his wife and two teens. Find out more about Steven at www.stevenpajak.com.

JANINE PIPE - Trading in a police badge and then classroom, Janine is a full-time Splatterpunk Award nominated writer, whilst also being a mum, wife, and Disney addict. Influenced by the works of King from a young age, she likes to shock readers with violence and scare them with monsters—both mythical and man-made. When she's not killing people off on paper, she likes to watch movies and documentaries and write about them especially for Fangoria. *SAUSAGES – The Making of Dog Soldiers* is out now from Encyclopocalypse Books. Her biggest fans are her loving husband and daughter. One day she will write that screenplay or direct that movie she keeps waffling about. Follow Janine on Twitter @janinepipe28.

SCOTT HARPER - The world was just a tad dull and unimaginative for a young Scott growing up in 1970's Southern California. He found a creative outlet in the world of Marvel Comics, fervidly devouring the monthly adventures of Iron Man, Hulk, and Captain America. Later, his tastes turned toward the Marvel black-and-white magazines' more esoteric horror province, faithfully following titles such as *Dracula Lives!* and *Tales of the Zombie*. Influenced by these works and such authors as Bram Stoker, John Steakley, and Marv Wolfman, Scott's unique writing style combines horror and fantasy elements with superhero-style action.

When not writing, Scott spends his time either reading, working out at the gym, adding to his model collection, or walking his two dogs. He lives in California with his wife and son. Find out more about Scott at www.scottharpermacabremaestro.com.

DAVID RIDER is the author of "Tweakers, Crane Girl and the Semi-pocalypse" on Kindle, as well as the novel series We Are Van Helsing.

He has never spent time in a mental health asylum on Route 47 in rural Illinois. Nor has he ever escaped from such an institution after forty-two hellish months where cruel orderlies handed him pills in paper cups twice daily and the oatmeal was cold and the lingering stares of his fellow patients judged him for a dark past they couldn't possibly fathom. No sir, David Rider is his actual name, and his wife and kids accept that to this day without suspicion. Find out more about David at www.facebook.com/davidrider author.

**JILL GIRARDI** is the best-selling, award-nominated author of *Hantu Macabre*, the first book in the occult/creature-horror series about Punk Rock detective Suzanna Sim and Tokek the Toyol. There will also be a film based on the characters in the book, set to shoot in 2022, and starring ex-MMA Fighter Ann Osman as Suzanna.

Jill is also the editor/owner of Kandisha Press and is the author of several short stories mostly involving small, wicked creatures and dark humor. Find Jill on Instagram or Twitter @jill_girardi.

**SCOTTY MILDER** is a writer, filmmaker, and film educator living in Albuquerque, New Mexico. He received his MFA in Screenwriting from Boston University, and his award-winning short films have screened at festivals all over the world, including Cinequest, the Dead By Dawn Festival of Horror, HollyShorts, and the H.P. Lovecraft Film Festival and CthulhuCon. His independent feature film *Dead Billy* is available to stream on Amazon.com and Google Play.

His short fiction has appeared or will appear in *Dark Moon Digest*, *KZine*, *Lovecraftiana Magazine*, as well as anthologies from HellBound Books, Dark Moon Books, Dark Peninsula Press, Sinister Smile Press, and others.

He teaches screenwriting and film production at Santa Fe Community College and the Seattle Film Institute. He is also the co-host of *The Weirdest Thing* history podcast with actor/theatre artist Amelia Ampuero. Find out more about Scotty at www.scottymilder.com.

**MIKE DUKE** - For the last fifteen years Mike has taught military, law enforcement, and bodyguards high speed, tactical, and off-road driving as well as hand-to-hand Combatives. He's practiced various martial arts since 1989. Filipino blade arts are his current favorite. Since he was a teenager he's loved reading, writing, and watching movies, particularly in the horror and sci-fi genre. He has a beautiful, supportive wife and a son and daughter who are both graduated. His babies now are a German Shepherd named Ziva, a daddy's girl who loves to play, and a Border Collie named Joey "The Bandit." Mike is a lover of music, as well, and it is an integral part of his writing ritual.

Mike writes an eclectic mix of horror stories, exploring dark supernatural entities, cosmic terrors, and natural monstrosities along with the wicked deeds of the human heart. He's skilled at provoking a significant response from his readers—whether shock, terror, dread, an uneasy sense of empathy, heebie-jeebie crawlies, or surprise at unexpected twists. Mike will make you feel while reading. As one reviewer said, when you read a Mike Duke book you don't just read about an experience, you have an experience. Find out more about Mike at www.facebook.com/mike.duke.author.

RICHARD CLIVE is a horror and science-fiction writer who lives in the medieval town of Conwy, North Wales, with his wife, daughter, and pet Labrador. When not writing fiction, Richard works as a journalist but originally studied film and scriptwriting in Manchester. Richard's work has been published in numerous horror anthologies, and his debut collection *Strange Frequencies* is available from Sinister Smile Press. Find out more about Richard at www.richardclive.com.

R.E. SARGENT is the author of three novels, four novelettes, and many short stories in the genres of suspense, supernatural, and horror. He is an active member of the Horror Writers Association, the Alliance of Independent Authors, and the Community of Literary Magazines and Presses. His short story, "Lucy," was featured in the 2021 Splatterpunk Award–nominated anthology *If I Die Before I Wake Volume 3 – Tales of Deadly Women and Retribution*.

R.E. lives in the Pacific Northwest with his wife and their Chocolate Lab. And the rain. Lots and lots of rain. He is thankful that writing is an indoor activity. Find out more about R.E. at www.re-sargent.com.

REBECCA ROWLAND is the dark fiction author of the short story collections *The Horrors Hiding in Plain Sight* and *White Trash & Recycled Nightmares*, of the novel *Pieces*, and of the novella *Optic Nerve*, and is the curator of five horror anthologies: *Ghosts, Goblins, Murder, and Madness: Twenty Tales of Halloween*; *Shadowy Natures: Stories of Psychological Horror*, *The Half That You See*, *Unburied: A Collection of Queer Dark Fiction*, and *Generation X-ed*.

Her short fiction regularly appears in a variety of online and print venues, and her book reviews may be found on Ginger Nuts of Horror. She is an Active member of the Horror Writers Association and lives in a chilly corner of New England with her family. Find out more about Rebecca at www.RowlandBooks.com.

**RICHARD CHIZMAR** is the *New York Times* bestselling author of the *Gwendy Trilogy* (with Stephen King), as well as *Chasing the Boogeyman, Widow's Point*, and many other books.

He is the founder/publisher of *Cemetery Dance* magazine and the Cemetery Dance Publications book imprint. He has edited more than 35 anthologies and his short fiction has appeared in dozens of publications, including multiple editions of *Ellery Queen's Mystery Magazine* and *The Year's 25 Finest Crime and Mystery Stories*. He has won two World Fantasy awards, four International Horror Guild awards, and the HWA's Board of Trustee's award.

Chizmar (in collaboration with Johnathon Schaech) has also written screenplays and teleplays for United Artists, Sony Screen Gems, Lions Gate, Showtime, NBC, and many other companies. He has adapted the works of many bestselling authors including Stephen King, Peter Straub, and Bentley Little.

Chizmar's work has been translated into more than fifteen languages throughout the world, and he has appeared at numerous conferences as a writing instructor, guest speaker, panelist, and guest of honor. Find out more about Richard at www.richardchiz-mar.com

**Novels / Novellas / Collections**

*Devil's Gulch: A Collaborative Horror Experience*

*Partum* by EV Knight

*Them* by James Watts

*Beast of Sorrows* by James Watts

*Shadows of the Damned* by James Watts

*Strange Frequencies* by Richard Clive

*Dark Days* by Steven Pajak

*Everything Went to Shit* by R.E. Sargent

*Lethal Lords and Ladies of the Night* by Scott Harper